DOUBLE DEAL

Also by John M. Green

The Trusted

The Tao Deception

Nowhere Man

Born to Run

JOHN M. GREEN

DOUBLE DEAL

PANTERA PRESS

This is a work of fiction. Names, characters, organisations, dialogue and incidents are either products of the author's imagination or are used fictitiously. Any resemblance to actual people, living or dead, organisations, events or locales is coincidental.

First published in 2021 by Pantera Press Pty Limited
www.PanteraPress.com

Please send all permission queries to:
Pantera Press, P.O. Box 1989, Neutral Bay, NSW, Australia 2089 or info@PanteraPress.com

A Cataloguing-in-Publication entry for this work is available from the National Library of Australia.

ISBN 978-0-6486769-2-8 (Paperback)
ISBN 978-0-6486769-3-5 (eBook)

Cover Design: Luke Causby, Blue Cork
Cover Images: Mark Owen/Arcangel, 135pixels/Adobe Stock, lornet/Adobe Stock, richardlight/Adobe Stock
Publisher: Lex Hirst
Project Editor: Lucy Bell
Editor: Linda Funnell
Proofreader: Sarina Rowell
Typesetting: Kirby Jones
Author Photo: Erica Murray
Printed and bound in Australia by McPherson's Printing Group

The paper this book is printed on is certified against the Forest Stewardship Council® Standards. McPherson's Printing Group holds FSC® chain of custody certification SA-COC-005379. FSC® promotes environmentally responsible, socially beneficial and economically viable management of the world's forests.

In loving memory of
Nigel Dunn (1948–2021)

‘Whoever holds Greenland holds the Arctic.
It’s the most important strategic location in … the world.’
– Director of Arctic Studies, US Naval War College

‘The United States [owning Greenland] would be nice.
It’s essentially a large real estate deal.’
– Former US President Donald J. Trump

‘Between two evils, I always pick the one I’ve never tried before.’
– Mae West

1

Barcelona, Spain

Tori Swyft's eyes were glued shut. Her head was pounding, her body quivering, yet this wasn't a hangover. Couldn't be.

At last night's celebrations she'd let barely a drop of alcohol touch her lips. How could she risk any misstep when the treaty – the one she had personally negotiated – was 'the first major shake-up of the Arctic's balance of power since the Cold War'? And that was *The New York Times* speaking, not her.

With Tori's help and guidance, Greenland – her client – chose China as its future polar partner, ending centuries of Danish colonial rule and decades as an American ally. If the US and Russia, the Arctic's two prevailing powers, kept out of the way … a very big if … this new accord would unlock a vast treasure trove of prosperity for the tiny population of this icy nation.

For chrissakes, her eyes … They refused to open, no matter how much Tori rubbed them. Her world was totally dark. Pitch black.

This wasn't eye gunk from sleep. It wasn't conjunctivitis.

Glue?

Was it actual glue? Was that even possible?

Had someone – *who?* – glued her eyes shut?

Her skin prickled and her breath shortened as a quake of terror surged through her. Panic wasn't the answer, she knew that, but her body wasn't listening, her hands taking it upon themselves to scrub and yank at her eyes, every muscle in her face contorting as she tried to open a crack between her lids.

With her heart hammering, sweat flooding from her pores, the locomotive of panic kept roaring through her.

Breathe, she commanded, but even her nose wasn't cooperating. Her nostrils were clogged too, so she inhaled through her mouth. Belly breaths, deep breaths.

Someone did this. To her.

Was it linked to the accord? Was it the Russians? The Americans?

Was this how they were going to play their hand?

The monster who'd done this, where was he? Close by, out in the blackness? Silently baring his teeth at her? Exulting in her terror?

She strained her ears but all she heard was the rumble of the air-conditioner and the sound of her own breathing.

No one was moving, no one crowing over what they'd done. To her.

She tried to sniff the air, to detect a scent – cologne, perhaps, the sourness of body odour, bad breath – but her nose was blocked.

She pressed a thumb over her nostrils, first one then the other, blowing hard, her hand catching the slugs of snot, which she wiped off on her pillow.

The rasp of her lungs, the pounding in her ears, the thump of her heart … she needed to slow it all down. Breathe, Tori, she told herself. Synch with something rhythmic, anything. The drone of the AC was the only thing.

Slow. Down.

Her heart rate *was* dropping and her nose began to sense an odour. It was not a welcome one. The first whiff was acrid, sour. The second was repulsive, stomach-churning, a stink Tori knew well but wished she did not, the same stench of death she'd gagged on two years ago in a Mosul hospital.

Her stomach heaved like it had that day in Iraq, the pit of her gut hurtling up to her throat. She whipped her head to the side, hoping her vomit would splatter the bastard who did this to her – if he was there.

He didn't flip out, didn't make a sound.

But that didn't mean he wasn't present, watching and smirking.

Tori knew the power of silences. Interrogation Techniques 101 at the CIA included a whole chapter on silences. She had applied them herself.

Now she brushed her fingers over her body. It was bare, varnished with sweat.

She understood.

Today, she, Tori Swyft, was the target.

She visualised her captor, leering at her from some vantage point, revelling in his handiwork as he calibrated his next move.

Confront him, she told herself. She wiped the puke off her lips with the back of her hand. 'What do you want?' She pushed out the question, her words dry and croaky.

She wanted his name, to make a connection, to remind the ghoul that *I'm a person, not simply your captive*, a standard tactic in hostage negotiation she'd also learnt from the CIA.

Except she knew it would not work. A man prepared to glue a woman's eyes shut would know that game and refuse to play it.

He'd proffer his name when it suited him. *If* it suited him.

'What do you want?' she repeated, her voice clearer, firmer.

The monster said nothing.

She pictured him holding a knife and silently stepping closer, almost felt him hovering over her and running his tongue along the blade of a KA-BAR. In her harrowed imagination she saw his fingers around the leather-washer handle, his reflection in the polished Cro-Van steel blade, brain drunk with his power over the naked woman he'd blinded, the tingle of cold metal against his tongue.

The fear welling up inside her was a dead weight, a barrier to action. She shook herself. There was nothing to be gained if she kept imagining the worst.

What if this silence signalled his absence?

If he'd stepped outside – a possibility – she'd have a small window to make her escape, or at least to try.

Again she pulled at her eyelids, but still failed to wrench them apart. This time, though, her fingernail caught on a thin lip of gum, a hard thread like plastic that snaked across her lashes and fused them together.

She picked and scratched at it, ripping clumps of eyelashes out. But not enough to see.

Without thinking, she opened her mouth to scream, opened it wide, drawing in as deep a breath as she could, and stopped herself. If he really had stepped out, the racket would bring him back and then …

That smell and her glued eyelids told her what he was capable of.

She exhaled, closed her mouth and groped sideways for a nightstand, hoping to find a phone. Hers. Anyone's.

As she reached out she experienced a sharp twinge in the crook of her arm. Felt a tiny lump, right over the bulge of a vein.

On top of whatever else the bastard had done, he'd drugged her.

2

Tori groped her left hand across the top of the nightstand beside the bed, its glass surface cold and strangely barren. She couldn't feel a lamp, a clock, not even one of those ludicrous fifteen-dollar bottles of hotel water that housekeeping left in her room every night – the kind she always refused to open on principle but would have paid ten times for right now.

Her hand nudged something metallic. It slid away, almost falling off the edge. She caught it in time and ran her fingers down its tapering length … an open penknife.

Did her captor leave it behind as a threat? Or was it meant to tantalise her, a possible weapon to use against him, only to have him whip it away at the last minute?

She swung her legs to the side of the bed, keeping her feet away from where she anticipated the puddle of vomit had landed, and sat up. With her head spinning – she assumed from the drugs – she sat still, waiting for the wooziness to settle, half expecting this to be the moment her tormentor would say his piece. Yet he remained silent.

She weighed the small knife in her hand as a new fear came over her. What if the glue had got onto her corneas? Almost in a panic she pinched the hairs on her left lids between her thumb and forefinger and pulled. The suction popped and her lids lifted off her eyeball. Thank heavens.

She repeated the procedure with her right eye and thankfully got the same result.

Her eyelashes had done what eyelashes were meant to do, they'd trapped the foreign matter and stopped it from getting into her eyes.

She balanced the knife in her hand again and decided her only way forward was to cut off her lashes. It would make her look weird, but weird was not blind.

With her left hand she pulled at her lashes and with her right took the knife and worked gingerly at the hairs, just tiny nicks, chipping as close to the skin of her lids as possible without slicing into them.

3

In the room across the hotel hallway, Tori's work colleague Frank Chaudry sat at the end of his bed, his eyes briefly on his left foot as he pulled on a sock then looked up again to catch the sub-titles scrolling across the bottom of the TV screen.

Yesterday had been epic. The best day in his post-MI6 career. He and Tori – well, Tori mainly – had tied up the Greenland–China deal in time to make the evening news bulletins in Europe and the mid-morning ones in America.

But this morning Barcelona TV was barely mentioning the story. That wasn't really strange, not with the state funeral this afternoon overshadowing everything, and the buzz of all the global politerati starting to converge on the city. Prime ministers, chancellors, a couple of kings. Even US President Isabel Diaz was coming.

Frank and Tori had been present three days ago when Oriol Casals – president of Spain's autonomous region of Catalonia and the host of the secret talks – took the fateful call. They watched the colour leach from his face as he dropped the phone.

His cousin's heart attack in New York City hit him hard. Not only had they grown up together on the same street in Barcelona, she'd also gone into politics, in her case to become one of Catalonia's – and Spain's – favourite daughters. Once the country's celebrated defence minister, it was only six months ago that Montserrat Vilaró i Mas was elected the youngest ever secretary-general of the United Nations. All of Spain loved her and called her Montse.

The bad news hit at a tense moment in the talks when Rao Songtian, China's lead negotiator, was at his most intransigent. So Tori, God bless her, whipped up the death, and the funeral, as a spur to bring the deal to a close. Their host, Oriol Casals – Uri for short to people who were close to him – was about to become completely preoccupied with the arrangements for his cousin's funeral. And, as Tori also knew, he had an election coming up.

The ante was upped even higher the next morning when America's president called both Casals and Greenland's newly elected prime minister. The US had got wind of the talks and was seeking a delay to give them time to put together a counteroffer to China's, one that Greenland would find compelling.

'This is brilliant,' Frank remembered Tori whispering to him and Greenland's leader, Nivikka Petersen, in a side room as she high-fived each of them. 'Let's go back in and really put the squeeze on China.'

Tori was class, thought Frank. She strode back into the negotiation room, sat directly opposite Rao Songtian, who was putting his own phone back onto the table, and regarded him coolly.

Not only did he return the stare but he spoke before she could. 'I know.'

'What do you know?' Tori kept her tone light, playing out a standard tenet of negotiation, *never assume.*

'I know that the United States knows,' he said, his eyes glancing back at his phone. 'You leaked these talks to them,' he added and pushed back his chair, started to stand and turned to Petersen. 'Madam Prime Minister, this breach of security is intolerable,' he said. 'On behalf of the People's Republic of China, I regret to advise you that we are done here.'

Frank watched. Tori's gaze was unwavering, her back straight. 'Rao,' she said, 'the leak did not come from us, you have my word. But Washington does know, that's a fact. The other fact is they want Greenland at least as much as China does. More, perhaps. So here's how we'll play this. Walk out of here if you wish. We won't stop you. But if you do I'll pick up my phone,' she put it on the table, 'and as soon as you slam the door shut we'll open talks with Washington. If you stay, we keep negotiating only with you but, with the US trying to bash down the door, your exclusivity will now end at 3 pm tomorrow. If you haven't reached a deal with us by then, we will invite Washington to come in and join the party.'

Rao Songtian had sat back down.

Frank stared at his socks. Black. Like all his socks. Bland. Plain. Frank liked to blend in. Unlike Tori, who shone even in black, which was her trademark. Everything she wore was black. She said it was purely utilitarian, so everything went with everything else, but he wasn't so sure, since it made the red of her hair crackle like flames across any room. At least he'd persuaded her to make a slight change for last night's celebration, even if it was only to move from black to black and white.

4

Oahu, Hawaii

It was just a month earlier that Tori had been on her surfboard, moving up and down on the swells, manoeuvring and waiting for the right wave. Time had faded the freckles that bridged across her nose as a child surfing on Sydney's famous northern beaches – these days her skin had a pasty bookish pallor. Yet out here the power of the sea offered her more solace than any book possibly could.

The incoming surge felt right and, grabbing her board's rails, she raised her torso and flicked back her hair, flinging out a sparkling curtain of spray. The salt on her lips cracked as she fleetingly looked back and, at the perfect moment, she started paddling hard and caught the wave.

Close to shore, Tori heard gasps from the beach as she leant forward, placing her hands on the board, then her head and, after forming this human tripod of support, she kicked her legs back and out, arcing them up into the air above her into a headstand. Balancing herself upside down, a manoeuvre that for most surfers was near impossible, she let the wave glide her all the way in to the shore.

An hour later, Tori was sitting in a sun lounge on a rooftop terrace looking out to sea, though unsure what she was hoping to spy. A whale? A pod of dolphins?

Her phone vibrated but she ignored it. She'd even switched off her voicemail. This month, this break, was meant to be sacred. She'd put everything else on hold. Tori needed the water, the waves. The solace.

The phone didn't care and vibrated again, more insistent this time.

She told her eyes not to look at it, but they disobeyed her. *Axel Schönberg III* the screen said.

She swung herself off the sun lounge and stepped closer to the rooftop's balustrade, debating whether or not to answer.

Gazing out, she watched the waves, low and slow, rhythmic, carefree. A giggling rabble of children leapt in and out of the lacy froth at the shore. She was here alone, which was exactly what she needed. At least that's what she told herself.

Axel was her boss at SIS, a secretive family-run firm that, under the one red-tiled roof in Boston, brought together the smarts of a Goldman Sachs and the wiles of a CIA. It was why so many MBAs and former security services personnel worked there. People like Tori. People like Frank.

SIS was a firm whose clients – kings, presidents and billionaires – only picked up the phone if their problem needed the special dose of discretion, guile or judgement that the publicity-shy Schönberg dynasty had been quietly mustering on their behalf for three generations.

She remembered that Axel – the third, and possibly the most successful of his family line – had personally signed off on her leave, agreeing to her request that no one disturb her. Yet here he was, calling her himself. 'The soul does need time out,' he'd nodded, 'a time when we can shut ourselves off from ourselves, as much as from what's swirling around us.' He'd taken a long draw on one of his Montecristo cigars and Tori wondered if he'd been speaking to himself as much as to her as she watched his smoke ring drift up to the ceiling.

Despite his wealth and influence, Axel was an incredibly thoughtful and respectful employer, her best, in fact, so if he felt he needed to intrude on her sanctuary, it must be quite important.

Axel was old-school so she expected he'd start off with an abject apology, and he did. It was genuine, she knew that, but she also knew his clients trumped everything. Their needs won out over anything else.

'Tori, it's the Arctic. Greenland, specifically.'

The Hawaiian sun was still high, almost directly overhead, but the mere thought of ice and snow and blizzards sent a shiver through her skin.

5

'Greenland?' Tori repeated, while she pondered what could possibly be behind Axel's call.

'Tori, what do you know about Greenland? Geopolitically?'

'Geopolitically? Didn't Donald Trump have some cockamamie plan to buy Greenland from Denmark a few years ago?'

'Not so cockamamie, actually,' said Axel pensively.

She heard water glugging into a tumbler. Once it would have been champagne, but Axel was a different, thinner man now and he'd taken to honing his new body shape like a man running a hot knife through the butter he no longer let himself slather on a morning muffin.

Apart from whales and polar bears and the impact of climate change on the ice sheet, and the blustering attempt by ex-President Trump to purchase it, Tori's mental search engine didn't have much on Greenland. 'Axel, can we stop the twenty questions? All I know is that Greenland is a huge icy landmass with a tiny population.'

'Yes, with a squeeze, Yankee Stadium could seat every single Greenlander, man, woman and reindeer, all 56,000 of them. It's such a small population that the country is only economically viable because they've got a *Juulimaaq* … to a Greenlander, that's Santa Claus.'

Where was this going?

'Every Christmas, Denmark slides down Greenland's chimney and pops a half-billion dollars into their budget stocking.'

'What's in it for the Danes?' she asked. 'It can't be charity.'

'Originally it was, kind of. A mix of altruism and post-colonial guilt. But in more recent times it's become a down payment on the future, staking a claim on the bounty that climate change is bringing to the Arctic.'

'*Bounty*?' Tori blurted out, thinking Axel's new diet must be making him too weak to think straight.

'Tori, our warming planet has grim downsides but for the Arctic there are a few positives as well. As the ice melts, a diamond mine of potential reveals itself. Remember, Greenland was actually green once.'

'So what's this about? Potential farmland?'

'And mining, oil and gas, fishing. Huge opportunities for tourism. With all that becoming possible, shipping and international trade will be early and huge beneficiaries. Russia got onto this years ago and already they've got forty icebreakers plying the Arctic with more on the production line. America, on the other hand, has been slow off the mark, a single operational icebreaker with a second that seems to spend its summers *and* winters in drydock for repair.'

While Tori still didn't follow where Axel was going, that was not unusual. He often approached a topic obliquely. 'Axel,' she said, 'you're not about to tell me SIS has accepted a job to work on Greenland for Russia, are you?' If Russia was his client, she'd sit the deal out. The country's current president, Maxim Vladimirovich Tushkin, was dark and primal, a chunk of dirty black coal as far from a diamond as she could imagine.

'Heavens no. It's our good friend President Hou Tao—'

She almost whistled into the phone. Putting China and Greenland together would be huge. Not necessarily a good thing, but it *would* be massive. 'You've persuaded China to step into Denmark's, er, clogs?'

'Actually, the word for clogs in Danish is *træsko*, but yes … President Hou is keen.'

'But isn't his attention on the BRI? China is spending trillions on it.' Tori had read a lot about China's Belt and Road Initiative. Via this vast infrastructure and investment project involving between sixty and seventy other countries, China was building the modern Silk Road – land *and* sea routes – to gain better and cheaper ways to ship its goods to Europe across Asia, the Middle East and North Africa.

'Tori, Hou is a deep-thinking strategist. Yes, he's building the BRI but he also wants to advance a Plan B, an alternative and competitive route that can zip his ships to Europe even faster, even cheaper. If he can seize an opportunity like that, China will be far less beholden to foreign powers. That Plan B is the new *Polar* Silk Road.'

'Are you telling me that Greenland is his key to carving that out?'

'Exactly. He'll pare twenty days off China's shipping times to Europe if their cargo freights go via Greenland instead of the traditional route that winds through the South China

Sea, the Molucca Straits and the Suez. That's a time-save of forty per cent. The current forty-eight days at sea cuts back to twenty-eight. It's not just the time-to-market benefit, it's also the savings in charter and fuel costs and dodging the huge port charges all those countries on the way are thrusting their hands out for. Shipping is the bread and butter of his Plan B, but the cream is mining and—'

'So Donald Trump wasn't a complete airhead.'

'On this issue.'

'If this is China's Plan B, why the urgency?' Tori asked, code for *why couldn't this wait till I got back from leave?*

'Because this is a charms race, Tori.'

She wondered if she'd misheard. 'Did you say *arms race*?'

'No. This is about charm, and resources, both of which President Hou has in abundance. The thing is, Russia won't accept a Chinese push into what they consider their territory lying down. America won't either. They've tried to court Greenland before – incompetently – and they'll try again. When Trump's thought bubble flew out of his mouth everyone slapped him down … Greenland, the Danes, the media, the Twitterverse, you name it. But here's the thing, Tori. The day after Isabel Diaz moved into the Oval Office we … I … gave Hou a call and, while I can't claim credit for the actual idea, we did fast-track his thinking. We told him that if a new administration in DC decided to dust off Trump's idea, they'd approach it properly and professionally so he needed to move before they did. The elections in Greenland last month gave us the perfect opportunity, so now it's all systems go, go, go. We started working seriously on this just after you went on leave and—'

'Whoa, Axel.' A scrap of intel from Tori's CIA days had come back to her. 'Greenland hosts a number of US military bases. DC will never countenance China wangling its way in—'

'Which is why we're playing Hou's cards very close to our chest. By the way, he's not our client. Greenland is. The new prime minister agreed this strategy with me long before she won the election. You'll really like her. Nivikka Petersen. She's quite the dynamo. An old family friend, actually.'

Of course she was. Tori smiled. For a century the three Axel Schönbergs had been gathering friends and influence as matter-of-factly as Elton John collected sparkly jackets and Grammy awards. 'How much of a friend?'

'When Junior took me to Greenland for our fishing trips Nivi was our deckhand. Her dad was our guide.'

It was bizarre, Tori thought, to hear her boss, not exactly a young man, referring to his late father, Axel II, as 'Junior' or his grandfather Axel as 'Senior'. It always reminded her of an old joke: What's the difference between an eccentric and a screwball? Money.

She pictured Axel holding up a glass of sparkling water, Badoit maybe, and watching the bubbles playfully rise to the surface the same way his family's connections inevitably did.

It wasn't only the past that was another country. The rich were too, Tori decided. They definitely did things differently.

6

'Nivikka's party romped in,' Axel was telling Tori. 'Won the election by a landslide, or an avalanche. Whatever.'

Tori detected a twinkle of pride in his voice. 'You funded her campaign?'

'Tori, please! SIS never has and never will soil its hands with grubby politics. Well, not *this* century.'

'Okay,' she said, 'but you've been advising her on this prospect with China since *before* the election?'

'Naturally,' he said, the word slipping off his tongue like a drop of morning dew from the petal of a pure white rose.

'And she genuinely believes Greenlanders will be happy to live under China's, er, patronage?'

Axel chuckled. 'I didn't exactly say that, Tori. The perfect outcome is we tie up a brilliant deal with China, one Greenland will be very happy with. But then we encourage America and Russia, ideally America, to barge in and … you know … overbid.'

'You're planning to run an auction for a country? That's actually a thing?'

'Not for their sovereignty. Greenland will keep that. But a race to win first dibs over pretty much everything else. Their ports, natural resources, military facilities, shipping lanes, fishing rights. Sotheby's will have nothing on SIS if we've got Tori Swyft banging the gavel. The richer the terms you strike with China, the better for our client, and the more the other two rival powers will fall over themselves to up the ante and come out ahead. At minimum, they'll be desperate to stop China gaining a firm foothold in the Arctic. At maximum, they'll want all that Greenland offers for themselves.'

Tori's mind was spinning.

Axel went on. 'Also, a globally significant deal like this needs an honest broker who—'

'Aren't we – *you* – the broker, Axel?'

'Absolutely not. Like I said, we're the trusted adviser to Greenland. China trusts us too, which is a bonus, but our actual client is Greenland. The broker sitting in the middle, the person who'll bring the two sides together and smooth the tensions that Tori Swyft will inevitably cause when she squeezes China for every drop of value, that person is the president of Catalonia. He's another friend, by the way.'

Of course he was. Tori shook her head.

'You'll like Uri,' he said. 'Everyone does. Well, the powers in Madrid don't but that's not saying much. There hasn't been a leader in Barcelona they've got on with for years.'

'Because of the independence campaign?'

'Exactly. But everyone else loves him. He's got one of those long Continental names, Oriol Casals i Castanyé. Oriol Casals for short or, to really close friends, Uri. We've known each other since we were boys. His father was a Catalan hero, you know. Garrotted by Franco's men. And now Uri is the president of Spain's richest and most prosperous region, and forever grateful for the pension Junior gave his mother and the scholarship that funded his education. Consequently, he's very happy to host our talks in beautiful Barcelona.'

'What does that mean, practically speaking?'

'He'll start with the ceremonial stuff and will be available whenever there's a sticky issue that you and China can't agree on. He is running an important Spanish region so he can't be at the talks all the time, but he will be close by. He's allocated us a convenient private section of the government palace for the negotiations, so you'll be away from prying eyes. I'm calling you from the courtyard right now. You'll find the palace a simpatico venue to do the horse-trading on a deal of this import. A stately neoclassical façade behind which you and SIS will bring two ancient cultures together, China and Greenland. We – you especially, Tori – will be making history.'

She noted that Axel hadn't asked her if she'd work on it, and she knew he wouldn't. Her boss had lost his paunch but not his cheek.

She planned to come back to that question soon enough but had a few others to ask first. 'Isn't Greenland the logical place to hold the talks?'

'If a Chinese delegation put a toe on the ice, it wouldn't take thirty seconds for the vultures of the global media to swoop in on it. In Greenland, Tori, everyone is someone's daughter, brother, sister, cousin, aunt, whatever. And before you ask, holding the talks in China isn't an option either.'

She nodded. 'That would show weakness on Greenland's part. Hence Barcelona: neutral territory, millions of visitors coming and going again, so no one stands out. But why me, Axel?' She watched the sea foam calling to her, glistening as it crept up the sand. 'You seem to have everything under control and, frankly, I'd really prefer to stay here.'

'Tori, if I had an alternative I—'

'You've been front, centre and behind all of this, Axel. You started it so shouldn't you be the one to finish it?'

'Until an hour ago that was my plan. I would never have called you, Tori. I know how important … But an emergency in Saudi Arabia has cropped up. The king phoned – he and I were at Harvard together – and the poor fellow is frantic. Just between us …'

As she listened to the details of the unfolding Saudi crisis she understood why Axel had to drop everything else for it and that, unfortunately, meant the same for her.

Which made an issue scratching at the back of her brain even more important. 'Axel, China's developed a pretty dubious reputation for drowning poor countries in huge amounts of—'

'You mean debt-trap diplomacy. Yes, a lot of world opinion, or should I say a lot of self-interested Western opinion, claims that China has a policy of seducing Third World countries with cheap loans for grand projects they want but can't afford, and that when those projects blow out, as they often do, the locals suddenly discover they can't even afford to make the interest payments to China let alone pay back the principal, so China forecloses, and they win a stranglehold over the projects as well as over the key components of the country's economy. Conquest by debt.'

'Exactly.'

'That's what people say but Hou doesn't see it that way. But as Greenland's adviser and his friend, I was upfront with him from Day One about that, making it plain that Greenland, and SIS, won't have a bar of any deal if there's even a sniff of that kind of thing. Not only does Hou understand, he's bending over backwards. He wants this to become the benchmark deal that proves to the world they have misunderstood China's past conduct.'

'How?'

'We've already nutted out some protections. Yes, China will be lending our client billions but Hou's already agreed for Greenland to have a ten-year holiday from having to pay any interest at all. Ah, Tori, my car is pulling up. I need to go, so Francis will update you with the rest. He's been working on this with me so he's, er, *full bottle* on everything. Isn't that what you Australians say? Whatever, he's all over the detail. He and I both think the two of you can wrap this up in two weeks, three at the outside, which means we'll get you back to Hawaii before your beach towels dry.'

That Frank Chaudry – or Francis as Axel always insisted on calling him – was up to speed and on the case was more than welcome. Frank was super-smart, incredibly diligent and a guy who always thought outside the box.

Tori couldn't help remembering her first day at SIS when he walked through her office door, devastatingly dark and handsome with a charming British reticence and a voice that thrummed like salted caramel on the tongue.

'So you need me in Barcelon—'

'Your first stop will be Nuuk, Greenland's capital. After my jet gets me back to Boston, it'll swing over to Hawaii with Francis on board to pick you up and take you both there. We've got a natural break in the talks. The Chinese team are going back home for Ancestor Day or Tomb-Sweeping Day, something like that. This way you get the opportunity for Francis to introduce you to Nivikka, for her and her people to get comfortable with you, as well as a few days for Francis to bring you up to speed before you all head back to Barcelona to wrap it up.'

A shadow floated over Tori and she looked up. A red-tailed tropicbird, otherwise silky white, was gliding in the thermal, its resplendent coral red streamers trailing behind it.

While she owed Axel and understood he needed someone to step in and run the deal, she really wanted to stay in Hawaii. She tried one last shot.

'Couldn't Henry step in?' Henry Harvey was an SIS veteran who'd worked there longer than any other director bar Axel.

'Henry is stuck saving Venezuela's bacon in Caracas. Tori, this will be over before you know it. The hula dancers won't even realise you've been away. Call me when you get to Nuuk.'

Even the name of the capital city sounded like someone beating their arms across their body to keep out the cold. She grabbed a beach towel off the deck tiles and wrapped it round her shoulders.

7

Barcelona

President Casals got to his office in the Generalitat Palace at 6 am despite the celebrations the previous night for the deal-signing. With two significant official functions on the day's schedule – one of them very personal – he needed extra time to go over the speeches and make them perfect. At 2 pm, he'd be giving the eulogy at the state funeral for his cousin, Montse. Earlier, late morning, he'd be cutting the ribbon for Catalonia's driverless car show, showcasing his region's tech prowess.

His faithful chief of staff Maria Noguera was waiting for him, as usual. No matter what time her boss arrived at the palace, Maria was always there with a steaming cup of *café amb llet* and a plate of *carquinyolis*, the crunchy almond biscuits he loved. She also had his daily stomach-turner ready for him, a print copy of the morning's *El Mundo* newspaper.

He could have read it online on his way in but he needed

the sugar from the biscuit to give him the fortitude to withstand the inevitable attack. Since his election, not a single editorial in Spain's national daily had rated him better than appalling. He dunked a biscuit in his coffee, popped it in his mouth and spread open the pages.

'*Fill de puta!*' he exclaimed, soggy chunks of biscuit spraying out over the paper. He looked up to apologise for his language but thankfully Maria wasn't in the room. Clearly, she'd already read the piece and knew to make herself scarce until he stopped shouting.

He put his head back down and read the opening paragraph in full:

> Catalan President Oriol Casals i Castanyé has learned nothing from his predecessors' mistakes. Despite all the work there is for him to do at home, we see him once again prancing about on the global stage. Yesterday he was bumping shoulders with China and Greenland. Today it will be a conga line of world leaders. The man sucks up any excuse to distract the public from his weak leadership and tarnished image …

Since when was brokering such a brilliant deal a distraction, he fumed. Bringing China and Greenland together was a masterstroke, and his efforts put Catalonia, and Spain of course, right at the centre of it. Without him …

And what were they implying about the state funeral for one of Spain's greatest daughters? Was Montse's death a distraction too? *Gilipolles!* Assholes!

He was about to call out to Maria when she walked in with a file of papers in her hand and a grim look that silenced him.

'It's the autopsy report on Montse,' she said. 'The coroner was up all night working on it. Uri, it's bad. Really bad.'

8

Air Force One, *over the Atlantic*

President Isabel Diaz smiled at the chief steward. For her, politics was similar to hospitality – the industry where she'd pulled herself up – and she appreciated the impact a simple smile or a nod could have on people.

The steward, dressed as always in perfect crisp white, was a five-year veteran of *Air Force One*. As he leant over to remove the dishes he winked at the First Man. Davey twinkled back, sucked the red sauce off his fingers then signed, 'Thank you, Chief Danny. The burger was good, but not as good as one of Isabel's.'

The officer looked quizzically at the president who, for once, was glad her crew's American Sign Language skills were still fairly feeble. She tousled her ten-year-old stepson's blond locks and signed to the boy, 'Chef Lisa's burgers are delicious, Davey.

Besides, it's not polite to diss her or Chief Danny when they've stayed up all night to please us.'

That said, she couldn't help thinking that the boy was actually correct. While Lisa's food was excellent, her burgers did lack the decades of devotion that Isabel had spent in perfecting her own, let alone the family restaurant chain she'd built to prove it.

The child signed back, a cheeky smile on his face, 'Isabel, did you know I can sign how your burgers are the best in the world in six languages! Six! Montse taught me.' He picked up his milk with both hands and guzzled it, then put the glass down.

Isabel took her napkin and wiped the white moustache off his upper lip. He gazed up at her with his big blue eyes. She knew what was coming. He'd been begging the same thing from the moment she told him they were flying to Barcelona.

'Can I sign your speech for you at Montse's funeral? Please? I've been learning it in International Sign,' a fact to which every passenger and crewmember on board *Air Force One* could attest. 'Please? *Please?*'

In truth, Isabel was as keen as Davey for him to do it, but she'd screwed up, asking the Catalan president about it during the same phone call with him two days ago when she'd raised the Greenland talks.

Oriol – only those close to him called him Uri – had exploded. Not about Davey's request, but about the leak – the talks were top secret. 'It was Madrid, wasn't it?' he raged; Spain's national government constantly spying on Catalonia was bad enough without them leaking its secrets to foreign powers, let alone secrets that belonged to two other friendly nations.

Point blank, she told Oriol he was wrong, which was easy to do because he was. She didn't tell him the complete truth, though. She'd have hell to pay if Greenland discovered that the five-star cybersecurity contractor they'd hired to protect their parliament's digital network was ultimately controlled by the CIA.

Raising Davey's request in the same call was imprudent, yet she'd done it and couldn't undo it.

Montse, like her stepson, had lost her hearing. In her case it was nine years ago when, as Spain's distinguished secretary of defence, she suffered a bout of meningitis after a mission to north Africa. Never one for half measures, Montse later perfected signing and gained fluency in six signing languages, making her a natural to take on the United Nations role.

There were still a few hours left before the service so Isabel hoped Oriol would recall the close friendship Montse had developed with her and, importantly, Davey, and change his mind.

Isabel first clicked with Montse years ago, during a Congressional Committee fact-finding tour to Madrid. Six months ago, when Montse got elected as secretary-general and moved to New York City, they became even closer, with Montse flying to Washington DC as often as both women's frenetic schedules allowed, once a month on average, when she took the third place-setting for dinner at the Residence.

Inspiring as a public figure, Montse sparkled in private, and especially with Davey. Their dinner conversations, all in sign language, were raucous. On one occasion, Montse held her hands up to stop the laughing, a serious look cast across her face, her eyes darting left and right as if she was checking no one was listening, and then joked how the infamous eighteen minutes missing from the Watergate tapes weren't blank at all, it was just President Nixon signing his okay to the conspiracy. Davey had no idea what a *water gate* or a *conspiracy* was but he laughed along anyway.

In her head, Isabel started playing back the opening line she'd crafted for the eulogy. *One of the world's greatest listeners has left us.*

She wasn't sure if people in the deaf community would welcome it as the tribute she intended or see it as a slight. Saying those words inside La Sagrada Familia – a basilica Isabel had yearned to visit since childhood – would amplify them, so she needed them to be perfect. To sing to Montse's song. *One of the world's greatest listeners has left us.*

The steward handed her the phone. 'Madam President, it's President Casals.'

She looked across at Davey, hoping Oriol was calling to say yes, but he began sharply and with no greeting, his tone short and clipped, like a man barely constraining his emotions. 'Montse did *not* leave us.'

'What?' Did a copy of her draft eulogy get leaked to him? Had *Casals* started to eavesdrop on *her*?

He continued. 'What I'm about to tell you – from the coroner's report – must stay confidential until after the funeral.'

Isabel knew there hadn't been an autopsy in New York when Montse died there last week because, as was standard practice for a diplomat dying on an overseas posting, Spain had flown the body home immediately. Oriol explained the local report had come through overnight and his call to Isabel was his first after breaking the news to his own country's president. 'Madam President, I know you and Montse were very close. It breaks my heart to tell you this but she was assassinated.'

Isabel felt as if her plane had suddenly dropped a few hundred metres and she gripped the edge of her table. In shock, she managed, 'But the doctors … they said it was a heart attack.'

'That was correct but incomplete.' Oriol sighed. 'Montse did have a cardiac arrest but the coroner found it was caused by an arterial embolism. A person unknown injected an air bubble into her bloodstream.'

9

Barcelona

Tori managed to snip just enough lash off one eyelid to get a slit of her sight back, not that it helped much since the room itself was pitch black. She needed some light and a mirror to complete the job safely, so she fumbled her way past the nightstand and felt along the wall until she got to a door she hoped was the bathroom.

The lights didn't work. The bastard who'd done this to her had either cut the power or removed the bulbs, though when she tapped around and found the makeup mirror above the sink, she discovered the one light he'd neglected to neuter. It wasn't super bright but it was enough to get the job done.

Finished, she blinked several times, big, wide-open blinks, and pulled her brows up high, relieved her eyelids were working perfectly. She took a deep breath, then leant forward into the mirror to check out her handiwork. Going lash-free wasn't as creepy as she'd expected and, except for a drop of blood where she'd nicked her bottom left lid, she wondered if anyone would actually notice.

She drew back from the mirror and when her eyes began adjusting to the room she saw the rest of the blood.

On the towel. In the sink.

On her, too. A river of crimson down her right arm. Splatters of red on her right breast. On her stomach. Down her right leg. All of it on her right side, none on her left.

She spun on her heels and poked her head back into the bedroom but it was still too dark inside even with the dim light from the makeup mirror and the sliver of light seeping in beneath the front door.

The smell, too ... all the effort to get her sight back had taken her mind off it. The reek of vomit was hers, but not the rest.

Bloody and naked, she gaped into her hotel room as the hazy outline of her bed and what was on it started to take shape.

10

Again, Tori wanted to scream but held it in, instead jerking back the drapes so that streaks of morning sun lit up a savagery that was beyond anything she'd witnessed before, in Afghanistan, Iraq, anywhere.

A man and a woman, or what was left of them, were right beside where Tori had been lying, their bodies hacked and mutilated. The bed was soaked with their blood and entrails.

The woman, naked, was face down in the middle of the mattress, her legs spread, rivers of red oozing out of her body and pooling at her sides. Her skull cleaved by a hatchet, her brown hair – was it brown? – caked in blood. Razor blades, twenty or so, stuck out of her back as if a crazed ninja had been flinging *shuriken* throwing stars at her.

The hatchet, with its half-moon blade, was familiar, a traditional Greenlander's ulu like the one Prime Minister Petersen always carried on her belt and which Tori saw her use daily to cut fruit, slice bread, even once to shock some sense into China's delegation.

The killer had posed the man on the far side of the bed in a sickening bondage tableau. A sheet was draped over his lower half, drenched in red up to his chest, and a studded black fetish hood obscured his face. His arms were hitched above his head, his lats thick and taut and slathered in blood, his wrists bound to the bedhead with yellow plastic cable ties.

Who were these people? Why were they in her room, in her bed? What monster had done this to them? To her? And why? Where was he? Lurking under the bed? In the walk-in closet?

She grabbed the lamp from the sideboard and, in a single move, yanked its cord out of the wall and raised it shoulder-high, ready to swing it. She crouched down and peeked under the mattress only to find that the bedframe was so low to the floor that even the single black sock she found there would've had trouble slithering in.

She got up, lamp still held high, and jerked open the door to the walk-in robe, ready to attack. Apart from her wheelie bag, backpack and her clothes hanging there, the closet was empty.

Whoever he was, he'd left.

She set the lamp down on the floor and slid the security chain across the front door. A useless gesture, perhaps.

She looked back at the bed. The only part of the sheet that was still white was the hollow where she'd been sleeping, the contour of her right arm and right leg proof of where her own body had acted as a dam, holding back the woman's blood.

Crime scene or not, she stepped over to the bed. The woman's face was buried in the pillow, her right hand flat beside it, the fingernails freshly painted gold like the sun streaming through the window, a sight the woman would never witness again.

Tori reached over. No pulse, the woman's skin chill.

Like anyone with even basic training in the field, Tori knew the Glaister equation, the formula used the world over to estimate a victim's time of death. *Normal body temperature minus current temperature divided by blah blah.* The victim's current temperature was supposed to be taken rectally but Tori wasn't doing that to the app on her watch. Approximation would have to do, so she pressed the clock face up against the woman's wrist, waited ten seconds, pulled it off and did the calculations.

The woman took her last breath five hours ago, maybe six, which meant she'd been murdered at around 1 or 2 am.

Tori was about to turn the woman's head, to check if she knew her, but the move brought her face close to the man's dead brown eyes, staring at her out of the holes in his face mask.

Her hand flew to her mouth. Frank? Was this Frank?

With all the blood it was hard to know. Only small splotches of his skin poked through, seemingly olive or tan. Thankfully, not Frank's deeper brown. To take herself to his side of the bed, she had to step over a crumpled pile of clothes. The outfit lying on top was hers, the black and white polka dot dress she'd worn last night, the one Frank had urged her to buy. Except now it was splattered red like a slaughtered Dalmatian.

'Black. You always wear black, Tori.' He'd said it with the same eye roll she reserved for the scratchy jacket he seemed to live in, a tweed in baby-poop green.

'I like black. I love black,' she'd told him, not for the first time. People often said it set off the fire in her red hair and the green sparkle of her eyes, but it was practicality, not vanity. Tori was no fashionista. She might have had the body for it but she didn't have the temperament. 'I'll tell you what,' she said. 'I'll splash out on this polka dot thingy – which is black *and* white – provided you buy a decent jacket, one that doesn't instantly evoke fusty armchairs, fox hunting or *Pip pip, dear chap*.' Frank's jacket had been a running joke between them. 'For the son of Pakistani immigrants,' she told him the first week they'd met, 'you're more Eton and Oxford than someone who actually went to Eton and Oxford.'

'Actually Tori, I graduated from both of those fine institutions.' He laughed it off, but then he was a gentleman so he would, if only to help her feel less awkward. For a woman who prided herself on never stereotyping, she'd really screwed up.

That was then. This time, she bought the dress and he bought a jacket.

She knew it was weird to be pondering trifles like that right now but looking down at the blood-spattered dress, taking in the carnage all around her, desperately hoping the man wasn't Frank, she needed to focus on trivia, to find a life raft of normality in a roiling sea of revulsion.

Nothing in this room was normal and it was dawning on her that nothing would ever be normal for her again.

Briefly she closed her eyes and held her breath before she checked the man's neck for a pulse, the man she couldn't bring herself to think of as Frank.

She felt nothing. Nothing except the chill of his skin.

She pulled back from the bed, trying to decide whether or not to unfasten his mask, when a glimmer flickered up from the floor – a wristwatch. She took a hotel pen from the desk and bent down, slid it into the band and picked it up, dangling it in the fetid air. The clock face, she saw, was cracked and the time frozen at 1.32 am, almost six hours ago, telling her she'd made a pretty good estimate of the time when the couple were slaughtered.

The watch was a Blancpain, a Fifty Fathoms 'bathyscaphe' model that looked very expensive, which meant it could not be Frank's. Moths would fly out of Frank's wallet before he'd ever stump up for a pricey piece like this.

So if this was the victim's watch he couldn't be Frank. But what if it was the assailant's?

If she unclipped the face mask she'd know one way or the other. Except she couldn't bring herself to do that. Not yet.

She took herself back into the bathroom to rinse her face again. This time, with daylight coming through the balcony doors, she could see how ropy and clumpy her hair was, the red dark and grubby, and the touch viscous and tacky, so nauseating that her knees began to give way. She reached out for the sides of the sink in time, only just managing to stay on her feet.

Breathe … in … out … in … out.

She clenched the lever on the faucet as if that might stop her trembling and she flicked it upwards, as if to make a plea to the God she'd never believed in and now had every reason to believe in even less.

She plunged her head under the stream of icy water, let it drizzle over her face and, feeling strangely detached, watched the liquid swirling in the bowl – at first red, then pink and finally clear. She took a handtowel from the rack and wrapped it around her hair, took another, which she soaked – the water still running – and patted down her face and body, not cleaning herself as much as checking for wounds or bruises.

Three scratches came up on her left shoulder, as though someone had clawed her. It couldn't have been the masked man, not with his hands tied. The woman? Suddenly her whole body spasmed, her stomach cramped and, turning her head fast, she spewed again, this time directly into the toilet.

She knew what all this looked like, the conclusion the police would jump to when they came. That she'd been part of a three-way, a saturnalian orgy. What they couldn't know, what they'd never believe, was that Tori didn't do sex with strangers. Never had. Nor drugs. The only coke she'd ever tingled her nostrils with came out of red cans.

She squatted, her head hovering close to the toilet, in case, and she pressed two fingers against the crook of her arm to squeeze a drop of blood out of the lump she'd found, where she guessed she'd been injected with some drug.

If she *was* a drug-crazed killer, someone who hacked an ulu into a woman's head and flung razor blades into her back, she'd have cut her own hands. But when she turned up her palms, hers were completely unmarked. Apart from the long lifeline that, years ago, a toothless psychic in a Hong Kong backstreet had smiled over.

Tori slowly pushed herself up from the floor, hoping the twenty bucks she'd paid that fortune-teller was money well spent, and inched her way back into the bedroom like an accident victim relearning how to walk, first one foot, then the other.

She stepped over the bloody pile of clothes to get to the man's side of the bed, and – *Please, please don't be Frank!* – she scritched the Velcro strap off the side of his mask and slowly slid it away from his terrified eyes.

Yes! He wasn't Frank.

But *no*! He was Rao Songtian. And to turn this already unspeakable situation into a grave international incident, not only was Rao the Chinese negotiator she'd gone toe-to-toe against in the negotiations, he was also the brother-in-law of the president of China, having taken the hand of the supreme leader's sister, meaning he also had President Hou Tao's ear.

Rao Songtian was dead. Butchered.

With him, all hope of a new future for Greenland was as good as dead too.

11

Mid-Atlantic, Air Force One

Washington DC's snow season was long gone but at 1 am the White House was in a flurry with scores of staffers dragging themselves into work from bars or beds. One team, bushed and bleary-eyed, was sloughing in behind their desks, charged with scanning the administration's digital databases for anything that mentioned a 'Project Gusher' or a project of any name with a connection to oil in Greenland. Another squad was opening up the archive vaults, sneezing from the dust as they opened file boxes from the 1960s. Yet more staffers were rushing in and out of conference rooms in the White House, Homeland Security, and State and Defence departments, scanning phones, shouting or being shouted at. They weren't just busy, they were frantic, the entire human whirlwind the result of a terse two-page media release issued fifty minutes ago by Endz of the Earth, a shadowy band of eco-terrorists.

When Endz of the Earth first publicly raised its head, the world had leapt to attention. That was four months ago, via a shock announcement from Russia's President Tushkin that his country's Special Forces had averted an international crisis by taking out the group's top echelon. The entire US security apparatus was dumbfounded. Until then, not a soul in the American intelligence establishment had heard of the group. There'd been no SIGINT, no HUMINT, no OSINT, no intel at all. 'Another massive intelligence failure,' the media raged.

In Tushkin's surprise media conference, he told the world that Russia's surgical intervention prevented Endz carrying out an imminent attack on two nuclear waste sites that, had they succeeded, would have killed hundreds of thousands of civilians.

Endz of the Earth's plan was chilling, and so was their manifesto. They maintained that the United Nations' efforts to reduce carbon emissions were futile because they would not arrest climate change fast enough. The Copenhagen Accord, the Kyoto Protocol, the Paris Agreement and the ones that followed, all of them, they said, were a waste of time, and time was the critical resource the world was running out of.

The root cause of climate change, as they saw it, was global population growth. The only sure-fire way to stop the planet warming was to slash the number of people polluting it. 'The planet is over-populated. Chop the people, save the planet.'

President Diaz first heard about the latest Endz media release in a call from her Secretary of State not long after take-off. The terror group, he told her, were claiming they'd uncovered a top-secret cache of papers that revealed a defunct CIA project called 'Gusher'. If it was true, he said, the revelation could damage the US far more deeply than the Edward Snowden leaks and the Vietnam-era Pentagon Papers combined.

The documents, Endz claimed, proved that illegal American actions were the direct cause of the rapidity of the melting of the Arctic ice sheet and the calamitous rise in world sea levels that flowed from it. All of that, they said, was due to a disastrous CIA operation in Greenland in the 1960s code-named Project Gusher.

The urgency to uncover the truth was sapping almost all the oxygen in Washington. Isabel's hope that the people working through the night back in DC would quickly prove it was a hoax was fading.

In a break in the rat-tat-tat of frenetic calls, her eye caught the reflection of her cashmere cardigan in the mirror opposite her desk. The aqua weave was washing out her olive complexion, making her look as bad as she felt. It had to go, she thought, and it would have except the tiling news headlines covering her computer screen captured her attention:

Eco-terrorists' alarming report:
Secret 1960s CIA program speeds up Arctic melt
– *Le Monde*, Paris

America's buried shame –
is Willard Buckingham, 93, the new Edward Snowden?
– *BILD*, Germany

Rising sea levels – US to blame, says revered scientist
– *The Times*, London

CIA's Project Gusher: 'peak oil' dream to king tide nightmare
– *Washington Post*

Project Gusher was supposedly a covert CIA-backed oil-drilling operation in Greenland that Denmark and Greenland never consented to or even knew about. When the engineers and scientists working on the project – and Professor Willard Buckingham was apparently one of them – saw the damage their drilling was doing to the ice shelf, they were forced to terminate the operation and send everyone home. The project's entire existence, including its dire consequences, was hushed up and had stayed that way for seventy years. Until Endz of the Earth dredged it up.

Washington's plan, said Endz of the Earth, was to stretch out as long a gap as possible between America's illegal actions and their devastating effects. That way no one would ever connect America's criminal negligence with a global catastrophe that would only reveal itself many decades later.

Isabel had skimmed three of the articles when her next call came through, a video meeting with her Director of National Intelligence, Robert Hirsty, and Vice-President Spencer Prentice.

Despite the early hour in DC, Spencer was immaculately dressed – no surprise – his trademark bow tie neatly in place, navy this time, a dark blue suit and one of the glaringly white shirts he liked to wear to contrast against the darkness of his skin. They were, he once confided to her over a late-night drink, his 'fuck you' shirts. 'Those racists we have to deal with in Congress – you know who I mean, Isabel – this way I remind them, constantly but silently, how proud I am that I'm African American.'

Her Director of National Intelligence, on the other hand, was tieless, decked out in a blue sports shirt and a rumpled brown sweater. The black shoe-polished helmet he tried to pass off as his natural head of hair was patted down, looking as unnatural as ever. He jumped right in and, far too quickly for Isabel's liking, began claiming victory.

It was a habit of Hirsty's that often rubbed her the wrong way. He was, she felt, like the bass drum at the head of a funeral procession, loud, bombastic and one-dimensional. 'No doubt about it, ma'am,' he said, ignoring the vice-president, 'these so-called *explosive* documents … they don't exist.'

'That would be wonderful if it were true,' said Isabel. 'What's the actual proof that justifies you saying that?'

He looked at her as if she had suddenly grown horns. 'Ma'am, conclusively provin' that somethin' we ain't seen don't exist … it ain't easy. But be assured that our best people are workin' on it.'

He smoothed back his gelled hair with the soft, uncalloused hand she always avoided shaking because it felt like a day-old fajita. That was one blessing of the COVID-19 crisis. There was a lot less hand-shaking afterwards.

Isabel didn't share Hirsty's breezy over-confidence and, unlike some, she wasn't comforted by his homey, apple-pie Southern drawl. As commander-in-chief, she had to brace herself for the possibility that if the Endz claim did stack up, if there were documents that no one in DC knew anything about, America's moral culpability for a global crisis *and* its legal liability might force her to go into defence mode. And if it did, she'd find herself forced to defend the indefensible.

The more she thought about it, Endz of the Earth's unlikely source was probably the best thing the US had going for it. Professor Emeritus Willard (Buck) Buckingham, now aged ninety-three, was one of the world's most respected glacial geologists. Why, she kept wondering, would a man with such a stellar record of service and scholarship turn against his country?

He had indeed worked in Greenland, from 1961 to 1966, but the bio in front of her said he'd been working on a US project called Ice Worm, not Gusher.

Isabel had a report on Ice Worm but hadn't yet had a chance to read it.

After Ice Worm, he'd returned home, taken a professorship at the University of Minnesota and over time had become one of the country's, if not the world's, most distinguished experts in glacial geology. His numerous projects had received millions in federal research funding.

Buckingham had retired only five years ago, straight after the tragic deaths of his wife and son. Since then he'd spent most of his time quietly collecting and cataloguing butterflies. Importantly, he'd never once lodged a complaint with any government department about his work in Greenland or what he'd seen there, and neither his name nor any complaint about Gusher had come up on any whistle-blower register.

Nothing in the professor's record hinted at a man who'd betray his country. So why would he hand over what the *Washington Post* was calling 'the stash of the century' to a bunch of extremists without at least trying to alert the new Administration in DC first? It simply didn't gel.

On top of that, the timing was very opportune for China, and Isabel couldn't help wondering if Hou Tao was behind it. If it was a program of disinformation designed to kill any chance of the US making a counteroffer for Greenland, it was pretty damned good.

'Could this be a put-up job by China?' she asked the two men on the call. 'That by the time the world finds out it's a hoax – if it is a hoax – the Greenland parliament has ratified the China deal and we're—'

'Out in the cold,' said Hirsty, trying for humour, but failing. 'We're explorin' all possibilities,' he went on, but Isabel saw him hastily jot something down, which told her that China being behind it had not occurred to him until now.

'What about that Endz of the Earth crowdfunding campaign?' asked Spencer Prentice. 'How much have they raised so far?'

'The websites keep poppin' up, despite us blockin' them. They say they got eleven million and some, sir. Enough to pay for a small army of mercenaries, but this Project Gusher thing'll probably see them double that level of support.'

Isabel wasn't listening. She was pondering Russia's reaction to the news. Max Tushkin had claimed he'd decapitated Endz, yet here they were, this time setting off a bomb under the credibility of the United States as well as wrecking any chance it had of winning over Greenland.

Tushkin was coming to the funeral in Barcelona. She definitely needed to talk to him. She'd previously invited him for a *tête-a-tête* after the funeral but he'd declined when he heard she wanted him to stand down the Russian forces at the Estonian border in exchange for dropping US sanctions. That was not a proposal he was willing to entertain. But Russia had unique insights into Endz, so she had to try again.

If this Gusher thing did kick the US out of the race for Greenland, Russia was the only credible counterbidder to China. For the US, Greenland coming under Russian *or* Chinese control was equally bad.

An hour later another video call from Hirsty and Spencer came through, this time with Secretary of State Linden joining them. 'Gentlemen,' she said, seeing the three faces pop onto her screen from separate locations, 'let me play out a new scenario for you. Just hours after Greenland's prime minister inks a deal that duds the United States, this shadowy terrorist group reveals a project that no one in Washington ever knew existed but which they claim is—'

'—directly causing a global climate catastrophe,' said Hirsty.

Isabel disliked people finishing her sentences and she was certain Hirsty wouldn't dare if she'd been male. 'Let's zero in on our weakest points,' she said, looking at the notes she'd scribbled. 'In 2013, scientists discovered a massive lake hiding beneath Greenland's glaciers—'

'As big as the state of Virginia, ma'am, three times the size of Switzerland.'

If she was a different woman she might have told him to shut the fuck up, but she wasn't and she didn't. 'Like I said, gentlemen, a gigantic body of water that's been melting the ice above it perhaps for centuries, which in turn has been creating more water that's contributing to the rise in global sea levels.'

'Which until now scientists were sayin' was a natural phenomenon.'

Maybe some, she thought. Her fingers were drumming against her desk. She'd probably crack her nail polish but she didn't care. 'Based on this Professor Buckingham's assertions—'

'If he's to be believed.'

She'd had enough. 'Robert, will you kindly hear me out? Based on the files Buckingham's supposedly given to Endz of the Earth, which we are yet to see, Endz are laying the melting glaciers and rising sea levels right at our feet.'

Her feet.

'Yes, ma'am,' Hirsty said, clearly not getting her message. 'Buckingham says ... the Endz people say ... that our drillin' and blastin' into the glaciers while we were lookin' for hydrocarbons was the cause. And when our people saw the damage they were doin' they stopped, hid the facts and vamoosed, prayin' no one'd ever find out.'

Mercifully, another paper came through from State. She clicked it open and read the first few paragraphs.

Secretary Linden spoke to it. 'Ma'am, as you can see in that memorandum, my department has undertaken as comprehensive a sweep as we can in the short time available. I'm assured there's not a single record anywhere within the United States government that refers to a Gusher project in Greenland. Likewise, any secret oil drilling project.'

'That's puttin' us on damn solid ground,' said Hirsty.

'Not in the court of public opinion,' said Vice-President Spencer Prentice.

'I'm with Spencer,' said Isabel. 'If this *was* a deep cover-up isn't that precisely the kind of thing we'd say? As I see it, this game is playing out as heads, Endz of the Earth wins, tails, we lose.'

'Ma'am, the truth will win out eventually. It always does.'

'Eventually can be a hell of a long time. We need hard evidence fast, and well before the next fourteen days passes.'

'Fourteen, ma'am?'

Hirsty really was an idiot, she concluded. When Nivikka Petersen phoned last night after the signing, she had gone out of her way to tell Isabel about the deal's ratification condition. 'Even as prime minister,' she'd said, 'I could never usurp my parliament's authority over such an historic agreement. In two weeks, parliament gets the final say on whether we partner with China or not.'

While Isabel felt that good democratic process was *one* reason why Petersen included the ratification clause, she was confident it wasn't the *only* reason. The real reason was tactical, to give America and Russia an opportunity to see what China had offered and quickly come up with better proposals.

But overnight everything changed. This Project Gusher scandal would taint anything the US proposed.

Which was why Isabel needed hard proof. 'Gentlemen, China's deal with Greenland only goes live if Greenland's parliament ratifies it, and their vote is in two weeks. If we can't kill this scandal well before then, the United States' Arctic presence is cooked. China or Russia, one or both of them, will control the region. Do I make myself clear?'

'Yes, ma'am.'

'So hard proof, Robert, and fast.'

'And Robert,' said the vice-president, 'it's the middle of the night in Minnesota but has anyone gone to wake up this Professor Buckingham? Have we talked to him directly?'

'A report just came in, sir.' Hirsty was reading from it. 'Folks went out to Buckingham's home … yadda yadda … He weren't there … Heck, this is … double heck … There weren't nothin' much there. No files, no computer, just the cables danglin' off his desk, makin' it look like he scarpered off like a jittery jackrabbit. All they rustled up was his walking cane, a mess of antique snowshoes, and trays and trays of dead butterflies … They roused his next-door neighbours, an' none o' them seen him for three days. Seems the guy just upped and disappeared—'

'Without his walking cane?'

'I'll check on that. Says he even left his chess buddy, guy next door, in the lurch. No call, no apology, an' they been playin' each other every week since his wife and kid died, same time, same place.' He looked up at the camera, 'Ma'am, our folks are doin' what they can to track Buckingham down.'

Best of luck, thought Isabel. A doddery nonagenarian drops a bombshell on the country he'd served his whole life with distinction then runs off without his walking cane?

She didn't think so.

12

President Diaz opened the memo from State. 'Here,' she shared the first page on the screen so Spencer, Hirsty and Linden could view what she was reading. 'See that second paragraph: *We have not yet found any record of a Project Gusher in Greenland in the 1960s. But the United States did conduct a Project Ice Worm there in the same period, and Willard Buckingham did work on that.*'

She read on. 'Oh, great, terrific, this is just what we need,' she grimaced as she leant towards her screen.

'Surely this can't be,' she said. '*With Ice Worm we were tunnelling* … I don't believe the insanity of this … *we were tunnelling under the Greenland glacier to construct* … hell on earth … *we were digging a network of nuclear silos* … And if that isn't bad enough, it says we hid the whole damn thing for thirty years from the

Danes *and* the Greenlanders, the very people on whose sovereign territory we were doing this. Thirty years. Hell.'

'Even worse, if that's possible,' said Prentice, 'we only fessed up in 1995 because we had no choice. The Danes called us out on it.'

'So if we come out now and claim Project Gusher never existed,' said Secretary Linden, 'the world will say *Here goes America again* ... that we're just doing a repeat of what we did with Project Ice Worm. Damn!'

All four of them were speed reading the memo. Project Ice Worm was a highly classified US Army project sanctioned by the Kennedy administration. The aim was to give America the capacity to launch a surprise nuclear attack on the Soviets from their near north, from Greenland. If geology had not stopped the project, the US would have installed a network of six hundred nuclear missile silos beneath the ice sheet, in complete contravention of international law.

'What was JFK thinking? The Cold War indeed,' said Isabel, her voice bitter, angry.

'Ice Worm was not America's finest hour for sure, ma'am,' said Hirsty. 'But the thing is, we didn't go through with it.'

'We didn't pull out because we got a sudden shot of morality,' said Prentice. 'We pulled out simply because our experts got the glacial science wrong.'

According to the memo, the US Army engineers were six long, secret years into tunnelling when their 'perfectly' designed shafts started to buckle and twist. Even back then the experts knew glaciers weren't static, that they flowed, but what these whizzes hadn't counted on was that the particular glacier they were burrowing into was moving a lot faster than their models predicted.

'If we'd actually got around to installing any nukes there,' said Spencer, 'the shifting ice would have crushed them, which in turn would have caused a nuclear holocaust. Jesus, Mary and Joseph!'

'It was of a different time, sir,' said Hirsty. 'Ice science was in its infancy.'

To Isabel, this defence of what was plainly an outrage was more than misplaced patriotism. '*Of a different time?*' She almost spat the phrase. 'The issue isn't the ice science. The issue here is our country's criminal misconduct *and* our naked hubris in doing whatever we liked on another nation's sovereign soil without their permission or even their knowledge. That is the issue. Morality is not relative, Mr Hirsty.'

Isabel was fuming. As she saw it, Ice Worm was yet one more disgraceful example of powerful men taking for granted that they and their enablers could escape censure for their corrupt behaviour by keeping it out of the spotlight.

'It was *of a different time*, you say? Well, this president will not stand for that as an excuse for behaviour that is, and always was, completely reprehensible.'

As Hirsty's mouth dropped open, a smiling Davey, his arms stretched out, flew into Isabel's office pretending to be an airplane. The boy was wearing blue, she noticed. The colour looked better on him than on her, probably because it brought out his gorgeous eyes, the ones she loved waking up to those mornings when she'd find him patiently standing by her bedside in the Residence, his head peeking just over the top of her mattress, his little hands cuddling his fluffy toy penguin, Pip.

After several fast but imaginary loop-the-loops of her office Davey handed her a mint and started signing to her, again asking about the eulogy.

She pointed to the video screen and signed back, 'Darling, I'm tied up and will be a while. Say hello to Mr Prentice, Mr Linden and Mr Hirsty before you scoot off.'

The boy saluted, then banked, turned and jetted out of the room. She popped the candy into her mouth but it was so strong her eyes immediately started to water.

Just after Davey flew out of the room, one of her assistants brought in a sheet of paper and placed it before her. It was a hard copy of a new Endz of the Earth media release, the second of the day.

She sucked on the mint and held the sheet up to the screen. 'It didn't take long. The Endz people are doing exactly what we were worried about. Here … *Earlier today we exposed Project Gusher in Greenland, a sordid American crime against humanity, which successive administrations have conspired to conceal for 70 years. When the US inevitably denies Project Gusher, remember that they have form on this* … And there they spell out, in all its elaborate finery, what happened with Ice Worm.'

She was about to put down the page when another paragraph caught her eye. '*These two projects, Gusher and Ice Worm, were but two corrupt elements in a 160-year US strategy to dominate and violate the Arctic. Over that period, America has repeatedly tried to buy Greenland outright but each time Denmark has said no. Refusing to see their naked imperialist ambitions stymied, America simply trampled on another nation's sovereignty. They did that with the Ice Worm nuclear program, which Denmark forced them to admit in 1995 and—*'

'Ma'am, that is utter bull dust,' said Hirsty. 'Anyone with a wit of knowledge about federal politics knows that kind of long-term thinkin' simply don't exist.'

Irony from Hirsty? That was new, thought Isabel, and ironic itself.

13

Endz of the Earth were claiming that the two projects were sturdy rungs in a tottering American ladder built over the past 160 years to attain Arctic supremacy. Four other rungs were the US's historic but futile attempts to actually buy Greenland – in 1867, 1910, 1947 and 2019. Each one was set out in a background note the State Department had sent Isabel before her own ineffectual intervention in the Greenland–China negotiations.

Owning Greenland was not a long-term strategy, it was merely a seductive idea that popped its head up every few decades.

The 1867 attempt came straight after then Secretary of State William Seward successfully negotiated the Alaska Purchase from Russia. Having bought control of Canada's western flank, he was keen to do the same to its north as part of a broader plan to prise Canada out of the despised British Empire. Buying Greenland would 'greatly increase [Canada's] inducements, peacefully and cheerfully, to become part of the American Union'. But his brilliant plan and the seventy-two-page report supporting it got leaked and Congress laughed it out of the Capitol, literally.

It took forty or so more years before America tried again, in 1910 during William Taft's presidency, and the rationale that time was to protect America's southern states via a tortuously complicated territory swap.

The first step was the US offering Denmark the Philippine island of Mindanao in exchange for two Danish territories – the Virgin Islands in the Caribbean and Greenland. Denmark, in turn, would swap Mindanao with Germany in return for territory Prussia had seized from Denmark in 1864.

But the combination of World War I and the deal's complexity killed off the idea. By 1917, the US was gripped by the fear that Germany would invade Denmark, which would mean the Kaiser would get control of the Virgin Islands and endanger America to its near south. So the US dropped its interest in Greenland and instead threatened to invade the Virgin Islands, thereby 'persuading' Denmark to sell them the islands for $25 million in gold.

The years marched on and three decades later, soon after the victory in World War II and with the new Cold War under way, President Truman's secretary of state James Byrnes got up a new head of Arctic steam and tossed down a bid for Greenland, offering $100 million in gold. America's objective that time was to flank Russia to its near north. Despite the Danes' gratitude for the Allied efforts in defeating the Nazis, they turned the offer down.

Then came President Donald Trump in 2019. Owning Greenland, he said, statesmanlike, 'would be nice. It's essentially a large real estate deal.'

His approach generated world-wide derision, especially from Denmark and Greenland. But, as Isabel now knew, that was the catalyst for China to quietly start working up its own plan to control Greenland.

While Isabel had been briefed on these attempts to buy Greenland, and now on Project Ice Worm, the only information she had on Project Gusher was from Endz of the Earth's two media releases.

According to them, JFK's covert effort to drill for oil under the Greenland ice sheet was not motivated by the Cold War. Instead, it was 'peak oil', a genuine alarm back in the 1960s. 'Peak oil' was fear that the world's oil supply would peak during the seventies and then rapidly start running out. For America's rapidly expanding industries, the search for new sources of oil became a desperate national imperative.

That her presidency was being tarnished with a sullied 1960s brush was burning a fire inside her. Isabel was politically committed to a different kind of 'peak oil' – not the mid-twentieth-century fear that the *supply* of oil would peak, but the current century's imperative for the *demand* for fossil fuels to decline.

According to Endz of the Earth and the professor who'd gone AWOL without his walking cane, Project Gusher was hatched when fossil fuel specialists pinpointed a vast sea of hydrocarbons hidden under Greenland's glaciers.

President Kennedy himself authorised funding for the CIA to mount a covert oil exploration and drilling program inside Greenland to run side-by-side with the nuclear missile project.

Project Gusher was so secret, said Endz of the Earth, that not even Project Ice Worm's top leadership knew about it.

The unexpected glacial instability that terminated Ice Worm was one of the reasons for stopping Gusher. The other was that Gusher's blasting and drilling program had critically destabilised the glacial floor.

Over the ensuing decades, claimed Endz of the Earth, what began as mere cracks became fissures which turned into caverns which grew into the gigantic underground lake that was melting the ice above it and accelerating the planet's rising sea levels.

The quote from Professor Buckingham in the Endz media release was blunt: '*I did it. I saw it. And I helped cover it up. But at ninety-three years old, I can no longer stomach the notion that our nation's dirtiest secret will die with me.*'

If this was a hoax, as Hirsty kept assuring her, then who was behind it?

China, Isabel calculated, was the obvious culprit. Hou else could it be? She almost laughed at her own pun. Instead she picked up her water glass and took a sip.

But what if it wasn't China?

Tushkin. Yes, it could be Russia. Easily. She put it to the men on the call.

'That'd be kind of perverse, ma'am. Endz of the Earth have been raisin' millions to hit back at Tushkin for takin' out their leadership so I can't see them doin' him no favours.'

Maybe. Maybe not. In Isabel's mind, Tushkin was as unpredictable as a drunk uncle at a barbecue but far more unpleasant and dangerous. For him, screwing with the US was as routine as downing a bottle of vodka. 'If Tushkin cruels our chances of outbidding China, he forces our bases out of there and stops us muscling in on his polar patch. Robert, do we have people checking out the clubs in Moscow?' she asked.

'Excuse me?'

'Perhaps they'll find Professor Buckingham is having a drink with Edward Snowden. You know, two traitors toasting to America's bad health.'

14

Barcelona

The grotesque mask dangled off the side of the dead man's face. Contorted and freakish as his expression was, he was unmistakeably Rao Songtian. His eyes were so bugged out that Tori could have been looking at the agonised figure in Munch's painting *The Scream*, his mouth locked so far open that she could almost hear the bloodcurdling shrieks as the gore spilled out of him.

Shrieks that Tori hadn't heard despite being in the same room. Or was too drugged to remember hearing.

A string of blood oozing off the side of the bed glooped onto her foot, creeping her out even more. As she scrubbed her toes against the carpet she noticed a dip in the bloody sheet that covered Rao from the chest down, a sopping red U-shape at his abdomen.

With the pen she'd used to pick up the watch, she gingerly pulled the sheet back.

Rao Songtian was sawn in half.

15

Tori desperately wanted to strip off her skin, to stop being the woman who'd woken up beside these two mutilated bodies.

She scanned every surface to see if she could find any evidence of what she'd been drugged with – a syringe, pills, baggies. Nothing, until she noticed the room service menu on the desk was slanted up. When she lifted it she found a syringe and a small bag of clear crystals that looked like glass. Crystal meth, ice? Probably.

She stepped back in shock, her foot accidentally kicking the pile of clothes on the floor, knocking aside her own dress so that the dead woman's clothes stared back at her for the first time. Tori knew that outfit, the traditional Inuit skirt, the belt she'd seen every day holding Nivikka Petersen's ulu, a blade exactly like the one sticking out of the woman's skull.

She went back to the bed and pushed the pillow away from the woman's face.

16

Nivikka Petersen was dead, in bed with Rao Songtian, both hacked to pieces. Tori's mind was racing, not just struggling with the why, the how and the who but with the way the world would view it, and her. *Sex for sovereignty scandal … Ice kills Arctic deal … China and Greenland in Spanish sex triangle …* And worst of all, *Tori Swyft main suspect in drug-fuelled double murder.*

That was how it looked, how it was set up to look, except she knew – didn't she? – that none of it was remotely the truth.

Think, Tori. Find an explanation.

Except she couldn't. The room, the bodies, the blood and the stink were overwhelming, suffocating her, pushing her backwards until she felt her spine pressing up against a blank space on the wall.

Her arm brushed against something metallic that stuck out of a side-slot in the TV, something warm.

A flash drive.

Her arm must have activated it because she heard the TV click itself on and, unable to stop herself, she craned her head forwards to see a naked brunette appear on the screen.

Porn.

Just seeing it seemed to thicken the stench, like a square of sandpaper scraping the insides of Tori's nose. She went back into the bathroom, ripped a couple of pieces off a tissue and stuffed them into her nostrils, and re-entered the room as the porn star turned her face to the camera.

Not a porn star.

Nivikka Petersen.

The image pulled back and Tori saw Nivikka was completely naked, astride a masked and also naked man, who Tori now knew was Rao Songtian.

'*No way*,' she called out involuntarily. 'Nivi would never …' She slammed her fist so hard against the wall that a remote control bounced off its bracket onto the floor. She left it there and forced herself to watch, trying but failing to understand. Nivikka was riding Rao, goading him with a riding crop, slapping his sides and his arms, stretching herself back and flicking at his legs.

The Nivikka Tori knew, and liked, would never betray her country like this. She would never do that.

Except there she was.

Tori squeezed her eyes shut, wishing the video away. For a time, because it was on mute – or there was no audio, she didn't know which – she had a brief respite until she cracked one eye open and saw a second woman step into the picture, her head out of the frame. This woman wasn't naked. She was wearing a dress, black polka dots on white. Tori's dress.

The camera, shooting from behind, tilted upwards as the woman drew the dress over her head, mussing up her hair.

Flaming red hair.

Tori's hair.

17

Tori bent down, scrabbled for the remote and, as quickly as her trembling fingers could, she pressed pause. This was not her.

Or was it the influence of the drugs, the ice?

She had no recollection of the three of them coming back to her room last night. Nothing. No memory of the drugs. But having never done hard drugs before, she had no idea what they might do to her, what she might do under their influence. Could they possibly force her to do *this*?

Desperate to work out what this video was, she stepped so close to the screen she felt her hair catch the static, a finger wavering over the play button. Hesitantly, she pressed it and the footage restarted, the camera zooming in on Nivikka as she glided up and down on his … on Rao.

She couldn't imagine Nivi doing this with a man they'd negotiated hard against and whose gallantry, even under pressure, had almost been cloying, yet there was Nivikka, lewdly smacking a riding crop against his face mask, her free hand reaching backwards and tickling his scrotum, squeezing his penis, while the second woman, the faceless redhead Tori couldn't bring herself to name, watched like a voyeur.

Viewed from the back and completely naked, she looked like Tori, not that Tori knew what she really looked like from behind. The slope of the woman's shoulders was similar, the cut of her hair, the same dumb dress tossed to the floor.

She peered into the image to scan for her scar, the small crescent-shaped mark under her left shoulder blade, the one she got in Kabul, but the pixilation wasn't fine enough to spot it. *You can't be me. You're not me. Turn around and show me your face.*

The video redhead wasn't listening, and instead provocatively wiggled the fingers of her left hand and reached out as if to move it to her breast while her other hand ventured lower, both her arms swinging, her hands obviously rubbing ... *Oh, God, no* ... Then, and only then, did she obey Tori's command and turn her head – what looked like Tori's head – to face the camera as she seductively licked her lips, what looked like Tori's lips.

Tori couldn't watch. Not this.

Covering the image of the redhead with her real hand, she looked beyond her, and beyond the Brunette – who Tori was refusing to think of as Nivikka – and put her focus on the Masked Man.

His hood was identical to the one she'd unhitched, his arms pulled back and bound with yellow cable ties the same as those securing the man cut in half on her bed.

The Brunette rhythmically lifted and dropped her lithe body, each movement faster than the one before. Her left hand reached out to her side, out of screenshot, her body tilting as if she was feeling around for something under the mattress. Suddenly her back straightened, her hand returned to view holding a bone saw longer than her forearm. Tori didn't need to guess what she was about to do with it. For a moment, the Brunette's fingertips held the saw vertically by its sturdy stainless-steel handle, teasing, showing it off and swinging it a little, its forty-odd centimetres of sharp, finely serrated teeth gleaming in the light.

The Masked Man's eyes drew wide beneath his hood, terrified, as he watched the Brunette wrap her fingers around the saw's handgrip. He was desperate, seeming to grasp for the first time that what had started as a frolic was turning deadly. Tori watched the fingers of his bound hands curl into fists, his nails dig into his palms and his body twist in panic as he tried to toss the Brunette off him but she rode him like a bucking bronco.

Fake Tori stepped forwards, her bare back to the camera, pried the saw out of the Brunette's hand, slid the long blade in front of her face, moving her head from side to side as if she was licking the steel.

The Masked Man continued writhing under the Brunette, panicked, his hood stretched out like he was shrieking beneath it.

As Tori imagined his agonised screams, sweat streamed down her face. It was all she could do not to vomit again. As she cried out, the crumples of tissue blew out of her nose and the stink of the room, its reek of violent death, engulfed her. On the screen the Brunette kept riding him, up, down, sideways, rolling, twerking her hips as he thrashed around, his arms squirming, pulling, tearing at his bonds, trying to release his hands, kicking his legs, bucking his hips to toss her off him, his suddenly limp penis flopping out of her.

Fake Tori moved in closer, her hands clenched around the handle of the saw, and set the teeth down on the bare skin of his stomach, then pushed.

And pulled.

Tori – real Tori – lashed at the wall, knocking the screen, slightly dislodging the flash drive so the horror movie freeze-framed, spurts of the Masked Man's blood suspended mid-air, an affront to anything remotely human.

Tori staggered backwards, tears streaming down her cheeks, her hands at her mouth. She was gagging, faint.

She brought her hands to her cheeks to calm herself but instead became even more frantic when she realised what this video was. It was a taunt, to let her know how deep a pile of shit she was in. And that whoever filmed it could release more copies … *would* release them.

She knew she had to unfreeze the video, to play it all the way through to search for a clue, a hint, any skerrick of evidence that 'he' or 'they' had carelessly left on it. Anything that proved the depraved redhead was *not* Tori Swyft.

Maybe the on-screen Tori wasn't a true redhead at all. If only she could catch a stray lock of hair – blonde, brunette, black, purple, she didn't care as long as it wasn't red – creeping out from under a wig, she'd have proof. Maybe a reflection in the glass over the painting on the wall might capture Fake Tori's face and reveal that her eyes weren't green, that her nose was big and broken, anything that was different from Tori.

She glanced over at the bag of crystals on the desk. Ice could make you psychotic, everyone knew that. Was that what she was seeing on the video? The terrifying possibility that she – the real Tori – had been in the grip of a manic ice rush she had absolutely no memory of?

She pushed the flash drive back in.

18

Frank flicked across the TV channels to find one speaking English. How many channels in Spanish or Catalan did Barcelona need?

If he'd held onto the FrensLens they'd brought to Barcelona with them – brilliant wearable technology, built into the frame of a pair of glasses – he could have used its instant language translator, but since Tori had kept them he had no alternative but to keep flicking channels. Where were BBC World and CNN when you needed them? Eventually he got a channel where the text ribbons scrolling along the bottom of the screen were in both English and what looked like Catalan … *Terrorist group accuses CIA of causing Greenland ice melt … World pays with rising sea levels … US denies …*

What?

Before he had a chance to take that in, a grainy video clip, time-stamped at 10.45 last night, started playing. It showed a man downing shots in a bar. Was it Rao Songtian? The image, dark and tinged with purple, looked like the club they'd gone to after the deal dinner, but Frank couldn't be certain. He'd only stayed fifteen minutes and for most of that time he'd been doubled over, stomach spasms forcing his eyes shut until he rushed out to race back to the hotel. Leaving was hugely embarrassing but staying and throwing up over Tori or Rao or Nivikka or Uri … Oriol … whatever, would have been far worse.

Frank couldn't understand what the newsreader was saying but he did hear Nivikka's and Oriol's names. The camera pulled back from the man to reveal a woman in a polka dot dress, obviously Tori even though he couldn't see her face. She was pouring iced water out of a jug, her pose stiff and inclined away from Songtian. He'd been a decent guy throughout the talks but Tori's posture wasn't a surprise since Frank knew too well how uncomfortable she felt socialising in a work context. Nivikka and Oriol were there too, somewhere, but the camera angle didn't catch either of them.

Frank had to re-read the text bar as its next headline crawled across the screen … *Chinese envoy missing in Barcelona after signing with Greenland* … and he sprang to his feet, almost tripping over his shoes as he sprinted for the door and into the hotel hallway.

19

The shower Tori took was the hottest and strongest of her life. The fastest, too, since she was on high alert in case her tormentor returned. In a robe, her hair still dripping, new wads of tissue stuffed up her nose to block the stink, she returned to the bedroom and uncapped a mini bottle of vodka from the bar fridge. She downed it neat, then pressed *play* on the remote.

She forced herself to watch the video the whole way through, the sex, Fake Tori hacking at the Masked Man then at the Brunette, later flicking razor blades through the air at each of them like a crazed ninja. In a weird, sick kind of way, Tori felt a twinge of relief. She had many talents but blade throwing was not among them.

Unless the crystal meth had done this to her.

No, she is not me.

She can't be me.

The lack of an audio track was a blessing, not hearing the shrieks, the crunch of the saw's teeth through flesh and bone, the whoosh of the razors through the air … But it also meant she couldn't listen for any clues, couldn't hear if the victims had yelled a name, begged someone to stop.

Tori took up the remote again, but her finger hesitated over the volume control.

She turned it up, but all she got was the hiss of silence, as if the video was mocking her.

Disappointed yet relieved, she took a deep breath through her mouth and restarted the video, playing fifteen seconds, rewinding, replaying, then moving forwards and backwards through the tape fifteen seconds at a time, scanning and rescanning every segment of the images, hunting for clues. It was hard to dissociate herself, to pretend she was watching actors and not a genuine, horrific snuff movie, but it was the only way she could push herself through it.

The camera operator and the editor had been meticulous. By the time the control bar showed sixteen seconds of runtime left, she'd found nothing helpful. It was either going to be the sixteen seconds where she'd find the hook to hang her innocence on, or sixteen more seconds of utter depravity.

The clip panned to the empty part of the king-sized bed, the third where Tori had been sleeping. On the video, her pillow and her part of the sheet were awash with blood and gunk, nothing like now. Fake Tori, naked, still with her back to the camera, sidled over to that part of the bed, reached down and yanked the blood-soaked sheet off the bed. A tell-tale glint told Tori it was plastic, a drop sheet.

'Damn, damn, damn!' Tori blurted out her frustration as the plastic slithered to the floor taking the red-soaked pillow and the mess with it, exposing an impeccably white linen sheet.

Fake Tori plucked a fresh pillow from off-camera and set it on the bed, climbed in face down and, with three seconds of runtime remaining, slowly, teasingly, began rolling over, the lens zooming in on her breasts, tilting upwards, the finale … her face, her smile.

Tori's face, for the second time. Her emerald eyes gave a wink to the camera, her hand a cheeky wave.

20

Tori scanned the room for her cell phone. Normally she'd leave it charging on the nightstand beside the bed but it wasn't there. The hotel phone sat on the stand beside Rao Songtian but it was plastered with bloody globs of slop. Her clutch bag was on the sideboard. She unlatched it, found her phone inside, its ringer on silent, and saw its screen light up with message tiles, most of them sent in the last few minutes: four texts from Frank, two from Oriol Casals, two more from the Chinese ambassador, and seven missed calls including three local Barcelona numbers she didn't recognise.

She was about to speed dial Frank when his number flashed up.

'Tori, where the hell are you?'

'My room. It's—'

'Why won't you open your door? I've been banging on it for three … four minutes. I've got people in the corridor staring at me, Tori. *Let me in.*'

No one was knocking. No one had been knocking.

Was it the meth? Was that why she wasn't hearing? Maybe that was why she didn't get any sound on the video. Maybe the person behind all this, who'd drugged her and Nivikka, maybe even Songtian, had done to her ears what he'd done to her eyes.

Then she realised how ridiculous that was. She could hear Frank's voice as clear as ever. If this was her getting paranoid, even without the meth, who could blame her?

'I'm coming to the door but be prepared, Frank, it's bad in here,' she said, desperate to see his face, setting the phone down on the sideboard next to her purse, tightening the belt round her robe and repeating *I'm coming* through the dark timber as she slid off the chain lock and swung the door open.

The corridor was empty, to the left and to the right. Canvas bags with newspapers hung off a few door handles and opposite, between the door to Frank's room and the one beside it, a lonesome room service trolley was parked with a platter of half-eaten strawberries and yellowish curdled cream, a champagne bottle shoved upside down into a silver bucket and a red sling-back stiletto hooked by its heel off the side. That wasn't remotely Frank's style. Besides he was ill last night, she recalled. He had been ill, hadn't he?

As she went to close her door, she noticed the *do not disturb* sign starting to swing on the handle. *No Molestar!* it said. *I wish*, she thought as she called out to her phone, still in the room. 'Frank, where the hell are you?'

She slammed the door and ran over to get her cell, slipping on something wet and slick. A knife. Reaching out for stability, her fingers unwittingly grabbed for Nivikka's ankle and as soon as she realised it, she yanked her hand back like it was on fire.

'Tori,' Frank was shouting, 'I can't magic your door open. The TV says Songtian is missing. The police want to interview a woman in a polka dot dress. A redhead. *You* ... obviously.'

'Stupid fucking dress,' she sang out, kicking it where it lay on the floor.

'Tori, the TV's showing a video from last night.'

She froze. In this room her world had already collapsed and apparently it was disintegrating in public as well.

'It's showing you,' Frank said, 'with Songtian. At the club last night.'

Strangely, she felt relieved. He was talking about a different video, maybe one shot by some social media addict who'd been drinking at the same club.

'Tori, what happened last night?'

Frank stood in his socks outside Tori's door. He ignored the elderly Asian couple gawking at him from down the corridor and stared at the phone in his hand. Tori only had a few minutes before Oriol, or anyone else from the dinner last night, notified the police that the woman in the polka dot dress was Tori. They'd rush here and kick down her door. The same door he'd been banging on. The room she was in, yet not in.

He pocketed the phone and crossed back to his own room.

All Tori remembered about last night was going to the bar, Frank getting sick and leaving, and she and Songtian drinking, and it was only water. Or so she thought at the time. She didn't know how to explain her situation to herself, let alone to Frank. Cutting him off was easier. It was probably for his own good, and definitely for her own. The fact she was in terrible trouble didn't mean she should drag him into it too. She needed to prove her innocence somehow and if Frank was in the dark, at least for now, it would keep him free to help her later. Assuming he believed her.

She went through her phone's settings to access the FindIt app that the SIS risk team installed on all company work devices in case they got lost or stolen. The last thing she'd want if she was going on the run – she *was* going to run, wasn't she? – was for the police to be able to track her down. She disabled the app and, for good measure, switched the device to flight mode to disconnect it from the cell network.

Nothing was making sense. The room, the video, Songtian and Nivikka, Fake Tori, Frank standing in the hall banging on her door but *not* standing in the hall and *not* banging on her door. Suddenly something about the door jogged her memory, something peripheral, so she ran back to it and, after putting an eye to the peephole to check no one was there, flung it open so quickly that the *do not disturb* hanger again started swinging from side to side.

The room number that she'd seen when she'd opened the door the first time – 420 – that was not *her* room number. It was not the room she'd been taken to when she checked in, not the room she'd stayed in the whole time since. That room was 2420.

She dropped her eyes to the floor expecting the missing number 2 had fallen there, but it hadn't. She ran her fingers over the spot on the door where the 2 should've been but the wood panelling was totally smooth, with no residue or flakes of glue to rub against her fingertips.

She glanced across the hall to the other doors, and all of them were also wearing numbers in the four-hundreds. This was the *fourth* floor, not the *twenty*-fourth.

She closed the door and went over to the balcony, looking outside for the first time, and yes, she was far closer to ground level than her actual room had been.

Which meant Frank *was* banging on her door, *was* ringing her room. Except it was the wrong door, the wrong room. The wrong floor.

21

Tori poked inside the walk-in closet, rifling through the hangered clothes, opening and closing drawers, checking her bag. All her things were exactly as she'd left them – except that she had put them 'there' twenty floors up. A phone started up close by, inside the closet with her, coming from her backpack. The ringtone was bouncy, playful.

The Rain in Spain.

If this was someone's idea of a joke, it was far from funny.

A screen lit up, hatched by the stretch netting on the side of her bag. An unfamiliar metallic red case held the edges of the phone and she could see the caller ID: *Guess Who?* She removed the phone and weighed it in her palm, debating whether to take the call. She did.

'A hale and hearty good morning.'

The baritone timbre was coated with the creamy richness of Frank's voice so it sounded like him except for two things – that they'd already spoken on the other phone, and *hale and hearty* was not an expression he'd use.

'Your robe,' he went on, 'it's rather elegant. Quite becomes you.'

This was unnerving. Frank never strayed from being the consummate professional, a complete gentleman and loyal co-worker.

But this Frank, this was not the Frank she knew, respected and, yes, liked. She shook her head and looked around the closet for a camera. There wasn't one and she was about to step back out into the room when Frank continued.

'In all the circumstances – and you know what I mean, Tori – you might put a bit more speed into getting dressed. By the way, those tissues up your nose ... a super touch. Now you smell it, now you don't, ha? And how you fixed your eyelashes. You're amazingly resourceful.'

What was going on? In their last call, Frank was worried, solicitous, what she'd expect from a concerned colleague, a friend. But this version of him?

'Frank? Are you watching me? Stalking me?'

As he laughed, a long, cackling laugh, she pivoted into the room and saw the camera almost immediately. An amber-coloured plastic dome about the size of a ping-pong ball, stuck to the wall above the TV. How had she missed it before?

Frank had seen everything.

The couple. Her. Everything.

Was Frank the devil who drugged her with ice? Glued her eyes shut? Made her do unimaginable acts? Was he really a sicko all along? The man who never swore, who attended Mass and confided once that he'd spent a year in a seminary studying to be a priest. The man who would not tolerate anything remotely unprincipled, such as when Tori wore the FrensLens glasses during the talks to eavesdrop a little better on the Chinese negotiators, until he called her out for it.

He continued. 'Tori, soon you'll have visitors. A swarm. They'll be garbed in blue uniforms, they'll be wielding guns and batons and Tasers and they'll be under orders to shoot to kill – to kill you. They might have dogs, huge, nasty, slathering animals with sharp teeth. Which reminds me, the media will be running close behind. You're about to become a star of the screen, Tori. The whole world is going to know you and what you've done, so if you don't get a gee-up and scoot out of that room, one of the first things people will see will be the police bundling you into a van, barefoot, hands cuffed behind you,' he sniggered, 'unable to prevent that fluffy white robe opening up and flaunting all your red-haired glory. I do hope for your sake that your little belt holds firm.'

It was definitely a snigger, an unsettling, ugly snigger, and the Frank she knew would never do that.

'Don't even think of putting your polka dot number back on, the one on the floor splattered with bits of Songtian and the once lovely Nivikka. Poor them. *Requiescant in pace.* Or is it more appropriate to say *requiescant in fragmenta.* Ha! May they rest in pieces.'

As Frank laughed down the phone, Tori was utterly stunned.

22

For the entire six months they'd worked together, Frank had been gentle, thoughtful, decent and chivalrous. Almost to excess. They'd seen eye to eye on virtually everything. Was that Frank a ruse?

Sure, he'd previously worked inside a dark realm of smoke and mirrors at MI6, but that hardly made him a torturer or a deranged killer. Tori had worked for the CIA and she wasn't like that. Well, according to the video she was, but she'd never been injected with crystal meth before. Frank couldn't possibly be behind this.

Nothing made sense, apart from being drugged, and right now she had to get herself dressed and out of here. But she'd do it without an audience. She got up onto her toes, stretched out with the pen she'd picked up and slid its point behind the camera dome to lever it off the wall. When it popped off and hit the floor, she bent over and smashed it to pieces with the base of the desk lamp then kicked it under the bed.

'Aw, you've blinded me,' he whined through the phone, 'tit for tat, eh?' He started singing, mimicking Stevie Wonder's voice, '*Very superstitious … camera's on the wall.*' Then in his own voice, 'When I did have my eyes, dear Tori, I saw you engaging in sexual activities that, speaking bluntly, appalled me. Worse, I watched you commit two callous and, frankly, depraved murders. Yet now you have the audacity to gouge out *my* eyes when,' again he started singing as Stevie Wonder, '*I just called … to say … they loved you, I just called to say I don't care.*'

The singing clinched it. The real Frank had the deepest, honey-dripping voice but he couldn't hit a note if his life depended on it. She knew that from the office karaoke party soon after she joined SIS, when peals of laughter had greeted his attempt to sing 'Sitting on the Dock of the Bay'.

This was not Frank. Most likely, she decided, it was someone using sophisticated voice-masking software.

'What do you want?' she snapped at not-Frank.

He didn't respond.

'What the hell do you want with me?' she asked again through gritted teeth. Frustrated and angry, she wanted to punch the wall since she couldn't hit the guy but instead, hoping to trap him into a confession, she set her own cell phone to record mode, pressed her phone up close to the one he'd been speaking through and said calmly, 'Tell me what you want from me.'

'Top marks,' said the voice finally, the voice that was definitely not Frank and now had a genteel Southern drawl. 'I see you're not wastin' time askin' who I am since you know I won't tell you.'

This voice was familiar too. Was he mimicking former US president Bill Clinton now?

'What do you want from me?' she pressed again.

'Not a thing, Tori. I've got everything I need.'

23

After Frank rang down to the hotel operator he was back in the corridor outside Tori's room, tapping his foot on a carpet that suddenly reminded him of what his stomach had disgorged last night. Why did hotels choose such revolting floor coverings? He checked his watch, eyed the door lock and, as the seconds and minutes ticked over, wondered if he should have simply picked the lock instead of calling for security, an idea that was becoming quite tempting until he spied a shiny black CCTV dome not far away in the middle of the hall ceiling. A moment later, the elevator chimed.

Two men in black pants and black open-necked shirts came bolting out of the lift towards him, one behind the other since the corridor wasn't wide enough to fit both giants abreast.

Frank pointed to Tori's door as the stampede got closer. 'My colleague's inside there. She's in some kind of trouble.'

The first man, wider than Frank and more than a head taller, slammed his meaty fist against the door.

'She won't answer,' said Frank, rubbing his forehead with an uneasy mix of distress and impatience. He glanced up at the CCTV camera again, reminding himself that he might need to ask them to check the tapes, depending on what they found inside the room. 'Just unlock the door. Please.'

The man banging his fist looked back at Frank, the baby smooth skin above his pinprick eyes scrunched up in irritation. '*És el protocol, senyor.*' He pulled back his shirt cuff to show Frank his watch as if that meant something and stood, waiting for what Frank counted out as an excruciating thirty seconds.

It was all he could do not to shove both men aside, plus the fact that one guy was as big as a fridge and his colleague the size of the whole kitchen.

At last, the first one pressed a card key against the lock and pushed the door open while the second gripped Frank's arm to stop him rushing in. '*Protocol*,' he said smiling, his bald head bobbing hugely, as if he saw Frank as an imbecile.

Seconds later, after his partner's voice bellowed out of the room with what sounded like an *all clear*, he let Frank step inside. 'Nobody here,' the first man said coming back towards him, his arms wide, his big hands empty.

The room was unoccupied, prepped for its next guest, the bed made up with a black throw rug across the white doona cover and the pillows plumped up like perfect soufflés. The citrus orange curtains were wide open to give the next guest the same spectacular sea-view welcome that Tori would have got when she checked in.

Frank pointed to the walk-in closet. The second man flung the door open to show him it was empty, no bags, no clothes, not a scrap indicating Tori had ever been here.

The bathroom too was pristine, no towels tossed on the floor, no toothbrush, no toiletries other than the standard hotel miniatures neatly lined up along the vanity. Frank ran his hand over the marble basin. It was bone dry, and there was not a single strand of red hair anywhere.

'When I spoke to her by phone, just a couple of minutes ago,' he told the men, 'she was here, she was definitely here.'

They shrugged and, on their way out, one pointed to the hotel phone on the nightstand, '*Recepció.*'

Frank waved a thank you and picked up the handset, 'It's Frank Chaudry from Room 2421 … That's correct, I *am* calling from 2420, which is my colleague's room. Your security people let me in. But she's not here … vanished … and all her belongings are missing.'

'Mr Chaudry, it was me you were speaking to before. One moment … yes, yes, now I see the problem. Your colleague … Can you give me her name, please? For security purposes.'

'It's Tori Sw—' He stopped, remembering how reception asked for their passports when they checked in. 'Victoria Swyft.'

'Thank you. I apologise I didn't pick this up when you called earlier. Dr Swyft moved rooms last night. That is why—'

'That's not poss—' he began. He squeezed his eyes shut.

'Please hold and I'll put you through to her new room.'

24

Tori ignored the insistent trill of the room phone and dashed over to the closet to get her backpack, one she'd bought from an online survivalist store a month before she quit the Agency. It was a triumph of science-meets-design and was sold as the perfect go-bag, with well-concealed inner compartments, a lining as bulletproof as Kevlar yet four times lighter due to a layer of graphene nanotubes. The original supplier swing tag claimed that if you slung the bag over your shoulders a kill shot from behind would feel no worse than a friendly pat on the back.

'Why didn't you kill me when you butchered Songtian and Nivikka?' she asked.

'The lady doth protest too much, methinks.'

Tori might once have thought that hearing those words

from *Hamlet*, especially in Bill Clinton's voice, might be funny, ironic even, but here, now, they felt sick, dirty.

'And don't forget, dear lady, it was *you* who killed them,' he said, chuckling. 'That trophy video of yours proves it for the world to see, and oh yes, the world's definitely gonna see that, baby.'

This maniac had handpicked her, had drugged her, to make her the star in his macabre snuff movie and she was mystified why.

She checked that her phone was still recording him – yes, the red *record* button was active – so she placed the two phones next to each other on the floor, a dry spot, and started unzipping the backpack.

'Why did you kill Nivikka Petersen and Rao Songtian?'

'For a PhD you're a pretty slow learner,' he said.

Stunned, Tori couldn't speak. What didn't this guy know about her?

'Cat got your tongue?' he asked. 'If you're thinking of scampering off – which I strongly urge you to do – don't forget about that video. The scene where you get yourself off at the same time as you're hacking them to death … it's Palme d'Or material, right? The folks at Cannes would love it. It's as good as any Tarantino film, better really because it's hyper-realistic – because it *is* real. You know what? Instead of you and I waiting to premiere it in Cannes, I'll get it to stream onto every phone screen in this city. Yes, let's do that. What time, Tori, what time would you like me to raise the curtain on our little movie? You're the star so you can choose. Five minutes from now … ten … thirty minutes? You choose.'

'How about never?'

She was shaking so much her finger almost missed the *off* button.

25

Tori only had two options, and both were bad.

Her Plan A, the I've-been-framed route, was straightforward: call the cops immediately, *before* they kicked in her door and tossed her to the floor, cuffed her and dragged her out by her hair. That would mean phoning 911 or whatever the Spanish emergency number was, throwing on some clothes, waiting out in the corridor, handing them the mongrel's phone and her incriminating recording of their conversation, and pointing them to the drugs and the wall camera she'd smashed. Purity proved. Go home.

All of that was fine and dandy except for a few crucial details. Like the video, like her hair in the bed, the bathroom, all over the bedroom.

Especially the video.

As well, the bastard could easily have refilled the syringe he'd used to drug her with her own blood and squirted her DNA all over the crime scene. After he'd put her under, he could have pressed any of the weapon handles up against her fingertips. Which meant that 'cleaning' the room was not an option, even if she had the time, which she didn't.

She took up her phone and pressed play:

'What do you want from me?'

'Not a thing, Tori. I've got everything I need.'

She had him, even if his voice was masked.

Her own voice was coming through strongly:

'Why didn't you kill me when you butchered—'

Mid-sentence, the audio stopped. Ended.

She tapped play again but nothing happened. Pressed it repeatedly, urgently, until it eventually resumed, but the words coming out were different:

'Now you hear it, now you don't. I'm pretty amazing, right? Call me Houdini, Penn & Teller, Joshua Jay, Andy Jerxman, any magicians you want to pick. Harry damn Potter if you like. But Tori, this recording is … hocus pocus, hey presto, abracadabra, alakazam … Poof! Gone forever.'

And with that, all the audio, including the hammy incantations, vanished off the phone.

As if their dialogue never existed.

The sole shred of evidence she had to corroborate she'd been framed by a remote mastermind had disappeared. Like magic.

The call register on her phone was empty too. She checked the log three times. The only thing she had to shift the pall of guilt away from her was her own word, which no sane person would believe once they saw the tape.

If she stuck with Plan A she'd rot in a prison cell for the rest of her life – if she was lucky.

26

Plan A was clearly no plan, especially after she'd seen how her nemesis had perfected the *Mission: Impossible* routine of this-tape-will-self-destruct-in-five-seconds. If the guy could remotely hack into a phone that was cut off from the network, a phone in flight mode, delete a recording on it then remotely embed a new one and delete that once she'd heard it, he truly was a magician, a hacking Houdini.

Her phone had to go. If he could do all that he could also use it to track her, know her precise location, what she was doing moment by moment. If he switched on her camera, he'd know who she was with, and if he flicked on her mic, what they were talking about.

She opened the phone's settings, went into reset and erased all its contents. When the data was wiped, she placed the phone on the ledge behind the lounge, hoisted up the desk lamp again and, this time shielding her eyes with her other hand, brought its heavy black marble base down hard, shattering the device, thin shards of glass and plastic and splinters of electronics spearing into the back of the chair.

Plan B, which had been the riskier option, was now her only option. She had to get hard, irrefutable evidence of the scumbag's guilt, track him down, tear the incriminating video apart, whatever it took. Her big question was how.

Even though she didn't have much time, first things were first, so she placed her backpack just in front of the door to the hallway, one of the few large carpet patches not splattered with blood. She crouched down and began unzipping the compartments, slipped the contents out and arranged what she planned to keep on the floor in front of her: the FrensLens glasses, her sunglasses, her US and Australian passports, a power adapter, her hairbrush – which was more than a brush – and a portable power bank that was almost fully charged with three of its four blue LEDs aglow.

She opened the laptop, erased all its data – she wouldn't be taking it with her since she needed to travel light – pushed her tablet computer to the side then reached back into the bag's innermost compartment for the Velcro tab, the one that released the false lining. She felt beneath it for the invisible tip-off thread, slipped a fingernail under it to give it some tension and, certain it was still intact, severed it with a sharp jag to free up the hidden flap behind it and tipped up the bag, allowing the contents to tumble out onto the carpet.

She'd packed them while she was still in the CIA and left them there after she'd resigned, as a kind of security blanket. A two-sided wig – black one side, blonde the other – vacu-shrunk into a tiny plastic bag no bigger than a change purse. Several fake passports she'd bought off-book with credit cards in the same names. Three rubber-banded wads of cash, US dollars, British pounds and Euros. Four pairs of differently coloured contact lenses and a spare burner phone with a battery that, unsurprisingly, was completely flat. She plugged it into the power bank, picked up her tablet and got to her feet, opened up the camera and started snapping photos of the grim crime scene from multiple angles and aspects. Wide shots first, then close-ups of the bed, the weapons, Songtian's face and the bindings tying him to the bedhead, Nivikka's hand on the pillow. When it came to recording their mutilations, she just pointed and shot, squinting her eyes, trying not to look.

Forty-three still shots and one panning video of the whole room later, she pulled the flash drive out of the TV and returned to the clean patch of carpet to send all the photographic materials to Thatcher, a virtuoso hacker who'd gone to school with Frank. Beating someone as tech-savvy as The Voice – how she now thought of her adversary – meant fighting his fire with her fire. And since she was about to go on the run, that meant asking for Thatcher's help.

For that she needed the internet and she also needed to make sure The Voice would not be eavesdropping, so she connected to her target destination, a high-security dropbox in the Cloud, one she shared with Frank and Thatcher, by using SIS's proprietary encrypted Virtual Private Network. The VPN was basically a lead-lined digital tunnel that blocked unwanted eyes, ears and fingers.

Tori didn't know if Thatcher was his first or last name. Frank had introduced him as Thatcher and that's what he answered to. It probably was his surname, an affectation harking back to their schooldays at Eton, two working-class boys on scholarships. Unlike Frank, who wore his schooling lightly, Thatcher cloaked himself in pretension as snugly as his tuxedoes, his preferred clothes *du jour.* 'One has to look the part,' he'd told her the first time they'd met. She didn't quite know what part he was playing but it certainly was not that of a stereotypical hacker surrounded by towers of empty pizza boxes and soda cans.

The man was eccentric, annoyingly so, but as Frank told her, it was worth putting up with him since he was brilliant, one of the best in the business. Even before Frank introduced them, she knew of Thatcher's legendary exploits, albeit under his hacker handle of Fig Jam. According to Dark Web folklore, Fig Jam was the only individual who'd successfully got into all the major intelligence agencies, America's CIA and NSA, Britain's MI5 and MI6, Australia's ASIS, ASIO and ASD, France's DGSE, Germany's BND, Russia's FSB and, most amazingly, Israel's Mossad. It was astonishing he'd managed to do all that and stay alive.

His unimaginative rivals, jealous of his prowess and aware of his arrogant self-belief, read his Fig Jam handle as short for the classic insult *Fuck I'm Good, Just Ask Me* but, as Frank told it, the reason Thatcher chose it was because he thought no morning was complete without a slice of toast slathered with the stuff. And it wasn't just any toast either. It had to be made from Royal Bloomer, one of the world's most expensive loaves, which Thatcher got the Orchard Pigs Bakery in Wales to ship over to him monthly. He didn't particularly love the bread, it was the fact that he was the only hacker on the planet who could afford sourdough that substituted the water and salt of the standard recipe with champagne and flakes of twenty-three-carat edible gold.

Tori plugged the flash drive into her tablet and pressed upload. While the forty-three photos and two videos were going through to the shared dropbox, she cut off Frank's access rights. It was more for his own good than for the remote risk that he really was The Voice, the bastard who'd done this to her. Assuming he wasn't, the less he knew or could find out, the less likely he'd be arrested for aiding and abetting the fugitive that Plan B was about to make her.

Thatcher, on the other hand, was a totally safe bet since he was physically located where the long arm of Spanish law couldn't easily reach him, in New York City. She started typing:

URGENT!

URGENT!

URGENT!

Thatcher,

I'm sending through 43 photos and two videos. What I'm asking you to look at will appal you ... it's horrific ... but please understand I've got no choice. I'm in trouble. I'm so sorr—

She stopped. Someone was banging in the hall behind her.

27

Tori scrambled to her feet. Peering through the eyehole she saw a bellman stepping back from the door opposite as it cracked open. His heel hit the room service trolley behind him and the jolt knocked the red stiletto to the floor. He turned to pick it up and, without comment, returned it to the champagne bucket like it was a regular accessory.

The hotel guest poked his head out, his shiny black hair hanging loosely over his bleary eyes, so long and stringy that it nipped the diamond stud in his nostril. The guest pulled the door wider, revealing a fluffy white towel wrapped around his waist and a chest that was bare apart from what looked like smears of cream over his nipples. The bellman began speaking to him softly, his words inaudible.

Relieved, Tori sat back down and continued typing. Saying she was in 'trouble' was too much of an understatement, so she replaced the word with 'emergency' then explained about The Voice and asked Thatcher to do whatever he could to prove that Fake Tori was a phony, that the video was what she hoped it was: a deepfake.

Her suspicion, her desperate hope, was that The Voice had spliced her face onto a different woman's body. If anyone could prove that, it was Thatcher, since he'd been making his own deepfakes for quite a while. An early one Frank had shown her was a macabre yet amusing video of Michael Jackson's head on Elton John's body singing 'I'm Still Standing'.

The photos of the room she'd sent through would help him to do spot-the-differences, comparing what was on the video against the actual scene.

She also asked him to hack the hotel's CCTV system. *See if you can get a time-stamped picture of anyone entering or leaving Room 420 in the past twenty-four hours. Anyone apart from me.*

Thatcher's skills made him a perfect choice for these jobs. If Tori had the time, she could've had a good crack at doing them herself. But time was an asset she was fast running out of.

She ended her message by explaining why she'd locked Frank out of their communal digital vault. She didn't dare tell Thatcher there was a possibility – very remote, it was true – that his best friend might be The Voice, so she kept it to: *Keeping Frank in the dark is the only way we can protect him. What he doesn't know etc. So if he calls you, tell him nothing. Promise me that, Thatcher.*

After she pressed send, she got some clean clothes out of the closet, ripped open the vacu-pack and took out the wig.

◐

Her disguise wasn't complete yet but so far so good. Her red gym T-shirt was wrapped over her head like a scarf. It hid the wig – she'd reveal that to the world later – and she'd tucked its ends beneath the collar of her black shirt. She couldn't see her eyes, not through the double cover of sunglasses and the pair of FrensLens beneath them. Her blue T-shirt was tied around her waist like a miniskirt.

Back at her tablet, the videos and photos were flowing like a torrent down SIS's VPN pipe, which was as thick as a fire hose, and the blue progress bar was showing 91 per cent … 96 per cent … and it was done. She switched the device off and, together with the flash drive, dropped it into her backpack.

She was about to finish off her outfit when she thought about the dome camera she'd smashed and kicked under the bed, worried the police might miss it, initially at least. She placed one of the spare pillows from the closet over the floor at the foot of the bed, leant down and slapped the plastic bits and pieces back out. She placed the fragments onto the sideboard and only now noticed a plastic card already lying there. It was the size of a credit card, one side white, the other emblazoned with a lewd graphic of a naked woman, her thighs hugging a fireman's pole, her hips thrust forwards and her spine arched back so her long hair dangled. The text underneath was scratched out but legible enough to read, *Bar Canona*.

Tori tapped the card with a fingernail, wondering who left it. Was it a previous guest, some small-town accountant who'd flicked it there, an embarrassing memento of his big city business trip, the last thing he'd want his wife to discover after he got home? Or was it The Voice? And if it *was* him, was the card a clue or a trap?

She put it into her pocket, then hoisted up her backpack and placed it in front of her stomach like a paunch, pulled its straps over her shoulders the wrong way around.

Her disguise needed a couple more touches. She pulled on her boots and, for something to conceal the backpack, she raided the stack of clothes on the floor. Out of the middle, and thankfully free of blood, she got Nivikka's gold cardigan, put it on, stretched the fabric over her new stomach and buttoned it up.

The fat frump with appalling dress sense was ready to leave.

28

Tori checked the location of the nearest emergency exit on the map screwed into the back of her door. She peered through the peephole to see if the corridor was clear, pulled the scarf down over her dark glasses, yanked the tissues out of her nostrils and left.

The fire stairs were to the right, after the elevators, and she scurried towards them like a dowdy old crone who was running late for her city bus tour or perhaps for breakfast, which, she reminded herself, was actually where she and Frank would have been if she hadn't woken up inside a slaughterhouse.

One of the lifts dinged behind her as her hand pressed against the fire door. She shoved it harder and entered, poking enough of her red headscarf back out to catch the backs of two men dressed in black pacing towards her room, their gait and brawn telling her they were more devoted to beer and burgers than barbells.

She waited and watched. The men reached her room. The shorter one picked up the stiletto from the room service cart parked opposite and, laughing, waved it around by the sling-strap. His colleague went to knock on Tori's door but his hand pulled back to his face – to his nose. He'd caught the stench.

She turned, letting the fire door close behind her as she took the banister loosely in her hand and, after checking there was no CCTV camera in the stairwell to record her, flew down the steps like a fit twenty-seven-year-old, two, three and four stairs at a time.

29

SoHo, New York City

Like father like son? Hardly. Thatcher's pa was a butcher in Nottingham, England, the beating heart of his working-class community, a small world where Thatcher felt suffocated; a life of bread and dripping and meat with three vegetables, all of them boiled to death.

The life he'd built for himself was one his unworldly parents could not conceive of. His opulent top-floor penthouse in distant New York City – New York City! – spanned an entire floor, one end fitted out as a hi-tech haven to nurture his genius and operate his business, and the other an apartment so lavish that a Middle Eastern sheikh would be tickled pink to stash any number of new wives there.

The outwardly derelict building was in one of the few remaining seedy parts of SoHo, its location and appearance part of a prudent subterfuge since Thatcher had every intelligence service in the world looking for him. This place was safe, the peeling walls and splintery boards nailed over the windows spelling 'abandoned' in every language, except the boards weren't boards at all. They were sheets of one-way electric glass, specially treated with an advanced heat frequency nullifier that ensured not even a breath of his lair's internal warmth could leak outside. If any agency sent a temperature-detecting drone or a spy chopper into the area to look for the infamous Fig Jam, this would be one building they wouldn't dream of wasting their time checking out.

Thatcher moved into his *palazzo privato* two years ago after a secretive anstalt in Liechtenstein paid for it on behalf of a Caymans trust that, in turn, was nominee for a shelf company in Nevis set up for Thatcher by a very expensive lawyer. Thatcher had never been to Nevis but he knew it was a small island that rose up out of the Caribbean, basically the nipple tip of a once-active volcano. It was home to 11,000 people as well as a fabled roomful of filing cabinets that, under lock, key and digital encryption, stored the business records and ownership details of 150,000 immensely opaque corporations, one of which was habitually very helpful to Thatcher's interests.

The criss-cross gate of his rickety elevator – installed in 1896 according to its brass plate – jangled shut and the car commenced its ritual jiggle and jerk upwards from the street, giving its usual unwelcome workout to Thatcher's chins and the abundant stomach that tonight pressed against the eighteen-carat gold buttons of his newest tuxedo.

He'd hurried back from the Lincoln Center uptown, from The Met's afterparty for its world premiere of *El lives for Ebrabeht*. He'd been mid-sentence with one of the stars when he saw that Tori had sent him an SOS, so he put down his flute of bubbles and excused himself.

Thatcher adored opera, unlike his parents for whom a great night out was a chippy tea in their local pub, and The Met's new production had been revolutionary. They'd taken a big risk but Thatcher thought it worked brilliantly. They'd appropriated the classic *The Barber of Seville*, and recreated it entirely in reverse, the orchestra playing every bar of Rossini's score backwards, the voices singing every syllable of Sterbini's libretto likewise. Even the title read back to front.

He'd loved it or, as he was about to say to the baritone, *Ti devoli*, a phrase he'd begun mentally perfecting the moment he got to his feet to join the standing ovation, but Tori's SOS meant he never got the chance.

The lift cage eventually reached his apartment and when it stopped bobbing up and down, he clacked the door open. Before stepping out, he leant over his stomach to check that the spatters of rain he'd encountered when he got out of his cab hadn't marked the shine on his patent leather shoes. Satisfied, he pushed back the few luckless strands of hair that had fallen forwards from his otherwise bald head and shuffled across the silk Isfahan rug to his kitchen.

Passing beneath his newest chandelier, an antique he'd chosen solely because Tiffany made it in the same year as his elevator, he made his way to the wine fridge. For someone so tech-savvy, the appliance was a dinosaur. All it did was cool wine. It didn't text a message when his supplies were running low or when the internal temperature was too cold or too warm. It couldn't play music. It had never met Siri or Alexa. In fact, there wasn't a single internet-of-things appliance in Thatcher's entire abode. He didn't trust them, the companies that made them, or the people who might hack into them to find him.

The cool air rolling out of the fridge felt good on his skin. Of course, he needed to solve Tori's crisis, but first things came first and that was bubbles, always.

He ran his fingers across the bottles, stopping at the *Charles & Diana*, a 1961 vintage Dom Pérignon had released twenty years later for the benighted royal couple's wedding. He'd been waiting a long time for the right opportunity to savour the $8200 bottle and, given the evening of pleasure he'd just cut short to deal with Tori's 'emergency', he knew she wouldn't object if he added the cost to her tab.

30

Barcelona

The fat lady was not singing. She was waddling eastwards from the hotel with her head down as a cavalcade of police cars whizzed past in the opposite direction, sirens blaring. Soon she arrived at Nova Icària Beach, its silky white sand scattered with sprawls of stoners recovering from their all-night binges, a place Tori was certain she'd blend into once she ditched her disguise inside the public toilet block.

Though its windows were high up and small, the walls were strobing red and blue as more and more police cars sped by outside. Minutes later, yet one more stoner staggered out, a young, thin woman with black hair, dark glasses, dressed all in black, dragging a backpack behind her and swinging her boots by the pull-loops.

Tottering unsteadily off the concrete path and kicking her bare feet into the sand, Tori stumbled down the beach until she was about ten metres from the shoreline, stopping near a six-pack of ex-partygoers, three of them taking turns swigging from a fast-depleting quart of vodka, two of the women sticking their hands into each other's clothes, and one of the men laid out on his back, dozing or passed out.

She'd only just plonked herself down on the sand, not close enough to encourage banter, not far enough away to look conspicuous, when a shadow loomed over her from behind and a hand tapped her shoulder. She froze, didn't look up.

'*Hola.*' A male voice.

Still she didn't look up, letting her head loll onto her chest, curling her legs beneath her, tensing them, ready to leap up and run.

'*Cervesa,* Coca-Cola, *aigua freda?*' A drinks hawker.

Without looking up, she vaguely waved him off and when his shadow moved away, she started to have second thoughts. Hiding in plain sight meant props and right here, right now, a cold can of something, anything, was as good a deception as any, plus she could use a sugar hit. She called out to him, '*Hola.*' He kept walking away. '*Hola,*' she repeated, louder this time, adding, '*una Coke freda.*' She watched him shake his head in frustration, turn and saunter back to her, a drinks cooler swinging off his arm and a sneer on his face that said, *What's wrong with these deadbeats?*

Silently, without giving Tori a price, he pulled a can out of his chiller – it was red but also gold – and tore open the ring-pull.

Before the froth ran over the label, she read it was a beer, an Estrella. '*No, una* Coca-Cola,' she repeated, hearing him grunt with disgust.

Flamboyantly, he raised his hand high above her and tipped the beer into the sand, a ribbon of the amber fluid waterfalling to her feet. She said nothing and pushed herself back from the splashes like a woman in her semi-smashed condition might.

He handed her the empty can as if to say, '*You* get rid of this, bitch,' and she took it, dropped it on the sand beside her, and raised her hand to the air where, palm open, she held it. 'Coke,' she insisted.

He stared at her for a few seconds, extracted a Coke from his stash and handed it to her, not bothering to pop the ring this time. He told her the cost, which was exorbitant, no doubt because he included the beer, but she shrugged it off, dug into her bag and airily handed him a few bills, then took the can, popped the ring, faked a smile and took a swig. As he moved away, she downed another mouthful. It was more refreshing than she'd expected, and she drank half the can, then pressed it to her cheeks and her forehead – being a fugitive was hot work. She'd only just dug the can a little way into the sand so it wouldn't topple when a shout came from down the beach.

Three uniformed police had stepped onto the sand at the far end, close to the hotel. She watched them split up and approach separate groups of layabouts, holding up phones and showing them something. A photo of Tori, most likely. *Have you seen this woman?*

Slowly, methodically, they moved along the beach, repeating their routine. On her count, they had thirty-plus groups to cover before they reached her. A drop of sweat ran into her left eye. Damn those lashes, she thought.

31

Frank had no idea why the two plain-clothes detectives were still interrogating him. They'd commandeered the hotel manager's office and he'd fielded the same barrage of questions three times in the last twenty minutes.

One of the cops, his cell phone face up in the centre of the desk, was recording the interview. An interpreter was standing to one side, a weedy-looking man who kept interrupting his translations with weak coughs and continually pulled at a black tie so thin it looked like it a cord that was strangling him. If anyone was guilty of anything, Frank thought, it was that guy.

'Answer the question, Senyor Chaudry. What is your relationship with Dr Swyft?'

'I've answered that,' said Frank, pausing for the translator before he repeated what he'd said twice before. 'We are business colleagues. She is my immediate boss, actually.'

Then another question he'd already answered.

'I started phoning her at 7.20 am. My cell phone log will confirm that if you extract the phone from that ziplock.' He pointed to the clear plastic bag lying to one side of the desk, his phone face down inside it and, even more inconveniently, on silent, so he couldn't know if Tori, their boss Axel, or anyone else might be trying to reach him.

Someone knocked at the door. The older cop – balding, wrinkled, crabby – called out what Frank assumed was 'Enter' and a female police officer came in. She pointed to the bagged phone and, when the senior detective nodded, took it and left. No words exchanged, no permission sought from Frank. He knew it was useless to protest so he continued.

'Yes, I spoke to Tori, and yes, she seemed confused … distraught even.' He paused again for the translator.

After the ritual cough told him the guy was done, he went on. 'I haven't got a clue why she was distressed,' he said, anticipating the next question, the same one they'd asked earlier. 'To be honest, I was perplexed myself. She was supposed to be in the room opposite mine, 2420, but she wasn't.'

He could see the detectives remained as sceptical of this retelling of events as they had been the first and second times they'd heard it. 'Like I said before, Tori also believed she was in Room 2420. No, I don't have the slightest idea why she changed rooms. It was news to me and it sounded like it was news to her. She seemed dazed, so I think she may have been drugged.'

He decided to repeat a question they'd so far ignored. 'The TV said that Rao Songtian from China is missing. Have you found him?'

The cops said nothing. Again.

'I want to know,' said Frank, pressing harder, 'if Rao Songtian is still missing.' He would have thumped the desk except that might take things too far, so he kept his hands in his lap.

The younger cop answered in excellent English, 'Senyor Chaudry, *we* ask the questions, yes? Your, er, little tale, it is very interesting. What is fascinating for us is that each time you've related it, you've been almost word for word the same. *Verbatim*, that is the English term, yes? You seem surprised that I speak English so well. May I say that you do too, especially since it is not your native tongue,' he said, obviously noting Frank's raised eyebrow. 'That would be what, Hindi, Urdu?'

'Punjabi, actually, if that is at all relevant. I was born in north-west Pakistan but I grew up in Britain, went to school there.'

The cop winked at his colleague like he'd won a bet. 'So let's walk ourselves behind your little charade, the story you and Dr Swyft so obviously concocted and rehearsed. Tell us about the club you all visited last night, the last time anyone saw Mr Rao.'

This wasn't the moment to protest his innocence but he still wanted to put it on record. 'Tori and I rehearsed nothing. Everything I've said is the truth, the complete truth. As to last night, Oriol – your president – took the four of us there for a nightcap, Dr Swyft, me, Rao Songtian and Nivikka Petersen. I felt ill quite soon after we arrived, something I'd eaten at dinner, I think, so I left early, about 9.30, and took a cab back to the hotel. Anyone who was there will confirm that. The barman. Your president. Nivikka Petersen. Wait a minute,' he said, reaching into his pocket, pulling out his wallet and thumbing through it. 'Here,' he held out a slip of paper, 'here's my taxi receipt.'

Before they had a chance to take it, Frank withdrew the receipt to scrutinise it for himself and only then handed it over. 'It shows my ride started at 9.25 pm and finished at 10.05 pm at the hotel. Look, I need a toilet break.' He didn't. What he wanted was time out. No one had told him a thing, neither the hotel staff nor the police. All he knew were scraps he'd picked up on the TV. It had all happened so fast. Once hotel reception had told him that Tori had moved to Room 420, he'd gone back to his own room and tried phoning 420 from there while hotel security went downstairs to check it physically. The phone remained stubbornly unanswered, and just after his open balcony brought him the sounds of sirens arriving he decided to go down to 420 himself except, when he opened his door, he found these two detectives standing there.

'You've been questioning me for a solid twenty-five …' The cops' body language told him he was about to get a refusal so he stood up.

The younger detective nodded to his colleague who also got up and escorted Frank to a nearby bathroom. After he checked the room was empty, he held the door open for Frank, at the same time unbuttoning his jacket so it fell open to reveal a gun in his shoulder holster. Frank got the message: *Don't play me.*

The detective smiled as he rebuttoned his jacket. 'I wait here, outside. With my little friend.' He tapped the bulge under his coat.

32

Frank hit the washbasins and splashed his face.

Annoyingly, the bathroom didn't have handtowels, only an air blower. He pushed open the door to a stall and pulled off a few sheets of toilet paper, patted them over his face and dropped them into the bowl. He closed the lid, and the stall door, and sat down, wondering what he'd do next.

Should he demand the right to call a lawyer? Could you even do that in Spain? Or make a call to Axel, give him a heads-up so he could begin working on damage control.

A loud exchange came from outside the main door. 'Hey man, what do you mean we can't go inside? It's a bloody toilet. See the sign. I'm fuckin' desperado, bro. If I don't take a piss in the next five secs, I'll be sprayin' it all over your boots.' It sounded like a New Zealander. 'Oh, shit. You're a cop. Sorry, dude, we're touristos. Don't want no trouble but the truth is, senyor, I've really, *really* got to pee. Sure, search us all you want ... Hey, man, that tickles!'

Frank heard the outside door creak as it swung open. The detective must've taken the line of least resistance after judging the Kiwi to be harmless.

The sound of flip-flops clomped in over the bathroom tiles. He listened ... two pairs. Two people?

'Why the fuck did dat cop have to frisk us? We're bloody guests in a five-star hotel. I've got half a mind—'

'Well, you are Irish,' laughed the Kiwi.

'Very funny. That cop was as edgy as a chainsaw.'

'Who wouldn't be after seeing that video?'

Frank heard two zips being pulled down as the Irishman spoke. 'If that video went to my phone and your phone, it musta gone t'every phone. Kids, too.'

'You're pissin' on my jandals.'

'Then wear wellies. They'll be handy for the next time you're cuddlin' up to your woolly sweetheart. Barbera, isn't it? Baaa-bera!'

'We're in lockdown in a hotel where some freak shot a fuckin' double-murder snuff movie and you're making sheep jokes? If I didn't see it with my own eyes ... Jesus wept.'

'That ginger bird. She was off her nut. The bloke was lucky she didn't cut off his knob.'

'Hey,' the cop called out. 'Wash hands and get out.'

33

Tori watched a strange version of a Mexican wave coursing along the beach, fingers pointing at phones, hands flying to mouths, a tide of gasps and chatter welling up with it.

The Voice had kept his threat. He'd sent the video out. From this moment, every single person in Barcelona would know Tori's face and more of her body than she'd ever want any stranger to see.

She guessed she probably had a minute, maybe two, before the sand got too hot for her, figuratively speaking, so she kept skimming the search results on her tablet. Bar Canona, a strip club that recently closed down, was a nineteen-minute cab ride away.

Suddenly, the beach erupted, people leapt to their feet, many shrieking, eyes glued to their phones; even the cops. Maybe a hundred faces were twisted in disgust or horror. She leapt up too.

34

The president of Catalonia sat at his desk with his head in his hands, a shocking image frozen on his cell phone in front of him. This was turning out to be the worst day of his political life.

He heard soft steps on the carpet and looked up to see his chief of staff entering. Maria's face was ashen, the tips of her fingers holding her cell phone in front of her as if it was oozing filth. 'You saw it?'

He nodded from behind his vast beechwood desk. It looked as blanched and sallow as he felt.

'This is bad for us,' she added, as if he didn't know. 'Your enemies will say—'

'Maria, two people, good people, are dead and another is missing—'

'Good people? Didn't you see what they were doing? And that Swyft woman! She isn't missing, Uri, she's a fugitive. They used you.'

'I can't dance on these people's graves just because it suits my political—'

'If you don't, the jackals will stomp over yours. Unless you take control of it, this is how it will go down. They'll slam you for lack of judgement, how you naively conducted a secret process underpinned by corruption, sleaze and sexual perversion. *How did he not know?* they'll shout. Then they'll drop you right into the middle of it.' She fixed her eyes on his. '*Casals must've been in on it. Is he the guy holding the camera?*'

'Maria!' he smashed his fist down on the desk.

She shrugged. 'That's the crap we'll be dealing with. The hate media's been out to get you from the day you were elected. They'll be playing yesterday's press conference on a loop, the part where you take each woman's hand and kiss it and—'

'I kiss the hand of every woman.' It was almost a whisper.

'You stopped during coronavirus. Maybe you shouldn't have restarted, even if palace protocol still gets everyone to sanitise when they arrive. Do you remember that moment in the talks? Second day, I think,' Maria said, holding his eye. 'Swyft turns up wearing black, as usual, and Rao smiles and cracks the only joke that ever fell from his lips. He says, "Whose funeral?" She smiles back, "Yours, if you're not careful." Do you remember that, Uri?'

He'd taken it as innocuous banter yet, given what had happened since then, it looked bad. Terrible.

Maria's phone started to ring and, mouth tight, she moved closer to his desk and held the screen out to show him it was the police commissioner, again. She tapped the speaker icon so they both could hear and without a beat she barked into the phone,

'Of course we've seen the video.' Uri watched her free hand rise up, as if she was conducting Allegri's *Miserere*, readying the choir for the soprano's impossible top C.

Have mercy upon me, O God, he thought, taking comfort in the text. *Wash me thoroughly from this wickedness and cleanse me from its sin.*

The commissioner interrupted Uri's silent prayer, 'Maria, please inform the president that—'

Uri leant forwards. 'I'm here, Miquel.' He heard the squeak of a chair being pushed back, a rustle of clothes, what sounded like the policeman standing up.

'Excellency. It's almost certain that the deceased male on the video is Rao Songtian and the female is Nivikka Petersen. Their delegations are sending people to the hotel room to ID them. Ah, sir, please wait a moment.'

Uri heard a hand go over the mouthpiece and then muffled speech. The commissioner came back on the line. 'My people are telling me that the crime scene in the hotel looks exactly like the video.'

'Miquel, how did this filth get to my phone, to Maria's?'

'To every phone in the building,' Maria added and, for Uri's benefit, pointed to the room beyond his door.

'Sir, apparently it went to every phone in Barcelona. We don't know how, not yet.'

'Tori Swyft,' said Uri, trying to keep his voice neutral. Despite the video, he wasn't prepared to accept he'd got her wrong, not yet.

'Mr President, she is missing but my officers have detained an associate of hers for question—'

'Frank Chaudry?'

'He claims complete ignorance. Either the man is a great actor—'

'Or he's telling the truth,' said Maria, saying what Uri was thinking. After ten years of working together she was good at that.

Uri had felt a rapport with Frank the moment they met, and throughout the negotiations what he witnessed was an honest man. A straight shooter. As was Tori, he reminded himself.

'Excellency, Chaudry's timings align with those you gave me earlier.' On Miquel's first call, when he told Uri that Rao was missing, the president told him that he'd taken the four people to the club, that Frank got ill and left around 9.30 and, while they were only on their first drink, Maria turned up and pulled him out, just minutes after Frank's departure. Uri couldn't say what happened to the others after that.

'My detectives are pursuing an angle that Chaudry's stomach cramp was a blind, a ploy so he could return to the hotel and set up the kill space. Our forensics people are examining his room as well as the other.'

'The hotel CCTV?' Maria asked.

'I'm waiting for a report on that.'

Uri leant backwards into his chair. 'Thank you, commissioner,' he said and waved a finger to his chief of staff. She hung up. 'Maria, cancel me out of the car show.'

'Uri,' she looked horrified. 'It's not a show. It's a showcase of Catalan innovation. We've planned this for months.' It was scheduled for eleven o'clock and, after Montse died last week, Maria specifically programmed the state funeral to follow it. The media's spotlight on the visiting dignitaries would give a boost to the local initiative and, of course, to Uri's re-election prospects.

'Cancel me,' he repeated.

She gave him her look. The classic icy stare, the slightly squinty eyes, the flared nostrils. He didn't need her to spell out her thoughts but knew she would.

'Uri, you *will* attend. You *will* cut the ribbon. The people need to see you have nothing to be ashamed of, that it's business as usual. Otherwise the opposition and, of course, Madrid,' which they both saw as the same beast, 'will bleat how weak you are, how you're running scared, got something to hide, are out of control.' She paused, then grimly shook her head. 'And even worse, Uri, that you were involved. Cancelling will fuel wild speculation that will play into our opponents' hands.'

He dropped his head and squeezed his eyes shut, trying to dispel the images his brain insisted on replaying. 'If you hadn't got me out of the club last night, if I'd stayed with them, Maria, maybe this wouldn't …' He couldn't finish the sentence and, instead, the words of the psalm filled the silence.

Make me a clean heart, O God.
Deliver me from blood guilt.

35

Tori put one foot onto the roadway and raised her arm to hail a cab. Three black and yellows passed by without slowing or stopping. She couldn't blame them. Picking up a stoner who might throw up in your car wasn't a great way to end your night shift.

'*Hola*,' someone shouted from behind her. A cop? Someone who recognised her from the video, despite the wig and dark glasses? Like the airy cokehead she was making herself out to be, she didn't look around.

Another cab was bearing down, so this time she shifted her pose, jutting one leg to the side like a model on a catwalk, a hand flicking back her hair, the other holding her boots and backpack by the straps.

'*Hola*,' The voice was closer, more insistent.

She steeled herself and turned around.

A man with leathery skin, a holey, dirty green T-shirt and mouth missing half of its teeth was holding his hand out to her. 'Help me,' he said, in English, somehow knowing she spoke it even though she hadn't said a word. 'Money … for breakfast?'

She was wary. He might be a genuine beggar. He might not.

The taxi veered out of its lane towards the kerb and screeched to a halt so close to her its bumper nudged against her bag.

'Five euros? Little money,' the man pleaded but Tori ignored him. 'You want I call police? Maybe it you they looking for … You with little bit red hair sticking out on forehead.'

As three police cars tore past, their sirens deafening, Tori saw the loose strand reflected in the cab window … Damn it. Quick as a flash, she pushed it back under her wig, swung open the cab's back door, slung her belongings onto the seat, hopped in, slammed the door shut on the panhandler and, fortunately, the driver pulled straight out.

She looked back at the beggar, watching to see what he'd do next. Hail down a cop car? Pull out a phone and take a snapshot of the taxi's numberplate? But he simply threw up his hands, showing his frustration at yet one more knockback from a tight-fisted backpacker.

When she turned back, she saw her driver assessing her, his eyes darting between the road and his rear-view mirror, so she was glad she'd fixed her hair. Had he even seen the video? If the street person had seen it, surely he had too?

She put on her best slurred French accent and gave him an address two blocks beyond Bar Canona's. That way, if he twigged to her identity later he wouldn't be able to tell the police where she'd actually gone.

He spoke over his shoulder in Catalan, her FrensLens translating his words into her earbud. 'Miss, are you certain you want to go there? That locale … it's quite seedy, not very safe. My daughter, she is your age, I would not want her to go there. Certainly not alone.'

36

The detective escorted Frank back to the room commandeered for the interrogation. The office seemed smaller this time, the air thicker and clammier.

The cop sat down and a shirt button popped off and pinged to the side, unburdening a few of his pounds to flop onto the desk. 'Senyor Chaudry,' he said, rearranging himself, 'what you did after return to hotel last night?'

Frank was not used to answering questions. In his nine-year MI6 career, he was the one doing the asking, and after so many interrogations he pretty much knew every technique, every angle. The one these cops were using was the old keep-the-subject-in-the-dark-to-unnerve-him routine, drip-feeding the facts, snippet by snippet, either to tease out what he actually knew or to trap him into making a mistake.

Until the conversation he'd overheard in the bathroom, he'd known nothing about the murders, nothing about the video. The notion that he or, for that matter, Tori, could be a suspect, let alone guilty of such heinous crimes, was absurd, and it washed a sudden, uncharacteristic anger over him, an emotion he would normally constrain. 'I'll tell you precisely what I did when I got back here. I projectile vomited in my bathroom!' he shouted. 'Then I showered and I threw up again. And again. After that, I threw myself down on my bed.' He glared at his accusers. 'You should be out there,' he pointed to the door, 'trying to *help* Tori, not in here—'

'Whose bed, Mr Chaudry?' the younger detective asked, scratching a note on his pad, probably a reminder to get forensics to give Frank's bathroom tiles a once-over to check his story.

'Bugger you. The hotel CCTV will show you every step I took!' he shouted again.

'Senyor Chaudry, if Dr Swyft is as innocent as you seem to think, why did she flee?'

Frank wasn't getting steamrollered. 'We are done here,' he said, getting out of his chair. 'If I'm not under arrest, I'll politely bid you farewell.' He went to the door, his body tensed, half expecting a set of handcuffs to be snapped onto his wrists.

37

The cops' caution as Frank left – or, more likely, their edict – was ringing in his ears. 'You are not under arrest, but we will need you for more questioning so, please, consider yourself our guest in the hotel. Do not even think of leaving your room, Mr Chaudry.'

The cop stationed outside his door was 'a guardian not a guard', they said. Against what, or whom, Frank wondered.

Inside, with the door closed, he surveyed his room. Drawers were open, black fingerprint dust was scattered over many of the surfaces and, judging by the skewed angle of the mattress and the crumpled bedclothes, they'd stripped his room.

Or had they?

As with Tori, habits he picked up in the security service

were hard to kick. He reached behind the bar fridge and pulled out his spare burner phone. The fools had missed it.

When he dialled Tori's cell, the call went straight through to voicemail. After three more tries he got to his feet, this time wriggling his hand into the gap between the TV screen and the wall. The cops had missed his tablet too.

He carried it to the bed, kicked off his shoes and sat on the edge of the mattress. He clicked open the FindIt app and watched a Barcelona street map slowly materialise on the screen, the hotel at its centre.

He stretched over to the minibar and took out a mineral water, unscrewed the cap and was about to take a slug when the app got a ping. It located his cell phone, the one the cops had confiscated. He watched it heading along a street named Dr Aiguader. The cop was probably cradling it in her lap, ready to pore over his logs, emails and text messages once she got back to HQ, looking for anything that might prove he and Tori were co-conspirators.

It's not your day, lady, he mouthed and pressed the app's wipe icon, standard SIS kit. Almost everything the firm worked on was highly confidential so, in a world full of prying eyes, this remote erase function was a necessity. In five seconds, every scrap of data held on the device would disappear permanently. Irrecoverably. Even the proof that he'd been trying to ring Tori since early that morning. Rubbing out that evidence might well make him look more suspicious, but he had no choice.

The second ping, unsurprisingly, came from the tablet he was working on. The third ping was his laptop, which the cops had taken without asking. It too was enjoying a trip down Carrer del Dr Aiguader. He pressed wipe a second time. He kept watching, waiting for one of Tori's devices to ping. None of them did.

38

Frank tapped his boss's direct number into the burner. It was mid-ring when he realised it was only 3.30 am in Boston so he hung up.

He got off the mattress and, after adjusting it to rest square on its base once again, he sat at the end of it and started flicking the TV from channel to channel. Not one was playing the infamous video. However, even though he couldn't understand what the announcers were saying, they were obviously talking about it, since almost all of them featured images of Tori, her face blown up so much it made her look forbidding. Evil. Not at all like the Tori he knew.

BBC World was different. Their backdrop was a man wearing a black bondage hood, his eyes so startled and full of agony that Frank had to turn his own away.

Barcelona … Brutal and sordid assassinations just hours after the Spanish city hosted China and Greenland signing a landmark agreement.

Greenland's prime minister and the brother-in-law of China's president are dead. Police are hunting down their deranged killer, a woman they believe to be Dr Victoria Swyft, a US-Australian dual citizen.

Thirty minutes ago, a shocking video of the murders was sent to every smartphone in the city, even phones belonging to children on their way to school.

While BBC World will not screen the video or post it to our website, we can confirm the unhinged killer is a redhead, as is Dr Victoria Swyft, and her likeness matches this shot of her taken …

No way! Frank shouted at the screen as an image of Tori taken at last night's media conference popped up. She was wearing the dress Frank had pressured her to buy because it wasn't all black and because she looked great in it – elegant, beautiful. But the TV people, the twisted bastards, picked a camera angle that made her look wanton, a seductress waiting to pounce.

Fake bloody news!

The video begins with a sadomasochistic sex-triangle. It ends with the woman believed to be Dr Swyft hacking the victims to death.

The murders have grave geopolitical implications. Greenland's opposition leader is calling for the country's landmark alliance with China, signed yesterday, to be scrapped.

We cross to Nuuk, the Arctic nation's capital …

The opposition leader was standing in a white hooded anorak with a glacier rising up behind him. He spoke in English.

> This video bares an ugly truth … that our novice prime minister allowed herself to be seduced, not only by China, but by her very own adviser, Dr Swyft …

'No way,' Frank whispered. This was crazy. Tori would never, nor would Nivikka or Songtian. From his dealings with Nivikka over this past month, mostly by Axel's side, he saw a savvy, independent woman devoted to her country and her people. A sex triangle with anyone she was negotiating with? Not possible. Utterly out of character. And for Songtian too. He'd been a complete gentleman throughout the talks. Tough, absolutely, but always decent. Frank looked away from the screen, unable to bear the sneering politician any longer, and only looked back when the announcer started speaking again.

> The shock waves coming out of Greenland don't stop at China.
>
> A fanatical eco-terrorist group, Endz of the Earth, is making a sensational claim against the United States … that actions America has concealed for decades have dangerously accelerated the melting of Greenland's ice cap. According to Endz of the Earth, a secret CIA-backed …

Frank kept listening but before that story had time to sink in, the announcer mentioned Tori's name again and a shot of her came back up on the screen.

> Newsflash … Police in Barcelona are advising the public not to approach Dr Swyft. She is considered extremely dangerous and may be armed …

Using the company VPN, Frank began checking social media sites on his tablet to see if he could find the video. At first, all he could find was an avalanche of outrage, a never-ending toilet roll of filthy, anonymous posts that raged against Tori ... *burn the witch at the stake ... track her down and end her ... carve the monster up.*

Eventually, he did find the video but after five seconds he wished he hadn't. It was worse than anything he'd ever seen, and that was saying a lot since he believed he'd already seen the worst of the worst when, at MI6, he'd led a team that chased down, busted and imprisoned the leaders of an international paedophile ring, and many of their followers.

With one hand partly shielding his eyes, he pushed fast-forward with the other, gasping for breath as he went. Forty seconds was all he could take before he shoved the tablet aside and ran into the bathroom.

After splashing his face with cold water, he walked onto his balcony and gripped the railing. He looked beyond the shoreline to where the rolling swells were capped with streaks of colour from the vivid morning sky, swathes of oranges and yellows and vibrant pinks forming a sweeping canvas untainted by blood and violence.

Out there, God and Nature were resplendent.

Behind him, inside his room, it was Hell.

39

Air Force One

The latest intel to reach Isabel was that Professor Buckingham had been found dead. A bartender jogging home across Stone Arch Bridge saw a body floating down the Mississippi. The medics who pulled the corpse out of the water identified Buckingham from the wallet in his pocket.

'Accident, suicide or murder?' the president asked her Director of National Intelligence.

'Our people got the local medical examiner out of bed and he's on it. The first responders reckon the old coot was probably dead *before* his boots hit the river. His external injuries were—'

'—consistent with post-death trauma,' said Isabel, 'his body smashing up against rocks and showing cuts but little bruising?'

'Exactly.'

Which sounded like murder to her. 'What have we got here? Buckingham goes public with a crazy conspiracy theory and threatens us with a cache of documents no one's ever seen and then he's dead. Any minute now, Endz of the Earth will come out and say we killed him to silence him. So tell me, did we? Did we kill him?'

40

Barcelona

When Axel's call came through, Frank heard the strain in his boss's voice, his pitch higher than usual, his Boston vowels rounder. 'Francis, we've been in the office here, worried sick, for almost an hour.'

For Axel to be at his desk outside of 10 am to 7 pm was almost unheard of. Four in the morning, or close to it, was unprecedented. '*We*, Axel?'

'Ron's here with me, and we've got you on speaker.'

Ron Mada, Axel's second in command, was a complete bastard. Frank understood how a man of Axel's decency, a softie, needed a hard man beside him, but Ron took hard so much to heart that Frank suspected he didn't have one. If it wasn't for Axel, and more recently Tori, he would have thought about quitting SIS long before now.

'President Hou got me out of bed,' said Axel. 'Not his office, Francis, but Hou himself. I roused Ron straight after and my driver picked him up on our way into the office. Oh my God, Francis. What a mess. We've been trying to call you ever since.'

'The police took my cell, my laptop. Still have them. They were questioning me—'

'You've wiped them, right?' said Mada.

'Ron, of course, he has. Francis, I can hardly speak.'

The line got crackly with static and Frank couldn't be sure who was talking. If it was Ron, they wouldn't be words of grief or sympathy for Tori. She and Ron didn't have a relationship, they had a stand-off. After her very first encounter with him, she'd told Frank, 'If I'd been his mother, I would've given him a toaster as a bath toy.'

'Francis, are you there?'

'Axel, I don't know how much you know but Tori is missing. I spoke to her by phone before she vanished, very briefly. She was … Axel, she was hellishly distressed, muddled. There's this vid—'

'We've seen it,' said Ron, his voice cold.

Axel came back on. 'If only we hadn't.'

'Like I've always said, Frank, Swyft is a conniving bitch—'

'Ron, shut the hell up,' Frank snapped, surprising himself since it wasn't his way to be disrespectful to a superior even if the man was a slop bucket of dung. He took a pause, then spoke again, 'Tori couldn't have—'

'Hell she could. Your problem, Chaudry, is perspective. Your lack of it. You and Swyft are too close, you're like the brown on her rice.'

Frank was stunned. Not so much by Mada's inherent racism but how his contempt for Tori overrode any concept of common decency. Frank drew himself back from the phone, taking a second to visualise the scraggy, physically insignificant man who was probably huffing out his sunken chest and heaving his pencil-thin shoulders back, proud of his filthy mouth.

In Frank's younger days, he'd let the poison of casual racism go past him, but that was then. He pulled up his sleeve and waved his bare arm at the phone, not that the slug in Boston needed to be reminded of Frank's heritage. 'That comment, Ron, is entirely … unbecoming. You need to withdraw—'

'Gentlemen,' said Axel, offering Mada a respect Frank didn't believe he deserved, 'no matter what superficial evidence there is against Tori we—'

'Axel,' said Mada, 'what's superficial about that video? It explicitly—'

'Ron! You know what Hou Tao said. I'll come to that in a moment, Francis, but the key point is this. The three of us, and SIS as a firm, will assume our colleague's innocence. We have to. We'll give her whatever assistance we can to prove it and we won't stop unless we are shown categoric evidence of her guilt. *Categoric. Unimpeachable.* This isn't just Tori's reputation at stake here, it's also our firm's. Have you got that, Ron?'

Bless you, thought Frank.

'The video, Axel—'

'Ron, are you deaf? Francis, what I'm about to tell you,' he continued, 'is in the strictest of confidence. Hou's brother-in-law could not have participated in the activities that video shows. Hou does not want it *publicly* known – he's relying on SIS's complete discretion – but, Francis, *you* need to know. Years ago, when Rao was a fighter pilot, he crashed into the South China Sea. He suffered serious injuries, including to his … He became incapable of … having sex. He simply could not have, ah, performed the acts that the man supposed to be him was performing.'

Frank was quietly overjoyed. Sad for the two victims, of course, but over the moon for Tori. 'That's all the proof we need, isn't it? That the tape is a fake,' he said. 'That Tori's been framed.'

Ron laughed down the phone. 'Just because a president tells Axel off-the-record that his brother-in-law couldn't get a hard-on doesn't mean it's true. The stakes are high for Hou. He might say anything to make the pall of corruption disappear. I've been thinking about it, Axel, and that story sounds pretty damn expedient. He invents it to put the heat on you to get the Greenlanders back onside and—'

'Except we'd be trying to do that anyway, Ron. Wouldn't we?'

'And we'd fail if they believed the tape was true. Let me finish, Axel. He tells you this snippet but makes you promise to keep *shtum*. And what does he do next, eh? He picks up the phone to our president, Diaz. He *doesn't* tell her what he told you, and instead he accuses the United States of being behind this … Shit, he's probably putting the heat on Diaz that Swyft did this because she's a CIA stooge. She did work for them before you had your brain freeze and put her on payroll.'

Axel stepped in before Frank could. 'First, Ron, in my experience Hou is a man of integrity. And yes, before you say it, I acknowledge my experience of him is limited, but if I'm good at one thing, Ron, it's judging character. Usually.' Axel paused, and Frank imagined him staring Ron down, putting him in his place. 'Second, I remind you of Hou's final words to me, *Save Swyft and save the deal*, which as you know, Ron, will also save our fee. Hou's insisting the deal goes ahead, Francis, come hell or high water—'

'Not a very appropriate expression,' Ron interrupted, 'with the ice cap scandal—'

'Francis, have you spoken to anyone from Greenland this morning?'

'I was being interrogated by the police until a few minutes ago.'

'Then we'll have to divide and conquer.'

41

SoHo, New York City

Thatcher's glass of gently bursting bubbles was untouched. When he'd originally read Tori's message, he'd cloaked himself in the stoic calm that a stressful job like this demanded, never expecting he'd be peering through trembling fingers at the video she'd sent though. He had to tap on the mouse twice before he could halt the footage. Desperate to shake it all out of his head, he twirled his chair away from the screen and rolled it over to another computer, one that would let him heave his best cyber battering ram up against the hotel's walls and bust into its CCTV network. If he could show that Tori was taken there already drugged, carried perhaps, he might never need to watch another frame of the horrendous video again.

The hotel network withstood his first assault, as most corporate firewalls usually did. What he didn't expect, and highly respected, was how the system immediately shifted into counterattack. Going on the offensive and 'hacking back' was a manoeuvre that was illegal in most countries, unless you were one of the state's own agencies. The hotel's possible malfeasance was not of any concern to Thatcher. A man in his line of work was in no position to snitch, plus he relished a challenge, and he would have enjoyed this one if it hadn't petered out in nine pathetically fleeting minutes. *Premature emasculation*, he sniggered, as he opened up the hotel's CCTV repository, terabytes of its video recordings. *Too easy*.

Smug, excited, Thatcher rolled up his sleeves, though only metaphorically since he'd never actually treat this precious mulberry silk shirt in such a fashion. The directories were set up conveniently into sub-directories, one for '*Passadissos*' – which his translation software told him were corridors, with separate sub-sections for each floor – another for '*Vestíbuls de l'ascencor*', lift lobbies, and more for restaurants, the main lobby, driveways, and other public areas. He clicked open the files for the fourth-floor corridor, the south end where Room 420 was, and braced himself for the thrill he expected to experience when he nabbed The Voice *in flagrante delicto*.

'Damn, damn, damn,' he shouted less than a minute later. Every coming and going in that corridor for seven days was there, neatly filed, except for the sixteen hours that started at 3.30 pm yesterday, Barcelona-time. From then until 7.30 am today the corridor tape was wiped, gone, vanished. No comings, no goings.

He clicked into the directories for the elevator lobby, the elevators and a selection of the public areas. All the tapes for the same sixteen hours were missing. Tori's adversaries had erased every second of footage for that entire period. He tried the logs but they were wiped too, so even the crumbs that Thatcher would ordinarily pick up to help him track down a miscreant were gone.

He closed his eyes and drummed his fingers on the desk for minutes as he pondered his next move. When he eventually opened his eyes, none the wiser, he saw he must have accidentally tapped his computer mouse, hit the play button, because one of the hotel tapes was running. The timeclock in the screen's corner was ticking over, telling him he was watching the corridor outside Room 420 at 7.33 am.

The image, in black and white, was crisp, clear. He pressed fast-forward and was soon watching a bellman hurry from the elevator to the room opposite Tori's, bump into a room service trolley and knock something to the floor, pick it up and put it back, speak to the guest inside and leave. Maybe ten minutes of elapsed time later – about thirty seconds on fast-forward – he saw a rather chubby woman sneak out of Room 420, her head down, wrapped in a scarf, as she scurried along the hallway, past the elevators and into the stairwell. The incident took eight seconds, eight seconds that screamed *Guilty, your Honour.*

Thatcher afforded himself a smile, finally. Tori's nemesis had screwed up. To let the tape capture one of his minions leaving was a huge mistake.

He replayed the eight-second segment on slo-mo again and again, scouring it for a hint of the harridan's identity. He was getting nothing. She kept her face scrupulously hidden with her head low, scarf covering most of it, sunglasses over her eyes, her shoulders hunched over her humungous stomach. What role might she have performed inside the room? The video camera operator, perhaps? Drug topper-upperer?

If he couldn't work out who this woman was, someone in Barcelona might.

He made a copy of the clip and started typing up a post on his least disliked social media site using a fake Barcelona police account he created on the spot. *Urgent: Can you identify this woman in Barcelona? Here she is fleeing the scene of the ghastly crime in the infamous Room 420 in Hotel …*

42

Barcelona

Tori's cab driver didn't speak for the whole trip. More surprisingly he didn't take a single one of the aggravating fusillades of calls or messages that kept pinging and beeping on his phone. *Have you seen the video? That evil witch is on the run. Don't pick her up.* Yes, she thought, the woman right behind you. The one with the hairbrush in her backpack that could kill you.

Until now, she hadn't thought too much about the brush, a weapon so brilliantly nondescript she'd carried it through airport security for years without challenge. It had become such a normal part of her carry-on she'd long ago started using it as a real brush. But in different circumstances all she had to do was rotate the toughened handle with a single twist and the bristle head would slip off to reveal a deadly twenty-centimetre shiv, its tip so sharp that just tapping her fingertip on it would draw blood. It was the dagger she had when she didn't have a dagger. The hairbrush from hell.

The cab squeezed into a deserted alleyway, the walls encrusted with graffiti, words even her FrensLens couldn't translate and pornographic images that were all too clear. The car brushed past a pile of black trash bags dumped at the side of the narrow lane.

This didn't feel right. It reminded her of a time in Kabul when a cab driver had sandwiched her in an alleyway just like this. With no words, she'd silently unscrewed the hairbrush and pressed the tip of the shiv into that guy's neck, a trickle of blood running down into his collar as she encouraged him to put his foot on the accelerator.

With the hairs on her neck standing up the same way, she reached into her backpack and unsheathed the shiv, ready to do what she had to.

43

SoHo, New York City

Thatcher was about to post the video clip of The Voice's helper scurrying down the hotel corridor when his champagne called him. He poked his nose over the bowl of the glass and sniffed the incredible aromas of biscuit and brioche that only a perfectly stored 1961 vintage could offer. For this wine he'd chosen a wide tulip-shaped glass instead of a flute. The broader rim allowed him to capture a richer, fuller hit of the Charles and Diana's flavours. Holding the glass away from his nose, he studied the bubbles, a process that always calmed him and helped him think. He liked to focus on one bubble from its birth at the pointy base of the glass and follow its life's journey, watching it slowly expand until it was big enough to tear itself away and begin its flight up to the top, getting larger and faster, joining its brothers and sisters, so many siblings that he'd no longer be able to identify his bubble any more. By the time they'd be popping at the top, dozens of them, they'd have cleared his mind, told him what to do, or not do.

Today was no exception.

The Voice, they reminded him, was not the careless type. It was unlikely that the CCTV caught the old hag because The Voice had been sloppy.

It was because he *wanted* people to see her.

Which meant one thing. That the old hag was Tori in disguise and if he'd gone ahead and posted the clip as he'd been about to – *Thank you, my dear bubbles* – he'd have as good as hung her out to dry. *Guilty, your Honour*, indeed.

Once again, his trusty tongue twister turned out true. *Pinot never pops purposelessly*. His bubbles proved their worth, deserved their reward.

He replayed the eight-second clip and this time he saw what he should have noticed before: the woman was wearing Tori's signature black riding boots. The elastic sides, the Cuban heels – an iconic Australian brand, she'd told him once, though he found himself wondering why any self-respecting Australian shoe company would choose to use a Cuban heel.

Given how absurd the boots looked on a woman wearing a miniskirt he couldn't understand how he'd overlooked them. But flailing himself wasn't going to help Tori. By finding this clip, he knew he'd find more, shots capturing her in other parts of the hotel as she scurried her way out. The Voice had left them on purpose, so the police would find them and add them to the weight of evidence against Tori, to be sure she'd be crucified.

'Well,' he said out loud, 'it's a good thing that it's Thatcher who got here first and not the police,' and with an elegant economy of clicks, he vanished the whole building's next half-hour of tapes, from 7.30 to 8 o'clock. 'Fat lady? What fat lady? Did anyone see a fat lady?'

He allowed the yeasty bubbles a moment to tickle his nose and tantalise his tongue. After making a toast to his genius yet again, he closed his eyes until a new thought came to trouble him.

What if Tori was actually guilty?

44

Air Force One

The president's chief of staff was a stickler for language, for punctuality, and even his dress. Gregory L. Samson – *don't forget the L* – never gave his Italian suits a vacation, not even on long-haul flights. His idea of casual was slinging a Zegna jacket over his shoulder; in an emergency he'd loosen the knot of his tie.

He wasn't like any other Australian Isabel had met. Gregory – or GLS to his staffers – didn't touch alcohol. Isabel had seen him turn down a glass of Penfolds Grange once, like it was two-buck chuck. He didn't say *mate* or *strewth* or *fair dinkum.* The only Aussies in his circle who did, he once told her, were politicians angling for votes.

Isabel knew plenty of American legislators who were like that too, the Ivy Leaguers who morphed into homespun Harrys or Harriets whenever they saw a TV camera hovering nearby. They'd drop their g's so they were *comin'* or *goin'*, they'd say *y'all* and call everyone *folks* but as soon as the camera or the crowd left, they'd start raving about the soufflé and sauterne the hapless taxpayer had paid for on their last Congressional boondoggle to Paris.

Isabel Diaz was not cut from the same cloth. She was a genuine rags-to-riches story. Not Ivy League or any league, she'd attended what she called 'the college of the customer', starting out as a runaway at fifteen, wiping tables in a diner in Half Moon Bay and, twenty-five years later, selling her ownership of one of America's most popular family restaurant chains so she could enter politics and serve America in a different way.

Gregory placed his can of Diet Coke on the coaster, centring it over the presidential seal. 'Madam President, it's my firm advice that we should turn around and head back to DC. With that Swyft woman on the loose and the media megaphoning her past years in the CIA, and the whole Endz of the Earth thing as well, the Secret Service is worried that your presence in Barcelona might incite a wave of anti-US protests.'

Isabel respected her agents, and Gregory too, but her response was firm. 'If President Casals postpones Montse's funeral, fine. If he asks me not to attend, also fine. But if neither of those happens, we'll land this plane in Barcelona and I will deliver my eulogy. Tell Chief Franklin I appreciate his advice. He'll just have to make the arrangements work.'

'This Swyft thing, it's potentially—'

'She's one of yours, Gregory,' she said, after referring to the note on her screen detailing Tori's background, including her dual citizenship. 'Why can't you, of all people, give her the benefit of the doubt?'

'I never gave one to Rupert Murdoch and he started off as one of ours.' He continued on another tack. 'The Service thinks the furore over the murders—'

'I've covered that. Anything else?'

He picked up his Coke can the way he always did to hide his frustration, his thumb and first finger circling the very top rim, his other three fingers splayed out like a Chinese hand fan.

45

SoHo, New York City

The phone tolled through Thatcher's apartment. He knew it was Frank calling as soon as he heard the ringtone. He'd dedicated eleven of his incoming lines to individual clients, with the twelfth for Frank. All of the numbers were registered in false names at false addresses, three each in London and Paris, two in Prague, one each in Budapest, Bolivia, Edinburgh and Venice. The one he'd allocated to Frank was the one in Venice, a city Thatcher kept planning to visit but never did.

Thatcher's regulars were not people who wished to be traced. So if one of them, or Frank, dialled him using their allocated number, the call would bounce randomly from country to country at least seven and up to ten times, making it virtually impossible for the authorities to follow.

Thatcher, on the other hand, would instantly know who was calling since he'd allocated each number a specific ringtone. What gave this call from Frank away was the initial upward sweep of violins and the martial horn refrain. It was the soaring intro to Wagner's 'Ride of the Valkyries'.

The great unwashed, as Thatcher liked to call the general public, knew the piece from Coppola's 1979 movie *Apocalypse Now*, when the Black Hawks made a vicious aerial attack on a North Vietnamese village.

Thatcher chose it because, while Frank was his dearest friend, his best friend, his one failing was that he was a Ring Nut, an aficionado of Wagner's operas. Thatcher loved opera, but hated Wagner.

Thatcher let the phone ring while he pondered how to play the call. Tori wanted him to keep his old friend in the dark to protect him. There was also the question of the fat lady. Thatcher didn't seriously believe Tori could be guilty of anything – apart from her tacky disguise – but the question was still circling in his head, and it wouldn't leave.

'Chowders,' said Thatcher when he eventually picked up, using the chummy nickname he'd given his friend the first day they met at Eton. He lifted his voice so it was as light as his bubbles, and went on and on about nothing, feigning ignorance that anything might be amiss.

Frank cut him off. 'Tori is in deep troub—'

'Thatcher is aware, Frank, but his lips are sealed,' he replied in his pinched adenoidal voice, using what Frank once had the gall to describe as his 'third person superior'. Thatcher preferred to think of it as a subtle way to underscore his dignity and modesty.

'Ah! She's contacted you then, Thatch. That's good. She probably told you not to tell me anything, right? Because it might compromise me?'

'That is Thatcher's quandary, old friend,' he said, although the words sounded more like *quandawy, old fwend* due to yet another eccentricity, the speech mannerism Thatcher had slavishly copied as a boy from a young royal who'd sat in front of them in Latin class.

'We don't have time for quandaries.'

Thatcher suspected Frank was right but Tori had been explicit, and in his dark profession the revealing of confidences, even to someone you'd trusted pretty much your entire life, was a grave taboo. Reputations were hard to build in hackerland and very easy to destroy. 'Dear, dear boy,' he said, 'she was most adamant—'

'That was *before* the Barcelona cops gave me the third degree. I'm in the clear now,' Frank said, though Thatcher wondered if he was stretching the truth. 'Thatch, you've got nothing to worry … *Thatcher!* Are you drinking?'

He put down his glass and listened to Frank recount his morning so far, what had happened last night, the video, the Endz of the Earth release, all of it.

'On that basis, Thatcher welcomes you inside the loop,' he said, crossing his fingers since he wasn't going to allow Frank inside the whole loop. For one, he didn't want to taint his friend's thinking with knowledge of Tori's suspicious-looking getaway. He'd almost convinced himself it was nothing, an innocent woman whose face was plastered all over Barcelona simply hiding her identity so she could escape and help Thatcher prove her innocence.

'Chowders,' Thatcher continued, 'Old Mother Hubbard was rather busy before you called. The thing is that when she broke into the hotel, she found its cupboards were bare. Someone, the people who framed Tori, emptied them and—'

'Thatcher, what the hell are you gabbing on about?'

Honestly, thought Thatcher, Frank could be rather thick. 'Francis, the real monster behind the ghastly goings-on in Room 420 is a man Tori calls The Voice. He wiped the hotel CCTV recordings from yesterday afternoon until, er, eight this morning. Thatcher went looking but he found nothing to help us identify the true miscreant. Nothing.'

'Was there anything to implicate Tori?'

Thatcher didn't mean to pause, but he did.

46

Barcelona

The Catalonian president's chief of staff had spent the last hour picking up so many phone calls she felt like a one-handed drummer.

Her phone started to dance on the table. Again. 'For the last time, no delays and no cancellations,' she snapped into the handset as she picked it up. 'Both events will start and finish on time.' As far as she was concerned, nothing was going to spoil the Cata-Cars launch, the hi-tech extravaganza she and Uri had started working on months ago – or Montse's state funeral. Both events were crucial to Catalonian pride and, as a bonus, they were certain to turbocharge Uri's re-election campaign.

She hung up and turned to her staffers, 'That was Madrid, again. Cancel, postpone, cancel, postpone. They're like a broken record. What do they care about a showcase of Catalan innovation? Or a tribute to Montse's memory? Postponing the funeral would be—'

'A slap in Catalonia's face,' said her aide. 'Turning away all these world leaders at the last—'

'An affront,' said Maria, wiping genuine tears from her eyes.

Over the years, before and after Uri's cousin lost her hearing, Maria had spent many late nights with Montse, the two women discussing politics, diplomacy, the Madrid–Catalan tensions and the parade of men they'd encountered in their careers who kept women down, though in their personal cases, those men had failed miserably. Uri was an exception. Exceptional, even. Maria and Montse couldn't have had a firmer supporter, not that either woman needed it.

'Has the president finalised the eulogy?' asked the staffer, a pushy young woman whose name Maria tried not to remember. The one who'd given Uri two good paragraphs and was only angling to find out if her words survived so she could add the success to her resumé and move on to her next job.

'He's still working on it,' said Maria. She encouraged ambition, especially among the women on her staff, but she was not one to waste time by holding people's hands.

She took the next call, listened for five seconds before she held the phone away from her head and barked into it, 'What good are you, Miquel, if your officers haven't got that Swyft witch in custody? Do your fucking job!' She slammed it down.

For the next caller, Gregory Samson – Gregory L. Samson – she switched to oily politeness, as necessary in a role like hers as brusque economy. She put the call on speaker so her staff could listen, and learn.

In Samson's last call, he'd given her the unwelcome heads-up that the US Secret Service were advising his boss to turn her plane around. This call would tell them his president's decision. Maria crossed herself and so did her staff. As Gregory spoke, smiles caromed around the room, as well as some quiet high-fives.

'Gregory, please give *your* president *my* president's deepest appreciation. He knows how big a place President Diaz and her stepson filled in Montse's heart …' Maria paused, momentarily appalled by her choice of words, given that she knew the real cause of Montse's death. She decided her best course was to keep talking. 'The Catalan people will view the presence of President Diaz on this most difficult day as the highest tribute to Montse's memory, since she will be here both as her dear friend and as the leader of the free world.'

Maria noticed one of her aides flinch. The 'free world' was still a loaded term for many older people in Spain who remembered how the West – the free world – had betrayed Spain by ignoring Franco's atrocities and condoning his dictatorship simply because he too was fighting against communism.

But Maria was a pragmatist. Uri needed the kudos he'd get from welcoming the first American president ever to visit Barcelona, let alone a president who was Catholic *and* Hispanic.

47

Tori's fingers gripped the shaft of her hairbrush but, luckily for her cab driver's neck, the street sign they'd just passed told her he'd brought her to the correct address.

He pulled up at the corner of a deserted cobblestone street, scraps of paper flitting and twirling upwards in the breeze.

Before she got out, her eyes quickly took in the rest of her surroundings. Slathers of graffiti, rows of abandoned buildings, most of the windows broken or boarded up.

The driver twisted around, showing a wide grin of yellowed teeth and skin peppered with a day's worth of bristles. Trying to be helpful to his tourist passenger, he mangled his words, borrowing from Catalan, French and English. '*Senyoreta*, are *vous* certain *vous* wish me to leave *vous içi*?'

'*Oui* … I mean … *si,*' said Tori. '*Gràcies, senyor.*'

He nodded, as if to convince himself he'd satisfied his obligation to a defenceless young woman. If he only knew, Tori thought, shoving her hairbrush back into her bag.

'Normally little traffic,' he added, 'but today Barcelona is many detours, long delays. Big funeral is later. Many important people come to our city.'

If there'd been detours and delays, she hadn't noticed. The trip had taken the same nineteen minutes her app had predicted. Smiling, and giving him another *gràcies, senyor,* she peeled a few euros off the wad in her bag, enough to round up the fare with a tip, an amount that wasn't so much or so little that she'd stick out in his mind. She got out, feigning a little unsteadiness until he drove off and disappeared around a corner.

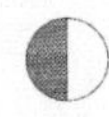

Once his passenger was out of sight, the cab driver pulled over and took the phone he'd been given out of his glove compartment, leaving his own, the one pinging with all the calls he'd ignored, on his seat.

Package delivered, he texted. That done, he removed the SIM card as instructed, opened his door just enough to reach out and drop both the SIM and the phone into a drain.

What a glorious day, he thought. His first trip and he'd got *two* tips, one from the woman and one from her worried uncle, a tip that was big enough to take him and his new girlfriend out for a dinner she'd never forget.

48

Through the peephole in his hotel room door Frank watched the cop outside yawn, swipe a finger down the screen on his phone and scratch his backside with his other hand. The poor guy was as happy being stationed there as Frank was being a virtual prisoner while Tori was out there alone, fending for herself.

At least Axel and Ron got to be useful, trying to keep the deal alive by working the phones from Boston and sweet-talking Greenland's acting leadership into sticking with it.

'Francis, I think you should abide by the police request,' Axel told him in their last call. 'Keep your head down and stay there until we get some clarity.'

He'd listened politely, but keeping his head down, lying low, sitting on his bloody bum ... There was no way Frank would do that.

He'd wait a bit, just long enough for Thatcher to wield the magic the pair had agreed on, so he kicked off his shoes, the new pair he'd bought in Barcelona, took the tea bag out of the cup he'd filled from his room's kettle, and sank back against the bedhead, cuppa in hand, to watch the local TV news.

How many times could they repeat the phrases *el suposat assassí*, *Tori Swyft* and *vídeo depravat* in the same sentence? He put the tea on his nightstand and got up to go to the toilet. He was halfway there when his burner beeped and then rang.

'Chowders, your humble servant has messaged you a link. Open it up.'

Though 'humble' and 'servant' were not words Frank had ever associated with his big-headed chum, he kept the thought to himself as he picked up his tablet and clicked the link he found there. That way he could more easily talk and look at the same time.

The link opened up on a fuzzy still image of a woman with dark – maybe black – hair, wearing sunglasses, poking her head around a street corner.

Thatcher was zooming the camera in on her, the pixels sharpening, the image enhancing. Despite the hair, she was unquestionably Tori. 'Am I watching this in real time?'

'As real as Thatcher's dulcet tones, dear boy.'

'So you know where she is.'

'Obviously.'

Frank sat on the bed, astonished. 'But how? How did—'

'Tori's adversary displays a penchant for wiping CCTV tapes so Thatcher hit the city CCTV network to look for – what do the crime dramas call it? – to see if the same MO turned up somewhere else.'

'Perhaps pointing us to where he might be hiding out?'

'Your dear parents would be so proud to know, finally, that your mentally celibate years at Oxford were not wasted.'

'Thatch—'

'Yes, yes, to the point. You're looking through a municipal camera located in a godforsaken square mile where all the recordings went *poof!* thirty-six hours back. The same cameras only came back online twenty minutes ago. That's the good news.'

'And the bad is … Oh my God. He switched them back on for a reason—'

'Exactly, to watch his back, to see who might pop by for a visit.'

'But if *we* know Tori is there … Thatch, turn the bloody cameras off again. Can you do that?' There was silence at the other end of the phone. 'Sorry. Of course you can. Please, Thatch, do it *now*! And keep the cameras switched off till I get there.'

Frank had made his decision. No matter what the police had demanded, or Axel suggested, he was done with keeping his head down. 'And Thatch, the chap in blue outside my room,' he said, his voice several notches quieter, 'can you accelerate what we discussed last—'

Frank heard a phone ringing through his door. 'Thatch, is that you calling him?'

'Certainly not, Frank. Most likely it's the head nurse from the local hospital's A&E giving him the bad news about his poor, poor mother. Something about a falling piano. If you look through your peephole, dear boy, you'll see the frantic wretch turn on his heels any second and run down that corridor. Go pack your toothbrush.'

49

Tori snaked through the last dim, narrow lane. She'd strapped her bag on her back this time, for protection as much as convenience. The pathway fed her into a vast open space, a demolition site with a fleet of construction vehicles parked on the far side. Fire-red dump trucks, Caterpillar-yellow bobcats, two bulldozers, and three orange excavators. She counted eleven, twelve, thirteen vehicles and, leaping from one to another, three mangy cats.

In the centre of the square, a single derelict building was waiting for these vehicles to flatten it. Around it, she saw the ghosts of kerbs and cobbles that hinted at three other buildings that once flanked it, all of them gone. The neon that hung precariously from the top of the building's front wall confirmed she'd come to the right address. It was the same semi-naked pole dancer that was printed on the card she'd found in the hotel room.

Apart from yowls from the cats and the pecks of a lone grey bird not far from her feet, the area was eerily silent. The dove or pigeon, she didn't know which, was nibbling at a half-eaten *flauta de jamón ibérico*, the local bread, tomato and ham speciality Tori had eaten every breakfast since she'd arrived in Barcelona.

The one-time strip club was a forlorn structure, long and squat, two storeys high, with no windows or, if there were, they were plastered over by posters of concerts and dances with dates from long ago or spray-painted with images of couples in absurdly athletic positions.

The asphalt between her and the building was cracked, bits of trash swooping and looping in the breeze above the smashed glass from green and brown bottles.

The bird flew away from the bread roll and flapped up to the neon sign, perching on the woman's toe, its wings fluttering just above the club's name: Bar Canona.

Tori stepped back into the shadows and let her eyes and ears crunch a path over the glass and gravel to the club's entrance, alert for any sign that The Voice might be lurking inside.

50

Air Force One

President Diaz wasn't changing her mind. 'For the last time, no, Gregory.' Her chief of staff sat opposite in her office on the upper deck. Unusual for a man, as she observed for the umpteenth time, he was ramrod straight. Gregory never slouched.

Isabel, tired of his toing and froing and perfect posture, was keen to be with Davey, who she knew would be trying out the virtual reality headset game she'd given him for his birthday.

'Today's agenda remains as is,' she said as she stood. 'We land, we do the one-on-ones at the airport,' the private half-hour meetings she'd set up with the leaders of Germany, France and, ideally, Russia in the unlikely event that Gregory could get Tushkin's people to change their leader's mind, 'we motorcade to Montse's funeral, deliver our eulogy – hopefully Davey gets to sign it – then we fly to Madrid for the talks with President Rubio and do our joint media conference.'

Santiago Rubio was the federal president of Spain. Her people and his had been negotiating changes to the governance at NAVSTA Rota, a joint naval station commanded by a Spanish rear admiral but fully funded by the US. Rota was strategically located near the Strait of Gibraltar at Spain's southernmost tip. Their talks this afternoon were meant to seal the deal on the new arrangements.

'Ma'am, I've said it before—'

'And I've heard you every time.' She stepped towards the door.

'I wouldn't be doing my job if—' He stood up. 'Look, there's a high risk that Barcelona will go into lockdown given these assassinations. And with Swyft on the run, an American …'

'Half-American.'

'And fully on the run.' He sat again, back at the pointy end of her V-shaped desk and lifted his drink can off the leather coaster.

Gregory's heart was in the right place, she knew that, but she'd had enough. 'We've got unique factors at work here. For one, we're making history. I'm America's first Hispanic president—' apart from Matt Santos, she reminded herself, the Jimmy Smits character she'd loved so much in the *West Wing* TV series, 'and I'm visiting Spain's two most important cities. But about Tori Swyft, if she—'

'—is guilty, which it looks like she is, ma'am—'

'I'm not so sure. The CIA's exit psych report says she's far more likely a victim than a perpetrator.'

'Not according to the head of the Agency.'

'Swyft quit the CIA. The upper echelon despises her for that, but the psych report is pretty damn conclusive. What you see on that foul tape isn't remotely who she is. I've tasked the NSA—'

'Yes, ma'am, I know, to check it's not a deepfake—'

'—like the one that showed me standing on the bridge of the *USS Gerald R. Ford* and declaring war on Russia last month.' That video, created by North Korean 'interests', had roiled the financial markets for the fifteen minutes it took the White House to issue a formal statement that it was a fake. Gregory had acted as fast as he could but a lot of financial damage still got done.

He put his Coke can back down again, as if the movement helped him think. 'Our Secret Service team on the ground—'

She'd wasted enough time on this. 'This hassling to go home, Gregory. It's a pretext, isn't it? Because you're scared you won't pass the Spanish drug test at the airport.'

'Excuse me?' he said, looking confused.

She pointed to his drink can and smiled as she left the room.

He sighed as the door was closing. 'I'll test positive for coke? Really? That's the best you can do?'

The door clicked shut.

51

Barcelona

Tori spied a street-cam on the corner. Though it wasn't pointing towards her it still got her worried that she might have missed one from the time she got out of the taxi until now. If the image got put up on TV or social media and the cab driver saw it ... She needed to change her appearance again.

She'd passed a women's clothes store one street back so she returned to it. The sign on the door said it would *Obert a les 10h* – open at 10 am – though she couldn't imagine why they'd bother, since most of the buildings nearby were deserted. The locals had been relocated, she guessed, paid off to make way for the construction project.

The front door was painted with a thick black lacquer, a yellow plastic smiley face stuck on it at eye level. She stepped into the doorway and rattled the padlock, cranky at herself for having given up carrying a set of lock picks. She went back to the building site and kicked around in the debris. Soon enough she uncovered a couple of thin steel nails that would do the trick.

As she pushed the door open, a wave of old-people smell hit her. It was what her aunt's house reeked of, what she later learned was the naphthalene flakes her dad's sister used to sprinkle in her drawers to stop the moths eating her woollens. Tori moved inside, pushing past racks crammed with clothes that, even in the dim light, she could tell would be more at home in a charity shop. Near the back she came across what loosely passed as a washroom, more of an alcove, with a shabby chenille curtain dividing it off from the rest of the store. She was about to pull the drape across when her burner phone started ringing.

Which wasn't possible since she'd switched it off when she left the hotel and hadn't turned it back on.

It kept ringing.

52

The caller ID read 'Frank', which was also puzzling since the phone was a burner and Tori had not loaded any of her contacts onto it. She held it up to her ear, her pulse pounding against the plastic or glass or whatever the screen was made of.

'Love that wig,' said Frank.

An unnerving image leapt into her head: Hannibal Lecter wearing his bite mask in *The Silence of the Lambs*, except the features belonged to Frank, not Anthony Hopkins.

'Tori, hold the phone out in front of you. I want to check if your delightful face still looks like the one on a certain video that's just gone viral ... Congratulations, by the way. You're super famous.'

He used the word *delightful* but his tone was menacing. The Frank she knew would never talk like this. 'Fuck you,' she said into the air, a chill scuttling down the back of her neck as she put her finger over the camera lens.

He ignored his sudden blindness and babbled on, but Tori was concentrating on the words, scraps of sentences, she could vaguely make out in the background. There was an echo too, like snatches of sound from a distant public address system. They were in Spanish or Catalan, she couldn't be sure, since she'd put her FrensLens in her backpack. She thought she heard *innovació* … *tecnologia* … *Cata-Cars* … definitely *Cata-Cars* and also *onze en punt*, which she knew was eleven o'clock in Catalan, two and a half hours from now. The time that President Casals was set to cut the ribbon at Catalonia's driverless car show, something he'd talked about last night.

She had no idea why The Voice or Frank or whoever this really was might be near the car show, but she was done with him. That was easily said, of course. Being done with a guy who could remotely activate a phone that was switched off and turn on its camera was complicated. Anyone who could do all that would most probably also be able to use the device to track her and know precisely where she was. Without hanging up, she dropped the phone to the store's tiled floor and stomped her heel on it again and again, as if she was crushing the air out of his throat.

'Hey Tori,' came a voice, this time from outside the door. 'It's me, Frank.'

Sure, you are.

'Tori, I know you're in there.'

If this 'Frank' was The Voice, finally about to step out of the shadows and reveal himself, she knew it was not likely to end well. Silently, she drew her hairbrush shiv out of her bag, gripped the handle and raised it high with the point forward and down, poised, ready to strike.

She waited.

He pushed the door in, slowly but steadily.

She moved her hand a little to the right, ready to plunge the shiv into the side of the bastard's neck before he had time to shoot her, stab her, or do whatever else he was planning.

53

'It's the Americans, again,' the police commissioner grumbled to Maria, his tone so frustrated she could almost hear his eyes roll. 'The Secret Service won't accept a motorcade for their precious president. Convoys are good enough for the Brit, the Russian, our own king and queen, for goodness' sake, but not Isabel fucking Diaz.'

'They can't walk her from the airport, so what—'

'Chopper. A fly-in to the basilica. All our planning thrown …'

Maria stopped listening to him. Miquel was an idiot. He'd clearly missed what was really happening. It wasn't the Secret Service behind this, it was Gregory Samson, the chief of staff from hell, from L, she corrected herself. He was orchestrating a scenario to get his boss to pull out. So he could tell her with a straight face, *We tried everything, ma'am, but the Spanish couldn't accommodate Marine One. I know you desperately want to be there, but our top people say that if they can't fly you in, you can't risk going.*

While the commissioner kept bleating, Maria had an idea and tabbed her computer monitor to the CCTV link that one of her interns had set up for the cameras surrounding La Sagrada Familia. The area was already perfect for international TV with the temporary flagpoles up and most of the United Nations members' flags already aflutter. But, damn, her idea was flawed. The park opposite the church's main entrance didn't have enough open space to clear a landing for a chopper. 'Plaça de Gaudí won't work,' she interrupted the commissioner. 'Too many—'

'Trees. Yes, I know,' he said. 'And the lake in there is too deep. The only place that might take a helicopter, two helicopters, is the street diamond where Mallorca intersects Marina.'

'Two?' she said, stepping away from her desk.

'Three in total, two of them touch down, one stays in the air. Two are decoys. No one knows which one carries the president till she steps out of it.'

With an upcoming re-election to win for Uri, Maria needed to trump American paranoia with Catalan pragmatism. She zoomed in on the street corner he'd mentioned. 'Miquel, if you get half the emergency vehicles filling up that diamond to pull back into Mallorca, that blacktop will be plenty big enough.'

'It'll disrupt our—'

'Miquel, we are safeguarding Montse's memory here. Find a workaround. We cannot give Diaz's people any excuse to pull her out. Her attendance today is crucial.'

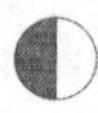

Their eavesdropper agreed completely.

54

Tori's blood was racing as the shop door slowly pushed inwards. Don't act rashly, she told herself, her arm held high. Keep calm, focused.

A hand slid through the opening. A large hand, a man's hand. His skin was brown, like the real Frank's, but that wasn't conclusive. The Voice could be any race, any colour. Any person. Maybe even Frank.

No, that wasn't possible. Not Frank. She'd worked with him. Liked him. But, she reminded herself, as Sun Tzu put it in *The Art of War,* 'all war is deception'.

The Voice *wanted* her to believe he was Frank. To turn her against her friend, deny her his support. By mimicking Frank's voice, he was playing her, making her believe her friends were her enemies. *All war is deception.* Misdirection. Illusion.

The shiv was high above her head and she gripped it tighter, tensed her arm, prepared to strike at any second.

His wrist came through the gap, his shirt white, the cuff doubled back but missing its cufflink.

She tightened every muscle in her body.

His sleeve started to come through and she couldn't stop the relief bursting out of her. It was like the air whooshing out of an untied balloon.

Tweed never looked so good. For the first time in her life, Tori *loved* tweed.

Or was she being too quick? Someone could slip on a jacket even easier than a fake voice. 'Who are you?'

'What?' he said, sounding bewildered. 'It's me. Frank.' He took half a step inside but stopped abruptly when the tip of her weapon came within a centimetre of his eye.

'Was that you on the phone to me just now?' The shiv glinted in her hand.

'Phone? I don't have a number for you. How could I call … Tori, you don't think … you can't think I have anything to do with this, surely.' He reached for her hand. His touch was warm and soft, though at the same time it felt electric.

'Tori, I can't begin to imagine how you're coping.'

The gentleness of his tone weakened her resolve. After everything she'd been through, she finally let go and allowed him to take the shiv and place it on the front counter. 'I'm sorry,' she said, slumping. 'For doubting you.'

'Given everything that's happened, you've got to doubt everything.'

She could have kissed him. 'It was Thatcher, right? That's how you found me?'

He nodded, making her happier than she ought to be, since she'd explicitly asked Thatcher to keep Frank out of the loop.

'Ugh, is that mothballs?' He sniffed at the air. 'I hate that smell. My aunt … never mind. Yes, Thatcher's been fantastic. A pain in the proverbial, but without him, I wouldn't be here.'

Frank was suddenly staring at her.

'What?' she asked, still wanting to hug him but knowing she wouldn't.

'Your eyes …' he started, his brow scrunching into a question mark.

She angled her head coquettishly. 'What? How they glimmer like emeralds in the moonlight?'

'Er, no,' he said. 'Your eyelashes. You don't have any.'

'They're overrated.' She decided to avoid the details, for both their sakes.

'Tori, we were supposed to have breakfast this morning. I've been worried sick and …' A cloud as dark as her wig came over his face. 'Why would you—?'

She was aghast. 'You think I did those … those things?' If he thought she could have, then maybe she did. The thought still petrified her.

'No, Tori. Never. Not at all. No. Why did you run? Not from the hotel, I get that. But why did you run from me?'

'If the cops questioned you—'

'So I wouldn't know anything. Sure, I get that, but why didn't you let me make that choice for myself?'

'You're here now—' she started, but stopped and looked at the phone she'd smashed on the floor. 'Frank, we've got to get out of here. You found me and,' she pointed to it, 'so did the bastard who's behind all this.' She grabbed the shiv and her backpack and ran past him out of the store.

55

Tori sprinted like a gazelle fleeing a lion. Three blocks on, she was out of breath and kicked in the front door of an abandoned apartment block. She needed a moment and bent over panting, hands on her knees, just as a rat scurried along the bare boards, swishing its tail on the floor and scattering cockroaches before it disappeared into a hole in the wall.

'Lovely digs,' said Frank, following her inside. He was breathing quite normally, but he hadn't had the morning she'd had. 'Are you thinking of putting in an offer for the place?'

Making light was one of Frank's hallmarks and she usually found it endearing, not so much now. 'We need to call Thatcher,' she told him. 'Is your phone encrypted?'

He nodded, pulled it out and dialled.

Thatcher answered. 'Frank and Tori, especially Tori—'

'Thatcher,' said Tori, 'how the hell did you know—?'

'Chowders, have you not explained?'

'Tori hasn't given me much of an opportunity, actually. Tori, Thatcher's taken control of the street-cams in this area and—'

'Hang on,' said Tori cutting in, 'if you could find me, see me, so could—'

'Tori, dear girl, what don't you understand about the words *Thatcher* and *control*? No one else, especially your adversary, has access. That Voice chap may think he is good, but he is no match for yours truly.'

She wasn't satisfied. Anyone who could remotely operate a phone that was switched off might not be so easily thwarted. He may well have tracked her location via the device's GPS. She decided to bring the two men into her plan. 'There's an abandoned strip club a few blocks from here. Bar Canona.' She saw the quizzical look on Frank's face so she pulled the plastic card out of her pocket and passed it over. 'Whoever is responsible for the murders dropped an entry pass for that club in my hotel room and—'

'It could be a bloody trap,' said Frank, staring at her like she was crazy.

'Or a previous guest might have left it behind and housekeeping missed it,' said Thatcher.

'Yes, to both. But if it *is* merely someone else's card, what's the harm if I go in there and—'

'How about catching a contact STD?' said Frank, handing the card back to her between two fingers as if it was tainted. 'But like I said—'

'A trap. It might be, for sure, but what if it's a clue? I won't know unless I go in.'

Two cockroaches had climbed onto Frank's shoe. '*Unless?*' He kicked them off, sending them into chaos. 'Tori, *unless* is the Catalan word for *crazy.* Going inside that place, that's a job for the police, not for you. Not for us.'

56

Tori and Frank worked together, curling their fingers under the grille that secured the club's front entrance, trying to yank it up. It simply would not budge. It just clattered and rattled and clinked like the coins that would have jiggled in the pockets of the hundreds of old men in raincoats who'd skulked their way into this place in its heyday, the brims of their caps low to shade their furtive eyes.

She picked up the crowbar – they'd pilfered it from one of the excavators parked at the far side of the site – and after sliding its chisel-edged claw beneath the bottom rail of the grating, tried to lever the grille up, but still made no headway.

Frank took the metal bar and got the same useless result. He arched his back into a stretch and cricked his neck from side to side. 'Hey, over there,' he said, pointing to the wall to their right.

Tori saw a faint light flashing, dim in the sunlight, no doubt the reason she hadn't noticed it before. Red then green then red again, like an access panel on its rostered day off. She turned her back to him. 'Can you get the FrensLens out of my backpack for me?'

She put them on. After glancing sideways and behind, satisfied no one had come into the area, Tori slipped the cardkey out of her pocket. She rubbed it between her fingers, the words *trap or clue* blinking in her head like the lights on the security panel, *trap* in red and *clue* in green.

She pressed the card up against the panel and the light went solid green, though only for a second. There was no click, no stutter of the grille to indicate that its rungs were about to climb up their tracks, no words in any language flashed up on the panel. She placed the card back into her pocket. 'There's got to be some other way to get in there. Around the back maybe?'

'Or better yet,' said Frank, 'we get the hell out of—'

His words froze as they heard shouts behind them, over near the trucks and the excavators. They spun around, and Tori realised what they'd heard wasn't yelling so much as squeals and giggles. Four girls, seven- or eight-year-olds, were bounding out of a laneway and rushing up to the vehicles. The first to make it, a child wearing a blue smock and clutching a teddy bear, pigtails jutting out the sides of her head like handlebars on a bike, pressed her nose up against the blade of a bulldozer and covered her eyes. '*Qui no s'ha amagat …?*' she shouted. The FrensLens instantly translated for Tori but she'd already got the idea from just watching. 'They're playing—'

'Hide-and-seek,' said Frank, his raised eyebrow telling her that he also didn't need an app to tell him what was obvious.

The other three kids were clambering over different vehicles and ducking down, finding their hiding places. One girl, in a red T-shirt and blue jeans, hid in a truck tray, the one in a green dress dropped herself behind the dozer blade, while the last girl stooped down behind a trailer to cuddle a stray cat which, from a distance, wore a coat as brown as her shorts.

Tori started moving around the perimeter of the building and Frank followed, each of them sporadically checking over their shoulder for anyone watching. Tori was knocking her knuckles against the wall as she went along, hoping that one of the posters might be covering a doorway. She stopped when she reached the corner of the building, and when Frank caught up she indicated a spot halfway along the next wall. 'There.'

A mound of debris about knee-high was piled up outside a niche. When she got close to it she made out broken glass, cigarette butts, sticks, newspapers, cardboard. Condoms, too. The breeze shifted and she caught the stink of urine.

The niche's opening was as wide as her body but only as high as her chest. She held her nose and bent down to crane her head inside, a move that blocked the daylight. 'Frank, can you give me your phone?' She shone its flashlight inside and saw a dark-coloured booklet on the ground. 'Hey, see that?' she said to him, shifting herself so he could step forward.

'Is it a passport?' He went to reach his hand in but she grabbed it.

'Wait.' She shone the light around the entrance, onto the niche's floor, the walls, the roof, checking for threads or tripwires. Satisfied, she rummaged through the rubbish pile outside with her foot, found a longish stick and tapped the booklet out into the open. A passport, its cover a dark navy blue.

'Canadian,' said Frank as he went to pick it up.

Was The Voice a Canuck? Did he drop his passport there? She let the thoughts sink in. Canada was, she reminded herself, a member of the Arctic Council. If Ottawa saw China stepping on its toes would Canada stand by or would they put up a fight?

'It can't possibly be the Canadians,' said Frank. 'They're so polite they'd have left their business card at the crime scene, probably embossed with maple leaves.'

She took the passport from Frank and flicked it open. '*Holy shit!*'

57

Tori knew the woman whose face was on the passport intimately. Knew her every feature as well as her own, how the woman thought, where she'd been. Her entire backstory. Where she'd grown up and gone to school in Saint-Constant south of Montréal, her lovers, her jobs, her last apartment on Sherbrooke Ouest, its décor, the names of her next-door neighbours, even their kids. She knew all of that detail without needing to read her name: Kathryn Mary Lisson.

Despite Lisson being a strawberry blonde with glimmering blue eyes, her photo bore a startling resemblance to Tori.

Because she *was* Tori, an identity she had crafted while she was at the CIA. This was one of the passports she'd got off-book and which she'd thought was in her backpack's secret compartment. The compartment whose protective invisible thread had been intact until she broke it herself. The compartment where she'd kept the burner phone The Voice, not so mysteriously now, had hacked. She'd underestimated him. Big-time. Silently, she handed the open passport to Frank.

He returned it, his scowl telling her what she already knew: that she shouldn't let herself be suckered into playing The Voice's game, that she and Frank should immediately run, or hide, or do anything except be drawn into following his lead. Except then, she told herself, she'd spend the rest of her life, probably a brief one, as a fugitive on the lam from the law.

'*Un, dos, tres, salvat!*' It was a jubilant cry from one of the children.

One, two, three, safe!

If only.

58

Frank was adamant. 'There's no way we're going in.'

Tori unslung her backpack and tossed it inside the alcove, ducking down and crawling in after it.

'No, Tori, no!' he called as she crawled forwards, drawing her feet in behind her.

The alcove was just wide enough for her frame and she was already one metre in, the cardkey in her teeth and her body blocking the light when she felt Frank tugging on her feet, trying to wrench her out. Resisting, she continued to nudge her bag ahead of her, pushing it in further, trying to twist her feet out of his grip. Instead of stopping her, all he managed was to pull off her boots.

She wriggled ahead quickly, not getting far before a steel barrier blocked her from going any further. Frank, loyal Frank, had given up trying to stop her and was grunting his own way in behind her. 'If you insist on being an idiot, Tori, you'll be safer if there's two of us.'

'Two *mugs*? That way we can really be in hot water.' She half-laughed as she took the card out of her mouth, switched the light on her digital watch and pressed the card all over the cold metal, hoping it might activate something to open it. Bent and cramped in the tight, claustrophobic space, she tried twisting sideways and pressing her shoulder against the steel, but that didn't budge it either.

Frank, close behind, shone the brighter light from his phone past her. The metal began to moan, as if his phone was Indiana Jones's flaming torch and it was rousing an entombed beast from centuries of slumber. '*Whoa!*' Tori cried out, banging her head on the ceiling as the barrier suddenly began to slide sideways ahead of her.

She squinted to see beyond it but the light from their devices was too weak to penetrate the darkness. She slithered her way through, expecting Frank to follow, but as soon as her feet cleared, the steel barrier slid back fast and closed with a clang.

If Frank was shouting, she couldn't tell. All she could hear were quiet thuds from the other side, presumably his fists banging on the metal.

Alone, no doubt how The Voice wanted her, she switched off her light and crawled a metre or so to her right, away from the barrier. There was no point making herself an easy target. Tense, alert for the sound of a step, a breath, the cocking of a pistol, a blade slicing through the air, she got up slowly, the wooden floor still cold through her socks.

Her eyes began to adjust to the gloom. She wasn't sure but she seemed to be at the side of a stage. She moved forwards slowly. One step. Two. Three, the floor so sticky that each time she lifted a foot it sounded like her sock was scritching itself off a patch of Velcro. Probably the tack from spilled beer, she hoped, since the alternative offerings in a strip club didn't bear thinking about. She moved ahead again, startling herself when she brushed up against something long and snaky that dangled from the rafters, leaping sideways so her shoulder whacked into a strippers' pole that she instinctively grabbed for balance, which she instantly regretted when she realised what it was, rubbing her hands against her pants as if they were covered in slime.

Beyond the stage, all she could make out was a blur of strange shapes, possibly rows of tables with chairs stacked on top. Her peripheral vision, though, picked up a dull red glimmer from the wall closest to her. She edged over to it and felt a switchboard with multiple rows of toggles and knobs. If she acted fast, she might gain the element of surprise, so she flattened her palm against the panel and swept it downward, flicking every switch she could.

No lights. No music. No curtains.

Nothing.

She listened beyond her own breath, trying to make out the slightest sound, the scuff of a shoe, the brush of an arm against a jacket, a puff on a cigarette.

Nothing but pin-dropping silence.

59

Frank leant on the wall outside the niche, venting to Thatcher and slapping the crowbar against the wall. 'Any sane person who found that passport, they'd go *let's bail.* But not Tori. Thatch, you remember when the three of us were debating traps and clues? It's like the discussion never happened. She just charges in, no backup, no one to protect her, and I'm stuck outside, useless.'

With one hand, he picked up her boots and dangled them by the pull-loops, and with the other tossed the crowbar as far as he could, watching it wheel through the air until it clanked onto the asphalt and kicked up a cloud of dust.

Down a corridor a long way ahead of her, Tori saw a thin greenish glow-strip at floor level, like someone had tossed down a *Star Wars* light sabre. Was it light creeping through the crack under a door? She slowly moved towards it, and when she got to the end of the hall, she bent over to pat the floor tiles which, thankfully, were dusty but not sticky. She dropped herself all the way down, stretched out lengthways and pressed her cheek against the floor, her backpack bearing down on her neck, the chill from the ceramic floor leaching into her skin and a draught of cold, acrid air streaming out through the gap under the door to the hum of what sounded like an air conditioner inside.

She couldn't see – the gap was too narrow – so she watched for movement, for the slightest smudge of a shadow drifting across to indicate someone was inside. The Voice, or maybe an accomplice.

In the face of the draught, it took her lashless eyes a lot of blinking to stay open. Worse, the smell the air carried out was rank. After two minutes of this cold, sour microclimate she got up. She twisted around to squint back into the corridor's dim emptiness, checking that no one was sneaking up on her.

The sweat rolling down her back clearly wasn't due to heat. Perhaps her body was reminding her how dangerous this was, how her only protection was a bulletproof backpack and the hairbrush shiv inside it.

She slid the bag off and slung it in front of her chest, as she'd done leaving the hotel. The fat lady was back, handy if Tori took a shot from the front when she opened the door. She fished inside for the shiv and held it up and ahead of her in a right-handed attack grip. She extended the back of her other hand to the metal doorknob, a precaution learnt at Langley that was now a habit and, greeted by no electric shock, she turned the handle and burst into the room, ready to jump whoever was inside before they had time to react, before they fired or lunged at her.

'*What the—*' she exclaimed, just before a slick on the floor sent her into a skid.

60

Tori skated across a slippery skin of red. She lashed her arm out sideways, grabbing at the only vertical object – a tripod of all things – and used it to stop herself toppling backwards into the sea of blood.

What confronted her was evil beyond weird. It was as if opening the door had whisked her back to Room 420.

Two bodies, hacked and mutilated – the same bodies – were splayed out on the bed – the same bed – in their same godforsaken poses. The masked man was on his back, his lower half covered by a red-drenched sheet, his bloodied arms stretched above his head, yellow cable ties manacling his wrists to the bedpost. The woman had an ulu hatchet buried in the back of her head, her hair caked with red; razor blades jutted out of her back, her skin oozing blood. On the floor lay a spattered pile of clothes, a polka dot dress draped over the top.

This was bizarre, surreal. The dead couple, the slaughter, the clothing. Had she been teleported back to the hotel room she'd just fled?

Everything was the same, except for two things. Big things.

First, the walls and the ceiling, which were a bright and luminous green, the colour so vivid that the more she looked, the more the bed seemed to float in it.

Was this a green screen? The technique film-makers used to drop exotic location scenes behind actors enjoying the comfort of a studio set – waves crashing onto a sandy beach in Hawaii, an icy precipice in the French Alps seconds before an avalanche. Or Room 420.

That also explained the second difference, the complete lack of furniture apart from the death bed. No nightstands, no desk, no TV, no wall art, no closet. Nothing apart from the pile of clothes on the floor, the tripod Tori was still holding onto and the butchery on the sheets.

The sex and the murders, she realised, must have been filmed here – with these two victims – and The Voice then dropped clean background footage from an empty Room 420 in behind it.

The Voice had accomplished a stunning sleight of hand, a filthy, murderous lie meant to vilify three people's reputations, sabotage the deal between two countries and frame Tori. This was proof.

Her socks were soaking up this unknown couple's blood from the floor, and she had no way to stop it. Tears began rolling down her cheeks. She let them fall. These people were innocents, human sacrifices, pawns in a lunatic's insane plan. Probably sex workers who'd bought some bullshit story about earning stacks of cash making a hard-core BDSM porn video. They might have families, might have planned to use the money to take their kids on vacation.

What was becoming clear was that nothing about this was spur of the moment. Tori ran through the steps in her mind. Locating and setting this place up, painting the room the right shade of green, hiring the two victims, tracking down an ulu knife exactly like Nivikka's, not easy to find if you weren't in Greenland, then accessing clothes that were similar to Tori's, Nivikka's and Songtian's … scripting the couple to act out a sadistic fantasy with Fake Tori, whoever she was, orchestrating a change of hotel room for Tori, drugging her and the others – maybe spiking their drinks while they were still at the bar – transporting them unseen into the hotel and up to Room 420 – for that The Voice surely needed inside help – murdering two of them, hacking at their bodies and arranging their corpses to mimic the scene already filmed here. A faithful but gruesome replica created for the police and public.

The person who stage-managed all of this was not just a monster, he was a master. His Master's fucking Voice.

If she got out of here – if he let her – she'd be able to point to this place as the irrefutable proof that she was a victim and not the sadistic, perverted killer the police were hunting down.

Which, she realised, meant she wasn't supposed to get out. Should have heeded Frank's warning that Bar Canona card was a trap, not a clue. A one-way ticket.

With Tori locked inside here, The Voice could get rid of two birds – three to be precise – with one stone.

Which meant she had to find some way to escape, and fast. And it also meant that she needed to take evidence with her, proof that this slaughterhouse actually existed.

She started taking snaps with her tablet as fast as she could, just like she'd done in Room 420. She got to the woman's hand, posed on the pillow exactly like Nivikka's, except she noticed a disparity. These fingernails were lacquered with pink polish, not gold.

As soon as she photographed that, she slotted the device back into her pack. She turned to leave and heard a click behind her.

She stopped. It clicked again.

It wasn't a gun since it was scratchy, not metallic, more like plastic against plastic.

A third click, and this time the lid of the camera on the tripod sprung open like a jack-in-the-box, and dark red flashes began radiating out of it.

61

The LED inside the camera was displaying the number 180. No, it was 179.

... 178 ...

The air con had stopped so the room was eerily silent, as if it was holding its breath. The LED was ticking over like her heart, far too fast. She felt bull ants were crawling all over her skin.

... 173 ... 172 ...

She raised a sleeve to wipe away the sweat streaming into her eyes, held her hand out flat, horizontal, and stared at it, amazed it wasn't shaking, then turned it over to see her wristwatch ticking its seconds over at the same pace as the LED.

Her mind was reeling. Who is this bastard, Stanley fucking Kubrick? With his smoke and mirrors, his video, his green screen – and now this ticking-clock movie cliché where in … 167 … 166 seconds … What? Was some flunky about to leap out of the darkness with a gun and shout, *Bang, bang, you're dead?*

… 165 …

Staying put for anything close to another 164 seconds, a little more than two and a half minutes, was not, she decided, a gamble worth taking.

… 163 …

… 162 …

Synching her watch's timer to count down like the LED used up a couple of those seconds, possibly crucial seconds, but she took them anyway, and when both timers showed the same numbers at the same time … 159 … 158, she flicked on her watch's flashlight, grabbed the polka dot dress – hoping Fake Tori's DNA was crawling all over it – stuffed it into her bag, took another item off the pile – a gold cardigan unsoaked by blood – then stepped out of the room, slowly, so she didn't risk slipping over.

Leaning up against the wall in the corridor she peeled her socks off, carefully from their very tops to keep the gore they'd sponged up from the floor off her hands. She dropped them on the clean floor first, then the cardigan, wiped her feet on it, pointed her watch light forwards and raced down the hallway.

Despite the dim light, it took her no more than twenty-six seconds to navigate her way back to the steel barrier she'd come in through.

She took out the cardkey and pressed it on the steel plate, around the architrave, everywhere she could, hoping that it might reactivate the mechanism that had opened it previously. It didn't.

At 94 seconds, she started waving the card around in case there was a motion detector. Nothing.

91 seconds.

89 seconds.

When she and Frank were pacing the outside of the building, she'd seen no windows, so there was nothing to smash and jump out of. All that was left was the roller grille at the front that they hadn't managed to budge even with a crowbar.

She charged back into the auditorium to find the grille from the inside, fast-tracking a turn to the left by grabbing onto the stripper's pole, no time for the distasteful thoughts she'd had last time. She twirled her body halfway around it, too hard apparently because as she leapt off the stage she heard it clatter to the floor.

At the toilets – unisex – she pushed open the door to double-check there was no window. There wasn't.

At 75 seconds, she swung a right, kicking open the doors to three dressing rooms – also windowless – and ran down another corridor.

At 52 seconds, she yanked back a curtain. It opened onto a foyer where smoke was billowing out of an AC vent on one side.

The public address system screeched and the guttural voice of a madman screamed out, something about being a god of hell fire, backed by pounding bass pedals and a blaring Hammond organ. The psychedelic sample kept looping, the smoke thickening as time was running out.

She dropped the curtain, took a deep breath of the cleanest air she could get, squinted to keep as much smoke out of her eyes as possible and tore through the split in the fabric, the drapes flapping behind her.

The glass doors ahead were only vaguely visible. As she got closer to them she could just make out the security grille on the other side, still reaching to the ground. She caught a hazy lime-green light pulsing through the smoke a metre or more to her right and, limiting her breathing as best she could, she waved the smoke away from her eyes and stepped towards it, relieved to see a security pad. Finally.

Maybe.

35 seconds left.

Spluttering, pressing her eyes closed to squeeze out the smoke, her eyes streaming, she pressed the passcard against the pad. When she thought she could hear the creak and rattle of the roller grille over the looping music, she pulled her shirt up over her mouth, felt her way to the glass door and pushed her nose up against it, but with her eyes weeping and stinging so much, she could not see outside.

She shoved the door – it was locked – and moved her hands over the surface to find the handle, then pulled and pushed it. Nothing. All she achieved was hearing the door banging up against the bolts that locked it to the floor.

25 seconds.

62

Frank was outside the alcove when he heard maniacal music booming from around the corner. 'Thatch, I've got to go.' He ran to the front, putting his phone in his pocket as he went, arriving as the grille was clanking its way up. The sound from inside was ear-splitting.

He ducked underneath the shutter, leapt up the steps and pushed and pulled on the glass door but it was locked. He couldn't see inside, the foyer so full of smoke it was starting to billow out from under the glass.

As he was looking around for something – anything – to smash it, he saw two hands emerge through the smoke and press up against the glass, then a nose … Tori's.

He flew down the steps, his head almost hitting the bottom of the rising shutter and sprinted to where he'd thrown the crowbar, and tore back.

Choking from the smoke, deafened by the thunderous music and with 17 seconds left on her timer, Tori didn't have to imagine what was about to go down. The place was about to blow, obliterating the truth about Nivi and Songtian's deaths – and her innocence – and purging the world of the evidence to prove it.

Beyond the glass, she could make out the grille rolling its way up. She stepped back and, turning side-on, ran at the door, hitting it with such force she almost cracked her shoulder.

15 seconds.

Turning, unable to see, she ran back through the curtain and into the auditorium, which was also filling with smoke, her knee slamming against the front of the stage. Dismissing the pain – she had no time for it – she scrambled up onto the stage, her feet tapping around the floor for the fallen stripper's pole. When she located it, she dragged it back to the foyer, picked it up and hoisted it under her arm like a medieval knight taking his lance into a joust.

At 5 seconds to go, the music stopped abruptly.

At first, the hush felt deafening. *Is this another mind game?*

Her eyes stinging and open only a crack, her lungs raw, she stepped back, one hand at the rear of the pole, one towards the front, and charged at the doors. At the same time as the metal hit glass, she heard more crashing, this time from the outside. The glass shattered, the cracks spider-webbing. She unslung her backpack, gripped it in front of her face and head-butted the crazed surface, smashing her way through it, chunks of safety glass crumbling around her and revealing Frank ahead of her, a crowbar poised in the air above his head.

'*Run!*' she screamed, with no time to thank him. He dropped the bar and they both jumped the stairs and hurtled into the demolition site, Frank making ground ahead of her since she was barefoot and had to dance around chunks of broken glass and stones and sticks. Not looking back, sucking in fresh air, the only sounds were their feet pounding the asphalt and the roller rattling back down behind them, until Tori heard snickers from the children.

Still running, she twisted around, saw the smoke dissipating, the roller three-quarters down and closing fast. When she saw the kids, she stopped suddenly, stubbing a toe on a rock, and watched the four little girls laughing and giggling as they chased after a cat that loped under the roller and up the steps. They followed fast behind.

'*No … Don't go in there!*' Tori shouted. She was still screaming when the howl of the explosion blew her backwards off her feet.

Debris started shooting out of the building, the blast wave picking her up and slamming her into the side of a steel dumpster a couple of metres behind her.

Disoriented, she scrambled around to the back of the skip, crouching under its lip as a torrent of rubble started raining down, chunks of brick, shards of tiles and splinters of wood landing all around her, and, at her side, the bloody, scraggly arm of a child's teddy bear.

63

The air was thick with dust and the stench of burning flesh. Dazed, with grit in her throat and her ears ringing, Tori got up, a little giddy as she looked back at the mountain of rubble where Bar Canona once had been. Clouds of smoke and dust were billowing into the sky, blotting out the sun.

Frank stepped out of a doorway he'd sheltered in, his hair and tweed unsullied. The anxious faces of onlookers were poking out of side streets, some of them, she fretted, probably parents of the girls, mothers and fathers about to enter their worst nightmare. As she moved backwards, dirt and who knew what else falling from her shoulders, she took Frank's hand and pulled him into the shadows of a deserted alleyway.

They ran over the cobbles, took a right and a left and hit a small strip of shops – none of them open yet – first a phone store, then a massage parlour, and last of all another clothes store. Frank checked that no one was around, nodded to Tori and while she gaped at the wild, dirty and dishevelled mess she saw reflecting back at her from the store window, he burst the door open with his shoulder.

64

Air Force One

President Diaz was on a video call with her vice-president when her DNI, Robert Hirsty, came through on another line. She joined the two calls up, her screen showing each participant in a separate window.

'Ma'am, sir,' said her DNI, 'turns out that old coot of a professor, Buckingham, he died from an arterial aneurism. Just like the UN Secretary-General.' Isabel had been a little elastic with President Casals' request for confidentiality about the true nature of Montse's death when it came to her closest advisers.

'Robert, that's one heck of a coincidence.'

'Or it's not, ma'am. We suspect that both deaths are down to Hermes.'

Isabel didn't have a clue what Hirsty was talking about. 'The luxury brand?'

'No, ma'am. The injectin' of an air bubble … whether it's under a toenail, behind the eye, inside the eardrum, anywhere you can hide a pinprick. That's a Hermes signature.'

'What is a Hermes?' Isabel and Spencer blurted at the same time.

Hirsty's head jolted back in surprise, as if what he was saying was common knowledge. 'Hermes is a contract killer, an international assassin. CIA profile says he's got a dark triad typology. Ain't one country that—'

'Dark triad?'

'A medley of three personality traits all cooked up into the one malevolent fruitcake. You get the psychopath added to the narcissist, an' all of it coated with the Machiavellian manipulator. Cold, callous, deceptive, zero scruples, ego as big as Mount Everest, the guy is evil unlimited. Like I was gonna say, ain't no northern hemisphere country where Hermes hasn't killed, threatened or ransomed at least one VIP. Everyone … us, Europol, Interpol … virtually every agency anywhere would love to lay their mitts on him. Unless he's doin' a job for 'em.'

'*We've* hired this monster?'

Hirsty shook his finger. 'Nope, ma'am. Could never happen. President Clinton signed an executive order blackbannin' that. August 2000 he signed it, puttin' a veto on any US government contact with Hermes, direct or indirect, unless we were takin' him down. Forty-Two wrote his order tighter than a …'

Isabel chose not to listen to the rest of his sentence.

Clinton's decision was personal, Hirsty went on to explain, coming straight after the assassin murdered one of the former president's rockstar playmates. He'd been flying out to an Adirondacks resort to sing for Clinton's fifty-fourth birthday party and died on board the jet.

Isabel recalled the death. She'd been a huge fan of the music herself. 'But I remember it differently,' she said. 'He died from an overdose while he was in his bath. The whole world was—'

'That was a blind, ma'am. Medics found the pinprick under his tongue. What alerted 'em to it was a piece of paper stuffed in his mouth with handwriting that copycatted Clinton's. *For Juanita, Kathleen, Paula and Monica*, it said.'

Isabel knew those names, the four women who reluctantly became famous because Bill Clinton denied ever having sexual relations with them. 'Are you telling me that this Hermes person is both an assassin *and* an avenger of women's rights? What kind of sick ethical code justifies murdering an innocent man just to get payback on another man who's—'

'Who's alleged—' said Spencer, interrupting.

'CIA reckons North Korea's Kim Jong-il hired Hermes to do it, to give a message that the Norks had the resources to get at whoever they wanted, even a buddy of the president. The note was a bait and switch, a deception to fuel disgust against Clinton.'

'It never did, though. Surely a hit meant to warn off Forty-Two would've made the headlines.'

'The whole thing was hushed up,' he said.

'*Covered* up.'

'I guess.' He went on to describe how the singer's body was 'discovered' at his home in Tennessee three days later, with the news reports showing what became a legendary photograph – the one Isabel remembered – a sad bathroom, the artist's body limp, slumped back in the tub, his mouth open, his tongue lolling, a small spoon with a white crystalline substance resting on the edge of the porcelain.

'The blind was a success. Not a single mention anywhere that he was murdered. An' nothin' neither about his missed gig for Forty-Two, the flight, the note in his mouth. Nothing about the prick under his tongue.'

And nothing, thought Isabel, about the prick who'd hired the poor man to sing at his party.

'So we've never used this Hermes since?'

'Not before, not after, ma'am. Even if we begged the guy to work for the US of A, he'd turn us down.'

Spencer cut in. 'To know that we must have—'

'Wasn't our finest moment, I admit,' said Hirsty, 'but that was before Forty-Two's veto. No one knows why Hermes's got a grudge agin' us. Somethin' must have happened way, way back.'

For decades, he explained, Hermes had operated freely as an elite global rent-a-kill, yet no one had the slightest clue as to his identity, not even his nationality.

'Do we have *any* facts about him?'

'Apart from that profile as a dark triad nutjob who don't like America, he's stayed pretty much invisible.'

'And the name … Hermes?'

'People s'pose he took it after the Greek Hermes, the mythical god who spent his time conductin' souls into the afterlife. The ancients called him the divine trickster.'

'So this time,' said Isabel, 'the devil wears Hermes.'

'Huh?' Hirsty didn't have a clue.

'Forget it,' she said and contemplated how this Hermes could again and again execute the most daring hits, thumbing his nose at the world's intelligence community each time, leaving not a single pointer to his identity. 'If no one knows who he is, how do his clients hire him? How do they make contact?'

'Ha!' Hirsty's expression brightened. 'Technology's changed it over the years, but the answer's always been that he'll contact you if he wants your job.'

She was none the wiser. 'How would he know that you wanted to—'

'You head over to the Dark Web, click into his encrypted site, leave a message. We've never been able to hack his site or even block it, the guy's that damn good. He's got these caduceuses all over it—'

'Which are?' said the vice-president.

Isabel called up the insignia of the US Army Medical Corps and shared it with the others on-screen, a stick with two snakes entwined around it. 'Spencer, that's a caduceus.'

'Anyhoo, you punch in a private message and ID yourself – he's mighty picky an' it's not just us he won't work for – you also ID your target, your time-frame and the fee you're offering. If the job don't offend his delicate sensibilities, if he's willin' to take you on as a client, if the timing works for him and the money you slap on the table is high enough, he'll let *you* know. Hermes never negotiates, by the way, which means you gotta pitch your dollars big, real big. Ma'am, this guy's gotta be worth mega-millions by now.'

'What did you say … your hit can't *offend his sensibilities*? So while the money is crucial, it's not his only motivator. Who else won't he work for?'

'The drug cartels. He'll hit 'em but he won't do a hit *for* 'em. Heck, he even works *low bono* if he likes your cause. You were on the right track askin' if he's some kinda moral vigilante. If someone he's willin' to work for wants him to take out a ring of child exploiters or human traffickers, that kinda thing, he'll do those jobs for expenses only.'

'What you meant by *low bono* versus *pro bono*?'

'Exactly. Here's an example from last year. The guy's a greenie, too – go figure – so, for free, *nada*, he took out a Brazilian lumber company's entire executive team when they were about to start loggin' an ancient forest in the Amazon. CIA says a green group hired him and he even covered all his expenses, which they reckon coulda been a cool couple of million.'

Isabel was looking for an angle. 'If Hermes killed both Montse *and* Buckingham as you think – two jobs he would *not* do for free – can't we simply follow the money?'

'Nothin' simple about doin' that, ma'am. With Hermes the money trail always goes dead pretty damn quick.'

'Then what about working out who might profit from these hits, *both* of them? That would surely be a tiny group.'

Hirsty blinked slowly, an annoying tell that meant he was about to take issue with her. 'Madam President,' he said using her formal title, in his case another tell, a flag for an 'incoming'. That was a code-word that she and her chief of staff used for the cloying condescension that some of the men in DC still piled up on her, despite her being the most powerful person in the world. 'It's true we got two murders and one murderer, but the workin' hypothesis of our intelligence community is the hits are unconnected.'

'Really?' said Spencer, clearly sceptical. 'The two hits were in the one week.'

Hirsty explained that Hermes had done that before, executing separate contracts for separate clients, and not only in the same week but even in the same city. 'Rumour mill says each client gets a fee-cut, so they share in his savin's on resources. Never tells 'em what the second job is, just that there is one. Matter of fact, same thing happened with the Clinton thing. Two days later, Hermes hit a New York congressman, Jerry Benson. Publicly, the guy died from a heart attack but privately he was a scumbag member of a ring of child molesters.'

When she was ending the call, Diaz asked her veep to stay on the line. 'Spencer, I get the feeling Hirsty is hiding something from us. His protestation that Hermes would never take a job from the US doesn't sit well with me. Why is our money untouchable when he's willing to do his dirty work for almost anyone else? North Korea, for example.'

'You're thinking it's camouflage,' said Spencer, nodding. 'Hirsty giving us plausible deniability.'

'Precisely. So if there's ever a revelation that the US *was* involved in these two assassinations, you and I can put our hands on our hearts and say we honestly didn't know.'

65

Barcelona

Tori left Frank perched on the edge of the shop's front counter, partly to keep guard while he sent the photos she'd taken inside Bar Canona to Thatcher, and partly to allow her a modicum of privacy while she used the washroom down the back to freshen up and change.

Her clothes, now piled on the floor and covered in dust and fragments of things she didn't want to think about, reeked of smoke. As she shook her wig out multiple times, she couldn't avoid visualising a little girl hugging her teddy bear as the blast tore it and her to shreds.

She'd scrubbed her face so hard it was feeling raw, and as she emerged out of the racks, washed, clothed and wigged, she hoped the dim store light would stop Frank noticing that she wasn't able to keep her eyes dry.

His hand went to his mouth. He'd noticed.

She wiped her eyes, again, with her sleeve. 'I can't get those kids out of my head,' she confessed. 'If it wasn't for me …' She let the words hang like a sentence, the judgemental kind.

'Tori, *he* did that, not you. All *we* can do for those kids and their families is bring him to justice, so let's get moving and stop moping.'

Tori looked down. He was right about the moving part. But she couldn't help feeling responsible. She looked back up and saw his expression had changed, like he'd sucked on a lemon. 'What?' she said.

'Your outfit. It's like you've got a green neon arrow pointing at you and it's flashing *Hey, look at me*! I was kind of expecting a more blend-into-the-shadows get-up.'

'Even the wig?'

'The wig's fine, especially now you've flipped it blonde side up. The hair is the least offensive part … You are definitely *not* the Invisible Woman you need to be.'

Was he right? She hadn't thought so when she'd picked the clothes out. Perhaps it was the incredibly poor light filtering through to the back of the store. Plus her tears. And her exhaustion. Or maybe the drugs were still in her system and clouding her judgement. She could attribute her gaffe to lots of things, but paying less attention to creating a disguise than was prudent was a rookie error.

She pulled her shirt – green paisley – over her head and held it out in front of her to check it out. Frank was right. Here, nearer the window, it was flashy. Garish, even. As she stood in her bra and slacks and reset her wig, she noticed Frank had turned his head away.

He really was Mr Decent, she thought, as she rifled through another rack of shirts.

She slipped another shirt off the rack, dark grey, plain, no pattern, long-sleeved. After undoing the top two buttons of its Peter Pan collar, she pulled it over her head. 'Ta da! You can look now.' She pulled the shirt cuffs down over her wrists and, as Frank turned back to face her, she spun on her toes in the sneakers she'd found in the washroom. Fortunately, they were close enough to her size, a pretty good fit. 'So, Ralph Lauren Chaudry, what do you think now?'

'Better,' he said, eyeing her. 'The blandness of the grey makes the mauve slacks less awkward. Nice shoes, by the way.'

She checked her watch. 'Shouldn't we call Thatcher?'

66

The bad news kept coming, and this time they heard it via Thatcher. The Voice, he told them, had briefly managed to breach Thatcher's control of the street-cams. 'He live-streamed the explosion over social media. Your escape, too, Tori. Frank, the camera didn't catch you, just an errant flap of your magnificent jacket, but Tori, the footage of you escaping and the little girls running inside – and Thatcher must be honest here – it gave the impression that you were looking back and admiring your handiwork. Like it was your bomb that killed them.'

'That's ridiculous.'

'Social media is on a rampage. Any crazy person who can type is pinning those kids' deaths on you. Hopefully you've had time to switch your clothes in that shop you broke into.'

'Thatcher,' said Frank as he poked his head out of the front door, 'if the street-cams allowed you to follow us,' he gave Tori a thumbs-up of an all-clear, 'could The Voice—'

'Francis, Francis, you really need to listen more carefully. Thatcher told you The Voice only got *brief* access to the CCTV. Your Saviour from SoHo cut him off just after the explosion, so he did not see the direction you went or the shop whose door you shouldered. But chaps, you really need to get moving. He might have people out there searching for you.'

'Before we go, Thatcher,' she said, 'I need you to access the CCTV in another part of the city. A square where the local president is launching a driverless car spectacular,' she checked her watch, 'in forty minutes or so.'

'Why?' said Frank, looking worried.

She told them about the call she got from The Voice on her now extinct burner phone and the Cata-Car announcement she thought she'd picked up in the background. 'Thatcher, I need you to case the place, or whatever your hacker-speak is for that kind of work. We need to find him before he finds us, or me anyway, and that's the only clue I've got.'

She dug down into her backpack, which was on the floor near Frank's feet, moved the polka dot dress, now in a plastic bag, to one side, and pulled out five one-hundred euro bills, placed them on the counter under the store's receipt book and on the cover scribbled, '*Gràcies per la* clothes & sorry *per la* door and the mess.'

'Frank,' she said, 'we're going to the car show,' then she grabbed her bag and ran out into the street and headed left, scaring off two pigeons that were pecking at a mound of trash.

67

El Prat Airport, Barcelona

Not more than a minute after *Air Force One* rolled to a halt, Davey slunk into Isabel's office, his face shrouded in misery, his chin tucked in, his lower lip jutting and his mooning eyes even more adorably blue than usual. Dealing with presidents and chancellors was way easier than trying to handle a whiny ten-year-old.

The funeral was still hours away but the boy was already dressed in his new black suit. His shirt's top button had popped open and his thin tie, yellow like his shoelaces – Montse's favourite colour – was skewed to the side, and with his spiky shock of blond hair he looked like a skinny Mini-Me version of former British Prime Minister Boris Johnson.

'Did they say yes?' Davey signed. He took a step forwards, crossed his fingers, his arms and then his legs so he almost toppled over and made it hard for Isabel not to laugh.

Before she could straighten her face, her chief of staff put his head around the door. He tapped the boy on the shoulder and waited for him to unfurl his limbs and look up at him. 'Sorry to interrupt, Davey, this is urgent.' Then Gregory manoeuvred his own face into a position where Davey could not read his lips. 'Ma'am, President Hou Tao is on the line.'

Isabel was dreading this call. She and Gregory had toyed with pre-empting it, calling China's leader first, but decided that risked Isabel coming across as defensive even though she had nothing to hide.

As far as she knew.

'Here come the accusations. *You killed …*' She paused. While Davey couldn't see Gregory's lips, he could still see hers. 'Davey—' she started signing, but the boy anticipated that he was about to be dismissed and left.

68

Plaça d'Espanya, Barcelona

Plaça d'Espanya is one of Barcelona's most important public spaces, with a monumental fountain and huge grassed area at its centre and a bustling seven-lane road encircling them, a massive roundabout heavy with the traffic that congests the six roadways that criss-cross the *plaça*. For today, all traffic was banned, and the city had erected a giant circle of grandstands, ten rows high, in front of the museums, exhibition buildings and shopping mall – a former bull-fighting ring – that lined the roundabout's perimeter.

Instead of cars, the *plaça* was bustling with thousands of people, locals and tourists who'd won numbered seats in the lottery. Tori and Frank weren't among them but Tori had snapped up a scalper's last two tickets. They were in section L, second row from the front and, luckily, facing north-west, so the glare of the sun was at their backs, ideal for a woman with no lashes. With only one row of seats in front of them, their view was virtually uninterrupted.

Around eighty autonomous cars – Cata-Cars, driverless vehicles designed and built in Catalonia – were fanned around the circle of the central parkland, their front bumpers almost touching the grass. A Catalan flag, the *Senyera*, draped each vehicle, the stripes of red and gold making the display look like an array of two-colour petals on a huge petunia.

'Tori,' said Frank, his voice low, as Tori went to sit, 'take one last look around. Here we are, out in the open, exposed to TV cameras and thousands of phone cameras. Remind me why we've come to the *last* place you should be? I really do think that we should leave.' He placed his hand on her shoulder.

She pushed it away. 'Enough, Frank. If *you* want to leave, you'll go with my blessing. Me? I'm willing to take the risk, to hide in plain sight.'

'Or you could give yourself up, go straight to those cops over there and—'

'So some pimply-faced, trigger-happy rookie who shits his pants when he sees the red-haired video killer shoots me before I can open my mouth? It's either that or they throw me in a Spanish prison cell and leave me there to rot for the rest of my life. By staying right here,' she said, taking off her backpack and sitting down to make her point, 'I get the chance to trip up the bastard who's behind all of this and clear my name.'

Frank shook his head. She knew what he was thinking because he'd said it three times on their way here: *If just one spectator catches on to who you are, the whole place will erupt.*

'Frank, either go or stay, but if you stay I need you to focus on the show.'

He leant in close. 'What if *you* are the show?'

'Enough! Besides, with my knight in shining tweed at my side, what could go wrong?' She tried a smile, but it wouldn't come.

Frank started typing on his phone. She assumed he was messaging Thatcher but didn't ask. Instead she said, 'We should update Axel.'

He looked up. 'I asked Thatcher to do that before I left the store to follow you. Axel, by the way, would undoubtedly agree that you're crazy being here.'

'*Deu minuts … deu minuts … Si us plau, asseuieu-vos,*' an official shouted over a loudspeaker.

'Tori, in ten minutes it'll be impossible to get away. Please, let's go now.' He took her hand this time but she wrested it away and crossed her arms. 'I know you don't want to hear this but—'

'Then stop telling me. Focus on the cars. Boys like cars. Hey,' she said, noticing blue sections woven into the flags covering the display vehicles. 'Those flags are *Estelades*.' As they both knew, the *Estelada* was Catalonia's separatist flag, identical to the official *Senyera* except for an added blue triangle and the five-pointed white star inside it. 'You know what that means.'

'The president's going to use this to make a statement, and it'll be about way more than innovation,' said Frank.

'Is he going to launch a new campaign for—'

'Independence from Spain,' they said simultaneously.

The secession movement was a recurrent stress between Madrid and Barcelona. Some of Oriol's predecessors had gone to prison or went into exile over it. Back in Franco's time, his father was murdered over it.

'What if,' said Frank, 'The Voice's next victim is Oriol and the reason you're here – the reason he led you here – is so you'll be his fall guy? Again. Tori, please, really. We've *got* to go.' He started to get up and pulled at her hand.

'Too late,' said Tori. She dragged her hand away and pointed to the dais.

69

The musicians started up. 'It's *Els Segadors*,' said Tori as the crowd around them roared and leapt to their feet and President Casals stepped onto the stage to lead them in song. 'Catalonia's national anthem, not Spain's.'

At the end, when the audience began to sit, Casals raised his fist in the air and shouted out the song's opening line, '*Catalunya triomfant, tornarà a ser rica i plena*.'

Much of the crowd was up again, going wild, as Tori translated courtesy of her FrensLens, 'Catalonia triumphant, shall again be rich and bountiful.'

'*La innovació és la independència*,' Casals continued, to thunderous applause, although as Tori observed to Frank, only half the audience was clapping. Catalans were split on the independence question. It was a divisive issue.

The president raised both hands until he got silence. Cata-Cars, the home-grown driverless car technology launching today, he told them, leapfrogged every competitor, the Americans, the Germans, the Chinese. Cata-Cars were so safe, he declared, that he'd authorised a trial on Catalonian roads outside Barcelona to start in three months. Barcelona itself was set to follow four months later.

'*After* the vote. That's smart politically,' said Tori, under the applause. 'His electoral chances get a bounce from the decision, but if something goes wrong with the trials, it won't be his ballot box that gets whacked.'

The audience hushed again when two children in traditional costumes came onto the stage and bowed to their president. The boy was wearing a red *barretina*, a sock-like woollen cap, and a wide red sash, a *faixa*, was wound around his waist. The girl wore a fine net over her hair, a *ret*, and a lace *mantellina* over her shoulders.

Casals gave them the nod and moved to the side as the boy took the loose end of his sash and handed it to his partner. She began to pull on it, and the boy began to spin around and around. As the sash got longer she kept stepping backwards until it was completely unravelled. With the long, wide red ribbon now held between them, Casals came forwards with a huge pair of scissors and cut it, repeating more words from the anthem, to more applause, '*Com fem caure espigues d'or, quan convé seguem cadenes*.'

'Just as we cut golden ears of wheat,' Tori translated, 'when the time calls we cut off chains.'

'He's quite lyrical, isn't—' Frank was starting to say when the entire plaza let out a collective gasp. The flags were whipping off the cars, snapped high into the air, apparently pulled off by wires that none of the spectators, including Tori, had noticed before. They fluttered back down onto the dais where the two kids picked up one of the flags between them and ran it in circles around the president, getting even more applause.

In unison, the cars, all of them driverless and passengerless, backed into the empty roadway, turned to the right and slowly circled, nose-to-tail, around the grass parkland. A moment later, again in synch, they accelerated, the ring of vehicles going faster and faster then, as one, they slowed and shifted into a figure-eight routine. The mob went wild, the clapping and cheering almost deafening.

Eventually, the vehicles came to a sudden stop, the space between each car identical, then they repeated their previous routine, this time in reverse, and faster. At the end, they screeched to a halt, flashing their headlights into the grandstands as if to thank the public for the tumultuous applause.

The red velvet skirt that draped the sides of the central stage lifted and men and women dressed as matadors came out and circled the perimeter.

'Didn't Catalonia ban bullfighting years ago?' said Frank.

Tori shrugged.

Still on stage, Casals took the *Estelada* from the children and waved it over his head, swooping the colours from side to side as all the cars started revving, like Grand Prix racers growling at their starting line. He started a countdown – *tres*, *dos*, *un* – and on zero the cars spun their wheels and smoked rubber, did 180-degree hand-brake turns and charged inwards towards the centre, as if they were bulls charging the matadors.

The matadors stood their ground and the audience, almost as one, leapt to its feet with a collective intake of breath, thousands of hands covering mouths and eyes.

'One of those guys is shaking like a leaf,' said Tori.

'This is lunacy. If anything goes wrong—'

It didn't, which gained even more massive applause, although the man Tori had noticed had collapsed. While the others took their bows, four paramedics rushed out from under the dais and carried him away on a stretcher.

As soon as the medics left, the cars swivelled around so their grilles faced the grandstands again. They were flashing their headlamps rhythmically, as if beating in time to a metronome. They rolled forwards slowly, inching towards the crowd but stopping a car-length short of the stands.

Excited children were waving at them, older people laughing. The lights of the two cars nearest Tori were beaming directly into her eyes, like a challenge. One that was making her feel quite uncomfortable.

70

On the distant side of the plaza, Tori saw movement, two cars moving out of formation. They circled the plaza slowly, one clockwise, the other counterclockwise, their red hazard lights flashing.

They pulled up either side of the two vehicles that were already idling in front of Tori and Frank's stand. These four cars began to rev their engines. Their bonnets went down, their boots rose, like snorting bulls about to charge. It was as if the cars were in gear and their non-existent drivers were simultaneously pressing on the accelerator and the brake.

'This does not feel good, not remotely,' said Frank, stating what Tori was thinking. The spectators in the front row just ahead of them grabbed their bags and their kids and peeled off to the sides, their heads bowed low, like embarrassed theatregoers leaving a show mid-performance.

The four cars began jerking backwards and forwards, their engines rising to a squeal. The remaining crowd was murmuring and shifting in their seats. More people around Tori and Frank were scooting away.

Tori nudged Frank's arm with her elbow and said, 'Let's go' at the same time he did but it was as if the cars had heard her. The two outside vehicles lunged forwards, smashing through the now-empty seats to flank Tori and Frank.

The passenger door closest to Tori opened. Her heart was banging against her ribs but she worked at staying cool. 'How very chivalrous,' she said, giving a weak smile to the car as she kicked away the seats in front of them, grabbed her backpack and Frank's arm and pulled him forwards with her.

As they ran to the right, she looked back over her shoulder. The four cars were turning to follow them but held back, a momentary benevolence to let panicked spectators scatter out of their way. It was Tori they wanted.

A woman nearby yelled, '*És ella*.' It's her.

Tori felt as if the woman had thrown a knife into the side of her neck. The mother, her eyes ablaze, was simultaneously holding her three children back and jabbing her finger in Tori's direction. 'It's the redhead from the video,' she screamed in Catalan. 'The killer in the polka dots.'

Tori saw that the onlookers had cleared away behind her and the four cars, now side-by-side in a squadron formation, had started to barrel forwards.

Further ahead, the frightened tide was splitting into two waves, a breach opening up in the crowd, and she quickly saw why. 'Frank, there in that gap,' she pointed, 'see that manhole cover? It's sliding open.'

'Could be another trap,' he said as they ran towards it.

'No choice,' she spluttered as they reached it. Calculating they had two seconds, three at best, before the vehicles mowed them down, she dropped feet-first into the hole. When she hit the bottom, she slipped on the watery surface below but managed to stay upright, ducked her head and sloshed her feet to the side to make room for Frank.

The hole was dank and sweat was pouring off her as she gasped for air. Frank also slipped but, as the motorised cover began to slide shut, Tori threw out her arms and stabilised him. The light from above was tapering off like phases of the moon and soon, in pitch darkness, they heard the thrums of tyres carom over the plate, then a stampede of footsteps.

Frank kicked a foot in the water, making a small splash. He switched on his phone's flashlight, sending its beam into what they saw was a tunnel.

His light was only on for a second when the phone buzzed.

'Thatcher or The Voice?' said Tori.

'Escape or trap?' said Frank.

71

El Prat Airport, Barcelona

Since coming to office, Isabel and China's leader had developed a strong and constructive relationship, one the entire world was grateful for. While Hou Tao always served his nation with strength and purpose, he mostly spoke, to her at least, with heart, contradicting the stiff, cold image often portrayed in the Western media. But today, in this call, he showed no warmth, his brow was furrowed and his hands clenched.

'Madam President, my people are telling me that the two assassinations were ordered by the United States.'

He was not directly accusing her but he was sending a clear shot across her bows, a warning. His anonymous 'people', he went on, were also telling him that the US objectives were twofold: to humiliate China, blocking its ambition of a strategic

Arctic foothold, and to poison the minds of other countries who might otherwise form alliances with China.

'Madam President, if these allegations I'm hearing are correct, they mean that the United States has made a direct assault on my nation's integrity.'

Hou's statements were strong, for sure, but they were also judicious, and she was grateful for that. He was a far more astute diplomat than, say, Russia's Tushkin, who'd toss accusations of calumny at her even if he had zero evidence. That aside, it was possible, she pondered, that Hou's phrasing was also cautious because he was concealing some crucial fact, which, if it came out, would later let him stand behind his words. *My people are telling me … If these allegations I'm hearing are correct.*

He'd been a chess master at eighteen and had clearly retained an ability to think several steps ahead. She, on the other hand, needed to be very clear, to speak plainly. This was not a moment to cavil, to give a qualified response, to hide behind advisors, even though she'd have preferred it.

'President Hou, you have my absolute, categoric assurance that the United States was in no way, *no way*, behind the assassinations.' Isabel hoped her denial turned out to be true. In her last call with Spencer Prentice, they'd entertained the possibility that one of America's agencies had gone rogue and was keeping her in the dark precisely so she had plausible deniability in a situation just like this. 'I am so sorry for your personal loss,' she added. 'I understand Rao Songtian was a—'

The sharpness of Hou's interruption surprised her as much as what he said. 'The assassin, Dr Swyft, she is one of yours. I'm told she is a sleeper who the US secretly and deceitfully implanted with Greenland to thwart that country's interests in favour of your own.'

Given the background papers she'd read detailing the CIA's hostility towards Tori, Isabel felt she was on far firmer ground. 'What you're being told is completely and utterly false.'

'Madam President, I hold you in the highest regard, and I know you would not knowingly lie to me, but I am afraid that the facts appear to be against you. For example, you personally called the prime minister of Greenland *before* the signing precisely to frustrate our negotiations. Until you did that, we had every reason to believe our negotiations had remained secret. If Swyft didn't reveal the talks to you—'

'Mr President, that's not—'

'If she didn't give you the information, then what prompted your call?' He'd put Isabel in check, and she could feel he was coming in for the kill. 'Was it perhaps information gleaned and passed on by the cyber-security contractor engaged by Greenland's parliament? Was it them who told you?'

Checkmate. Isabel noticed she'd unconsciously clenched her own fists, though luckily they were out of sight, under her desk. 'Mr President, you—'

'We both know that company is a long-standing CIA front. So how, Madam President, do you think the Greenlanders will react when they learn that the United States, their loyal friend and ally, has for years been spying on their most sensitive communications? And that's saying nothing about the impact of today's revelations about your Project Gusher.'

Isabel tried not to flinch or blink in case Hou caught her out, which was difficult since he was partly correct. Not about Gusher, that was a truly cheap shot, and not about Tori Swyft, but about the CIA's shameful eavesdropping operation. She'd only heard about it herself in the past few hours.

'President Diaz, America's double standards are unbounded. On the one hand, your people spread false and grossly offensive claims that Mingmai, one of the world's leading and most admired tech companies, is a puppet of my government. They defame Mingmai to get it banned from bidding for government contracts all through the West, despite its world-beating know-how. At the same time, you operate a cyber-security firm that has the highest clearances to secretly do America's dirty work and, before you protest, Madam President, I have proof. This,' he was waving a sheet of paper at the screen, 'is a list of thirteen *other* countries whose parliaments and congresses rely on that same firm, *your* firm, to protect their most classified data and communications. Shall I tell their leaders what you've done?'

Isabel didn't take the bait and instead returned to territory where she still had a chance. 'Tao,' she said, using his given name, 'the video from Room 420. We have good reason to believe,' she glanced at Gregory, 'that it is a deepfake, though I'm still awaiting confirmation.' Out of the corner of her eye she saw Gregory raise both his eyebrows. She'd gone a little far but in essence it was true. *She* had reason to believe the tape was fake even if Hirsty did not and the test results hadn't come back. She moved her hand off-screen and made a circle motion, which Gregory knew meant *Speed up the results*. He slipped out of the room.

'We are also examining it, Isabel,' his use of her first name suggesting she'd possibly softened his stance. He also looked pensive, another good sign, so she went in with her best shot. 'Tao, it's on the public record that your agreement with Greenland is conditional, that it needs their parliament to ratify it, which is scheduled – *was* scheduled – for two weeks from now. The thing is, that delay meant the United States had absolutely no need to sully our hands with what happened in Room 420. That two-week hiatus was more than enough time for us, for any country, to put together the bones of a counter-offer that, in turn, would persuade Greenland to delay the ratification vote further.'

'I don't think so. If they pushed beyond the two weeks, China would walk away. Greenland would lose its leverage.'

'You say you'd walk away, but would you? Really?'

72

Barcelona

Tori took the burner phone from Frank, pressed accept and put the call on speaker.

'This man,' Thatcher started, though for the first couple of seconds Tori didn't really hear him, she was so relieved he wasn't The Voice ringing to gloat. '… these people you're up against are highly capable. Those cars knew precisely where you were sitting.'

'We were there, remember.'

'Which means this device you're talking on, any other devices you're carrying, could be beaming your location to him. Which therefore means that in a few moments you'll be ditching everything electronic that you're carrying. Phones, tablets, those FrensLens glasses, too. But before you do, Thatcher needs to bring you up to date.'

Tori had already taken off her FrensLens and crushed them underfoot, and she was now wiping the data off her tablet.

'Before you leapt into the tunnel, Thatcher cut all nearby signals, the street-cams, the outside-broadcast TV, cell towers, even the signals to those cars. No one who was watching remotely – your nemesis or the cops – could have seen you leap through that manhole. You're welcome.'

'The cars,' said Tori, thinking about all the people above ground. 'If you poked out their driver's eyes they might've hit innocent—'

'While Thatcher has never thought it necessary to possess an actual driver's licence – he remains a ghost to the authorities – he did manage to slip behind the wheels, virtually, and ensured public safety. Again, you're welcome.'

'But this phone we're talking on?'

'It's the only open signal, highly encrypted, specifically directed, a Thatcher one-off. At your service.'

'Thatch, a woman up there identified Tori,' said Frank. She might've seen us drop down here, and by now, she might've found a cop.'

'The female of Rubenesque proportions? The one with three snotty-nosed children at her heels, all dolled up in the colours of the *Estelada*? Yes?'

Tori and Frank looked at each other. Thatcher was so full of his own brilliance it was often excruciating to talk to him, even if his ego-trips were almost always justified.

'Her name is Agnès Blanxart. As we speak, she and her brats have rushed onto a crowded train that is pitching and lurching its way to Bellvitge Hospital. Turns out, dear friends, that straight after she identified Tori, she took a call from 112 – the local 911 – and a paramedic gave her the shocking news that her sister had suffered a coronary and was being rushed to that same hospital.'

'How did that call get through if you—'

'The same way this one did. You're welcome, yet again. It was a garbled call, naturally, due to the time lag for the translation software to wing its way from New York to Barcelona, but Agnès picked up enough of it to rush her kids down the escalator into the plaza's Metro station. There was more bad news for her, too. Her Vodafone account was suddenly cut off so she has no way to contact the police or the media, at least for a little bit.'

Tori was so relieved she spontaneously hugged Frank. But when his arm tightened around her waist she quickly pulled away.

'Thatcher also bears you both good news about that unmentionable video,' but before he could finish, the manhole motor began to purr and a splinter of light came through.

'Thatch,' said Frank, cutting in. 'Why are you opening the cover?'

'Hello, folks. And Mr Thatcher, nicely done, letting me know your name *and* your city. That knowledge might come in handy if I need to track you down. A little advice, sir. If you hear a knock at your door anytime soon, don't assume it will be the Mormons. So … *Who am I?*' He sang the words, the classic line from the musical *Les Misérables*. 'But no, I'm not Jean Valjean. Wrong sewer, wrong city.'

The trio were stunned, Tori and Frank looking at the phone like it was a sorcerer's talisman, then up at the manhole as it closed again.

Thatcher broke the spell. '*Ditch the phone and run!*'

As the pair charged down the tunnel into the blackness The Voice's laugh echoed behind them. 'Catch you later,' he called.

73

Two security guards, possibly the beefiest men in Barcelona, were trying to lift Casals off the stage but he managed to wriggle out of their grasp and scuttle down the stairs by himself. The rest of his security detail were lined up at the bottom, guns drawn. What he'd planned as a glorious stride towards independence had morphed into a debacle, a personal disaster, a public humiliation that his political enemies would remind him of every day until the election.

His people were trying to bustle him into the SUV that had screeched into the centre of the roundabout, but Oriol was done with cars and he could only imagine the photograph *El Mundo* would run on its front page tomorrow: 'Hi-tech president fails. Slinks off in "old-school" vehicle.' He'd risk an enormous electoral backlash. He sloughed off the guards' arms and said, 'I'm walking,' even managing to push away his bodyguard Guillem, a human fridge twice as wide as Uri and easily half a head taller.

The palace was a thirty-minute walk away, forty allowing for the crowds, but hopefully less if he went quickly. With Guillem following and his other guard Jordi clearing a path ahead of him, Casals strode down Paral-lel.

His phone tingled. 'Maria, it was a total fuck up,' he said. 'Did you see?'

'Where are you? How close to the palace?'

He looked up, 'I'm on Paral-lel at Floridablanca. I want Lluïsa—'

'You're *walking*?'

'I want Lluïsa waiting for me when I get back.' Dr Lluïsa de la Riva was the inspiration and chief engineer for the Cata-Car program. 'She needs to explain how she let this debacle happen.'

'Uri, get in a damn car. Forget the optics.' Maria knew him well.

Casals' assistant handed him a coffee at the palace's front entrance, strong and black and, he hoped, with a shot of *vermut*. He sipped it as he walked. No *vermut*.

'Where's Maria?' he snapped and brushed past Dr de la Riva into his office. He put the mug on his desk, threw himself into his chair and fumed, unable to find the right words, glaring at Lluïsa.

As beautiful as always, she looked unruffled in her white coat, more like a thirty-five-year-old lab technician than a fifty-three-year-old Nobel Laureate whose life's work had just imploded.

She spoke first. 'Uri, we got hacked.'

'Don't say.'

'We don't know how but we're looking.' She brushed back her blonde fringe, the same hair she'd let Uri toy with a couple of times after his wife died, though that was as far as it went. 'We've got the toughest, most advanced encryption known to protect our Cata-Car system. Quantum key distribution. It's unbreakable.'

'Apparently it isn't.' Uri picked up his coffee then put it down again, some of the liquid slopping onto the draft of his eulogy.

After what just happened, his speech would come across as pathetic at best, a farce at worst. He recalled the relevant sentence word-for-word, *Of the many things Montse stood for, Catalan innovation was …* But he stopped, unable to finish it, even in his head. He bellowed towards his door, startling Lluïsa. 'Maria, we need a new eulogy.'

Her voice came back. 'We're already on it.'

He turned again to Lluïsa. 'So, this encryption?'

'The encryption wasn't the problem.' She sighed. 'Last night, we had a thing.'

'A thing?' he said, banging the desk, then apologised when he saw her take a step back. Casals was famous for not losing his cool. He spoke softly. 'Lluïsa, I'm sorry. What thing?'

After her head of security got home last night, she explained, he thought he'd misplaced his cell phone somewhere around the house. Strangely, an hour later, it surprised him by ringing in the pocket of his lab coat, the pocket that he'd checked and rechecked multiple times. Yet his wife had called five times for him and it hadn't rung once. 'When he answered the call, the screen briefly flashed up what he thinks was a caduceus—'

'Which is?'

'An ancient symbol, a stick entwined by two snakes. But he isn't certain, it was fleeting and it vanished almost immediately. We can't find any trace of it on his phone. Now he's wondering if he imagined it.'

'Who was calling?'

'No one. The line was dead, the number unidentified and untraceable.'

Maria put her head round the door. 'President Diaz's office is on the line, so is Chancellor—'

'Fuck it, Maria. Tell them all *yes* to whatever they want. Tell them *yes* the funeral is going ahead, tell them *yes* we are beefing up security, and get Guillem to instruct the commissioner to do that if you haven't already—'

'I have.'

'And tell the Americans that *yes*, her boy can sign her speech. The kid can sign for me too if he knows Catalan. Assuming I get a decent speech from you.'

He turned back to Lluïsa.

74

30,000 metres above France

President Tushkin luxuriated in his spa bath with Natasha and Valentina, his two favourites among the flight crew. While he watched the news, this time via CNN so he could hear the parochial American angle, he let the women soap his arms, and other appendages.

The news anchor, a New Zealand woman whose voice he found particularly beguiling, loomed out of the MicroLED TV screen spanning the wall from the mirrored ceiling down to the gold taps. '*Shh*,' he hushed the women.

> ... Eco-fanatics Endz of the Earth are making yet another explosive allegation, claiming that US President Isabel Diaz herself illegally authorised the professor's assassination. If correct, the implications are far-reaching.

For an American president to sanction the murder of a US citizen on American soil …

Tushkin lay his head back against the rim of the bath. Endz of the Earth were becoming a force to be reckoned with. He smiled as a thought in English came to mind, *The Endz justifies the means*, then he placed Natasha's hand where it could do its best work.

75

Barcelona

'How long is this damn tunnel,' huffed Tori. They'd been running in the dark, in fits and starts, for four minutes, Frank slipping twice and Tori once, during which time she ditched her digital watch, having forgotten to do that before. Her forehead was throbbing from a thump into a low-hanging beam, and her eyes were stinging, but at least it was sweat and not blood.

Up ahead a shard of light appeared out of the blackness. As they got closer, the sliver swelled into a beam and, closer again, broke up into a cluster of smaller beams. 'If it's a grate,' said Frank getting close, 'watch out, there might be—'

Tori braked herself not a moment too soon. Less than a metre ahead of her the tunnel floor started to rake down into the stormwater trench where Frank had landed on his butt in a puddle, tiny circles of light speckling over him from above. 'One halo's not enough?' She couldn't help laughing.

He pushed himself up, the back of his pants glistening, his shoes drenched, but his beloved tweed bone-dry. He got up onto his toes, poked his fingers through the vents in the grate ready to push it open. 'Could this be one of those Schrödinger's Cat moments—'

'Where we know we're alive down here but to someone up top we could be alive *or* dead—'

'Unless it's The Voice up there, in which case we *will* be dead.'

'That's a comforting thought.' Tori sloshed past him, moved his hands away and grabbed the rim of the grate herself and began to push it open. 'If we're talking about cats, you'd better remember Heisenberg's Uncertainty Principle.'

'What?' said the Oxford graduate. 'That the more accurately you measure the velocity of a cat, the less accurately you know its position?'

'No,' said Tori, as she kept pushing the grate aside. 'Curiosity either killed the cat or it didn't.'

76

'The cat lived,' said Tori, peering back down into the drain hole from above. 'All the cats. The alleyway up here stinks and … You'll see.' As she lowered a hand to help Frank clamber out, she glanced up and down the passageway. Tomcats and tabbies leapt from dumpster to dumpster. The bins were spilling over with paper, boxes, rotten apples, bananas and other produce. A mountain of empty fruit boxes was so high it was almost toppling.

Frank got one knee up onto the rim of the grate just as a rodent scurried over his fingers. 'Maybe I should've said Schrödinger's Rat.' He lifted his other knee, stood and shook himself off. 'I need new pants … shoes.'

'Don't forget the jacket.'

'It didn't get wet … Oh, it's just your usual witticism.'

Tori touched the label on one of the boxes. It showed the destination address Mercat de Sant Antoni. 'You'll probably find what you need in the market behind that wall. I'll wait here. Go crazy. Buy us some new burners.'

He came over and took her face in his hands. 'That's a heck of a bruise on your forehead.' He moved her head gently from side to side. 'You okay, Tori?'

She pulled away. 'Apart from dealing with a maniac who's out to kill me, yes I'm okay.'

'How do I look?' Frank asked Tori, who was holed up inside a scrappy delivery box, the only large one that wasn't reeking of decaying fruit.

When it came to clothes, Tori knew Frank was no risk-taker. When he spun around on the toes of his new shoes, she knew nothing much had changed. They were the identical utilitarian black style he wore all the time. One difference was his new slacks. They were grey, of course, but they came with a sharp front pleat. For Frank, that was a radical fashion statement.

'Here,' he said, swinging a large white shopping bag through the air to her.

She stood up inside her box, caught the bag and looked inside. 'Men's clothes? Are you trying to tell me something?'

'Barcelona's Most Wanted is a woman. It might be smart if you stopped being one.'

She nodded and rummaged through the bag. 'This jacket, it's—'

'Tweed, yes. And that tedious joke of yours … now it's on you too, so enjoy.'

The fabric was in greenish tones whereas his was a palette of browns and, in her mind, pukes.

'There's a hat and shades to go with it.' He drew a gold-rimmed pair of knock-off Ray-Bans and a pitch-black fedora out of a bag he'd left on the ground. 'It's quite fetching,' he said, running his hand round the brim of the hat, 'and with this silvery band it's … I don't know … elegant yet a little raffish? The stall owner says it's the best quality rabbit.'

'It'll make me look more *rabbi* than rabbit.'

'Rabbis don't wear tweed,' said Frank.

'No one does.'

'How droll.' He pulled a wig out of the same bag and threw it to her. 'Rabbis don't do dreadlocks either.'

'Actually, they do,' she said as she caught it. 'Sort of. You know, those long side bits.' She held the wig up to her ear, the dreads dangling down onto her shoulder. 'You don't care about cultural appropriation, do you?'

'Your culture's been appropriating mine for so long it's become part of my culture.'

There was some wisdom in that, she thought. 'Did you get the phones?'

He brought out three, in different colours, blue, gold and pink. He threw her the gold one. It had four bars of charge. The others did too apparently. He'd paid for them in cash, no ID required.

'I bought a fourth as well. Messaged Thatcher on it then chucked it. Gave him the numbers for all of these so he could set up the encryption. That way your guy can't monitor—'

Tori snapped. 'He's as much *my guy* as coronavirus was my disease. If you want to refer to him, try fucking murderer, voice of Satan, but *never* my guy.'

77

Air Force One

Most days, Isabel loved being president. Not for the trappings of power. Not for the crisis management. It was the times when she could make a difference, improve people's lives, give solace or work at rekindling a national tone of civility that years of belligerent politics had squashed. Today was not one of her good days.

Emails, papers, reports and memos were tiled over her computer screen. Despite taking up pages and pages and thousands of words, they all said the same thing: Project Gusher wouldn't, couldn't, and therefore didn't happen.

Isabel wasn't one to be comforted by claims on paper, by anodyne reports or faceless research, especially when all the pages and words boiled down to a single but equivocal fact: no one could find a single government record that gave even a hint of a possibility there'd ever been a secret oil drilling project in Greenland, whether it was called Project Gusher or anything else.

What she needed was proof, at the very least an unambiguous denial from an original source, a person she could trust, someone who'd actually know what they were talking about from their own lived experience.

The same applied to Endz of the Earth's claim that she'd ordered Professor Buckingham's murder. While she absolutely knew that *she* didn't order it, what she needed was verification that no one else had done it 'for her'.

Gregory was counselling her not to press, not to poke, not to go beyond the documents in front of her. He was urging her to apply the classic wisdom of the courtroom cross-examiner, *Never ask a question you don't know the answer to.*

While she dreaded what the truth might actually turn out to be, she feared even more the risk that whatever it was would fly out of the blue and turn black on her.

78

Sant Antoni Market, Barcelona

The two men strolled through the aisles past stall after stall of T-shirts, gym clothes, phones, spices, fruit. Whatever you wanted, this market seemed to have it. Tori caught her reflection in a mirror and, without stopping, not wanting to attract any more attention than her outlandish looks might already, she saw how good Frank's shopping job had been. People in Barcelona, tourists and locals, came in all shapes, sizes and get-ups, and while the dreadlocks flopping around her eyes and ears felt strange, when seen under the black fedora they gave off an aura of calm. Likewise, the tweed jacket and, a bonus, it wasn't as scratchy as she'd expected. 'Hey, Frank, what am I now – Rasta or rabbi?'

'Sing Desmond Dekker's "Israelites" and you'll kill both birds with one stone.'

'Stoner, I'd say.'

He laughed and pointed through the exit ahead of them to a pizza cafe across the road. 'We were supposed to have breakfast, remember?'

Tori pushed open the cafe's swing doors. 'Mmm,' she said, inhaling deeply. 'What is it about the aroma of freshly roasted coffee beans that tells your brain to ignore how totally shit your day is?'

'If you really want to know,' said Frank, 'it's furfurylthiol, methylbutanol and dimethylpyrazine.'

'You really did hit those chemistry books at Oxford, didn't you?' She sat and pulled in her chair. 'Look at us, the Terrible Twins in Tweed and not a bloodhound or a dead animal between us.'

'There is that rabbit on your head,' he said, flicking one of her locks.

A waiter came over. 'Two *café bombóns*, please,' said Frank, as Tori gave him a nod. Despite his usual preference for tea, and that they both hated the local version of coffee when Casals introduced them to it – a fifty-fifty mix of espresso and sweetened condensed milk – they both craved the sugar hit.

'A pizza, too,' Tori added, her voice as deep as she could muster. 'Large please. That one up there,' she indicated the chalkboard, 'with *jamon* and wild *bolets*. That's ham and mushrooms, right?' The waiter nodded, turned over the glasses on the table, poured them some water and left. Tori picked up her glass.

'The votes are in,' said Frank. 'You're definitely Rasta.'

She looked at him over her drink. 'What?'

'Rabbis don't order ham pizza.'

Under cover of her brim, she scanned the cafe. What was missing was conversation and what was abundant was a proliferation of white cords dangling from the customers' ears while they tapped on their phones or other devices. 'That woman there,' said Tori, tipping her head towards a customer whose foot was rocking a baby stroller in time, Tori supposed, to the music coming through on her earphones, while she typed on a laptop. 'I bet she's writing the next *Harry Potter*.'

'It's Harry in the stroller. I saw the scar on his forehead when we walked past.'

Frank, bless him, was doing his best to bring light into her darkness. Sitting with him was the first normal, human thing she'd done all day, and while she wanted to savour it, she couldn't allow herself to relax. They had a lot of ground to cover.

She leant closer to him, her dreads swinging a little, one of them dunking into her water glass. 'There are three things we don't know.'

'And there's something *I* know,' said Frank, 'but *you* don't. The law of gravity.' He undunked her dread and pushed it back behind her ear.

'Three unknowns. Who murdered Nivikka and Songtian?' She held his gaze. 'Why did they do it? Why are they framing me for it?'

'We can narrow down the *who* question,' Frank said. 'It's got to be someone who'll benefit from the deal falling over.'

She nodded. 'Which puts the United States at the top of that list. This has all the hallmarks of a CIA black op.' Frank was shaking his head, about to speak, but Tori continued. 'Diaz's phone calls to Nivikka and Oriol. She wanted in, obviously.'

He cleared his throat. 'America didn't need to go dark. If she wanted to knock China out of the park, all she had to do was make a better offer. Which, I remind you, was why we, you, insisted that China agree to that two-week hiatus for the ratification process.'

Tori came at her point another way. 'But Diaz couldn't have known about the vote condition at that stage. Not until we announced the full details. And what if she'd decided the US *couldn't* beat China's offer? We got Beijing to really stretch on this, remember?' She looked around, but no one seemed to be listening, no one was watching them, not even a single furtive look away.

Frank was thinking. 'True,' he said eventually. 'That is a possibility, except for one thing. Endz of the Earth—'

'Whose top brass Russia buried down some deep hole in Siberia months ago. They're defunct.'

'Apparently not. You haven't seen …' He pulled one of the phones out, switched it on. 'They issued a media release this morning. Just a second.' He did an internet search for it. 'Here,' he handed her the phone. 'Operation Gusher.'

Tori started reading as he kept talking.

'America denies the operation ever existed, of course, but while that allegation is out there, no incoming leader of Greenland would go near *any* offer from the US. Diaz could offer them California and they'd give her the finger, or whatever Greenlanders do. In other words, with this Project Gusher thing in play, America was screwed regardless.'

79

The list of remaining possibilities was short and Tori was now putting Russia at the top of it. 'If it's not the US, this has Tushkin all over it.'

Frank nodded. 'He's got form, that's for sure. He's taken out enemies before, inside *and* outside of Russia. But he's not the only possibility. Denmark has to be on the list. If Greenland cut ties they'd probably lose their prized seat on the Arctic Council.'

'I doubt it's them,' said Tori. 'They're as wimpish as the Canadians. The last time the Danes did anything audacious was when their king wore a yellow star and told Hitler to—'

'That,' said Frank, 'is an urban myth.'

'Which only strengthens my point,' said Tori. 'Give me one daring thing the Danes have ever done.'

'The Sydney Opera House?' He paused. 'Yeah, okay, it's not the Danes. There's Spain. Casals blamed Madrid for leaking the negotiations to the US, so—'

'Only because it would humiliate him,' said Tori. 'But by helping the US, Spain might also extract some favour back in return.'

'Or to build up goodwill with Russia. Europe still hasn't got over your President Trump scaling down NATO.'

'He was never *my* president. Besides, Trump is ancient history so I don't …' She stopped.

The waiter placed two glasses of steaming liquid on their table, each one containing a double shot of espresso floating on top of a thick white sludge of sweetened condensed milk. Frank took up his spoon and Tori watched him swirl the milk and coffee the way Casals had guided them. 'Stirred but not shaken,' he'd joked.

Frank took a sip and grimaced. 'This drink exemplifies why a gentleman would always prefer tea.'

She swirled hers, raised the glass by its metal handle and held it up to her mouth to blow across the rim. This wasn't just a drink. It was liquid sugar and, as bad as it tasted, she drank most of it down. 'Lucky I'm no gentleman, despite my, what did you call it? My elegant and raffish appearance.'

She stood up and stretched, caught the waiter's attention. 'Where's the, ah, *men's* room?' she asked, and wandered off.

Tori sat back down. 'Turns out this place is gender-neutral. Anyhow, I got to thinking, we have to put the US back on the list. That Gusher thing, from Endz of the Earth. It's irrelevant.'

'Why? Greenland would never parlay with America after that.'

'*After* that. Precisely.' She waited for the penny to drop, which it did when Frank slapped his forehead with the flat of his hand.

'Of course!' he said. 'Washington could still have orchestrated the murders. They wouldn't have known that Endz of the Earth were about to hammer them over an operation they thought was dead and buried.' He took a sip of water and Tori waited for the cogs to spin in his brain. 'No,' he said after a few seconds. 'That theory's got a hole in it. Isabel Diaz would never have authorised those hits.'

'Only if she knew,' said Tori. 'What makes you think those creeps at the CIA would ask her, or even tell her? The Agency gets to play dirty, she gets to stay clean with plausible deniability, and the US comes out on top. They use a double-whammy strategy, execute the hits to stymie China *and* lay the blame on someone they despise, someone expendable. Me.'

'It's a perfect strategy,' Frank admitted, 'until Endz of the Earth turned up and put a bomb under it.'

80

Air Force One

As an aerial Oval Office, *Air Force One* worked fine. But being parked on an airport apron 4000 miles from her key advisers when they had no answers made Isabel crabbier than usual.

DNI Hirsty was reporting back. At her direct request, he'd quizzed the directors of every agency face-to-face about the Buckingham hit, including two agencies not a single member of the House Intelligence Committee even knew existed, nor Isabel, until he told her.

He'd got each man – they were all men – to sign a statement, on oath, confirming that his agency 'did not commit, authorise, or know anything about' the professor's murder. Once Isabel sighted the sworn denials, she told Hirsty to destroy them, and watched him slide them into the high-security, P-7 cross-cut shredder he kept beside his desk.

On Project Gusher, which he annoyingly kept referring to with air quotes, she'd asked him to personally drill into DC's most sensitive databases, caches of files that were classified top secret, restricted data, and sensitive compartmented information – records that very few people had access to. 'I ran dry, ma'am. Nothin' on any program called Gusher in Greenland, and nothin' like it. If that dang project ever existed I'd a found it.'

He was definitive yet she didn't completely trust him and, after she clicked off the call, she picked up the sheet Gregory had given her with the phone numbers of two of the oldest surviving CIA directors. These were two of the men who had headed the Agency in the 1990s, men she'd never met, never spoken to. They'd served under presidents with different party allegiances to hers and so were not likely to agree with her politics and, worse, given the era they'd operated in, she suspected they might have a problem with a woman sitting in the Oval.

All of that plus having to rouse two cranky old codgers out of bed in the middle of the night made these calls very chancy.

She was wrong to be worried. As soon as she identified herself and apologised for the time of her call, each man, as patrician and crotchety as he came across on pick-up, snapped to attention, neither one uttering a single word of complaint.

These were people who, when a president phoned them – even if it wasn't *their* president, or their party – they respected the office. These were the dedicated kind of officials that DC used to be full of before the mud rose up to swamp the place. It was people like them, she reminded herself, who did make America great. Since then, instead of people who spoke truth to power, the Beltway became full of people for whom the truth was whatever their bosses wanted to hear.

Both men gave her the same message. 'The way the Agency ran back in those times,' said one, 'if any of my predecessors had run this Project Gusher under that or any other name, I'd personally know about it. It was protocol, director to director. We might not keep any files, but I'd know. And I'm telling you straight, ma'am, I didn't know. I don't know. Never heard of it. Never heard of anything like it. So in short, ma'am, it never happened. Period. It's total bull. Fake news.'

Being a hoax wasn't the end of it for Diaz. It threw up other troubling questions, such as who'd manufactured the 'evidence' – if Endz of the Earth ever got around to producing it – and why. And Hermes: why would a bizarre international assassin kill a nonagenarian professor so that Endz of the Earth could pin the death on her? There was also Montse. The same assassin killed her. Again, why?

Did Hermes have one client, as Isabel suspected, or was Hirsty correct, that Hermes was working for two clients, the timing purely a convenient coincidence?

As she nestled back into her chair to think through what she knew, Davey once again poked his head in, his arms wide, not playing at being an airplane this time, just a kid shrugging and inclining his head towards her in silent query.

She'd neglected to tell him the news. She jumped up out of her chair with a wide smile, a thumbs-up and signed that Casals had okayed the boy's role at the funeral.

Before she could go over and hug him, Davey saluted her, turned his arms back into wings, banked left and zoomed out the door.

Isabel glowed. Davey was her greatest gift, her one bright note on a dismal day.

81

Barcelona

The napkin on the cafe table was vibrating. Tori lifted it off the phone, took out a long, white earpiece cord, and plugged it in. She passed one of the buds over to Frank and fitted the other into her own ear.

Thatcher's voice boomed out at them, his excitement palpable. 'Tori, your photos from inside Bar Canona – brilliant. No, sorry, horrendous. The blood, the violence … You *taking* them, *that* was brilliant. And most important, the Room 420 video, as you suspected, it's one hundred per cent a deepfake, a digital sleight of hand. This call is bringing you a rolled-gold Thatcher guarantee that you are not that woman.'

Frank's eyes were popping out with excitement. 'I knew it. I knew it,' he said and threw himself across the table to hug her, but Tori pulled away. 'Sorry, sorry,' he said, shrinking back into his seat. 'What will people think? I didn't mean …'

She didn't mean it either. Truly, she was ecstatic at Thatcher's corroboration and thrilled, really thrilled, that Frank's blind faith in her had proved justified, that he'd believed in her, regardless of … everything. Even more than all that, she was psyched she could finally silence the harrowing howl of paranoia that had filled her head since she woke up, and which irrationally, neurotically, continued to hound her even after she'd been inside Bar Canona and seen the evidence that disproved she had actually done it, the fixation that her moral fibre was so feeble that the merest jab of some drug could tip her over the edge to commit such awful crimes.

And yet, despite all the relief, she couldn't relish the moment because Thatcher's news also washed a heavy fog of heartbreak over her. It was a repellent reminder of the nightmare she'd woken up to, the horrific deaths she could never unsee, the murders of two people she'd grown to admire and respect. And two more she didn't know, who'd been pawns in some evil bastard's plan. Not to mention the four innocent little girls.

A fear hung over her, too. What if Thatcher's self-confidence was misguided? What if he'd made a mistake, and she'd be stuck trying to disprove her guilt with a few photos and little more than her word? The word of the monster on that video, the word of a woman who'd been whacked out on ice?

And finally there was the slow, suffocating terror, like someone holding a pillow over her face, that this thing wasn't over. That The Voice was not done with her, and was coming after her.

She dearly wanted to squeeze Frank's hand in thanks. But she simply couldn't do it. She knew she was fucked up. She just didn't know how much, not until she heard Thatcher gloating how it was all over, when clearly it was not.

Frank looked up at her, a muscle twitching at the corner of his eye, his lips taut. He leant forwards. 'Thatcher,' he said, 'we'll ring you back.' He ended the call, took up the napkin and wiped away the tears Tori hadn't realised were streaming down her cheeks.

82

In the skies above France

President Tushkin gripped the handset, his knuckles as white as the towel wrapped around his waist. His eyes narrowed and, despite Natasha's tender pats with a fresh cloth on his back, his skin felt like it was on fire. 'Where did you get this number?' he snapped into the phone. 'Who are you?'

'The real question, Tushy – may I call you that? – is who the hell are *you*?' The unnamed voice was speaking in Russian, though with a perceptible Chinese accent.

Tushkin now knew precisely who was calling. He reached back and brushed Natasha away and, pumping with rage, he shouted down the phone, 'How dare—'

'Your ravings and rantings might silence your apparatchiks but they won't work on me. You chose the wrong bunny to make a fool out of, Mr President. You assumed I'd take your blood money no questions asked, except Hermes always asks questions. You defrauded me, sir.'

On a small screen located below the light switches on the wall of Tushkin's spa, he tapped out a message, *Oleg, have you got a trace on this call yet?* 'That's nonsense,' Tushkin said into the phone. 'I don't know—'

'Tushy, if you think your flunky Oleg is going to track me down, you're so dumb you could blow your brains out with a Kleenex.' All Oleg would see, Hermes explained, was this call flitting around the world. First from a farm in Novosibirsk, a moment later from a pub in Manchester, then back over the Atlantic to a schoolhouse in Kansas, a slum in Dar es Salaam, a wine bar in Hobart, and so on.

How, Tushkin wondered, did this arrogant prick know he'd messaged Oleg, specifically Oleg, to run a trace? He pressed the device against his chest, opened the door and signalled for both women to leave. They weren't dry or dressed but that was their problem. '*Go!*' he ordered them. They hunched over, their arms covering their bodies, their eyes darting down the corridor checking that no one would see them. He pulled a couple of towels off the rack and tossed them at the women through the gap as the spring-loaded door started to close.

'Tushy, I told you two years ago, after our last encounter, that I would never accept another job from you. So what do you do? You masquerade as Endz of the Earth—'

'You are mistaken. They are my sworn enemy.'

'Except they don't exist.'

'Only because I took out their leadership—'

'*You* are their leadership. The account you paid my fee out of two years ago – *your* account – is the same one that Endz paid my fee out of this time. That's damn careless of you, Mr President.'

Fucking Oleg had messed up! Tushkin inventing Endz of the Earth and conning Hermes into believing *they* were his client was a genius move that had saved him a fortune – except now, it turned out, Oleg had screwed up with the payment. Denial was Tushkin's only course. 'Hermes, those Endz *blyati* … they are a scourge—'

'Are you always this stupid, Tushkin, or is today an exception? Quit the phony outrage.'

The president fell quiet, a state he wasn't used to.

'You planned this out. You almost got to commit the perfect crime – against me, that is. You invented these freedom fighters for the planet, knowing Hermes would never work for you again but would have a soft spot for them, and you kept them on ice until you needed them. You preyed on my good nature, coaxing me to help Endz save the world from scum like you and the Americans and, what's more, you got me to discount my fee as well. Tushkin, so far I've taken out six people to advance the Endz plan, except I now find out it was *your* plan. I wasn't saving the Arctic *from* climate criminals like you, you were getting me to save it *for* you.'

'Hermes, I—'

'That's a lot of damage you've done, to my reputation *and* to my self-esteem. How do you propose to repair it?'

'This is ridiculous.'

'What's ridiculous is that you got almost everything you wanted *and* you got it with a fucking discount. I charged Endz five million all-inclusive when I would've charged a commercial client fifty plus expenses. So, Tushy, I'll tell you how you're going to fix this. First, you'll pony up the difference. That's $45 million, and I'll cover the expenses. After all, Endz, or rather you, supplied me with the drones for free. Second, you'll top up that forty-five with punitive damages of another forty-five.'

Tushkin picked up the bathtub's extendable shower head and smashed it into the wall. 'This is madness.'

'The only madness is you trying to swindle me. So, in case your math is as poor as your judgement, that tots up to $90 million in cold, hard American greenbacks, and it's all due and payable right now.'

Tushkin did his own calculating. Hermes was right, that he'd got virtually everything he wanted already: the viral sex video, Petersen and Rao dead … which meant China's Arctic ambitions were too. The Project Gusher hoax, the lie buried with Buckingham. And Swyft painted as an American puppet. Whatever aspiration the United States had for Greenland was also in tatters. And last, with the UN Secretary-General dead, Diaz would most conveniently be attending her funeral.

Hermes' job was done apart from that one last hit. And that was only a nice-to-have, a final flourish. If Isabel Diaz didn't get assassinated on live TV with an anguished Tushkin sitting beside her, it would not be a disaster.

He still could relish how gullible Hermes had been to buy the pretext that killing Diaz would 'literally cut off the head of the planet's worst polluter'.

In reality, Tushkin couldn't give a shit about all that climate stuff, but it was the best excuse he could come up with for getting an idiot like Hermes to take out Russia's fiercest rival for global supremacy.

It was time, he decided, to put this prick of an assassin in his place. 'Hermes, yes, I misled you, so shame on me. But what about the shame on you for falling for it? Do you really want your client base to find out how naive you are? Listen, we agreed a contract. You took the job *and* my money, so complete the fucking job.'

The line seemed to go dead but he could see it was still open. Tushkin waited, said nothing, gave Hermes time to let his demand sink in.

A video call was coming through on another line, from a number Tushkin knew well because he called it every day. It was his daughter's number, her office at Oxford University where she was a professor of Russian literature.

Zoya was on her knees, her hair a mess, her face streaked with tears, her hands zip-tied behind her back. A man in a grey balaclava loomed behind her, one hand pointing a gun at her head, the other pulling on a thin wire halter that he'd looped around her neck. Zoya was looking up into the camera, trying to speak but no words were coming out. The man yanked on the wire and jerked her head back against the muzzle of his pistol.

'Daddy,' she struggled to say, 'if you don't pay … what they're asking … they're going to kill me—'

That line went dead too.

83

Barcelona

Tori came back into the cafe. She'd needed air, a lot more than air, truthfully, but she had no time for that. 'Thatcher,' she said when they called him back, 'the encryption on this phone. Could he be listening?'

'Impossible,' and he rattled off some technical gobbledygook that even for Tori was incomprehensible but which Frank understood well enough to give a nod of approval.

'How solid is your proof? The police will need more than the say-so of a ghost.'

'It's rock solid,' he said. 'And yes, you're most welcome.' He began to take them through it. 'The EXIF data is key—'

Tori interrupted, 'EXIF?'

'Exchangeable Image File Format,' Frank told her, quietly so no one nearby could hear.

'Chowders, please,' said Thatcher. 'Tori, you know how your phone automatically labels your photos with the time and place you took them? That's the phone's inbuilt clock timestamping every shot and its GPS geo-tagging, attaching the location coordinates of where you were standing when you took it. And all that metadata gets recorded in EXIF format.'

'Pretty standard stuff,' said Frank.

Standard to him. Tori's pulse was beating so fast she felt a little dizzy, a sensation that was far more welcome than the plunge into utter despondency she'd just lifted herself out of. 'So this metadata attached to the video proves it was not shot at the hotel?'

'Not quite. Actually, they deleted the EXIF data, specifically to prevent someone of Thatcher's genius from—'

Tori thought she must have misheard him, 'Then why are we talking about it?'

He continued. 'Because, Tori, these lowlifes were too smart by half. They wiped the data *after* they edited the video … *after* they'd cut bits out that made it too long or—'

'—or frames,' supposed Frank, 'that revealed images they didn't want us to see?'

'Right,' said Thatcher. 'Like if Fake Tori's real face got reflected in a mirror.'

As they were talking, Tori visualised long strips of film falling onto a cutting-room floor, including clips identifying the woman who'd posed as her.

'But then something beautiful happened,' said Thatcher. 'Their boss, this Voice chap, he wasn't happy with the finished product so he gathered up one teensy bit off the cutting-room floor, ordered his flunky to splice it back in and, wonder of wonders, the numbskulls neglected to delete the EXIF that was still hanging off it. It's only two seconds of footage, a segment, dear friends, that a lesser mortal would have missed, but not yours truly. It tells us precisely where and when they made the video—'

'Which was?'

'Inside Bar Canona and, most crucially, *not* at your hotel, *not* in Room 420. And timewise, they shot it *before* your media conference, when Prime Minister Peterson and the Chinese fellow were still very much alive, as witnessed by countless TV cameras.'

Tori and Frank high-fived, then quickly looked around. Sheepishly, Tori picked up her glass and guzzled the dregs of her coffee, which was all condensed milk since the two liquids had separated and the sweet white slop was all that was left.

'Then there's the metadata on the photos that you managed to take inside Bar Canona, Tori. They show a different timestamp, obviously, just before the explosion, which reinforces your account of events. More important, the GPS data says you shot those photos within a tight radius of where the original video was made. And wait, dear people, back to the video's EXIF, the gift that keeps giving. It tells us the make of the video camera – a Canon – together with its model and serial number. If the Spanish cops are half good at their job, they'll be able to track down where it was purchased, maybe who the customer was. Next—'

'Stop,' said Frank, so suddenly that Tori froze.

84

Frank apologised when he saw the fright on her face. 'I didn't mean to freak you out.' He'd halted the conversation because the waiter was approaching with their pizza.

He pulled off a slice, thin strands of gooey cheese stretching from the plate to his mouth. 'Thatch, you were saying?'

'Sorry, Chowders. It's your turn to wait.'

While Frank's teeth were breaking the cheese strings, Tori could hear Thatcher popping a cork. Just as she was about to finesse her own slice of pizza into her mouth, its tip sagged and a glob of yellow cheese grease oozed onto the table. She wiped it up with a finger and brought the morsel to her mouth. 'Frank, since you knew about Heisenberg's Uncertainty thingy, are you on top of Einstein's special theory of pizzativity?'

He looked at her like she was indeed nuts and picked a mushroom off his slice and popped it into his mouth, 'I guess you're about to enlighten me.'

'It's $E = MC^2$, obviously, like his other theory.'

He kept looking at her.

'Ecstasy = Mozzarella x Carbs x Crust.'

'Which proves,' said Frank as he scooped up another slice, 'pleasure diminishes as the crust disappears.'

Thatcher came back online. 'Can we continue?' he said, smacking his own lips. 'Those parts of the video that show your face, Tori. It is truly your face, by the way—'

Frank cut in, 'But you said—'

Tori gestured for him to wait. She expected they were about to hear what she'd hoped from the start.

'It *is* Tori's face *and* it *is* her head, but the hands doing all those …' Thatcher grunted his disgust. 'They're the hands of a different person, on a different body. The same goes for Greenland's prime minister.' The people who created the deepfake video, he explained, had lifted real images of Tori's and the PM's faces – perhaps taken while both women were drugged – and using artificial intelligence tools they'd pasted them onto the bodies of other people. 'If it wasn't for Thatcher's keen eye they'd have gotten away with it.'

'More accurately,' Frank whispered to Tori, 'it was your keen thinking in asking him to check the video out for you.' A scrap of mushroom flew out of his mouth and plopped into his drink, which she noticed was largely undrunk.

'If you want the detail—' said Thatcher.

'We don't,' Frank whispered again, no spray of mushroom this time.

Thatcher wasn't listening or, if he was, he wasn't about to spare them a show of his brilliance. 'Thatcher found some tell-tale flickering in the video's temporal smoothness, a tiny change of skin tone near the edge of the supposed Tori's cheeks, also at the tip of the PM's nose. For a split second, Tori, they gave you a double chin.'

'You didn't find a loose pair of eyelashes lying around, did you?'

'What?'

'Forget it,' she said. She was feeling a hell of a lot better now and while she was doing her best to make light, something was nagging at her, and she needed to be diplomatic how she raised it.

'Thatch, how do we answer an argument, from the police, say, that you, as my friend, created that scrap of EXIF data and planted it on the video so as, you know, to throw the scent off me?'

Thatcher laughed. 'Tori, there's no way anyone can claim that. You weren't the one who sent the video out to a million phones, yet they've all got the EXIF data on them. The copies people posted to social media, they have it too.'

All up, it did seem like Thatcher had given Tori a genuine stay-out-of-jail card. Frank was beaming again, and for the first time today, her heart wasn't cracking her chest open.

'Tori, Thatcher has one more nugget for you, his *pièce de résistance*—'

For once she knew what he was going to say. 'The prime minister's nail polish. I know.'

85

Oriol Casals was at his desk, checking through the city's street-cams via his monitor. Demonstrators were massing across the city, their numbers growing fast, their chants loud. The protesters weren't coordinated – rather, a farrago of diverse, even clashing objectives. One group, waving placards like *Gusher is a Crime Against Humanity*, was congregating at Plaça de Pablo Neruda. They were demanding that Spain arrest Isabel Diaz for Project Gusher and place her on trial at the International Criminal Court, despite the inconvenient details that she had not been president at the time or that America had never recognised that court's jurisdiction.

Across town, anti-Tushkin activists called on people to *Avenge the Endz Five*, the leaders of the group who Russian Special Forces had killed months ago.

At three other locations, crowds of pro-Catalan independence advocates were coming together. Not as pleasing to Casals was the large group of Federalists, locals opposed to secession, who'd chosen to congregate – ironically? – at Plaça de les Glòries Catalanes. Another crowd, at Plaça de Catalunya, was shouting, *Greens say No to Greenland's Yes*. Another group was demanding *Halt China's Economic Imperialism*. And a second anti-US assembly wanted *American Bases Out Now*.

The president had signed off on the city's security arrangements two days ago. The face-to-camera broadcast he was about to make – going out live to TV, radio and online – was part of that plan. His director of communications snapped the clapperboard, 'Fifteen seconds,' and the makeup guy who'd been trimming a few wild hairs above Casals' ears took the towels off his shoulders and left.

'Senyor President, five seconds, four, three, and we are … *live*.'

'My fellow citizens and family, friends and admirers of Montse,' Casals began, 'today is her day. Barcelona is a city where we celebrate peaceful protest. That is our civil right. But with that right comes obligation,' he paused. 'We have a solemn duty to honour Montse, her incredible achievements and her lifelong devotion to Catalonia and Spain that made her one of our country's greatest daughters.'

He lifted a greyish-green sprig of weaver's broom off his desk, its fragrant yellow flowers in full bloom, and brought it to his nose.

'This is a spray of Montse's favourite flower.' The script on the autocue told him to close his eyes, inhale and pause, and he did. 'Whenever I smell its delicate honeysuckle perfume I remember how, when Montse and I were children growing up together, these golden yellow buds would burst out of the drains and cracks in our street. You know,' he said, letting a wistful look come into his eyes, 'she would tell me that they sang the scent of summer ... *sang the scent of summer.* Her words, not mine. How they reminded her of the *Senyera* that we fly from our flagpoles. Later today when I pay formal tribute to this inspiring woman at La Sagrada Familia, you will see how the basilica will also be alive with these beloved flowers of hers, and you will see me wearing this one here as my boutonnière.'

On script, he broke off a length of the stem and threaded it through the hole in his lapel; slowly, to make sure the camera operator could bump up the yellow filter intensity to make it really pop.

Seeing the lens pull back to crop his head-and-shoulders, Casals looked deep into the camera with his warm bedroom eyes, the eyes Maria told him were better vote-catchers than his policies.

'If you go into our streets, you will find hundreds of our city's magnificent policewomen and men, and what will they be doing? They'll be distributing tens of thousands of Montse's gorgeous blooms so each of you can remember her by placing one of them against your heart, like me.'

He held up a badge, adorned with a sunny photo of Montse's face and her fingers aloft in a sign of peace. One of Maria's interns had photoshopped the fingers in. 'All our police have this badge pinned to their uniforms today, also reminding us of Montse as we walk our streets. She will be all around us, smiling, wishing us love and peace today, just as she did when she was alive. Thank you.' And with that his media director clicked off the broadcast.

Uri turned to Maria. 'It was corny, but will it work?'

She shrugged and put a new draft of his eulogy in front of him.

86

When Tori asked Thatcher to package up the evidence – to give it to the police and, as comfort to Greenland, to Axel as well – she didn't count on the intensity of his reaction.

'For Axel, certainly, but for the police, no, *nyet*, *nada*, never. If you didn't know it before, Tori, you need to know it now … Thatcher suffers from a debilitating case of coprophobia.'

'Thatch, just because a word's got *cop* in it does *not* mean it's about the police. You do know that, don't you?' She whispered to Frank, 'It's a fear of—'

'Excrement.' He nodded.

Thatcher heard them. 'Which, dear Tori, is precisely the point.'

'I know he's a genius *and* a true friend,' she told Frank after they'd ended the call, 'but he can be insufferable. If you'd stayed with the Church, they'd probably canonise you for tolerating him. St Francis of Thatcher.'

'Hmm.' He wet a fingertip and tapped up the last few flakes of *bolets* from the plate between them. 'Now we're onto religion, what's the difference between Jesus and pizza?' He gave the answer without waiting, 'Jesus can't be topped.'

Axel and Ron Mada listened silently as Tori and Frank walked them through Thatcher's evidence. At the conclusion, Frank said, 'That should answer any doubts about Tori.'

'It does, yes, but I never had any doubts,' said Axel. 'Ron, you?'

Silence.

Axel pressed. 'You do agree, Ron?'

Tori adored Axel.

'Ron?'

'Er, right, sure.' He took so long to say it that Tori was imagining Axel had roused him from a daydream where he was enjoying himself by ripping the wings off angels.

'You're positive, Ron. About Tori?'

'Positive. Yes, absolutely.'

She loved Axel.

The waiter came over, this time bringing dessert and decent drinks. The server put the peppermint tea in front of Tori, the *café solo* before Frank and, between them, the *crema Catalana* to share. After he left, Frank swapped the cups. Tori sniffed at the dessert. It looked like a *crème brûlée* but the nose was more lemon and cinnamon than the French version's vanilla. 'Axel, can you give us a minute? We need to take in some fuel.'

Tori cracked her spoon though the top crust of caramelised sugar, took a scoop of the dessert and dolloped it onto her tongue. Heaven.

Frank did the same and gave one of those ethereal eyes-closed, deep-inhaling grins that universally translated as bliss. 'Did Einstein have a formula for this, too?' he whispered.

She took another mouthful.

'We're good to continue,' said Frank, taking his second portion.

Axel ran through what he lightly tossed off as 'a few random ideas', typical Axel-speak for an exhaustively thought-through inventory of next steps. In Tori's experience, Axel and *random* were never in the same room.

One key question he raised was who should go to the police, since no one was the perfect choice. Frank shut down Axel's first idea, that it should be Thatcher, before Tori could get the spoon out of her mouth.

Ron suggested Tori. As he would, she thought. Frank was shaking his head and was about to say 'no' when Axel himself vetoed it, '*Believed to be armed and dangerous* … that's what the news report said, Ron. If a police officer sees Tori and *doesn't* shoot her, it will be 50,000 volts of taser with questions later, next decade probably. If she's lucky.'

To Tori it seemed Axel had articulated the precise reason why Mada had suggested her in the first place.

The only viable choice was Frank, even if the police would be sceptical of a man who'd slipped away from the hotel against their wishes. Plus, he could take them the bloodied polka dot dress that Tori had swiped from Bar Canona. It was still in her bag, wrapped in plastic together, she hoped, with some of Fake Tori's DNA.

The plan was to divide and, hopefully, rule. Which meant that once Thatcher had packaged up the evidence, Axel and Ron would run the Greenlanders through it and Frank would take it to police headquarters.

Tori's role, said Axel, was to lay low.

'That's the one thing I can't do,' she said, her voice flat.

'Can't or won't?' Frank spluttered.

'Why can't you, Tori?' asked Axel.

Frank looked at her, horror all over his face. 'Axel, she's planning to track down the perpetrator herself. The Voice. Tori, he almost killed you in that explosion, and he came pretty close at the car show. He might not fail next time.'

She was toying with a sachet of sugar.

'Third time lucky,' said Mada ambiguously, though Tori knew what he really meant.

87

Axel was insistent. 'It's the job of the police, not you, to go after The Voice, and they will surely do that once Francis enlightens them.'

Tori was not so confident. 'How long will it take before someone high enough in the chain of command has the guts to clear me? Me, the person every set of eyeballs in this city saw committing unmentionable acts. Will the cops take hours? What if it's days? Or weeks?'

For Tori, this was about more than clearing her name. Part of it was justice – to see the bastard who'd done all this behind bars. Another part, one that Axel and Frank might not understand, was retribution. Not just for the murders, though there was certainly that, but for making Tori doubt herself, for mind-fucking her into thinking she might actually have committed those terrible acts of evil.

It was also about how Tori would live the rest of her life. If he escaped whatever net the police eventually got around to throwing out, he could do it again. She'd never feel safe. Every street she walked down, she'd be peering over her shoulder. In a supermarket aisle, in an airport, a train station. She'd constantly be worried he was the guy in the black hoodie ducking behind that red car, the shady-looking driver with the five o'clock shadow behind the wheel of the yellow cab, or the dad in the Chicago Bulls number 23 sweater taking off his glasses to check the use-by date on the milk carton, or the old lady with the pink hair and green blouse standing behind her in the line at Grand Central while she was buying a train ticket to Greenwich, Connecticut. Until The Voice chose his time to strike, he'd be everywhere and nowhere.

Tori knew she could not afford to rely on the police, so she went in with her killer punch, which, to satisfy Axel, had to be about business. 'Axel, with the proof Thatcher's given us, plus the polka dot dress, you should be able to convince Greenland's new leadership either to stick with the deal or wait for the counteroffers we were hoping for—'

'Absolutely, Tori.'

'But that's not enough. If The Voice did all this, not just to push China out but so that his friends or clients could come in, it means that one of the countries who makes a counteroffer might be the one who was behind all of this. The very party who paid for the assassination of our client's prime minister. So if we don't track down who that is, Axel, you could find yourself asking Greenland to tie itself forever to the people responsible for—'

Ron Mada cut in. 'Except we *don't* know that, *can't* know that. If it is the truth and it comes out later, we can simply say we just did our job with the facts we had at the time.'

'Ron,' said Axel, 'the truth always *comes* out, eventually. It might take years but when it does, if it is indeed the scenario that Tori is painting, SIS's reputation would be—'

'Trashed,' said Tori.

'Exactly, but even so, Tori,' Axel continued, 'I cannot for one moment abide you risking your life any further.'

The phone vibrated. Tori feared for a second it was The Voice until she saw the caller ID: *Bearer of Truth*. 'Axel, Thatcher's calling. We'll phone you back.'

'Tori, before you go, listen to me. If you're not willing to get that idea out of your head, at least wait. With Francis peeling off to take the proof to the police, give me time to get you some backup. We have contacts we can trust in Barcelona. Let me—'

'We'll talk soon.'

When she picked up, Thatcher was shouting down the line. 'Tori, take this phone and go outside the cafe. Walk up and down the pavement. Then go across the street to that market and recross. Frank, you wait at the table with the other phones.'

'Thatch, you sound kind of crazy. What's this all—'

'Do what Thatcher says. *Now!* Tori, *stand up and go outside!*'

She got up so fast her chair fell backwards and the earbuds pulled out of both her and Frank's ears. She put her bud back in and went outside, leaving Frank to deal with the chair. 'Thatcher, what's happening?' she said as she pushed through the door into the street.

'Too many competing phone signals in that place. Thatcher couldn't be sure if he saw what he thinks he saw. Go left, good, keep walking … more … more … stop. Turn around … walk … more … more … Okay, if it's safe to cross the street, do it now. Thatcher's hacked into the local cell tower and he's plotting you and that phone against the street map. No … No, no, no.'

'What?'

'You've got a GPS tracker on you. It's not the phone. Thatcher's run a check on that. Maybe The Voice sewed it into an item of your clothing—'

'Impossible. Nothing that I'm wearing is mine.'

'When you woke up this morning, did you have any mosquito bites, cuts, anything new like—?'

'One in the crook of my arm where I think he drugged me.' She felt the spot, pressed it, pinched it. 'There's nothing under the skin, I'm certain of it.'

'You've definitely got a tracker on you. You've got to find it. That bastard has been laughing at us all damn day. He's known your every move. Go back to Frank. Your backpack. What about that? Get Frank to check over your body *and* your bag. Go *now!*'

She ran back into the cafe with Thatcher screeching into her ear, 'Cut the thing out, wherever it is but, Tori, do not damage it. Clean it up and—'

She understood. 'Slip it into a bag, someone leaving the cafe – a decoy.'

Tori put her hand up to her head as she approached Frank, feigning she was sick in case any of the other patrons lifted their eyes off their screens, which they didn't. 'I'm going to throw up.' She winked at him. 'Take me to the restroom. Fast.' She scurried off. 'And bring my bag.'

88

Tori explained as they went down the stairs and, midway, Frank ran back up and approached the waiter. 'First-aid kit? For my friend. Sh—*He* has a cut …'

The waiter looked worried, like Frank was about to accuse the cafe of being responsible. Frank tried to reassure him. 'He tripped in the street, just now, fell onto some glass.' The waiter wasn't getting it so Frank grabbed his leg and made a slashing motion. 'Glass. Cut. I need first-aid kit,' and he drew a box in the air with his fingers and paint-brushed a cross over the top.

'*Si*.' The waiter reached under the counter and pulled out a red box with a white cross on it. 'Bring to me back when finish.'

'Bite on this,' said Frank handing her a roll of white bandage he'd got from the kit, which he'd left open at his feet. The nick he'd found in Tori's skin, just below her left shoulder blade, was small and neat, almost invisible. There was no redness or even pain when he pressed on it. 'I'd say he jabbed you with a local anaesthetic, an antibiotic too.' He wiped the small silver tweezers with a sterilising pad. 'Okay, here goes. Bite hard.'

Once they were done and Tori was dressed again, they took to the stairs. She left her backpack in the bathroom, her money and other valuables stuffed in her pockets, the polka dot dress in the plastic bag shoved down the back of Frank's pants. 'I'll miss that backpack,' she said, thinking more of its defensive qualities than its design or storage capacity.

She went back to their table, limping slightly for the benefit of the waiter, while Frank headed to the counter to return the emergency kit. She sat quietly fuming. The Voice had outplayed her again. No way was she going to let the bastard get away with it. Not now, no matter what Axel said.

Frank was waiting in line behind Harry Potter's mother, her little wizard burbling in the stroller. As she turned to go, Frank leant over the kid and slipped the tracker into a shopping bag the woman had hung off the handlebar. 'Cute baby,' he said as she wheeled out of the cafe.

'You friend, he okay?' the waiter asked, glancing at the man with dreadlocks.

'*Si*, thank … *gràcies*.' Frank handed him the kit and returned to the table, where they watched the woman leave with her baby and the tracker.

'I hope nothing—'

'If The Voice puts eyes on her,' said Frank, 'he can't possibly mistake her for you. She's tiny, barely taller than her stroller, and three shades browner than me.'

The phone vibrated again and they reinserted their earbuds. 'Good work, team. Elvis is definitely leaving the building,' said Thatcher, obviously feeling pleased with himself, again. 'But you can't stay there. He'll work out what we've done soon enough and when he retraces the signal's path you need to be gone.'

Tori suddenly knew what she had to do, and she didn't have time to wait for Axel's backup, and she couldn't tell Frank. He'd try to stop her. She leant back and 'accidentally' pulled the earbud out of Frank's ear and, turning her head as if she was stretching, asked Thatcher in a whisper if he knew where the tracker was transmitting its signal to.

'Just a mo … Yep. Got the GPS coordinates. It's in Barcelona, no surprise there. Wait, the street address … Got it. Thatcher has texted it to you. Hang on, Tori, why do you want it? You're not planning to go there? Tori? … Tori?'

The text came through. She hung up and switched the phone off. 'Frank,' she said as she got out of her chair, 'show me those other phones.'

He pulled them out. 'Why?'

'I need them.' She took them, checked they were switched off too, and put all of them in her jacket pocket. 'When you get a new phone, call me.' She turned to leave.

He pushed his chair back. 'What are you doing?'

'I need to buy a new wig,' she lied, walking off. 'This one scratches the hell out of my scalp.'

Close by the door she spun her head back, her dreadlocks flicking out like whips. 'No woman, no cry,' she called out in her best baritone voice, leaving him to pay the bill before he could chase after her.

89

Local police had cordoned off a tic-tac-toe-shaped grid of nine city blocks, with the iconic basilica of La Sagrada Familia at its centre.

President Casals clicked over to the street-cams inside the cordon where, thankfully, he could see the crowds were placid. So much so that some of the riot police were occupying themselves playing cards on makeshift tables.

While it was a different story outside the cordon, his strategy seemed to be working. At one police barricade, he watched the troublemakers being charmed by Montse-loving members of the public wielding armfuls of flowers. As far as he'd heard, not a single canister of tear gas had been fired so far, no water hoses unfurled, no batons brandished.

Mounted police were going up and down the streets in a classic four-beat walk, the crowds opening and closing around their horses like hugs, the animals getting more kisses than a bridal couple on a wedding day.

The atmosphere was mostly festive, apart from two locations. One was close by the modern art museum, where Uri watched police arrest a handful of militants brandishing Molotov cocktails, handcuffing them before they'd had a chance to set their missiles alight. 'Art critics,' said Maria, coming up behind him. 'Who'd blame them wanting to throw bombs? The current exhibition in there is total shit.' She reached forwards and took the remote control for the TV on his wall, turning up the volume.

> The extraordinary spirit of peace, love and fellowship being felt all through Barcelona today rivals San Francisco's legendary Summer of Love. The president of Catalonia is being hailed as a modern-day Allen Ginsberg.

For those who didn't know, which was virtually all of Barcelona, the commentator explained that when Ginsberg, an American beat poet, coined the term 'flower power' in 1965, he planted the seeds for a political movement that became famous for passive, non-violent protest.

> President Casals' bounty of beautiful golden flowers all over the city has defused what looked set to be an explosive situation after the dangerous fiasco at his driverless car show this morning.
>
> It's an outcome that augurs well for him in the upcoming election campaign.

Uri couldn't afford to let the good news make him complacent. He switched the sound to mute and focused back on the street-cams, this time the one at the Arco de Triunfo, where riot police were lined up on one side of the street, their shields locked. Opposite them, twenty black-masked radicals armed with crowbars and baseball bats stood behind a pile of tyres and tree branches, one of their number brandishing a flaming torch.

When a group of aged nuns in serene white habits filed out of a nearby alleyway and paraded right between the opposing forces, turning to face the agitators, Casals feared the situation was going to explode. Holding his breath, he watched the sisters kneel and raise their pasty, wrinkled hands in prayer as their mouths began to move. He turned the sound back up. They were singing, *All we are saying* … and he began to laugh.

'What's so funny?' said Maria. 'It's a John Lennon classic. Everyone loves "Give Peace a Chance".'

'They love the chorus. But if those nuns knew the actual verses, about *bishops* and *fishops* and *masturbation* and *flagellation*, they'd end up spending their afternoon waiting for absolution in a long line outside the confessional.'

An hour later, police had made only sixteen arrests citywide and there were no reports of injuries. Maria had been sceptical of Uri's plan from the get-go but, as usual, he'd picked the public mood perfectly. His speech, the flowers and badges, the nine-block cordon, they were actually working. No wonder, she reminded herself, that he was the politician and she was the chief of staff.

As she carried in the plate of biscuits for him, a reward of sorts, she mentally reviewed the list of protocols he'd personally designed.

The only people permitted inside the grid, apart from officials and police, were residents and other locals who'd submitted to strict ID screening and body scans and wore colour-coded photo ID lanyards around their necks. And flowers, too, which was a typical Uri touch.

The only vehicles allowed on the grid's streets were police blue-and-whites, emergency rescue vans and transport for mourners who had official access passes into the church. Any cars that had still been parked inside the grid at 6 am were towed away.

Maria, already nibbling one of the *carquinyolis*, pointed to Uri's TV, which was showing a squadron of the Spanish Army's Tigre attack helicopters circling above the basilica on high alert. 'I think it's safe to let the choppers go back to base, don't you?'

He took one of the thin, crunchy biscuits and broke it in half. Like her, he loved hearing them snap. He popped one half into his mouth and held the other half to his nose. Maria smiled. He'd noticed that this batch had something extra, topping off the traditional aroma of almonds. He sniffed at it, smelling the anise, just a hint of it. Crumbs flew out of his mouth. 'You say it's safe?'

She knew he wasn't really asking her, he was making the point that his plan had worked. 'Yes, Uri, you were right and I wasn't. Happy?' Her phone beeped and she looked at the screen. 'Your eulogy. The redraft is in your email.' She pointed to his screen. 'I'll print a copy and you can edit it on your way to the basilica. You've got to get going.'

'What if I don't like this draft?'

She took another biscuit. 'Don't worry. It's going to kill,' she said, then wished she hadn't when she saw the look on Uri's face.

90

For Tori, this was an odd Metro carriage. It wasn't so much the weirdo she saw reflected back at her from the window, the guy with sunglasses and the black, big-brimmed fedora and dreadlocks pretending to bop to the music that wasn't actually streaming through his earbuds, it was that all the other passengers were doing what passengers rarely did – smiling, laughing, chatting to each other, chatting even to strangers. Almost the whole carriage was decked out with yellow flowers, either pinned to people's shirts, pushed into their hair or tied to the straps of their bags.

Frank would have been amused too, except he wasn't here. Tori had successfully slipped away from him. She was going to disembark at the stop for La Sagrada Familia, walk half a block to the address she'd got from Thatcher and, if The Voice really was there, she'd confront him, face to face. She wasn't sure how, not yet, but she'd made a career out of improvising, so she hoped it would carry her through now.

After nine minutes and three stops, the train was approaching Monumental, the last station before the stop for the basilica, and a long announcement blared out over the public address. Judging by the flower waving and hugging going on, the other passengers seemed delighted with whatever they'd just heard. Tori was glancing up at the air vents to check for happy gas when an old grandma broke the spell. Despite three shopping bags at her feet and two children crammed either side, she managed to throw her arms in the air and yell out a long and bitter protest. Other passengers shushed her, two handed her flowers. Tori had no idea what was going on until the train was actually pulling into Monumental and the announcer repeated the message in English.

'Route change … La Sagrada Familia station, the stop after Monumental, is closed today. Passengers for Sagrada Familia should alight either here at Monumental or at Encants … We have made this temporary change to help Barcelona give Montse the tender send-off our city's favourite daughter deserves. Flowers are available for free inside these stations. Please share them with other citizens and visitors. May you go in peace and love … For Montse.'

91

The *whump-whumps* from TV station La 1's news helicopter carried through the open balcony doors. Hermes could easily have looked out and seen the eye-in-the-sky take the place of the Army's Tigres as they left their posts above La Sagrada Familia, but preferred to stay unobserved and keep watch via one of the six screens.

The five other screens, tuned in to cameras inside the basilica, were not official feeds. 'Florists', contractors hired by Hermes, had planted these cameras at the tops of five of the columns during yesterday's flurry to decorate the church. Casals' directive to create a floral tribute to his cousin inside the church was a heresy according to Gaudí devotees, who argued that the majesty and simplicity of the architect's design was itself a sublime ode, and obscuring his work with a forest of flowers was an insult to his vision and to God. The president pulled rank and rode over their objections, which suited Hermes' purposes perfectly. The cameras hidden among the flowers gave the assassin eyes over every square metre of the basilica's interior.

Simply by swiping two fingers on a touch pad, Hermes could zoom in almost close enough to pinch the cheeks of anyone sitting inside. The mic in front of Hermes was patched into the basilica's audio system via voice-masking software. When the master schemer had something to say, the entire congregation would hear it.

The camera feed to Hermes' eyrie piggybacked the frequencies that the emergency services believed they'd reserved for themselves. Listening in, Hermes heard that UEI, Spain's elite counter-terrorism unit, was about to switch on their electronic geofence. It was designed to encase the grid, jamming signals from any unregistered devices. No unauthorised drones would be able to fly through. They'd either drop out of the sky or bounce off the geofence and return back to their base.

Hermes used the audio mixer to turn up the sound while eavesdropping on UEI's line. 'Yes, Agent Franklin,' – who Hermes knew was head of the American Secret Service team on the ground – 'you have UEI's guarantee that everyone inside the geofence, inside the basilica, will be safe.'

Hermes found the Spanish unit's confidence endearing and hoped Agent Franklin had a good pension plan. After today, he would be needing it.

92

The man whose dreadlocks were now festooned with golden flowers was skipping along the street, a roving bush of a tourist throwing himself into the city's spirit.

While the flowers would have got Tori up to the security barriers, she needed a pre-issued lanyard with a red border to get past them, one that displayed her photo, her name and a unique security barcode. Each of the nine blocks inside the grid was allocated a different colour, and a temporarily erected street map told her the address she'd got from Thatcher was located in the red zone.

She hung back from the knot of police at the corner of Mallorca and Lepant and leant against a bus stand, not too far from the two Portaloo trailers that had been wheeled in for the day. The long stainless-steel boxes, each a row of six stalls, two of them mobility-enabled, glinted in the emerging sunlight. Parked in parallel lines with the passageway between them discreetly angled away from the scrutiny of the nearby guard station, offering a modicum of privacy. The toilets were already fully occupied, judging by the waiting line.

Tori leant back, chillaxed like a modern-day hippy, and watched the comings and goings. Police sauntered up to the checkpoint or rode through it, members of the general public got visual one-twos of their lanyards and faces, followed by cursory swipes of their barcodes. A few people, seemingly at random, got ushered behind a makeshift curtain, she assumed for body searches, though they were remarkably brief.

Tori chose her moment, joining the line to the toilets right behind a young cop she'd just watched parking her motorcycle. She was from the Mossos d'Esquadra, according to the logo on her hi-viz and her bike, an electric BMW C-Evolution.

Tori had ridden Harleys and Hondas, Ducatis and Triumphs but never a BMW, gas or electric. Today felt like the perfect time to try one out.

The cop, her helmet on, turned towards Tori, the photo ID and security pass pinned to her jacket giving her name as Constable Joaddan Akono. She lifted her visor to give Tori a once-over, not realising that Tori was doing the same to her.

Her gold-flecked eyes, no doubt once keen and vibrant, were lifeless, and Tori guessed at why. A black woman in uniform, plodding a thankless, humdrum beat, would undoubtedly have suffered racism and sexism.

But Tori didn't choose to line up behind Akono to offer her solidarity. It was because, first, she was a cop and, second, she was pretty much Tori's height and build. Provided Tori was wearing Akono's helmet and gloves, as she planned, they could easily pass as twins.

The cop spoke, something beginning with *Hola.* Tori pulled out one of her earbuds. 'Dude, I don't speak Spanish,' she said, in as deep and lazy a voice as she could muster. Taking a small risk, she picked one of the yellow buds out of her dreads and slotted it behind the cop's security pass.

At first Akono jerked back then, seeing Tori meant no harm, gave her a wink and, when she got a smile in return, turned back to face the toilets.

From under the brim of her fedora, Tori studied Akono's duty belt, imagining the heft of the kit, her own hips weighed down with the handcuffs, the baton, radio, what looked like a can of pepper spray, the taser, flashlight, the pistol and spare ammunition, the gloves clipped onto the side. Heck, how much gear did cops have to carry? Ten kilos, she guessed.

Akono's pistol was a Heckler & Koch USP, a 9 x 19 mm gun that Tori knew well from her days at The Farm, the CIA's training facility at Camp Peary. Due to their oversized trigger guards, HK USPs were perfect for motorbike cops facing an emergency where they needed to fire fast but didn't have time to dismount or unglove.

Tori knew what she was planning was wrong and, worse, illegal. A *true* crime to add to the litany she was falsely accused of, the first she'd actually be guilty of.

By the time Officer Akono reached the front of the line, they were the only two left. Akono was jiggling slightly. Maybe she'd left her toilet run a bit late. One of the stall doors swung open, a disabled toilet, wider than the others. The door was spring-hinged, but the elderly man who exited chose to tap it closed behind him with his walnut cane, making it clang. In his neat crimson flat cap and camel hair jacket, this was a man, thought Tori, who reached his twilight years without ever leaving anything to chance, the type who'd sniff the ham slices in his fridge even if the use-by had a week to run.

Akono moved forwards, removing her helmet as she walked and shaking out a thick mass of black curls. Tori followed silently and as soon as the cop opened the stall door, she jumped her.

In a quick, graceful move that she'd practised many times in training but had never used in the field, Tori looped her right arm around Akono's neck, placed her left behind her head and pressed it forwards, hard, into a sleeper hold.

In the struggle, Akono freed her hands by letting her helmet drop, reached up to pull Tori's hands off her and kicked back. Tori expected the shin kicks so she'd already spread her own legs wide, booted the helmet into the stall and, at the same time, used the full weight of her body to shove Akono inside too, letting the door swing itself closed behind them.

93

On the terrace outside the basilica, the official welcoming party comprised the city's archbishop and two men who were normally political adversaries, the president of Spain and the president of Catalonia's Generalitat.

Russian President Maxim Tushkin strode up the steps from his motorcade, gave each man a curt nod, avoiding the proffered handshakes and ring kissing, a habit of haughtiness he'd embraced long before the last pandemic made it acceptable. He posed with them for the obligatory photos but didn't smile and offered no pleasantries. This was Tushkin's perennial pose. *I am Russia. Russia is me. Go fuck yourself.*

No one had mentioned there'd be flowers and he slapped aside the yellow bloom that one of the idiot presidents tried to pin onto his lapel. Merely thinking about the pollen made his eyes moisten.

The wind shifted and he heard the *whoop, whoop* of an incoming helicopter. He looked up to see it was from the local TV station, not the American president doing her damnedest to upstage him.

Two ushers escorted him inside, and as he went down the aisle his eyes were watering and he could feel the fingers of a wheeze limbering up to strangle his throat. Fucking flowers.

When he reached the front row, the head usher pointed him to the third seat along from the centre aisle, past two others that were also empty, seating him next to Chancellor Brinkmann from Germany. Tushkin had no time for Brinkmann and had only last year shared his disdain publicly during a flare-up on a panel at Davos.

While standing, he tapped the smartwatch on his wrist and spoke into his earbud. 'Why do we not have the aisle seat?'

The two free seats, he was told, were reserved for Isabel Diaz and her stepson. As a close friend of the deceased, Diaz was giving a speech so needed the easiest access to the lectern. 'The kid will sit between the two of you. That way you can avoid her whingeing.'

As he went to his seat, he wiped his eyes with a handkerchief, preventing him taking the German chancellor's outstretched hand, not that he needed an excuse.

Brinkman didn't get the message, and tried to engage Tushkin in talk but, as the Russian sat, he brought a finger to his lips and tapped his ear, like he was listening to a feed from his security team. Rebuked a second time, the German looked down at the backs of his hands and kept his mouth shut.

Tushkin pressed the handkerchief back into his pocket and looked up, away from Brinkman, and noticed the cross of Jesus hanging above the altar, just below the baldachin, a canopy of gold and ochre.

Unusually, this effigy of Jesus was looking upwards, to the vaulted ceiling and the flowers up there. They were above Him, in front of Him, and wreathing the coffin beneath Him. Buds blazed in the aisles and on the congregation's lapels. The perfume was intense, more pungent than jasmine even, the aggravating flower with the stench his idiot cousin in Minsk insisted on calling the 'aroma of calm' just to annoy him.

He reached into his inner jacket pocket for the foil of antihistamines.

Tushkin's invincibility had limits, not that he'd ever let it be known.

94

Her visor down, the cop exited the toilet stall, letting the door slam shut behind her, the heel of her palm resting, ready, on the handle of her pistol. She looked sideways several times, satisfied no one would notice that her service belt no longer had a set of handcuffs swinging off it.

Tori turned back to face the door and, using the cop's marker, drew a large red circle and slashed an oblique red line across it. *No entry.* She didn't know how to write *out of order* in the local language so the pictogram would have to suffice.

She reclipped the marker to the vest pocket of her newly acquired hi-viz and, clinking the cop's keys, sauntered over to Akono's bike, thrummed the engine and rode the thirty metres to the security gate, touched her glove to her security pass, saluted the guards and drove through.

She'd entered the red zone.

95

After the second-last motorcade pulled out, a flurry of American Secret Service agents scattered across Carrer de la Marina. Six of them paced down the street from the diamond at Provença to the one at Mallorca. Two ran electronic sniffers along the pedestrian barricade opposite the basilica. Another six eyed the sky, while four more were talking into their sleeves or into walkie-talkies.

American presidents did not travel light.

It was only when Chief Franklin – the special agent in charge of President Diaz's protective division – gave his thumbs-up that the TV helicopter moved away from the airspace overhead and three VH-60N White Hawks flew in.

One of the choppers carried a squad of eleven combat troops, the second more artillery than Spain wanted to know about, and the president was in the third. No one on the ground knew which was which.

One did a sharp vertical drop until its landing skids brushed the asphalt a few metres from the basilica steps; it wobbled momentarily from ground effect then climbed straight back up.

A second bird swooped down and it was only when the media caught the president's hand waving out of the window that they began broadcasting, *This is history in the making as Marine One touches down in Barcelona and brings the first American president…*

Isabel stepped out, followed by Davey, the downdraft from the rotors tousling the boy's hair, a short black veil protecting hers. The lace lifted off her face momentarily and the cameras caught her eyes, dark and solemn.

None of the TV commentators had paid any attention to the get-up worn by the male dignitaries but had gone into great detail for the few women, as if their viewers couldn't see the clothes for themselves. They gave Diaz the same treatment, NBC reporting: *she's wearing a hip-hugging black Vera Wang suit and matching gloves, patent Stuart Weitzman pumps and a matching clutch with a golden yellow clasp. It's the president's all-American homage to her dear friend Montse.* As if simply being there wasn't an homage itself.

Davey's yellow tie was straight. Isabel had adjusted it just before they stepped out of the chopper. She'd got him to retie his yellow shoelaces too, so he didn't trip over them.

They moved away from the rotors and, after waving at the public behind the barricades, took to the grey stone steps. Isabel felt the pull of Davey's hand, a signal he was about to break off and either hop his way up the stairs or scamper off to scatter the pigeons. Or were they doves? Scores of the drab birds were pecking at the steps, like conscripts from the Secret Service employed to test every scrap of bread, worm or bug for any taint of explosive.

She gave Davey's hand a little jerk, a reminder to stick to the plan and make their walk from the chopper up to the Nativity Facade a solemn affair and not one for childish play. He complied.

The archbishop, a bald man, his scarlet *zucchetto* the only adornment on his head, was the first to offer Isabel his hand.

'Congratulations on your elevation to cardinal, Your Eminence,' she said, dropping Davey's hand while giving the boy a stern eye. Even through her glove, the priest's palm felt slight and silken, like the boy's, as if an extra sixty years of life hadn't touched the man. On a ten-year-old it felt natural, on the prelate a little creepy.

His other hand touched the pallium on his chest, a band of brilliant white wool adorned with gold crosses that was draped like a Y from his neck to his abdomen. Was this, she wondered, a hint of sinful pride? Vanity that the Pope himself had presented the archbishop with the vestment at a consistory in Rome a month ago?

'Madam President, you are not only the first president of the United States to visit our city, you are also its first Roman Catholic president to do so. Although the reason you are here brings deep sorrow to all of Spain, we especially welcome you.'

She glanced at Casals, who was wearing a black tie with a gold hatch and a yellow boutonnière in his lapel. She wondered if he'd shared the news of Montse's murder with the priest.

She turned to the third man in the welcoming party, Spain's federal president Santiago Rubio. He went to kiss her on both cheeks, but she held out her hand. He took it and whispered that he'd keep his words for later when they'd be flying to Madrid together on board *Air Force One*.

Casals bowed and then, unlike the other two, kneeled down and spoke to Davey. 'Young man,' he said in English, slowly in case his pronunciation made it difficult for Davey to read his lips, 'I am excited that you will be signing President Diaz's speech for her. Montse,' he crouched a little more, 'would be thrilled you came today. She told me many times how very special you were to her.'

Davey beamed.

96

The two presidents escorted the last of the bigwigs, Spain's king and queen, down the aisle and left them at the coffin, taking their own seats in the front row. The king, in a simple black suit and black tie, with a yellow boutonnière poised just above his medal of the Distinguished Order of the Golden Fleece, bowed his head and poked his fingers into the garlands, as if he was trying to create a physical bond with Montse through the mahogany of the casket.

The queen, in *a high-cut two-button black Dior jacket with welt pockets, and a knee-length pencil dress*, as one reporter described it, just stood there. Like Isabel, the queen's outfit had a touch of lace, hers at the neckline of her dress. She showed remarkable stoicism, though Isabel, sitting fairly close by, detected a slight tremble in her hand – not surprising, given the queen and

Montse went back a long way, a friendship that had begun when they were college roommates.

When the royals turned to walk up the steps to their seats, located to the left of the altar, Isabel noticed the queen's heels. As thin as the legs of the pigeons outside the church, they were three times taller, and their colour, she was pretty certain, was Jimmy Choo's liquid fluorescent yellow, one of her favourites. Montse was big on stilettos – Jimmy's, Manolos, you name it – and once confessed to Isabel that her shoe collection, her only vice, boasted more heels than Carrie Bradshaw's in *Sex and the City*. Montse's philosophy was simple: if the shoe fits, buy it in every colour.

Montse towered intellectually over many of the men she had to deal with but, conscious of her diminutive height, by wearing stilettos she could do it physically as well.

Skyscraper shoes stopped being Isabel's thing last year when, with the world watching, she'd stumbled as she stepped out of *Marine One* onto the deck of the USS *Gerald R. Ford*. Hence, she was wearing pumps today.

The organ started as soon as the royals got to their seats, a canticle Isabel didn't know. She looked back down the aisle to watch the procession approach, the priests first, then choristers, then children carrying candles in glass jars, and the archbishop last of all.

After the kids passed by they circled the coffin, some placing their candles on the floor, the flickering lights adding an even warmer lustre of gold to the flowers draped over it. Other children put their candles on the steps leading up to the altar as they took their seats in the wide U-shaped pew behind it.

The archbishop was carrying his crosier and now wore his mitre simplex, a spare, pointed hat of unadorned white linen damask.

While Isabel knew most of the details of the service – the catechisms, the prayers – she'd taught herself to wear her own Catholicism lightly. It wasn't for faith or prayer that her mother had taken her to Mass every week, it was for the free wine.

97

Casals' eulogy soared from his first words. He likened Gaudí's lofty columns to the strength and beauty of Montse's character. He compared the bluish rays raking through the stained glass of the south-western transept to the spotlight she shone on disadvantage and societal dysfunction. The intricate stone carvings of the facades paralleled Montse's dedication to making change for the good, in contrast to the vapid, arm-sweeping rhetoric of so many other politicians. He shot a glance at President Rubio when he said it.

This building, this edifice, he said, was her favourite church, and its unfinished state was an analogy for her own unfinished work; for a good life cut short.

His language, the timing of his pauses, his gestures, his eye contact were as masterful as Isabel had ever seen, better than her own would be if she was juggling a speech in five languages as he was. She had mastery of two, but he was giving each sound bite first in Catalan, then Spanish and English, followed by French and an African language she did not recognise. It was, he explained, a mark of respect to the millions of Montse's admirers around the world.

The sound system gave his address even more power. Isabel was seated as close to Casals as anyone and was fascinated that all his words came to her through the speakers dotted throughout the church, not a murmur carrying direct from his mouth to her ears. The result was a perfectly balanced acoustic, no echoes, no voice overlap, no aural confusion, just crisp, stirring oratory.

When she saw the white boxes positioned either side of his lectern she realised he was using inverse acoustics, the same technology her own team had demonstrated to her three weeks ago. The boxes produced voice-cancelling acoustic holograms, a complex technology that her people explained cancelled out the speaker's sound by beaming back at it the exact opposite anti-sound.

Inside the boxes were a directional microphone, a directional transmitter and a computer. As the mic picked up Casals' voice, the computer did two things: it pumped his words out of the speakers at the same time as it was reverse-engineering them and pulsing the mirror version back at his mouth.

The result was even better than she'd heard in the White House. Davey, of course, was oblivious to it. He was sitting cross-legged on his chair, his yellow shoelaces lapping over the edge. He was fully absorbed, one minute his attention on Casals' mouth, lip-reading when he spoke in English, then moving his head to focus on the International Sign translator, a woman standing a metre to the local president's right, then he'd swivel again to watch Casals on one of the two monitor stands nearby. That way, he could see his lips in close-up and could also read the scrolling subtitles, which, thankfully, were in English.

Isabel noticed Maxim Tushkin stealing glances at her over the boy's head, but she couldn't read him. That man was insufferable. He'd cancelled the one-on-one she'd asked for today because putting Estonia on the agenda was apparently 'another offensive American attempt to meddle in Russian sovereignty that won't be tolerated'. As if his repeated attempts to rig US presidential elections weren't exponentially worse.

Casals' speech suddenly took an unexpected turn when he used Montse's name to make a strident call for action on climate change. 'March for Montse. March for the planet,' he called out, asking people watching around the globe to picket their parliaments, to protest in their streets, and demand that their leaders and those present in Barcelona put an end to their talk-fests and excuses and start taking real action.

A collective gasp of surprise seemed to empty the air in the church and, judging by Casals' own facial expression, the response came as a shock to him, yet he spoke on, raising his tempo and his rhetoric even higher.

Isabel fixed her expression to hide her own surprise, to make sure she'd look thoughtful and not at all defensive if any camera zoomed in on her, despite being as startled as everyone else.

'Our Montse … she would have wanted this,' Casals said.

Isabel knew, from her private chats with Montse over the years, that there was at least an element of truth in what Oriol was saying. Montse, like Isabel, was frustrated by the glacial pace of action on climate change, but they both knew that operating in a hard-headed, pragmatic world, they couldn't push too hard. Unlike in physics, they'd agreed that the shortest path in politics was rarely a straight line.

On Isabel's flight, in between the stress over Project Gusher, the assassinations and the extra matter of running a country, Gregory had had her practising her stony camera-face. The more he'd spoken to Casals' office, the more he was concerned that he might hijack the funeral for his electoral purposes, with independence for Catalonia his most likely cause.

While that was a benign issue for America, it carried the risk of Casals making some bold demand, and that was making her protective detail more paranoid than usual.

'With both you and Rubio there,' Chief Franklin told her, 'if Casals does call for independence, he could spark riots in the streets.'

Franklin had not been convinced by Casals' 'peace and love' TV address or by the blanketing of the city with flowers. It was why he'd insisted on using *Marine One* for Isabel's arrival and more especially for her exit. If she had to get out, it might have to be fast.

It seemed Franklin was right to be worried. He'd just picked the wrong cause.

She glanced down her row of seats to President Rubio, a climate belligerent. He was holding onto power in Madrid by the fingernails of a precarious one-seat majority. She'd been privately hoping he'd lose at the next election.

Casals' demands were a direct challenge to Rubio. To Isabel, too, even if she shared his sentiments. Her problem was Congress, the reason why she kept reminding herself of Otto von Bismarck's remark 150 years ago: 'politics is the art of the possible'. With the current Congress, there wasn't much about climate policy that was possible at all.

Chief Franklin, she knew, would have already recalculated his security posture and she checked her smartwatch to see the outcome. Except she had no signal.

Davey, his face screwed up, tapped her leg, and when he'd got her attention, he started signing, 'This is weird.'

'I know,' she mouthed back.

'No. You don't,' he answered.

98

A semi-circle of eight of Casals' staffers were munching on *xuixos* as they crowded in front of his wall-screen. Apart from a smattering of snide comments about priests and altar boys, which Maria hushed, they were as respectful of the church service as anyone could be while stuffing their mouths with deep-fried pastries oozing custard.

All of them knew the thrust of Oriol's speech, and a couple knew the last draft verbatim. Five of them had worked on Team Casals for years, so they were attuned to his beats, the lifts that led into the dramatic flourishes his public lapped up. Whenever Oriol teared up in a speech – which was often – even these professionals couldn't help tearing up and, when he laughed, they laughed. He had the knack. If he placed his hand on his heart, they would too. A finger to a trembling lip, the same. A breath and a lengthy pause for emphasis. His beautiful bedroom eyes raised to the heavens, his arms opening in peace, and the clincher, his ten-carat-diamond smile, the best vote-catcher local politics had witnessed in years.

But *this*. What was this?

'Maria, where is this speech coming from? We did not write these words. Did you know about this?'

She did not. The Uri she knew often went off-piste, but this was so wide of the piste that he was tumbling over the side of the mountain.

This was nothing like the call to arms they'd pored over, amended, rewritten and signed off on, the words Maria had personally sent through to him.

'Maria, what happened to the call for independence?'

There was a barrage of *Maria, what?* and *Maria, why?* but she had no answers for any of them. She was even more in the dark than they were. Uri consulted her on everything and he'd never once, in all the years they'd worked together, made a major policy announcement without bouncing it off her first. He didn't always accept her point of view but he always asked for it, and he always listened. Until this.

'He's being so extreme.'

'So fanatical.'

'So un-him.'

'He's just thrown the election.'

Maria had her head in her hands. 'All our work, everything we've spent years building, our agenda—'

'I didn't come here for this! Maria, I'm done.' The newest recruit, a careerist fresh out of Harvard's Kennedy School, chucked his pastry at the screen, grabbed his satchel and stomped out.

'Harvard shmarvard. Ignore that prick,' said one of the older hands, a polling expert from Girona who'd worked for Maria for eight years. 'The thing is, what Oriol is saying is actually honest. It's raw. Maria, you're the one who's always telling him to be authentic. Well, it doesn't get more authentic than this, so, hell, if he's lost us the election, then fuck the election. As of this moment, I've never been prouder to work for anyone.' She flipped the rest of her pastry up in the air, opened her mouth wide and caught it in her teeth.

99

Hermes yawned. Being forced to listen to the first half of Casals' eulogy was even more tedious than reading it. If it was put to music, Hermes would've ranked it with Billy Ray Cyrus's 'Achy Breaky Heart' as one of the most turgid songs ever written. What were the speechwriters thinking when they penned all that teary sop? Montse this. Montse that. The fawning. The saccharine-sweet hokum.

Displayed on Hermes' screen was the rest of the text, lifted when it was winging its way from Maria's computer to the autocue in the church.

More than anything, Montse wanted our beloved Catalonia to be independent.

But friends, the way she saw secession was not through rupture, not through conflict.

Montse saw the peoples of Catalonia and Spain as brothers and sisters, parents and children, cousins, friends, co-workers, co-investors.

She would always say that, like the best of friends, like any family, we have our differences, different needs, different wants, but we should never ignore how much we share, how much we agree on.

Which is why she felt that now is the time. The time to celebrate all our heritages. The time we choose to live both together and separately.

To live as the best of neighbours, sharing our fruits and our bounties, our joys, while at the same time each of us making our own rules and respecting the other's.

Equals, neither subservient nor superior ...

'Blah, blah, blah.' The congregation, thought Hermes, should be grateful that they'd never have to listen to these unctuous globs of hooey. Instead, the words coming out of Casals' mouth, almost literally, were words Hermes had crafted for him, words that radical environmentalists like Endz of the Earth would be proud of ... If they'd ever existed.

Hermes' brilliant, and high-priced, tech team in Silicon Valley had worked hard to ensure that the new text coming out was in Casals' own voice, that it was synched to his lips, to his pauses, his beats and his cadences. It wasn't all down to them, though. The NSA had a hand in it, although they didn't know so they couldn't take a bow. Hermes had pilfered the artificial intelligence software her people were using from them. As a result, the task wasn't anywhere near as difficult or as time-consuming as it would be otherwise.

Only a few months ago, scanning the terabytes of Casals' speeches and interviews on the internet and isolating the precise snippets of words and phrases needed for the new speech would have taken weeks, and the output would've still been clunky.

Today, Hermes' people had taken just an hour and they'd achieved near perfection.

Bless you, NSA, for the bountiful gifts that your taxpayer billions keep bestowing on me.

100

The Russian pulled back his sleeve to check the message coming through on his smartwatch. He pressed the alert button to make sure his security people saw it too.

10-MINUTE WARNING:

Tushkin, your funds haven't arrived.

You obviously haven't grasped the force of my ultimatum, so I suggest you fix your eyes on that droning Catalonian.

Once you see what your little birdies do to him, you will know what will happen to you if you don't pay me.

The Russian raised his eyes to the ceiling and closed them to pray. His watch vibrated again and he looked down.

Idiot, I'm watching you. Prayers won't help you. Only paying me will do that.

Heed this warning.

While I've got Casals mouthing your bullshit Endz of the Earth script, he'll be taking a little diversion and I want you to appreciate every nuance of it.

When your birdy bots start toying with him, be sure you keep your tight little backside glued to your seat. If you don't, a stray bird might lash out at you.

So ... do NOT stand up. Do NOT signal for help.

If you do either, I'll do to you what I'm about to do to him.

Send me my fucking money.

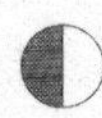

Outside, the basilica steps were a battleground. Tens of annoying pigeons pecked at the feet of a line-up of pushy reporters who were pretending to ignore them as they spoke to camera about the unexpected turn of events inside.

The CNN correspondent, wishing she hadn't decided to go with open-toed shoes, looked back to camera from the basilica.

'Behind me, President Casals is demanding an urgent step-up in climate action. It's a huge slap in the face for US President Isabel Diaz. And the question on the lips of locals who'll be heading to the polls in a month is whether Casals has cut his own electoral throat—'

The reporter stopped mid-sentence when several of the pigeons flapped up in front of her face, hovered, then flew over her head. 'Shit, what's with these birds?' she said, forgetting that the camera was live as she waved them away.

Her cameraman kept filming, capturing at least a hundred more birds forming a swarm above the reporters' heads. They divided, one flock heading towards the apse at the front of the church, the other flying to perch on the stone ledges beneath the stained-glass windows on the northeast facade. For a moment, the cameraman imagined he was filming a scene from Alfred Hitchcock's *The Birds*.

101

Tori sat high in the motorbike saddle. Rigged out in police hi-vis, gloves and helmet, she was regretting not also taking Akono's boots. No one had noticed the sneakers, not yet.

She drove slowly beneath flag after flag of the countries of the United Nations, the avenue of towering aluminium flagpoles fluttering their welcome for the benefit of the international media and the dignitaries who'd been driven past them on their way to the funeral service.

The address Thatcher had given her was up ahead, a narrow seven-storey row house diagonally opposite the Sagrada Familia and directly across from a landscaped park. She pulled up on the park side of the street and flicked a leg over the bike to dismount.

The flag flapping outside the house wasn't one she recognised. Colombia's flag was the one to its left and Costa Rica's to its right, so if they were in alphabetical order, this one probably belonged to the Congo. A sky-blue ensign slashed by a thick stripe of red. Like a river of blood. Yes, probably the Congo.

The kerbs were cleared of cars apart from a scatter of emergency vehicles further up the street, so Tori had a clear line of sight to the building's upper levels, though a long red dumpster immediately outside blocked her view of the ground floor. Four or five metres wide, it took up almost the entire frontage. A fluoro-orange trash chute snaked out of a hole in its lid and slithered up the exterior wall, eventually coiling its way in through a window that, if she moved her head sideways, she could just make out behind the flag. It was on the sixth level, second down from the roof.

Renovating a building in a prestige location like this made sense. East-facing windows for the sun to skip into across the tops of the trees in the park opposite. French doors on the wide balconies to draw in an even more dazzling stream of morning light and give the occupants a breathtaking side-view back to the basilica.

But why, she pondered, would The Voice choose this particular place to track her from?

She propped herself against the bike to contemplate the answer, watching and waiting.

102

Davey nudged Isabel, indicating that she look at Casals' translator. Isabel's International Sign wasn't as good as Davey's, so she found herself quite confused. The woman was signing about independence for Catalonia, not climate action.

Davey, who must've seen her puzzlement, tapped her leg, this time pointing her to Casals. *Read his lips*, he mouthed. *He's talking in English now.*

She saw it immediately. Oriol's speech was being hacked. Someone was manipulating the acoustic hologram technology, but only she and Davey were close enough, and had the skills, to see it.

She glanced a second time down the row. Tushkin's smug self-confidence had gone. He was gripping his seat like a man on the edge of a cliff. Chancellor Brinkmann, a cool customer with his arms folded and his lips pursed, was indifferent, a man whose only care in the world might be holding back a pork-knuckle burp. Her eyes stopped at President Rubio, his fingers clasped like a steeple, his cheeks redder than his name, a curl of a smile on his lips. Was he actually enjoying this?

Isabel was raising her smartwatch to her mouth to alert Chief Franklin to Davey's discovery when the word '*Traïdor!*' boomed through the speakers.

Casals stopped mid-sentence and stepped back, looking around to see who had called him a traitor. The voice continued, this time in English, over the same speaker system.

'President Casals, your words today, though welcome, are cheap. You, and politicians like you, have wasted years doing nothing. You have all betrayed our planet. You are all traitors.

'So it is now my solemn duty, President Casals, to inform you that Endz of the Earth has put you on trial for the crime of high treason.'

This didn't make sense. The people who'd hacked the speech – who'd switched it to climate change – were now attacking him over it.

Was this truly Endz of the Earth, Isabel pondered, the same group who only that morning had made false attacks on America?

People throughout the church, though not the dignitaries in the front rows, were rising from their seats.

The voice started shouting through the speakers, terse, ominous, loud. '*Everyone … Sit down. No talking. Stay quiet.*' He added, '*Or else,*' just as two of the stained-glass panels at the back of the apse smashed inwards. Sharp chunks of coloured glass sprayed over the priests and children sitting directly below, and flew out to shower Casals and the king and queen.

Security guards raced out of nowhere, weapons raised. Some rushed up to the royals, others to flank Casals, still others surrounded Isabel and the other leaders, but none of them knew what to do or even where to look. Her mind involuntarily replayed horrific images from the incursion on Washington's Capitol in January 2021. She knew this was not going to end well.

An ear-splitting sound erupted behind Isabel, like a car crash in a tunnel, as the windows on the nave's north-eastern side exploded. Shards of flying glass sliced into necks, faces and hands raised protectively. Chunks of it smashed onto the stone floor and splintered. People everywhere were screaming, throwing their arms over their heads or trying to shelter loved ones.

Dozens, maybe fifty, of the screeching pigeons – they were moving so fast they were a blur – shot into the basilica through the shattered panes. They flew low, hurtling around the interior of the church, so low that at one point Isabel had to duck, until, with a thunderous squawking, they rocketed up to roost among the flowers festooning the tops of Gaudí's double-twist columns.

Davey was shaking in Isabel's arms. They both looked up, mouths gaping, only to see the beady, glassy eyes of the birds glaring back down at them.

103

The shouting from the speakers – *Relax, they're only birds!* – made the crowd even jumpier. Chairs were tipped over; children, men and women of all ages became hysterical, many racing for the doors, past security guards whose eyes and gun barrels sought an invisible and impossible target.

Davey had leapt to his feet crying. Isabel rose to comfort him, hugging him, burying his head in her tummy. She tried to look calm, stoic, a woman who, even if she was not in command of the situation, was in charge of herself. Tushkin, she noticed, was the only person still seated, but then he didn't have to comfort a distraught child.

'Return to your seats immediately. Everyone. Do not try to approach the doors. If you do, you will die. Endz of the Earth does not wish to

hurt you. Our sole goal is to make the leaders, the traitors to our planet, pay for their crimes.'

Most people did stop and go back to their seats. They righted them, slowly sat, and dabbed at cuts with whatever cloth they had. Hundreds of pairs of eyes were nervously looking around, up at the birds and back at the doors. The entire church was straining as people whispered, argued, cried, and tried to make sense of what was happening.

Beyond the doors, Isabel heard new blasts and muffled shouting coming from outside the church. As if to explain, the screens cut away from Casals to cameras panning outside the church, accompanied by the words INSTANT REPLAY. The camera tilted up, showing a police tactical unit cable-dropping from an EC135 helicopter onto the terrace. The troopers' visors were down, and their guns – which to Isabel looked like MP5s – were up. As soon as their boots touched the ground, they stormed the basilica's giant bronze doors.

As the first commando tried to yank the doors open, a flock of birds flew down from the roof and swarmed like bees around his head. When he tried to swat them away, they exploded, blowing away his hands and his head.

Inside, at the back of the church, a man who was either crazy or brave – maybe both – ran down the centre aisle and pushed through the people still crowding there, to aid the commandos by pushing the doors open from the inside. Other people tried to hold him back but he tore away and pressed his shoulder against the doors. He was screaming in English, 'Open up, save us!' when two pigeons nosedived from the ceiling and detonated at his knees, blasting his legs off. His body collapsed to the floor, blood spraying out of his stumps, his face in shock as Isabel – though not Davey, whose eyes she was covering with her hands – saw the light of consciousness leave his eyes.

'We warned you not to defy us. You have seen what we can do. So return to your seats … Now!'

104

After five minutes, Tori had seen no movement inside or around the building. No workers had gone in or out and the balconies were clear, even the one whose French doors were open on the sixth floor.

The dumpster clogging up the footpath in front had the usual building site safety pictograms slapped all over it, the kind forbidding entry to anyone who wasn't decked out in protective gear. Thanks to Constable Akono's involuntary generosity, Tori was fully kitted out, except for the steel-capped boots.

She was about to push herself off the bike and cross the street when a series of crashes and blasts came from the nearby basilica and, shortly after, a squad of riot police began running up the steps from the street and a helicopter swooped down to hover just above the terrace. Akono's helmet radio started to crackle. She didn't catch it all but the general message was clear.

Sagrada Família … emergència … immediatament … microdrones.

A blare of sirens and horns, whistles and shouts thickened the air and, from her right, two blue-and-whites and three police motorcycles were whizzing past to the basilica.

Whatever was happening had one upside. The police focus would not be on her, at least for a while. Tori stepped across the road.

105

Inside and outside the basilica was pandemonium, not least in the temporary security hub, an enclosed marquee pitched that morning and shared by virtually all the foreign agencies who had leaders attending the funeral. The swing door flew open and Chief Agent Franklin burst out onto the roadway holding his phone up to the air.

He could no longer reach his president, or any of his agents inside the church with her. All comms going in or coming out of the basilica were cut off, apart from the TV broadcast, which, also worryingly, the network had lost control of.

He re-entered the marquee. The call he needed to make demanded absolute privacy, and the hub's three purpose-built SCIFs – Sensitive Compartmented Information Facilities – were still occupied, the reason he'd run outside in the first place. Luckily, he only had to wait twenty seconds for his Saudi counterpart to exit one of the SCIFs.

The prince – everyone he'd ever met from Saudi Arabia seemed to be a prince or a sheikh – gave him a nod. 'Franklin, the landline is working fine. I expect you'll be wanting to advise your people back home to make a call on the Twenty-Fifth. That is the relevant Amendment, isn't it?'

Franklin gave him no more than a raised eyebrow as he entered, but the Harvard law graduate had picked it in one.

Franklin dialled. 'Mr Vice-President, it's—'

'Your phone hasn't been answering, Franklin, nor is POTUS's. I've been trying to reach you both. The broadcast—'

'Sir, forgive me if I get straight to the point.' This was history in the making so Franklin was choosing his words carefully, aware the only precedent for the counsel he was about to give the vice-president was from Hollywood movies. 'Mr Vice-President, terrorists operating remote-controlled drones have seized control of the Sagrada Familia. They've blocked all comms in and out. I am unable to communicate with President Diaz or any of our agents inside and it's the same for every country with a leader in there. Sir, at this time I, the Service … we cannot guarantee the president's security nor can we extract her safely. Therefore, sir, I believe I have no choice,' he bit his lip, wishing he did not have to say the words, 'Mr Vice-President, it is my considered judgement, my solemn advice to you as the nation's second-in-command, that President Diaz,' he was almost choking on her name, 'that our president is unable to discharge the powers and duties of her office.'

Prentice was silent. Franklin assumed he was gathering his thoughts or his composure, or both. 'Franklin, surely your CAT team,' he said, meaning the Counter Assault Team that always travelled with the president, 'surely they—'

'Mr Vice-President, we are past that. My urgent advice, sir,' Franklin could feel his heart pounding against the pistol in his shoulder holster, 'is that you immediately convene an emergency meeting of Cabinet to initiate Section Four of the Twenty-Fifth Amendment.'

After a lifetime of devoted service, at the moment of his president's greatest need, Franklin felt he'd let her and their country down. He unpinned his Secret Service lapel pin, brought it to his lips and kissed it, then placed it in his pocket.

'Franklin, no Cabinet has ever—'

'Sir, I cannot see any alternative. I am …' his words caught in his throat. 'Sir, I am truly sorry.'

It was a momentous step. In the Republic's almost 250-year history, a majority of its Cabinet had never voted to remove a president's powers.

106

Hermes was ad-libbing and loving it and, if Tushkin's intransigence meant the Russian's own microdrones would be turned against him, the day would get even more delicious.

Endz – in truth, Tushkin – had spun a lie to Hermes, claiming that they'd stolen the breakthrough Nano-Air-Vehicles from a high-security facility in Siberia operated by the country's elite Advanced Research Foundation.

Until then, Hermes had only heard rumours about NAVs like these, tiny robots modelled as birds that could hide in plain sight, as they'd done today, their long-life batteries letting them coo and peck for hours on the basilica's terrace, on the steps, the roof, in the park opposite. And no one had noticed.

Ordinarily, an electronic geofence would have blocked Hermes from operating these rogue drones, but Endz – Tushkin, as it turned out – told Hermes Russia had a mole inside Spain's intelligence agency. He, or she, Hermes didn't know or care which, had created a breach in the fence, one wide enough for Hermes' signals to penetrate and operate the drones as well as the cameras, computers and speakers planted inside the church.

It was yet another opportune example of the asymmetry of digital warfare, the state of affairs that meant governments and corporations had the impossible task of keeping the bad guys out 100 per cent of the time, whereas people like Hermes only had to find the tiniest crack once and squeeze their way through it, just like today.

Hermes put Casals back on the screen, the patsy's hair glinting with chunks of glass and his face shiny from the sweat beading on his brow and above his top lip. As the president leant forwards into the microphone, Hermes chose to interrupt him, and started typing into the voice-masking software, smiling when the text came out in a gravelly, meat-and-potatoes Bronx accent that would have made Robert De Niro proud.

'President Casals. Keep your mouth [the word came out as mowt] *shut. If you say a single word* [woid] *our birds* [boids] *will choose a family in that church* [choich] *at random and top them. Their murders* [moiders] *will be on your head.'*

Hermes tilted the cameras inside the church up towards the ceiling and zoomed in on three pigeons as they swooped down, following them until they hovered above the heads of a young family cowering at the back of the church. Three people, *tree* Hermes mouthed, the blathering child no more than eight years old. This was superb theatre, a performance Hermes thought worthy of an Oscar if assassins had the time or inclination to form their own Academy.

Isabel Diaz hugged Davey close with one arm, her other hand tapping her smartwatch behind him, futilely trying to communicate with Chief Franklin. From the baffled looks on the faces of the security guards and police inside the church, all of them tapping earpieces or wrists like she was, their comms seemed to be suffering the same problem.

However, Maxim Tushkin, she saw, *was* reading his smartwatch, and whatever he saw there made his brow crease with desperation, his eyes bulge and his mouth open as wide as a dying catfish's. Until now, Isabel had only ever seen his lips snap-frozen into a thin straight line, one that always made her think of a spike he probably kept at the ready to impale his nearest enemy.

This was not the Tushkin she knew.

The Russian shut out the chaos and reread the message on his watch for the third time.

You've stalled long enough.

Three minutes – that's all you've got left.

Casals first.

If that doesn't get you to pay me, then one minute later, it's your daughter Zoya's turn.

Start visualising a sharp, cold blade slicing across her throat.

Two minutes after that, if I still can't see your funds in my account, Mother Russia will need to appoint a new big daddy.

For you, it will be death by pigeon. Your own, of course.

Flap, flap. Squawk, squawk. Bang, bang.

I'm leaving your comms open so you can fix this.

His heart was racing as he tapped his watch and spoke quietly via his earbud, 'Have you read it? Their threat?'

'I have,' said the real Tushkin, speaking from the comfort, and safety, of a white leather armchair as his jet began to taxi towards the runway. 'Vitali Ivanovich Fetinov, you are my most loyal friend and supporter—'

'Mr President, I apologise for asking but do I still have your assurance?'

'You have that and more. Russia will forever be in your debt. Your cosmetic surgery, acting as my double these past months ... Whether your cancer takes you or it's the hand of our enemies, know that your family will never want for a thing. You have my word on that, Vitali. The mortgage on your home was cleared this morning. Your wife has no debt hanging over her head and her pension is secure for life.'

'My son's scholarship, for his doctorate?'

'He will make us both proud, Vitali. He received the university's confirmation ten minutes ago.'

'Thank you, Mr President. Again, I do apologise for asking, but here among the chaos, the birds, the madness ... Until today, risking death as your double was hypothetical. I'm sorry, sir, I mean no disrespect.'

'None taken,' said Tushkin. His plane moved away from the apron and as he looked out his window to give the troops encircling *Air Force One* a cheeky salute, two seagulls flew by.

'Vitali, a moment, please.' He picked up the phone to the cockpit. 'Captain Boris, seagulls to starboard.'

Tushkin had been wary of gulls at airports ever since a tragedy he'd witnessed at Moscow's Domodedovo airport in 2007. Still an FSB officer back then, his flight was landing at the same time birds struck the engine of a cargo jet taking off on the parallel runway. He watched it crash, later learning that all seven people on board died instantly. Ever since, he always studied the 'airport' tab in his security briefing folder. Like this morning, when he read that Barcelona's El Prat was built on a former bird sanctuary, a drained natural wetland, so that, like a number of European and North American airports, it maintained a stock of raptors to scare off the pesky birds that refused to find another habitat.

'Boris, tell the tower to release their falcons.' He put down the cockpit phone. 'Vitali, my apologies. A few logistics.'

'What about the girl, Mr President. Your daughter's double?'

'Of course. You met her at the plastic surgeon's. We are taking care of her family too. You do not need to worry on her behalf. Vitali, remember that whatever happens in that church, you are there to represent our Mother Russia. Hold your head, my head, high.'

The president put down the phone.

Hoodwinking Hermes by exploiting the sap's soft spot for the planet was still a beautiful thing, even if the plan hadn't succeeded all the way.

He checked his watch. Casals would be first – good riddance – and a minute after that Hermes would kill Zoya's double and two minutes more it would be Vitali's turn.

So be it.

He leant forwards and took two shots of vodka from Natasha's tray and handed one to his daughter. 'Zoya, take this. Let us make a toast.' Zoya put down her book, a proof copy of his upcoming autobiography, which his publisher, he'd told her, had said was 'a masterpiece' that would outsell the Bible and Tolstoy combined.

After father and daughter downed the liquor, Tushkin put his glass on the console and took up his phone again, messaging Hermes in English so the clown could not possibly misinterpret him.

Hermes, you won't get one more rouble out of me, you greedy fuck. Do your worst.

107

Tori knelt behind the dumpster until the next squad of cop cars passed. She rattled the padlock on the gate, locked, slid Akono's belt under the fence and vaulted herself over the top.

The front door was open, but not enough to see inside. She reclipped the belt, took off her gloves, and drew the weapon out of its holster. With the muzzle pointed at the ground, she pressed the paddle on the grip to release the magazine into her left hand – ten rounds, fully loaded, *Bless you, Akono* – unclipped the release and pulled the slide rearwards to check the chamber was empty, no cartridge or casing. She re-slotted the clip and cranked the slide to chamber a round. The gun was primed.

She raised it up in a two-handed grip and nudged the door open with her foot. It didn't creak but she still let a few seconds pass before stepping over the threshold. Outside, more sirens whizzed past, but the interior was quiet. So far. She knew that wearing the helmet wasn't ideal for listening but decided to keep it on, a protection against a surprise blow from behind.

The front room was fairly dark thanks to the hoarding outside, though her eyes adjusted quickly. She lifted her visor and took a sniff. There was a chalkiness in the air, a smell you'd expect from the demolition of bricks and plaster inside a building site. A hint of wood shavings, too, and a lingering tang, quite sharp, probably from paint-stripper solvents.

Nothing about the place suggested an assassin's lair, not so far.

She scanned the room for wires and threads, tripwires, lasers, cameras, her eyes sweeping up and down the floorboards like a cleaner's broom, then she checked along the skirting boards, up the walls, around the cornices, the ceiling.

Nothing, except for some short worms of coloured wire dangling out of holes in the walls and ceiling, their live ends taped over.

The space behind the front door was clear, no cables or touch plates to set off an alarm.

She had a good line of sight up the stairs and most of the way down the corridor. She closed the front door behind her and tiptoed down the hall, the sneakers she'd filched finally coming into their own. Moving beyond the staircase she passed a small elevator, the kind that would fit one person comfortably and two at a pinch, but it was not in use according to the red 'X' taped over the glass of its door. Further along were three rooms, doors removed, spaces empty, floorboards also bare, wallpaper stripped.

What did start to puzzle Tori was how tidy the place was. Too tidy. No tools lying around. No piles of debris waiting to be wheelbarrowed out.

Her pistol up, she headed back to the stairs and inched up the first flight, giving each step a look over before she placed so much as a toe on it.

The next floor was much the same, gutted yet tidy. But when she got to the second flight of stairs what looked like a gold-backed playing card was overhanging the edge of the bottom step.

She flipped it over with the muzzle of her pistol. It wasn't a playing card. It was a photo of Freddie Mercury in one of the Queen frontman's iconic poses. She'd seen it many times, the one with his right fist held high above his head, his left holding the mic, the stretch pulling on his yellow military jacket to reveal the deep vee of his skin-tight white T-shirt.

Another flurry of sirens whizzed past outside as Tori stared at the card. His left hand. He wasn't holding a mic. It was a pistol.

The Queen Killer.

Was it a message? A warning? Was she the queen, a killer, or the one to be killed?

She picked up the card and studied the gun in the picture. An H&K USP. The same as Akono's. She suddenly felt as if her skin was shrink-wrapping her bones.

If she went upstairs, she might well find The Voice, but what use was that if the truth died with her? Creeping back downstairs and running the hell out of here seemed no better, not with the carloads of police whooshing past. They might have something else on their minds right now, but that could change in a flash. They were, after all, under orders to be on the lookout for her and to shoot her on sight if they had to.

In hindsight, coming here without backup, without Frank, without the help that Axel had offered, was more than impulsive, it was crazy. She'd put herself in a position where either choice – to stay or go – risked death.

Tori didn't believe in fate but, even so, she flipped the Freddie card up in the air. If he landed face-up she'd continue upstairs. If he landed face-down she'd take her chances with the cops outside.

108

Boston

Axel and Ron were still working the phones. It was just after 6 am in Massachusetts, 8 am in Greenland. The Arctic country's deputy prime minister and justice minister had moments ago hung up to rejoin the emergency Cabinet session that Axel had dragged them out of.

'At least they didn't say *no*,' said Ron hopefully.

'How could they once we gave them Thatcher's proof?' Axel looked to his doorway. His long-time personal assistant Lucille stood with a platter in one hand he hoped wasn't full of those awful crackers that tasted like dried plaster.

He nodded to her and she entered, going over to the bay window first, her blue eyes sparkling in the glare of the sunrise coming across Boston Common. She turned the slats on the venetians down a little and then placed the salver on the desk between Axel and Ron.

Argh. He hated these insipid Swedish crispbreads even if, as Lucille incessantly claimed, they were good for his '3 Ds' of diet, digestion and disposition. He couldn't speak to the first two Ds, but he knew for a fact the crackers did nothing for his temperament.

Lucille, as always, was immaculately dressed: her one concession to today's early hour was that she'd pulled her silver hair back into a ponytail instead of her usual French roll.

She picked up the remote for his wall TV and switched it on. 'You'll both want to see this,' she said, and left.

An NBC newsflash logo was swirling at the top right corner of the screen and the picture showed Axel's friend President Casals inside the Sagrada Familia. Uri's eyes were wild, and chunks of glass – yellows, blues and greens – were scattered through his hair and over his shoulders.

> In Barcelona, Spain, a swarm of killer micro-drones – slaughterbots – have killed five people at the Sagrada Familia, the iconic church where terrorists calling themselves Endz of the Earth are holding five hundred funeral-goers captive, including American President Isabel Diaz and other world leaders.
>
> A few moments ago, a spokesman for the extremists denounced Catalonia's President Oriol Casals as a traitor and ...

Axel's usually rosy cheeks paled. He put the TV on mute, unconsciously took one of the crispbreads and snapped it in two. 'Five dead, Ron. Our president a hostage. And Uri ... That man is a saint, not a traitor.' He turned over the two halves of the cracker and put one in his mouth. 'With everything else that's happened today,' he nodded, a few crumbs blowing out of his mouth onto his desk, 'I'm thinking this has to be—'

'The Voice.' Ron shifted his wraith of a body on the chair and a pinkness came to his insipid skin as if he'd sucked it out of Axel. 'That's if such a person actually exists.'

'Ron,' said Axel, the sharpness of his tone a clear warning to lay off his contempt for all things Tori. 'What if this Endz of the Earth group and The Voice are fellow travellers?' He put down the rest of the cracker and dialled Frank's latest burner. He put the call on speaker. While the number was trilling in the background, he went on, 'Until this,' he pointed to the TV screen, 'I believed Francis's new plan was smart. Risky for sure, but smart even so. It's just become a whole lot riskier.'

'And a whole lot less smart.'

After Frank lost Tori, he'd raced back to the market to get a new phone and got Thatcher to tell him where Tori was headed. He convinced Axel that instead of taking Thatcher's evidence to the local police, the best way forward was to win over public opinion first. Through Axel's connections, they'd got a TV network to agree to run through the proof package on air. They wouldn't play the depraved video, only the frames that showed it was a deepfake. Then they'd display the metadata that identified where and when the recording was made – i.e. not in Room 420 – and blurred photos of the sex workers' bodies in front of the green screen at Bar Canona. That way, the public would at least be open to the possibility that Tori was framed, which in turn would place considerable pressure on the police to start looking for the real killer, and to withdraw the order to shoot her on sight.

Frank, meanwhile, had set off to find Tori and explain what they were doing, and stop her from risking everything by confronting The Voice. Once he'd found her, he was to call the police and give them the address. But he and Tori wouldn't wait there. Instead, he'd escort her to the TV studio, where she'd go on air to tell her side of the story. With the whole world watching, they'd all agreed the cops couldn't possibly come in with guns blazing when they turned up to arrest her.

Frank's phone kept ringing.

'Francis, answer your damn phone. Ron, why isn't he picking up? Lucille,' he called out, 'something's wrong with my phone.' He slammed his hand down and crushed the crackers.

109

Barcelona

The thrust of the take-off pressed Tushkin back into the soft white luxury of the calf-leather seats. He allowed himself a smug grin, an indulgence he was prepared to give himself since the crew were belted up in the galley and Zoya was his only witness.

'What is it, *papushka*?' Zoya asked, smiling back.

The president adored his daughter but leadership was a lonely place and he couldn't share his satisfaction in calling Hermes' bluff, not even with her. He settled back and was about to close his eyes when his smartphone buzzed. The phone identified the caller, in Russian, as *You definitely want to take this.*

'So, Tushy, you're sitting back, seatbelt fastened, patting yourself on that muscular back of yours over how you pulled the yak's wool over my eyes. Correct?' Tushkin's mind was in a whirl. He said nothing as he tried to calculate his next move. 'Tushy, have you been bragging to Zoya about how brilliantly you slipped off my hook? Not the *you* you, the *Vitali* you. Cancer-guy. The poor dupe who only you and I know is shitting himself in the church because, for the first time since that plastic surgery you paid for, he's actually expecting to sacrifice his life for yours. Except the thing is, Tushy, poor old Vitali is not the boob who fleeced me. And the Zoya I kidnapped is not your daughter. Yes, I threatened them both but that was my little game, a misdirection. Your two doubles are safe. You'll be pleased to know that they are not in my sights.'

Tushkin's smile had long dropped off his face. The jet engines were roaring as the wheels lifted off the ground, the dials on the console showing him the climb … 75 metres above sea level … 95 … 230 … 480 … and the speed at 180 knots … 250 … 460. He heard then felt the landing gear retracting, too late to get the captain to abort take-off.

'Cat got your tongue, Max baby? It's so strange for such a rich and powerful man as you not to have all the answers. You've got your own planes, army, navy, hypersonic nuclear missiles, secret police, six or is it seven billion stashed away in secret bank accounts. And despite all that, you're still a measly prick who swindles an artiste like me and tells *them* to fuck off. Except, Maxy, *nobody* fucks with Hermes. Oh, I almost forgot, I've got a little gem of information for you. You know those little drones you gave me? They have a truly *amazing* characteristic, one that real birds don't. Airport falcons can't scare them off. You do know about airport falcons, don't you?'

'*Papushka*,' said Zoya, leaning over and placing her hand on her father's wrist. 'What's wrong?'

He shook her off.

'Maxy, is that the lovely Zoya I hear in the background? She has her late mother's gorgeous eyes, don't you think? But enough chitchat. Crane your head back out of your window. Do you see how your microdrones have magnetised themselves to the outer casings of your engines? Hey, do you feel that slo-mo constriction in your sphincter? Well, suck it up. You're in good company. Goliath felt the same thing watching the pebble from David's slingshot fly towards him just before it smashed his giant skull open. Get ready to blow, big boy. Here goes, three, two—'

The Russian held the smartphone in front of him and screamed into it, 'Hermes, you said Casals was first! You gave me your word!'

'You gave me yours, and look where that got me.'

'I'll pay, do you hear me? Hermes, I'll pay double what you asked. Do not do this. I'll pay triple.'

'The window for atonement was closed, but I'll re-open it. For Zoya, not for you. So, yes, do *double* the money – I'm not greedy – but do it right now. You've got twenty seconds. Tick, tick, tick. You know the drill.'

Tushkin glanced at Zoya, who was about to speak. He shook his head, looked down at his computer screen and logged into his account. 'I'm doing it, Hermes. Right now, I'm typing in my password … I'm in … Ninety—'

'Times two is $180 million.'

'Transferring it … Here goes. The money, all of it, it's on its way to you.'

'Such a shame you won't be able to buy that British football team or that penthouse in Paris you've been looking at for Zoya's birthday.'

'How did you—?'

'I'm a magician. But enough about me. As I started saying before, three, two—'

'But Hermes, I *paid* you. I did what you asked. You can't—'

'Actually I can, and I will. In fact, I am. Tushy, you can't possibly appreciate how much of a kick this is giving me. Where was I? Oh yes … two, one, and *kaboom, baby*.'

110

Freddie Mercury won Tori's card toss, which was supposed to mean *stay* except his outstretched arm was pointing *down* the stairs. Was that a sign? Was he telling her to scoot? While Tori didn't believe in signs or omens, weirdly it did feel like the dead singer was warning her.

She still had to make her choice. Upstairs, downstairs … which?

After thinking for another moment, she had a different idea and turned on her heels, leaving the fallen rock star to sing his heart out. Thirty seconds later, she was at the elevator on the ground floor, jimmying the door open with one of the blades on Akono's multi-tool.

She stepped inside the cabin and swung her arms out

sideways, pressing her palms flat against the opposite walls, her elbows bent and, thankfully, they had plenty of give.

She placed her helmet on the floor and stretched up to the hatch in the cabin roof, shifted it to the side and … *one, two, three, bob and spring* … pulled herself up through the opening.

Standing on top of the cabin at the base of the narrow shaft, she looked up, six wedges of light filtering through the glass doors above her. It was a long way to the top.

The lift well was the perfect width for what she was going to try, a *dà* ratchet. It was a technique her parkour coaches mostly described as a split-leg body-wedge, but Tori preferred her tag. She'd named it after the Chinese character *dà* – 大 – because the symbol mimicked the shape of the required body stance: hands and legs out to the sides, the four extremities pressed against opposite walls.

The first time she'd used it in the field was in Tunis, to sneak up on a suicide bomber who'd been spotted vesting up on the fifth floor of a heavily defended apartment building. When Tori looked at the images beamed down from their drone and saw the tight, unguarded alley at the building's rear, she killed the plan to precision-strike the place and, after zig-zagging her way through five alleys to get there, did a *dà* ratchet up the exterior walls, reaching a terrified fourteen-year-old girl and saving her as well everyone else in the block.

After that, Tori had no more call for *dà* ratchets until she took her job with SIS and started doing it for fun, spending quite a few of her weekends scrambling up walls all over Boston with a local parkour group.

She pulled her duty belt up a little higher on her waist to give her hips more freedom and slipped Akono's gloves back on. The more grip the better. After taking three long breaths she sprung up off her feet and, momentarily airborne, thrust her four limbs out sideways into the classic *dà* shape and crammed her toes and hands against the walls to give her a strong four-point hold.

Then she did her first ratchets, hopping her feet up a few centimetres, then the same with her hands. Repeat. Feet, hands. Repeat, each time hoisting her body a little further up the shaft.

When she got to the base of the first door she stopped and held, pausing to catch her breath and prick up her ears. This door, like the one she'd jimmied open, was translucent glass, so she peered through the airgap at the floor. As she expected, since she'd been on this floor only a few minutes earlier, she heard and saw nothing. So she continued upwards. She stopped at each level, listened, looked, then resumed ratcheting up, puffing, sweating, until she got to the fourth floor where, this time, she did hear someone, a man.

He was distant and the sound wasn't coming from under the door, but from down the shaft. She began to ratchet again, and as she went up the voice became louder, though not clearer. It sounded like he was speaking in Catalan. As she passed the fifth floor, he changed to English and became strident, a vocal bellows stoking a raging furnace.

'President Oriol Casals, you stand convicted before the People's Court of Endz of the Earth, a criminal, a traitor to your planet.'

This was crazy. Oriol was no traitor.

And this man, the speaker. Was he upstairs? Or was it a broadcast coming from the church?

'The People's Court sentences you to … immediate death. Death by drone. Bring on our birds.'

Isabel pressed Davey's eyes into her tummy. The buzzing in the vaulted ceilings drew her gaze up to the tops of the columns where she saw the pigeons – one, two, three … seven – diving off their perches, one after the other, beaks first, wings hugging their bodies like a squadron of tiny feathered kamikazes, all plunging down towards Casals.

He was trying to swat them away but they persisted like wasps, pulling up near his ears and manoeuvring themselves into a ring formation where they began to fly in orbit around the top of his head, spinning so fast that for the briefest moment Isabel thought the whirr looked like a halo.

Their orbit trajectory dropped a couple of centimetres, so they circled at his eye level, then lower again at the tip of his nose … down to his mouth … and lower still, and all the while, no matter how much Casals tried to dodge or weave, the hoop of birds moved with him, shifting with his head as if some higher intelligence – artificial intelligence? – was directing them to keep a lock on his cranium.

The birds were spinning faster and faster, shrinking the radius of their ring, now closing in, like a noose tightening around his neck.

The blast happened so quickly that Isabel didn't have time to look away as Oriol's head blew into a million pieces, his blood and bone and brains spraying upwards like a geyser, splattering the Jesus sculpture hanging from the canopy.

Desperate not to scream, her whole body numb with shock and terror, Isabel clamped Davey to her while she watched Oriol's headless body crumple to the floor just metres away.

111

Tori felt the explosion through her gloves, heard the screams. With a gaping fifteen-metre void below her, all she could do was grip the walls for dear life ... and weep as she heard the voice – The Voice? – continue.

'Death to Casals. Death to all other traitors! Everyone in the church, sit ... down!'

Tori didn't know precisely what was happening in the church, but she was imagining the worst.

'Diaz. President of the Benighted States of America. Your boy as well. Take a look at President Tushkin. How quiet he is. How obedient. How seated*! Diaz, sit the hell down!'*

Tori could feel a cramp coming on. She had to stop speculating. Her immediate challenge was holding her stance.

'If anyone in the church disobeys us – president, priest, mourner, child – you will suffer the same fate as the traitor Casals. No exceptions.'

Tori seemed to be hearing everything twice, first a whisper then, before the sentence finished, it seemed to repeat but louder. It was as if the fanatic doing the talking was upstairs, his words coming back to him after a lag, perhaps over a TV.

'Everybody, in one big voice, chant with me. First in Catalan: 'Mort a tots els traïdors! Visca el planeta!

'Now in English: Death to all traitors! Long live the planet!

'Louder! Repeat after me: Mort a tots els traïdors! Visca la planeta!

'Louder in English! Make the church ring out with your voices … Death to all traitors! Long live the planet! And long live Endz of the Earth!

'And again …'

Tori's muscles were burning up. The strain from keeping her four-point hold, constantly trying not to cramp or to slip and fall was becoming excruciating. Her eyes stung from sweat and tears, and blinking was useless. She tried craning her head sideways to a shoulder to wipe her eyes but couldn't stretch far enough.

She squeezed them shut for a few seconds, then started ratcheting up again, ignoring the pain, working her limbs again and again until she reached the lip of the sixth floor where, as before, she went to peek through the airgap under the elevator door.

What the …?

112

Isabel didn't sit down or join the chanting, nor did any of the other leaders. Like her, they knew defiance was a risk, that it might bring wrath down on their heads, like Casals, but as proxies for their countries none of them was willing to humiliate their national pride by cowering before these fanatics. It was not heroism. It was duty.

When the Endz maniac stopped speaking, a stunned quiet fell over the church, as if the place had entered a kind of limbo, a no-man's-land between hell and a hell yet to come.

At the massive bronze doors to Isabel's right sat three police, guarding the body of the man bleeding out on the floor. A civilian – presumably a doctor – was kneeling beside them, looking grim, shaking his head.

The monitors were panning over the hundreds of terrified faces, husbands and wives, friends and strangers, people comforting each other, parents hugging children like she was, strangers holding hands, handkerchiefs dabbing eyes.

No one was speaking. For some it was the stoicism needed to calm a loved one who was even more frightened – and that was partly so for Isabel – for others it was shock, or fear. Or respect for the dead.

A humming started above her. Five drones. Her eyes followed as they swooped back and forth along the centre aisle, staying at eye level so they couldn't be missed. Airborne ushers intimidating the congregation, keeping control, until … Until what?

Isabel drew Davey even closer.

113

An opaque strip of white electrical tape blocked the view space under the elevator door. Tori, her limbs on fire, was only just managing to keep herself braced above an eighteen-metre drop. She couldn't see into the sixth floor.

The release mechanism for the door – as for the floors below – was a simple latch that a cam affixed to the elevator cab would trip and unlock when it moved into position. With the little energy she had left, she ratcheted herself up to the latch and tried tripping it with her nose, except her sweat meant her nose kept slipping off.

There was a way to do this, there had to be. The only way she could think of meant trusting her legs alone, already weak, to support her, but she had no other choice. With her left hand on the side wall for balance, she lifted her right, first to wipe her eyes then to unclip the multi-tool pouch on her belt. She pulled out one of its blades with her teeth and slid its point under the latch.

She was about to lever it open when a kind of clacking started up behind the door, fast, no rhythm, like someone typing. A voice, the one she'd heard before, came through, though this time it was so soft she could only make out some of the words:

'President Diaz. If … want your boy to reach … next birthday, tell … to stop signing.'

A fraction later, the same words came back in a shout, and more followed:

'Diaz! Are you as deaf as your stepson?'

This racket was the cover Tori needed, the click of the latch unlocking the door one of the most beautiful sounds she'd ever heard. She re-pouched the multi-tool, pressed both hands firmly into the side walls and pivoted her weight on them, swinging her legs backwards to connect against the rear wall so she was almost horizontal. After positioning her forehead against the glass, she bent her knees and kicked, propelling herself forwards like a suddenly decompressed spring, forcing the door to fly open and *oof*-ing herself into the room. She landed face down on the floor and, without missing a beat, she rolled onto her side, drew the pistol and thrust it out ahead of her to point at …

The room went black. She couldn't see a thing, couldn't hear a thing, apart from her heart pounding into the floor.

She lay flat, silent, her finger poised on her trigger, Akono's utility belt pressing uncomfortably into her stomach.

Something metallic clinked high up, and a circle of intense white light, a spotlight, burst onto the wall to her right. A man with his back to her – maybe two metres tall – and garbed in a long black coat, stepped sideways into the beam. He slowly turned, the hem of his coat bizarrely billowing out as if he was standing at the edge of an Irish cliff in a squall, not the feeble breath of wind Tori detected brushing against her cheeks. A dark hood cast a shadow over his face. When she saw his arms were bent, his hands gripping a pistol, the muzzle aimed at her – what was it, a semi-automatic Glock 19? – she swivelled to the right, pointing her weapon back at him.

Once again, she heard clicking and clacking. It definitely sounded like typing this time. It was coming from her left, to his right.

'Do you want to call the cops?' he said, his voice deep, face still hidden. 'Oh – you *are* the cops.' He laughed.

Tori wiped the sweat from her eyes – where were her lashes when she needed them? – and bit down on her lip, not only to stop her saying something she'd regret but to steel herself for taking a shot. Despite the stress, she forced herself to breathe, slowly, deeply, as she tightened her grip. Squinting her right eye, since she was left-eye dominant, she focused her vision on her gun's three-dot sights and aimed at the man's centre mass.

'You look kind of sweaty in that uniform, Tori Swyft. Can I help you slip into something more comfortable? How about a coffin?'

114

Tori got her shot in first yet when he slumped to the floor she heard no cry, no thud of his body hitting the boards, no clatter of his gun.

The light snuffed out. Apart from the spot's afterimage burning into her retina, she was again in total darkness.

She unclipped Akono's torch and got to her feet but, before she could switch it on, the spotlight flashed back on, this time lighting up a space a couple of metres ahead of the elevator shaft, in front of what looked like a black curtain.

The same man, apparently unhurt – was it him? – stepped into the circle, though front-on this time. He wore the same long, weirdly billowing coat, the same hood, had the same gun held high. 'Like I was saying …' he began, but when a second spot snapped on, he stopped. This one illuminated a wall to Tori's left, where what looked like the identical man, in the identical coat, the identical hood, with the identical gun, stepped into that circle.

Then two more lights, two more men.

115

Tori's legs were shaky, her arms more so. Four men with weapons aimed at her and a fifth, a bullet in him, lying unseen on the floor to her right, not making a sound. None of them were. The four-man firing squad were glowering at her from beneath their hoods, she could feel it. She again wiped her eyes on her sleeve, unsure what to do now, where to shoot, who to shoot. Her only possible exit was the way she had arrived, via the elevator shaft. But what was the point? These men were probably itching to kill her after what she'd done to their partner.

Then the spotlights went out. She stiffened and fired four shots into the blackness where the men had been standing.

All she heard were the thuds of her bullets and a swish. Was it one of their coats? Or someone moving towards her through a slit in the curtain? She fired again. The room lights snapped on and a breeze filled the black drape ahead of her, but there were no men. None standing, none on the floor.

This time she did take a step back towards the lift well. Coming here had been a bad idea, a crazy idea, possibly the worst she'd ever had.

She was about to turn and drop herself into the shaft to ratchet back down when she heard some more typing and one word, '*Stop!*'

She stopped.

Typing. 'Tori, you know that song "YMCA"?'

'What?' she said, baffled, then snapped her mouth closed. Saying even that one word was a mistake.

The Voice – she assumed it was him – laughed. A real laugh, then more typing. 'Your police uniform,' he said. 'Did you think you were auditioning for the Village People or something? Hey, let me give you a little-known factoid. Did you know that the Falling Man, that guy photographed from the Twin Towers on 9/11, might have been the brother of one of the original Village People?'

Tori recalled the image of one of the many desperate heroes who chose to freefall to the ground when they were forced to make an unthinkable choice.

'So, Dr Swyft,' The Voice continued from behind the curtain before Tori could answer, 'I guess you found my tracker. Not such a big deal really, but back-hacking it to find me … *that* is impressive.'

'What the hell are you? Assassin? Terrorist? Endz of the Earth? Dirtbag of the Universe?'

'Didn't your daddy teach you to respect your elders?'

'What's with all that typing? Cat got your tongue? Have you even got a tongue?'

More typing. 'In good time.'

'What happened to your goons? Are they skulking back there with you, hiding behind that curtain?'

'There are no goons, Tori. No spotlights either.'

Tori looked up and immediately understood. Instead of spotlights, there were video projectors. The five men didn't exist. Neither did the wind that filled up their coats. No wonder she heard nothing after she shot them. It was another of The Voice's many misdirections.

'Playing me like that. You think you're pretty smart.'

Typing. 'Not think, Tori. I know it. Now listen carefully. I'm unarmed so when I come out to introduce myself, please … I'd really be grateful if you didn't shoot me. Deal?'

Tori said nothing.

The curtain rustled and a hand pushed through a split in the middle. It lingered for a moment, as if waiting to see if Tori would shoot or not, then withdrew. More typing. 'Tori, would you mind closing your eyes? I do love to make a dramatic entrance.'

As if, thought Tori.

More typing. 'I assume that's a *no*?'

Tori gripped the pistol with both hands and spread her legs wider for better balance.

The Voice pushed his hands through the centre slit of the fabric, holding them high, both hands empty, then a leg, then his whole body.

Except … he was a she.

116

The Voice, the depraved killer who doubled as Endz of the Earth and had murdered Oriol Casals, *he* was a woman. A blonde, at least for now, in a skin-tight black jumpsuit that made Tori think of Catwoman, except for her mask, which was a glossy royal purple and missing the pointy ears.

The woman – Caucasian, judging from the scanty amount of skin she was showing – started swaying. She opened up in song and, for the first time, Tori heard her natural voice, not one of the multiple versions she'd synthesised via her typing into some kind of software. '*I fake … just like a woman. Yes, I do / But you, Tori … you break … just like a little girl.* In case you missed it,' she said, 'that's a Bob Dylan parody.'

'So you *can* speak.'

'I'd prefer you called that magnificent performance *singing*.' Her accent, finally unfiltered, was American, Midwestern. 'I remind you, Tori, I'm unarmed. Here, please check me out,' and she bent both knees, crouched into a deep *plié*, then sprung up, her legs in a classic four-shape, and pirouetted *en pointe* three times.

It seemed she was telling the truth. Tori couldn't see any weapons, nothing shoved down the back of her pants, or strapped to her back, or slipped into the side of a boot. Even so, Tori kept her gun up and stayed alert. This, after all, was an adversary who'd proved herself capable of the most gruesome murders, fake videos and all kinds of tech whizzbangery, including fooling Tori into believing she'd shot five thugs who only existed digitally. To cap it off, she'd also been tricking Tori all day into thinking she was a man.

The woman might well be unarmed but, for all Tori knew, the wall of curtain draped behind her was hiding a firing squad of *real* hoods.

Tori kept her aim straight. Her finger was itching on the trigger, primed in case the slide of a gun told her to get off a fast two-to-the-body-and-one-to-the-head.

'Listen lady, how about you cut the crap? Who and what are you?'

A wry smile came over the woman's face.

'And take off that mask,' Tori added.

'I will, but only when I see you fluttering those big, beautiful eyelashes of yours. Oh, gosh. Apparently, you don't have any. I guess the mask stays.'

The woman sniffed at the air. 'Phew! Tori, that uniform of yours is pretty rank. You really should've taken the stairs,' she said and, without warning, dropped onto one knee and, out of nowhere, a huge bunch of long-stemmed roses materialised at her fingertips. She tossed them to Tori, who looked on in disbelief but still had the presence of mind to step back, leaving the flowers to complete their arc and scatter across the floor in front of her.

She kicked them away.

'Oh,' said the woman, touching her ear like she was adjusting a comms earpiece. She tapped the watch on her wrist. 'It's time for a newsflash from the BBC, Tori. This is live, by the way.'

An announcer's voice came through from behind the curtain.

'Eyewitnesses at Barcelona's El Prat Airport report that a jet has just exploded during take-off. Airport sources have told the BBC that the plane is Russian President Maxim Tushkin's.

'At this stage casualties are unknown but the BBC can confirm that Mr Tushkin was not on board.

'This feed streaming live from the Sagrada Familia shows Tushkin as one of the five hundred people terrorists are holding captive—'

The Voice tapped her wrist again and the broadcast stopped. 'The BBC is wrong about one thing. Tushkin *was* on that plane.'

Tori was befuddled. 'The newsreader said—'

The woman laughed, her teeth flashing like tiny orbs, and held out her hand. 'My name. It's Hermes.'

Tori kept her weapon up. 'Why *Hermes*? Because you're dressed to kill?'

The assassin raised her arms to the side and curtsied. 'Sorry to disappoint you but my name has nothing to do with the fashion chain, though I'm sure the designer who made this glorious outfit will be flattered.' She did a little twirl on her toes. 'For the record, my name is pronounced Herm-eez. The clothes brand is French and that's Air-mezz. Surely a modern woman like you should know that.'

'Do you think I give a fu—'

'A girl like Tori Swyft should always give a fu, whatever a fu is, so let me enlighten you. In ancient Greece, Hermes was the divine trickster, the god who ushered mortals into the afterlife, like what I do for a living. Homer was quite poetic about him, you know: *bound on my glittering golden sandals with which I fly like the wind over land and sea / I take the wand by which I seal men's eyes in sleep or wake them just as I please.*'

'Hence gluing my eyes shut. And how impressive, quoting Homer to justify your demented stunts. If my hands weren't committed to holding this pistol I'd give you a slow clap.'

'I wouldn't seem so demented to you if you saw my client list. Tori, I operate in a simple world, a marketplace where demand looks for supply. When people want to buy, I'm happy to sell, provided the price is right and the buyer meets my standards.'

'Standards? If you turned up at a freak show, they'd offer you top billing.'

'Tori, you completely misread me. We're actually kindred spirits, two former CIA girls out to smash the patriarchy. Peas in a pod.'

'Us? The same? What the hell are you smoking? And do you really expect me to believe you're ex-Agency? If you were, how could you ever threaten your president's life? You're the only traitor around here, not Casals.'

'To be a traitor, you need a country, and when those CIA pieces of shit sent me packing, they took mine away.'

Unexpectedly, the curtain swept open and Tori flinched, suspecting she'd pushed Hermes too far and she might have decided to let her goons loose on her. If this was how it was going to end, so be it. She pulled the trigger.

117

From out of nowhere, a thin white cord whipped towards Tori, so fast that it wrapped itself around the muzzle of her gun and tugged at it before her bullet had a chance to leave the chamber. Instead of hitting Hermes, the shot went into a wall. 'What the …?' Tori yanked the weapon free.

'That's just me checking if your reflexes are up to scratch,' said Hermes casually, as if someone trying to kill her was little more discomforting than finding a pebble in her shoe. 'Maybe I should sing that Elton John number for you, "I'm Still Standing". It's quite catchy, don't you think? Like my lasso.'

'How did you do that, with the cord? And before, with the roses? What *are* you, a witch?'

Hermes shrugged. 'The divine trickster, remember? To slightly misquote Blanche DuBois in *A Streetcar Named Desire*, reality sucks, magic is better. So to honour my ancient namesake, I've trained myself to be quite a dab hand at most of the magical arts. Skills of dexterity and misdirection are pretty useful in my profession. So, the roses? They're just ornamental fripperies, one girl's gracious welcome to another. The lasso, clearly, is more functional. But it's also a bit of fun. How about this for a bit more? You've heard of sawing a woman in half?'

Tori stiffened, tightening her grip on the pistol. This was no idle threat. Tori had already seen a *man* sawn in half today. Two of them.

Hermes noticed. 'Relax. It's not you, it's me. Watch this rope cut right though my body.'

Hermes passed the rope over her head until it was behind her back, the ends held between her hands.

'Tori, one minute, you see the rope behind me and then … you'll see it moving through my clothes, through my spine, through my stomach … don't blink.' Then, keeping the rope firmly in her grip, Hermes snapped both hands forwards and the rope, to Tori's astonishment, sliced right through her waist like there'd been nothing to stop it.

Hermes hadn't let go of the cord, not for a second. Or that's what Tori thought she saw. The witch had somehow yanked it through her body, effectively cutting herself in half.

'That's impossible,' was all Tori could say.

'In case you think you missed something, I'll do it again, slowly this time,' said Hermes with a smirk. 'Watch and learn, Tori.' For a second time, Hermes passed the rope over her head so it was behind her back, still between her two hands. 'One, two, three,' but this time Hermes added a half-twist of her body, and the rope stopped partway through her, flowing from one hand into her stomach, the rest sticking out of her back and into her other hand.

'What the f—'

'But enough of that,' said Hermes as she pulled the rope out of her body. She turned her back to Tori, apparently satisfied that the rope, or some other trickery, would prevent Tori trying to send another bullet her way. 'The thing is, you've caught me at rather a busy moment. I've got a captive audience down the street who are literally dying to hear what I've got in store for them next, and they can only keep hearing my rantings on auto-repeat for so long.'

By now, the curtain had pulled across completely, revealing two tables set up with five, no, six computers, and no goons, nobody at all. Of the two screens facing Tori, one was scanning the street in front of the building, probably from a camera set up on a vantage point on the roof, and the other was showing a feed from inside the basilica.

Further back, the balcony doors were open and the orange trash chute she'd seen snaking up the building's facade was poking in through a window.

After Hermes tossed the rope into the trash chute, she tapped on one of the keyboards. 'The congregation's probably getting a bit tired of chanting *Long live Endz of the Earth* with my baby birds flitting around their heads. In case you're wondering, they're darling little exploding drones I got from Mr Tushkin before they killed him. And your friend Casals, too. Oh, dear, I see the German is at it again. Well, let's show him, Tori.' She started typing and Tori heard what she assumed were the words coming through a speaker.

'Hey, Chancellor Brinkmann, if you ever want to eat a slice of Helga's kirschtorte again, stop your fidgeting.'

Hermes patted one of the computers. 'Tori, this marvellous box here is translating that into German for me. Helga is Brinkmann's mistress, by the way, a woman who Frau

Brinkmann, back home with the kids and the dogs in Berlin, has no idea exists, not until now. We girls do have to stick together, right?'

As Hermes lifted a bottle of water from the table and took a swig, Tori noticed that the Congolese flag outside was picking up a gust. The balcony doors swayed and the breeze came inside to lift a few sheets of paper. Hermes placed the bottle on the pages and wiped her lips with the back of her hand. 'Tori, you do know that if you hadn't quit the Agency when you did, those pricks would've booted you out anyway? But look at what you've done with yourself, a big-time hired gun just like me.'

'Except I don't kill people.'

Hermes laughed. 'Not that you haven't tried. And how's your game plan of working for the rich and famous actually working out? What have you got out of it? Your shitty little apartment in Boston. A few bucks in your bank account. A loveless life. Whereas me … I've built an empire, I've got contractors all over the world working for me, significant investments in Silicon Valley and Switzerland, and a few other places. Hey, here's an idea. Come in with me. You're a fugitive. What else are you going to do with your newfound free time?'

Tori shook her head in disbelief. Hermes was either kidding herself or high.

118

Hermes kept jabbering. Tori brought her hands close to her body, her elbows thrust to the sides – a cramped pose for holding a weapon but the best stance she could manage to protect herself from another lasso.

'Hermes, bad luck that cord of yours didn't get my gun, because I *will* make you pay for your crimes.'

'Not with all those fairy lights zipping and zapping over those scrappy sneakers of yours, you won't.'

Tori's peripheral vision told her something was indeed happening at her feet and she dropped her gaze to see a dozen red laser dots dancing at her toes. But when she looked back up, damn it, Hermes was pointing an automatic assault rifle back at her. A Colt M4 Commando. With a three-round burst on a single trigger-pull, Hermes would be able to cut Tori down before she got off a single shot.

She was unable to hide her astonishment. 'You *literally* had that thing up your sleeve?'

Hermes kept a lock on Tori's eyes. 'Sleeving an M4 isn't easy when a jumpsuit's hugging a body as glorious as mine.'

'You're both a narcissist *and* a deranged psychopath.'

Hermes slapped her weapon. 'That's not what the unicorn I share my bed with says.'

Tori tipped her head towards the red laser sights at her feet but kept her eyes on the madwoman. 'The lasers …'

Hermes shrugged. 'Maybe they're just fairy lights, maybe they're not.' She stamped her foot and the lightshow shifted from Tori's feet up onto the walls. 'Take a look up there … and there,' she pointed her muzzle at two spots on the ceiling.

Tori didn't look, guessing it was another misdirection. If Hermes was about to shoot, so would Tori, even if she was outgunned.

'Fine, don't look. If you did, you'd see a couple of tiny cameras up near those video projectors. If you'd been more diligent earlier, you'd have noticed the camera inside the elevator shaft. I loved your performance in there, by the way. Great effort. I suppose it was my Freddie Mercury card that put you off taking the stairs. But back to *these* two cameras, dear girl. You're probably thinking I'm trying to distract you with them, so know this: if my two guys watching you via those cameras detect your finger inching towards your trigger, they'll unsheathe a very sharp blade and carve it across the throat of a very close friend of yours.'

'Sure they will,' said Tori, fronting a confidence she did not feel. She moved her finger well away from the trigger, just in case.

'I can tell that you don't believe me so here, catch,' and a phone that Tori would've sworn wasn't in sight a second before flew out of Hermes' hand towards her and started ringing. 'Answer it.'

She caught it. A video call was coming through. The caller's head was covered in a black hood, not like those of Hermes' video goons, more like a balaclava but with no holes. The fabric completely covered the caller's face and draped down onto the shoulders of his jacket.

Tori's stomach clenched into a tight ball. It was a tweed jacket.

She looked back at Hermes, but what she could see of the face behind the mask was blank. The man's muffled grunts drew her eyes back to the small screen. A gloved hand was pulling the hood off his head revealing that he *was* Frank. A dirty rag was stuffed into his mouth, gagging him, one eye was swollen shut and blood was dripping down from a gash on his temple.

Tori was on the knife-edge that separated terror and rage, even more eager to shoot Hermes – except she knew what would happen to Frank if she did.

'Stay calm, Tori, unless you want Frank's death to be the first today that you're *truly* responsible for.'

119

Tori tried to convince herself that what she was seeing on the screen wasn't really Frank. After all, this was Hermes the trickster, the mistress of misdirection, the doctor of deepfakes. She'd tried to fool Tori using Frank's voice before. Who was to say this really was Frank and not more lies? But was Tori going to let herself risk that? What if, this time, what was in front of her was real?

She had no tricks up her own sleeve. All she could exploit was time, dragging this out somehow to expose some gap in the psycho's agenda. 'Look, Hermes, if you release Frank … as a sign of good—'

'Not happening.'

Buying time to take Hermes' attention off Frank was one task, but she was also keen to gather evidence that she, or Frank, could use if one of them did manage to get away. Hermes was a narcissist, clearly, so she was going to play that since she didn't have much else. 'Your video this morning, which I admit was—'

'Brilliant?'

'Truth be told, yes. What I don't get is why you deepfaked me into—'

'Great guess, but not so great since you have the advantage of being the only other person still alive who's been inside Bar Canona.'

Tori instantly thought of the little girls but shook them out of her head. Stay on track, she told herself. 'Why did you make *me* the assassin? Why would a megastar like you want to share the limelight?'

'You're wondering why I didn't kill you as well. But don't you see? You're the hare everyone is hunting, not me. And besides, I so love to watch a good chase.'

'Then why show me Bar Canona? I'm impressed, of course. Your incredible attention to detail …'

Hermes yawned. 'And your point is …?'

Tori could hear Frank grunting, trying to speak.

'Take off his gag. Please,' said Tori.

'Yeah, nah, as you Aussies like to say. Ooh,' said Hermes, her eye catching a movement on the street-cam, 'we seem to have visitors.'

Two motorcycle cops were pulling up at Akono's bike. One powered up his radio mic. 'This is Officer Virella and Officer Cardona. We've located the bike at Plaça de Gaudí, on Provença near Marina. We'll be commencing our search for the offender. Send backup.'

Cardona swung his leg over his bike and looked across the street, his eyes following the line of an orange trash chute as it snaked upwards from the dumpster into the sixth-floor window.

'Tori, if you've been trying to buy time – which you have, right? – then parking that cop's bike down there screwed that little strategy right up. You couldn't have done a better job of leading the cops to my door. I'm not happy with you, Tori. If you don't want me to end Frank's life right now, and yours for that matter, you better give me a good reason.'

Frank was grunting, shaking his head, trying to spit the gag out of his mouth.

'We both know what he's trying to say … *Shoot the witch, even if they kill me.* Frankie,' she said, lifting her voice, 'am I right?'

Tori saw the light drain out of his one good eye. She was definitely seeing Frank in real-time.

'Swyft, if I'm a witch, I'm a generous witch, so I'm going to give you a choice: to sacrifice *one* life to save *many*, or *many* lives to save *one*. It's your call.'

'Meaning?' Tori asked, afraid of the answer but needing to hear it.

'Just give the word and my boys will kill Frank but you'll save all the people in the church. I'll let them go home – *after* I extract a huge ransom from the Yanks and the Europeans to drop into my – I mean Endz of the Earth's – coffers. It's a pretty fair trade, no? Frankie for the five hundred?'

Hermes turned her back on Tori, plainly confident that with Frank in custody Tori wouldn't be shooting her any time soon. The woman coolly placed her weapon on the desk and swapped it for a tablet computer. 'Your other option,' she said, turning back, 'is that Frankie gets to live, you and he can make kissy-kissy and move into some charming three-bed walk-up where you'll have babies and grow old together, and all you have to do to win that prize is press your pretty little finger up against this button.' She held up the tablet and showed Tori a red icon with a large white '90' displayed on it.

'And what happens if I do that?'

'For ninety mind-numbingly slow seconds, nothing. But then, *boom!* My little birds go nuts, zooming around the church and blowing up the people, the building – everything and everyone, including the leaders of pretty much everywhere. The world's political and financial system collapses, though conveniently I've set myself up to make a small fortune out of that.'

If it wasn't for the blade at Frank's throat, Tori definitely would have shot Hermes. 'They're innocent people,' she said, her voice low, calm.

'Most of them, sure. But we all die some time. So, Tori, what's it to be? One for all, or all for one? Like in *The Three Musketeers*, except not boring.'

'If I refuse to play your sicko game?'

Hermes shrugged. 'Everyone dies: lover-boy, the five hundred, those cops downstairs – and you.' The red laser dots were back, whizzing in circles, but this time they were playing on Tori's chest.

120

The assassin put a finger to an ear and began nodding. 'You've just had a bit of luck, Swyft. My newest deepfake is hitting the airwaves. It'll answer a few questions for you, it might even help you play God and make that decision about who lives and who doesn't.'

Tori let out the breath she'd been holding.

Hermes turned a screen around so Tori could see a report from Sky TV that was coming through. 'Hold that phone up, Swyft. I want Frankie's good eye to see this.'

> Russia's strongman, President Maxim Tushkin, has committed suicide ... leaving behind a videoed confession that will rock world capitals.

Despite earlier reports that placed Tushkin inside the Sagrada Familia, Sky TV can confirm he was definitely on board his plane when it exploded ...

'That's what you told me, before,' said Tori. 'But how did he sneak out from the church?'

'He didn't. It's his double in there, and that version of Tushkin is still in there. Poor fellow sold his soul, and his face, for a few pieces of Tushkin's gold.' Hermes began to frown. 'Damn those Sky bastards! They're refusing to play my video.'

'You play it for me, then,' said Tori, still hoping to eke out a little more time.

'I would, but with those cops you brought here about to breathe down our necks, we'll just go with Sky's summary.'

Tushkin confesses that he was behind the gruesome murders this morning of Greenland's Prime Minister Nivikka Petersen and Chinese diplomat Rao Songtian. The Arctic accord the two countries reached yesterday, he said, was a direct threat to Russian supremacy in the Arctic.

His operatives held a gun to their heads and forced them into a depraved orgy, which Tushkin ordered to be videoed ...

'It's only a matter of time before people work out that your video was a deepf—'

'Swyft, shut the fuck up and listen. You're witnessing high art here.'

The only thing true on the video, said Tushkin, was that his assassin – the now infamous woman in the polka dot dress – was indeed the fugitive currently being sought by Barcelona police, the renegade ex-CIA officer Dr Victoria Swyft ...

'Unbelievable!'

'There's more.'

> Tushkin goes on to say that he collaborated with eco-terrorist group Endz of the Earth to crush any ambitions the United States might have of stepping into China's Arctic shoes …

Hermes muted the report.

'That last part is a little bit true. The full truth is that Endz of the Earth are a total Tushkin fabrication. And now I've made them *my* fabrication. That way, it's them, fanatics aligned with a rogue Russia, who are holding world leaders hostage, demanding action on climate change they should get but never will and ripping a huge ransom out of the bastards as minor recompense.'

Tori took a deep breath. 'Very clever. You can make anyone believe anything. So why should I believe you've really got Frank? Why should I play that game?'

Hermes looked at her pityingly. 'Oh, honey. Do you really want to take that chance?'

The silence stretched out between them. Then very slowly, so as not to alarm Hermes, Tori began bending her knees. She placed her pistol and the phone on the floor. She rose just as slowly, showing Hermes that her hands were empty. 'You win, Hermes.'

'Good move,' said the assassin, smiling. 'If you've made your choice, let's hear it. We don't have all day. Who gets the chop? Lover-boy or the quivering masses at Mass? Tick, tick, tick. And your answer is?'

'I've been thinking about what you said before,' said Tori as she shot her left hand forwards, Akono's taser in her grip, firing its two barbed darts into Hermes' torso, the electroshocks crackling the air.

Hermes fell to the floor, convulsing, squirming, screaming as the fine copper wires delivered 50,000 volts into her body.

'That misdirection thing,' said Tori, keeping her finger pressed down on the taser trigger, 'that was a great tip. Thanks.'

Tori crouched, grabbed her gun with her other hand and shouted into the phone at her feet. 'You people with Frank. Put that blade anywhere near him, and your boss here gets 9 mm of steel in her fucking brain. Untie him and remove his gag. I want to hear him speak. *Now!*'

121

Suddenly, Hermes leapt to her feet, seemingly oblivious to the electric pulses still going into her. A two-metre silver cane materialised in one of her hands and she whipped it through the air, right then left, whacking both gun and taser out of Tori's grip, then lashed the cane back again to whack it against Tori's right ankle then her left.

Hopping from foot to foot, her hands and legs stinging, Tori screamed, 'How—'

'Boys,' Hermes shouted, directing her voice up to the ceiling cameras, 'give Frank a taste of a tase. On three. One—'

'*No … Please!*' yelled Tori. 'Leave him. Please.'

'*Two.* In my world, Swyft, actions must have consequences. You taser me, I taser Frank. *Three.* Tase him.'

Tori squeezed her eyes shut as the moans and crackles came out of the phone.

'Enough, boys. Now, Tori, listen and learn. In my business, appearances count, which is why I use only the best dressmakers. Like the one who made this jumpsuit.' She splayed out her hands and curtsied. 'A stunning cut, don't you think? Makes me look like a potential Miss Universe, right? But its real magic is in the fabric, not the cut. This material,' she said and snapped the sleeve at her wrist, 'is one of man's wonders. It's a wafer-thin sandwich of stretchy Lycra and a multi-thread carbon fibre, making it the world's finest anti-stun-gun textile. If a taser's charge hits these fibres, like yours did, they absorb it and the electricity never reaches my delicate skin.'

'You were convulsing on the floor. I saw—'

'One distraction deserves another. My yin for your yang, or whatever.' She yanked the taser's two prongs out of her stomach and flicked them and the wires away from her. She picked up the tablet and tapped the screen. 'Time's running out.' She pointed to the cops on the street-cam, one speaking into his radio mic, the other walking across the road towards the dumpster. 'We don't have a lot of time, Tori, and my five hundred church mice are getting restless, as am I, so I'll make your choice for you. Despite you tasering me, Frank gets to live but in … ninety seconds,' she tapped the screen and held it up so Tori could see the countdown, 'my slaughterbots blow up the Sagrada Familia and all who wail in her.'

Tori, her ankle and wrist pain agonising, tried to work out what to do. If she went for her pistol she risked Hermes shooting her first or changing her mind about Frank, or both.

'Tori, I want you to picture another video, one recording how it was the already reviled Dr Swyft who pressed this button. What's the countdown at so far? Ah, 81. Anyway, the video shows you setting the very timer which, 90 seconds later, activates the signal that gets those birds to kill all those fine people. Sure, I was the monster who actually pressed it, but that's a secret between two girlfriends. Tori, because I'm such a fine individual, I'm going to give you one chance to alter that history I've pre-made for you.' She held the tablet up again. 'The big red button that started off with the number 90 – now, look, it's 66! It's kind of thrilling watching the digits count down, don't you think?'

'Get to the point,' said Tori, no angle coming to her mind.

'Sure. We're done here,' Hermes began to step backwards, 'so here's the deal. If you do somehow manage to give this button a second tap *before* the number reaches zero, you'll get to do some abracadabra stuff yourself. You'll have reset my little birds and instead of Tori Swyft committing mass murder, you'll see them whoosh out of the church's windows and wing it to an altitude of three hundred metres, where they'll self-destruct. Do that and all those people in there get to go back and continue making a mess of the world.'

The number was down to 41 seconds.

Hermes was a desk-length away from the balcony when Tori dropped to the floor and went for her gun.

'That dumb move just cost Frankie his life,' said Hermes placing her free hand on the rim of the orange trash chute at the window, the other still hanging onto the tablet. She dared a stare at Tori as she backed one foot into the chute behind her, then the other. 'Boys,' she called out, 'slice his throat.'

Down at Tori's feet she heard the *shick* of a knife and a loud gurgle. 'You promised he'd live,' she said, her voice a whimper. She bent down to pick up the phone and went to look at Frank but couldn't. Dazed, distraught at what she'd done, she put it into her pocket.

122

The timer on the tablet was down to 23 seconds. The upper half of Hermes' torso was still out of the chute. 'Actions have consequences, Tori. I did warn you. Time's running out, girl, so I'm out of here. If you want some friendly advice, you better scoot too or you'll end up the same way as your buddy … ex-buddy, I guess. Hey, here's an idea for you,' she said, and tossed the tablet, its cover flapping as it flew out through the balcony doors. It hit the flag and seemed to tangle in the halyard.

Hermes slid the rest of her body into the chute and, as her head disappeared, she started singing the chorus to Queen's 'Another One Bites the Dust'.

Tori desperately wanted to collapse, to curl up into a ball and sob, to bang her fists on the floor and scream out Frank's name but when she saw the tablet work itself loose of the halyard, she remembered the photo of the Falling Man and knew what she had to do.

She sprinted across the room and flung herself headfirst over the balcony railing, arms back in a swan dive.

'Holy crap,' said Cardona down on the street, grabbing Virella's arm and pointing to the upper floors.

'Officer down. Officer down,' Virella yelled into his radio. 'Dispatch an ambulance. An officer's been pushed off a sixth-floor balcony.'

Tori plummeted. The tablet was spinning and tumbling, its cover flapping, just out of reach. After what seemed an age but was less than half a second, she stretched out a hand and snatched it, slipped it inside her hi-viz jacket. The lowest corner of the flag flicked her face. She grabbed hold of the fabric, knowing it would rip but hoping it would slow her down. She swung herself towards the lowest balcony as the flag shredded, twisting her body at the last second so it was her shoulder and not her head that crashed through the French doors, splintering the wood, shattering the glass. Instinct cut in and somehow she managed to arch herself forwards, tuck in her head and manoeuvre herself into a dive roll.

Spread out on the floor, her heart thrashing a mile a minute, blood pounding and sweat pouring out of her like a broken dam, it was so hard to breathe she feared she was about to black out. Knowing time was not on hers or anybody's side, she reached into her jacket for the tablet and, with … 13 seconds left, she jabbed her finger on the red icon.

… 12 …

She jabbed again.

… 11 …

She pressed her finger against it again and again, but the countdown wouldn't stop.

The 11 became a 10.

'Fuck you, Hermes!' she screamed.

The two cops looked up, their mouths open. 'Who the hell was that?' said Cardona. 'Superman?'

'Super*woman*,' said Virella. 'Do you think it was Akono?'

123

Isabel Diaz, like everyone, sat firmly in her seat. She wasn't taking any risks, not with her boy beside her, not with the birds flying to and fro and intimidating the crowd.

A few minutes ago, when a man further back stood up to stretch his legs, five slaughterbots dropped from above without warning, swarming and buzzing around his head like bees until a woman sitting beside him dragged him down and, to the relief of the entire church, the birds darted back up to perch at the tops of the columns. Waves of murmurs and snuffles and sobs were still washing over the crowd.

Isabel had no idea what was coming, what her security team was doing outside, but she knew they'd be throwing every resource into this.

Stuck here, she had no choice except to keep a steely face and maintain her dignity – her country's dignity – and keep Davey safe. What she'd wanted to do, what she felt was her duty, was to activate the Twenty-Fifth Amendment and put Vice-President Spencer Prentice in charge, except with her comms down she had no way to do it. Agent Jenkins, sitting over at the left side of the transept, had signed that all comms were down, his included.

Jenkins was a man who always went the extra mile. He had been learning ASL in his spare time to be of better service to Davey. Isabel had never dreamt that one day, and so soon, it could be of vital use.

Tushkin, seated two down, was fiddling with his smartwatch, constantly checking and re-checking it. If he was anyone except the world's tough guy Isabel would swear it was nerves. The man who famously never let a smile cross his face was hunched over, head low and – was that a sob? It was, she was sure of it. Tushkin was cracking. Instinctively, she reached across Davey's lap and put her hand on the Russian's leg and gave it a squeeze. He looked back at her, his eyes glassy, a corner of his mouth quivering. He unstrapped his watch and, under the guise of a stretch, he slipped it to her.

The four full bars of signal she saw on it made no sense, but then neither did Tushkin the Terrible passing her the only working communications device in the whole building.

She glanced back at him, confused, and he pursed his lips like he was steeling himself. He reached over Davey and tapped the screen. The Cyrillic letters changed to English.

Russia's President Maxim Tushkin dies on plane after leaving video suicide note … reveals man in church is double …

Isabel glanced back at him in alarm but he turned away. She looked back down at the watch.

> Tushkin confesses to a staggering conspiracy against China and Greenland ... admits to assassinating Greenland's leader and a Chinese diplomat ... reveals ex-CIA officer, already wanted by Spanish police, is secret Russian agent ... collaborated with eco-terror group Endz of the Earth ...

The revelations kept coming. They explained a lot but not enough. She quit the news feed, tapped the voice recorder icon then coughed, an excuse to bring the watch to her mouth, hoping whoever was operating the cameras wouldn't catch what she was doing. She whispered her message, typed in the Secret Service's emergency number and pressed what she hoped was send.

124

The countdown icon was at 7 seconds.

It flipped to a 6. Sweat was pouring off Tori's brow, stinging her lashless eyes, drops of perspiration falling off her face onto the screen.

She was messed up, a wreck. Who wouldn't be after freefalling through the air, almost crushing her skull and snapping her spine? Worse, none of her jabs at the red icon were having an effect and Tori, not thinking straight, was at a loss.

She started damning herself for not shooting Hermes when she had the chance … if only …

Downstairs, men were yelling; the only words she understood were *policia* and *Akono.* The sweat kept stinging. She wiped her sleeve across her forehead.

… 5 …

More sweat dripped onto the screen … on her fingers …

That, she realised through her haze, that was the problem. The same way Hermes' jumpsuit stopped the taser, her sweat was also a conductor, soaking up her finger's electric charge, shielding the touchscreen, stopping her touch from registering.

… 4 …

The empty room was echoing with the men's shouts and the thuds of their boots running up the stairs. 'Don't step on Freddie Mercury,' she muttered in her stupor as she wiped the screen across her pant leg and rubbed her finger dry.

… 3 …

The screen was smeary, she wiped it again, then pressed her finger down on the icon as her eyes closed and everything went black.

125

Tori winced at the unwelcome stink of garlic in her face, the bed so hard that the lumps cutting into her back as she shifted around got her wondering how the princess ever solved the problem of the pea.

Her eyes blinked open and the forest of hairs straggling out of the man's nose were way too close, his breath awful, his dark eyes concerned but lacking kindness and his beard speckled with greys and browns and an assortment of crumbs.

He was kneeling beside her. Was he a doctor?

She couldn't tell if he was speaking in Catalan or Spanish, or English for that matter. He handed her a flask of water, his other hand sliding under her shoulders, raising her up off the – what? The floor?

This wasn't a bed. She wasn't in a hospital.

Her head was light and fuzzy, her body limp. She didn't know where she was or how long she'd been out. She smiled at him feebly, twisted the cap off the flask and began to take a swig, the water cold, refreshing. She felt hot, sweaty, and held the flask to her forehead to cool herself down, poured a little over her head.

She looked back at him and the security pass pinned to his chest came into focus. Virella, it said. A cop. And everything rushed back to her.

She tossed the flask aside, a ribbon of water flinging out of it, and she sat up, her butt crunching into more of what she now realised was broken glass. She patted her hands around her, feeling for the tablet, but it wasn't there, and scrambled to her knees.

'The tablet!' she shouted, drawing a rectangle in the air and wiggling a finger into the imaginary shape like she was swiping the screen. 'The iPad, Galaxy, Surface, whatever the fuck you call them here. Where is it?'

A second cop came into view. 'You search for this?'

Tori grabbed the tablet out of his hands, wrenched the cover open and saw the screen flashing with the red icon … frozen at 2.

She put it on the floor and leapt to her feet, ran to what was left of the balcony doors, slivers and splinters of wood hanging off the hinges.

The Sagrada Familia was still standing, hundreds of people were streaming out, some going to a line of ambulances, others to buses, and a pall of grey smoke was roiling in the air high above the tops of the spires.

'I did it!' she screamed and skipped back to the cop, kicking at chunks of glass and bits of wood like mini-footballs and giving him a hug.

He pulled away, his hand on his side-arm, sizing her up. He pointed to Akono's pass on her chest. '*Senyora*, we placing you under arrest. Many charges … assault police, impersonate police, steal vehicle. But most big,' he added severely at the same time as he snapped the cuffs on her wrists behind her back, 'for assassinate the—'

She stopped listening and moved her cuffed hands to her side so the back of one managed to make contact with the pocket where she'd put the phone to muzzle Frank's dying moments. It wasn't there. It wasn't on the floor either, so she imagined she'd dropped it when she leapt out of the window. Her heart was tearing, rip by rip, and she fell back down, a blubbering mess.

She pictured the moment early last night when Frank arranged to have breakfast with her. His last touch of her wrist in the cafe. His fingers brushing over her neck when he found the tracker. All of it seemed like a lifetime ago.

A hand gripped her shoulder and brought her out of her daze. '*Senyora*,' said the cop, 'we must go now.'

He was helping her up when his partner, holding up the tablet, called out 'Cardona!' and started running towards them. Instead of the screen displaying the frozen red 2, Tori saw a text message, in a font big enough for her to read even as the cop approached.

Wow, girl. I didn't think you had a do-or-die leap in you.

First the good news … you're alive.

Next, the bad news … sorry, but it won't be for long.

That building that you and Mutt and Jeff are lolling around in is about to BLOW, baby.

Cheers,

Your friend in crime (for another 15 seconds),

Hermes

It was going to be Bar Canona all over again, Hermes aiming to destroy every shred of evidence that would corroborate Tori's story and prove her innocence.

She knocked the device out of Virella's hands and scrambled to her feet so fast that Cardona fell backwards. '*Run … now!*'

126

Soon after the hundreds of huddled, terrified people flooded out of the Sagrada Familia, Hermes watched Spanish President Santiago Rubio take to national TV.

Rubio stood on the steps in the shadow of Gaudí's distorted Gothic edifice, the smashed stained-glass windows as lifeless as the four SWAT commandoes being wheeled away on gurneys in black body bags.

Unscripted, speaking from the heart – or as much heart as a politician possessed – and with tears welling in his eyes, he hailed the late Casals as 'a great Catalan and a great Spaniard', and committed Madrid to working with Catalonia 'to bring the despicable killers, enemies of our people, to justice'.

'Inside this hallowed church, Tushkin and his cronies committed a treason against all humanity ...' Rubio let the sentence trail off and shed his first tear. 'Like Montse, the wonderful woman whose life we all came here to celebrate, Oriol proved himself a hero.'

It was the first time Rubio had ever used Casals' first name and he went on to promise he'd dedicate the rest of his term to making Spain the kind of respectful, united nation that Casals would have embraced.

Hermes gave the grubby opportunist a slow clap and switched off the broadcast.

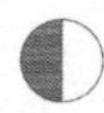

Isabel Diaz allowed no time for recovery. With Davey sedated, courtesy of the White House physician who always travelled with her, she took a chance and set *Air Force One* on a north-westerly flight path even before she dialled Greenland's acting prime minister.

This was her third call to him that day, her first straight after the news of Nivikka Petersen's death, her second to tell him Project Gusher was a hoax – the call when he 'took note' of her assurance and hung up on her.

'I can be in Greenland tonight,' she said this time. 'Your nation is in mourning, I understand that, but I'd like to come and personally express my country's deepest sympathy and show, by my presence, that the American people will always stand with our friends in Greenland.'

This time his voice was warm, his tone genuinely compassionate. 'Madam President, you've suffered an extraordinary ordeal yourself today. Shouldn't you be flying home with your boy, not—?'

'Sharing Greenland's grief is my priority, to put my hand on my heart in front of your people and assure you that Gusher—'

'Ma'am, I don't wish to be indelicate by raising state business at a time like this,' which, of course, was a lie, 'but I assume you will be bringing in your … back pocket, is that the expression? … the bones of a proposal for us to compare against China's.'

'I was about to—'

'Good. We've been speaking to our adviser, Axel Schönberg, and—'

'Schönberg? How could you, after Tushkin so specifically named one of his people as the assassin? The same woman Schönberg employed to work *for* Greenland was the one who murdered your prime—'

'Madam President, the Schönberg family's history with Greenland goes way beyond politics and party. It began when the current Axel's grandfather started visiting us in the 1920s. Their friendship with this nation has lasted longer and, might I say, is even more trusted than America's. Axel has shared evidence with us that categorically refutes Dr Swyft's involvement. It may not have come to your attention yet but, be assured, his people are making it available to your State Department as we speak. One last thing you should know, ma'am, before you arrive, and in the spirit of full disclosure. We owe you that. When you land, you will find President Hou Tao will be here too.'

Isabel was not expecting that. She kept listening in case, in the same spirit of full disclosure, the acting prime minister had any more surprises up his sleeve.

'Ma'am, I hope you will join me and President Hou at a banquet tonight. Your presence will give even greater gravitas to marking Nivikka Petersen's short but inspirational contribution to public life. I do hope you like fermented seal.'

Russia's ambassador to the US, Dmitry Avdonin, arrived at the White House and was immediately escorted to the secure videoconference room. Inside, Vice-President Prentice and Secretary of State Linden stood to greet him. Isabel was online. She could just as easily have placed a call from *Air Force One* to Avdonin while he was at his embassy but she wanted to make a point.

'Madam President, on behalf of—'

'Mr Ambassador, I offer the Russian people our condolences on the death of their president. I can't say anything good about Mr Tushkin so I will simply get to the purpose of this call. I expect Russia is investigating Tushkin's collaboration with Endz of the Earth, his conspiracy against the United States—'

'Madam President, the Russian government is as stunned as—'

'Hold that for another day, Dmitry. I have two demands for you to take back to whoever is in charge in Moscow. First, Russia will issue an official, public and unconditional retraction and apology for Tushkin's malicious and criminal defamations of the United States.'

'Ma'am, with respect—'

'Second,' said Isabel, cutting him off, 'within seventy-two hours you will deliver to us the names of every person involved in Tushkin's conspiracy together with the punishments Russia proposes to mete out to them.'

'Madam President, I understand how you feel—'

'Mr Ambassador, you'll understand America's position even more clearly once you read the text of this sheet of paper I'm holding.' She waited while Secretary Linden pushed a copy across to Avdonin and for the ambassador's eyes to scan down the page. 'As you can see it's a facsimile of the Executive Order I have in front of me and which I am about to sign with this pen.' She held it up.

'Ma'am, surely not. Please let me speak to Moscow first and—'

'Watch me put my signature on it, Dmitry.' She uncapped the pen and wrote her name. 'These sanctions against Russia take immediate effect. I will lift them only after Moscow complies with both my demands. In full. That is all.' She clicked off the call.

127

The prison cell was cold and dank and Tori, in dirty brown fatigues, a wreck physically and emotionally, huddled on the hard metal bunk. When the cops brought her in to the station, the guards strip-searched her, tossed her the jumpsuit and led her naked, no shower permitted and with shards of glass and splinters of wood still strewn through her hair, into an interrogation room.

It was standing room only when she entered, six men and two women, two with rifles at the ready, sneering and sniggering – even the women – as they leered while Spain's most wanted stepped herself into the regulation brown outfit.

One of the women shackled Tori's hands and legs to the table – they were taking no chances – and when she snapped on the last cuff she brought her face up to Tori's, spat in her eye and called her *La Bèstia de Barcelona.*

The Beast of Barcelona.

Tori was weak but she wasn't stupid. Justice was going to be a nuisance in this room, her audience obviously angry that the arresting cops wimped out, didn't shoot her when they had the chance.

She'd been kept manacled in that room for hours, first with Spanish police interrogating her, then security officers in grey suits, after them three American consular officials and, eventually, the US ambassador, who'd flown in from Madrid that morning to greet the president when she disembarked from *Air Force One.*

Whatever wheels were turning – justice or vengeance – Tori had no more to give. She'd recited her story nine times so far, and for seven, maybe eight of them the eyes looking back at her were a cold fury of disbelief and disgust.

In her cell she no longer had to talk, to answer the same questions over and over. Here in solitary, curled into this tight ball on her bunk, her arms wrapped around her legs, her head pressed against her thighs, she at least got some kind of respite.

She raised her eyes, red from exhaustion as much as crying and looked up to the camera. She wanted to scream out her innocence again, to bang her fists against the walls, but protest was pointless when even the police were calling you the Beast of Barcelona.

If I was guilty, why would I leap out of a window to save five hundred people and your landmark? she'd asked them. Repeatedly.

'The Russian said you were in on it. Prove that you weren't.'

The evidence is under the rubble of the fucking building that I got your two officers out of. And it's with Frank. Who's dead. Probably. With Hermes' DNA on the polka dot dress he'd stuffed down the back of his pants.

'Chaudry? If that man stayed in the hotel like he was told, if he kept away from you, he'd still be alive. You kill whoever you touch, Swyft.'

If Frank really was killed. Tori couldn't help wondering, wanting to believe that Hermes had pulled one last sleight of hand, one last deepfake, and that Frank was still alive. But if he was alive, where was he?

Whatever had happened to him, she blamed herself. She slammed her fist against the bunk. *It's all my fault.*

She pounded the bed, smashed her fists into her legs.

Hermes, you despicable fuck.

For the past hour, two, three – she didn't know how long she'd been in here – she'd been replaying her time with Hermes, trying to work out what she could have, should have, done to save Frank. If it was Frank. But if she'd shot the witch when she first saw her, would that have made a difference? What if she hadn't reached for the gun when she did?

She ran through scenario after scenario, but in no version did the Frank on the phone screen end up alive. Hermes always intended to kill him. Yet that was no consolation.

The police hadn't found his body, didn't know where to look for it. The thought of him rotting in some basement chilled her.

The shrieking inside her head was so loud she almost didn't hear the cell door creaking open, but when the glare of the hall light spilled onto the concrete floor she looked up. A warder reached into the room, quickly slid a phone across the floor – cordless, so she couldn't suicide – mumbled two words, '*Una* call,' then slammed the door like he was bolting before the Beast of Barcelona had a chance to strangle him.

She unfurled herself and sat on the side of the bunk, a lattice of tarnished steel mesh framed by black angle iron that was bolted into the bare cold wall, and waited for the pins and needles to drop out of her legs. She tramped over to the phone and flopped down beside it cross-legged, the floor as chill and unforgiving as the excuse for a bed.

She didn't call a lawyer. The US ambassador already promised her he'd do that. She didn't call Axel. He'd probably been the ambassador's second call.

It was Thatcher she needed to call.

Frank was Thatcher's oldest and dearest friend, possibly his only friend. If Frank was truly dead, the news would devastate Thatcher. She owed it to Frank's memory that Thatcher heard it directly from her, the last person to see him alive, to hear him die. On the other hand, if Frank had somehow survived, Thatcher might know.

She dialled Thatcher's 'crisis number', aware it would route around the globe, bouncing off mirror sites until it finally chimed its arrival in SoHo. The cops would probably be tracing the call. Good luck to them. They'd find out who she was talking to, his name at least, since his idiosyncratic third-person mannerism would guarantee that. But they'd never learn his location.

'Tori, you're safe! Thank goodness. Thatcher's been worried sick. He read they arrested you in that building but you got out in the nick of …'

She wasn't listening. She was trying to work out how to begin. 'Thatcher.' He'd already given his name so it didn't matter if she repeated it. He kept talking. 'Thatcher.' She had to repeat it three times before he stopped.

'Have you heard from Frank?' This was her last, desperate hope, that Phone Frank was not Real Frank, and that Real Frank had made contact with his trusted friend.

'You don't know where he is?'

Searching for the right words after that, and giving air to them, was hard. With each syllable she felt more and more certain that Frank was dead, and that she was the one who had drawn the blade across his throat.

For what seemed like minutes she sat on the floor, waiting for Thatcher's response, the phone a dead weight in her hand, the cold creeping up into her spine, numbing her legs.

The breaths over the line were hollow. Then a sniff, a whimper, before finally a whisper came over the phone. 'Thatcher loved him, Tori. No, that's not right … Tori, I … *I* loved him.'

128

Two weeks later – the Oval Office

Isabel lifted her eyes from yet another NSA report, leant back in her chair and buttoned up her cardigan, suitably black. From across her desk, she sized up her Director of National Intelligence and spoke before he did. 'Swyft's been in custody two weeks. With the treasure trove that she and her people in Boston gave us on Hermes she's clearly innocent. Why the hell is that woman, a US citizen, still locked up in a Spanish prison?'

DNI Hirsty bent over her desk, his hands wide on the wood, a familiarity she did not welcome as she leant even further away from him. 'I keep tellin' you, ma'am. That woman cannot be trusted. We still got that video of Tushkin confirmin' she was in on it.'

Either Hirsty was an idiot or he thought his president was. 'The suicide video was bogus,' she said. 'The NSA confirmed that was a deepfake, as was the earlier one, the video supposedly revealing her as a crazed killer.'

'That's right about the videos, ma'am, but we ain't got nothin' that proves she still wasn't Tushkin's proxy.'

Actually, that wasn't correct. Russia's Ambassador Avdonin had called on Diaz privately twenty minutes ago. He'd given her a heads-up that while Moscow's investigations weren't complete, it was as good as certain that Swyft was *not* a Russian agent. He could have been lying, but he had no reason to, and Diaz chose to believe him.

'Listen, Robert, this vendetta our agencies seem to have against Swyft, it ends now.' She tapped her finger on the phone to buzz her secretary. 'Get Madrid on the line. President Rubio.' As she said his name, Hirsty's face turned a shade of beetroot.

129

Six weeks later – Praia do Norte, Nazaré, Portugal

Tori flew straight to Portugal after the dedication ceremony at Oxford University, Frank's alma mater. His parents were there, of course, relatives and friends too, colleagues whose trench coats and furtive looks suggested they'd worked with him at MI6. Either that or they were subsequently defrocked priests who'd attended the seminary with him. Axel and Ron flew in from Boston and brought half the SIS office with them. Tori wasn't sure Thatcher would come until a black cab showed up and she watched a rotund man in a black coat, sunglasses and grey broad-brimmed hat shuffle out. He'd flown to the UK on a false passport.

It was over two months since she'd seen Frank, since anyone had. His body hadn't turned up and, under pressure from the White House, and Axel, the Spanish authorities hadn't given up on finding him. There couldn't be a funeral, of course, or even a memorial since no one who knew Frank, who respected him, was yet willing to acknowledge what the local police were already suggesting was the truth. At the same time, his relatives, friends and colleagues wanted – needed – to celebrate Frank. His loyalty. His bravery. His friendship. So, in Frank's name, Axel funded a massive scholarship program at Oxford.

Tori had known Frank less than a year, yet there was so much she desperately wanted to say – to his parents, his friends, to him. She stepped to the front of the crowd to speak and stood there, looking at his photo on the stand, at all the faces looking back at her. Kind, warm faces. But every time she opened her mouth, her body heaved and nothing but deep, mournful sobs came out.

Axel eventually came forwards, took her shoulders and hugged her, led her back to Thatcher, where she stayed, the pair comforting each other, their arms entwined.

Axel returned to the front, his speech unscripted yet eloquent, sympathetic, generous. He spoke, as if he'd known them as friends, of the struggle of Frank's immigrant parents, how they came from Pakistan to a new country, how they'd worked two, sometimes three jobs each yet managed to bring up a model child, their beautiful boy winning a King's Scholarship to Eton where he made 'a lifelong friend', a phrase that got Thatcher wailing into Tori's shoulder, how Frank had come to Oxford to do a double-first in theology and mathematics, then joined a seminary, later leaving the Church, though not God, to work 'in government', which was as close a descriptor to Frank's nine years in MI6 as Axel could say out loud.

He ended with Frank's achievements at SIS, but not in terms of the deals, the clients or fees. It was all about character. 'Francis's decency, his sense of what was right, shone out to all of us like a beacon.' He spoke about Frank's loyalty, honesty and dedication and gave touching examples. Frank's mother, a statuesque woman who'd had a hard life, was probably hearing for first time what a remarkable man her modest, self-effacing son was, and she crumpled into her husband's arms.

Axel was about to leave the podium when he tossed a smile at Tori. 'Francis's last known act was typical of him, an act of the utmost loyalty, standing in the face of danger to rescue a friend and colleague. Like Francis,' he said, 'Tori Swyft was the victim of a shocking conspiracy. She spent weeks in a Spanish prison cell, her name sullied, her reputation trashed. But she is with us today because her friends, Francis and others,' – he directed his gaze at Thatcher – 'and even the president of the United States, we all relentlessly pursued the truth and ...'

Tori couldn't bear to hear the rest and buried her head in Thatcher's coat. She left before the drinks, unable to bring herself to join in. She'd taken the first flight out of Heathrow for Lisbon and had a car waiting to bring her the ninety minutes here, to North Beach at Nazaré.

Nazaré hadn't been her first choice. She'd thought of flying back to Hawaii – where all this began, where she'd been when she took Axel's fateful call – but she wasn't ready to even contemplate what her psychologist called resolution, let alone closure. Going back to Australia, to old friends, had also been an option, but if she did that, she told herself, she'd also be giving up on Frank.

A quick flight to Portugal was the answer. Nazaré. Where she'd confront some of the most treacherous surf on the planet. The waves crashing in front of her were not thirty-metre winter monsters like those she'd experienced the last time she'd come here. They weren't even half the size, yet at the height of a five-storey building with hundreds of tonnes of water powering them forwards, they were still frightening, still deadly.

Changed into her wetsuit, she leant against the fire-red lighthouse on the roof of the cliff-top fort, a vantage point for mariners since 1577 and for surfers from much later.

She was among a crowd of strangers, thankfully. Fifty or so, some of them surfers, most of them day-trippers, but all of them craning to watch the board-riders, cheering if they got through or shrieking if their waves spat them out.

Tori hadn't ventured out herself yet. She'd hired a board and arranged her tow, the requisite safety vest at her feet. Equipped with CO_2 cartridges and four inflation pull tabs, it meant she'd be prepared even if she really wasn't ready.

'Dude, did I get axed out there,' said a guy behind her, a Jersey boy she guessed from his accent.

She turned her head. She didn't really see him. Just one more guy in a wetsuit, his hair dripping.

'Worst moment of my life, and then the best,' he said. 'That's why we do it, right? To draw out our miseries and crush 'em.'

He was right. It was why she couldn't stay at Oxford, the reason she'd flown here. To face terror, to stare down Frank's likely death, to rage at the heavens about Hermes, to remind herself that she was still breathing when a man who'd been more special to her than she'd allowed herself to know was gone, and it was solely because of her.

She tried to smile back at the surfer, but even that was too much and she fell to her knees as a torrent of ache and fury crashed down on her.

EPILOGUE

A private Pacific island

He had no idea how long he'd been here. Time wasn't obvious when you were effectively sightless, incarcerated alone inside a windowless cell. Before they flew him to this island, wherever *here* was, they'd whisked him out of Barcelona in a van, drugged and blindfolded, driving for hours, four or maybe five.

The first thing to hit him when they dragged him out of the vehicle was the sunny smell of fresh-cut hay and the pungent wafts of cow manure. He didn't know precisely where they'd taken him but it had to be a farm somewhere in the Catalonian countryside.

The glow of the late afternoon sun helped him discern vague blurs through the weave of the fabric covering his eyes and he heard the plane before he saw the glints of light from its windows in the sun as its wheels hit the airstrip. The flashes suggested six, maybe seven side windows, a small private jet, the size a rural runway could easily take.

The bucolic air and the fuzzy outline of big wheels next to his captors' van told him the vehicle they'd pulled up beside was a tractor.

They dragged him out onto the grass, two men flanking him. He heard the buzz of a mosquito apparently before they did. No, it wasn't a bug … it was a motorbike in the distance.

'That's annoying,' said a woman still sitting inside the van, a Midwestern American accent. 'You gave me a guarantee that the farmer wouldn't be here, that this was his regular day in town.'

'Hermes, that was our intel.'

While they argued, he pondered the name Hermes. It seemed to ring a bell, though at that moment, in his drug-induced fog, nothing was ringing very clearly.

As the bike rode nearer, the two men started shouting and took off towards it, leaving him standing near the tractor. He wasn't sure where the woman was, if she was still in the van, had gone with them or was watching him. He tentatively stretched out a hand and touched the tractor's side, the metal warm from the day's sun. He ran a finger over the surface. Rough, encrusted with the seasons, with years of dust and dirt. A gritty door handle. A few bubbles of rust. A ding and a gash in the metal panel, perhaps from skidding the vehicle across mud into a tree last winter or taking a hind kick from an indignant cow or whatever animals they had on this place. Wherever they were, he hadn't heard any.

He pressed his palm over a jagged curl of metal, aware it might be rusty but infection was the least of his worries. He swiped his palm across the edge, to and fro, feeling the coldness of the cut as it broke his skin. A warm drizzle of blood. A smear he purposely left to dry there.

He took his hand back, slipped it into his pocket. Wherever they were taking him, disappearing him to, his blood was here. Which meant *he'd* been here.

It was a silent victory, a blessing in waiting.

A grisly memory of a knife slicing across his throat was pushing through his haze, the recollection getting clearer, as if he was somehow witnessing his own death in a mirror. He knew it was ridiculous, but still he rubbed his throat to check. A little stubble but no stitches, no bandage.

The woman, Hermes … She was the one he'd heard give the order. One of the men holding him – the guy who punched out his eye – had held the knife.

When it happened, he started to recall, it was strange. He hadn't *felt* anything. Like he was numb to it, as if it was an out-of-body experience. Something he was watching on a video.

Why didn't they really kill him? Why bring him to this farm, to the landing strip? What use could he possibly be to them?

A gunshot burst out of the distance, a single blast ricocheting through the rural emptiness. The incoming bike stopped. The drone of the mosquito died. The woman's laughter drifted over from that direction.

Certain he was alone, he pulled his hand out of his pocket, pressed down on his palm and rubbed more of his blood over the tractor's door, praying that if people eventually came looking for the dead farmer – a local who ventured into town rarely so it might take a while – they might also stumble over his blood. Discover his DNA.

Then they'd know, *Tori* would know, that he'd survived.

Inside his solitary cell, that was the one hope keeping him sane. Sane-ish, he corrected.

A sound he hadn't heard before broke into his mental meandering. The cranking of his cell door opening. Not the food flap at the floor, the actual door. The whole door. The rays of sunlight raking across his walls were so dazzling he had to cover his eyes.

'Frank Chaudry,' said a woman. 'Your vacation is over. Come with me and earn your keep.'

ACKNOWLEDGEMENTS

'Don't tell me the moon is shining;
show me the glint of light on broken glass.'
Anton Chekhov

My love affair with Spain, and Catalonia, was cemented on a couple of trips. A hike up the Spanish Pyrenees and along the Costa Brava with two effervescent Backroads tour guides bubbling with stories about their history and culture, Oriol (Uri) Muns and Gloria Castañé Carrera. You'll see echoes of their names in one of my characters. Marta Bonastre Aguilar helped me initially with some Spanish and Catalan idiom. But my memories of Catalonia would not be as fond or as striking without Laura Coch, not only a brilliant tour guide (www.LauraToursBarcelona.com) but Laura cast her keen eye over the entire manuscript to nudge my portrayals of Catalan culture, locale and idiom in the right direction.

Spoiler alert: Whenever I am in Barcelona, I visit La Sagrada Familia to savour the ethereal, the sensation that springs out at me from this place's magical fusion of folly, genius and sheer dedication. It's in that light I point out that what happens to the basilica in my story in no way endorses what George Orwell wrote in *Homage to Catalonia* (his 1938 chronicle of six months fighting with the Catalan militias against Franco). 'La Sagrada Familia is one of the most hideous buildings in the world,' he wrote. 'It has four crenelated spires exactly the shape of hock bottles. Unlike most of the churches in Barcelona it was spared because of its "artistic value". I think the Anarchists showed bad taste in not blowing it up when they had the chance.'

Several magicians kindly peppered me with advice for creating a master assassin who is equally talented in the dark arts of magic, misdirection and illusion: Joshua Jay (who shared his thesis, 'Tragic Magic – A Survey of Fatal Conjuring: 1584–2007'); Stephen Bargatze (international president of the International Brotherhood of Magicians); Dr Gene Anderson; Steve Valentine; Larry Wilson; Marcus Denton; Sreekanth; Roger Snirt; Doug Krueger and Mike Mound. Also, thanks to Jimmy Fingers for his permission for Hermes to perform part of *Rope-u-tation*, his rope-through-body effect.

David Hambling, author of *Swarm Troopers*, advised me on drones. Bestselling author Steve Berry offered insights in his ITW Thrillerfest masterclass. Ronald Ross, again my go-to guy for expertise in WiFi and tracking technology. For help with Tori's escape from one of Hermes' fixes, Roan Chapin, thriller writer and doctor, and ophthalmologist John Kennedy. John and Hiraani Clapin sleuthed the hotel environs of Room 420 for me in Barcelona. (By the way, it's not true that all of the clocks are set at 4.20 in Quentin Tarantino's *Pulp Fiction*.) Jordi Muñoz Mendoza, the Ramón y Cajal Research Fellow in Political Science at the University of Barcelona, gave advice on presidential succession in Catalonia. And Edmund Blenkins, Batlow firefighter, truffle hunter and trail builder, for inspiring Tori's prowess at parkour and free-running.

Most of all, Tori Swyft and I thank editor Linda Funnell, the incredible team at Pantera Press, especially Lex Hirst and Lucy Bell, proofreader Sarina Rowell, Luke Causby for the book cover and, of course, my co-founders and co-lots-of-things, Ali Green and Marty Green, and the ultimate co-founder of all that's good in my life, Jenny Green.

ABOUT THE AUTHOR

John M. Green is the author of *Double Deal*, *The Tao Deception*, *The Trusted*, *Born to Run* and *Nowhere Man*.

He left his day job as a banker two years before the global financial crisis – enough of a lag so no one could accuse him of starting the whole mess! He wrote his first novel about it.

His childhood years roaming the back alleys of Sydney's infamous Kings Cross set the stage for his later careers, in law and finance. He became a partner in two major law firms and then an executive director in a leading investment bank.

Today, he straddles writing, business and philanthropy. He's a director of several organisations, listed and unlisted, including cyber-security, financial services, engineering, publishing and not-for-profits. He's been a Council Member of the National Library of Australia and a director of two publishing houses. And, like one of his story characters, he's a magic aficionado.

He lives in Sydney with his wife, the sculptor Jenny Green.

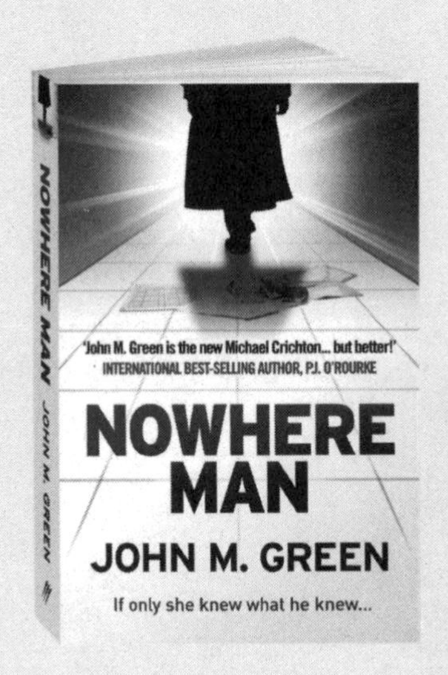

More great reads from John M. Green

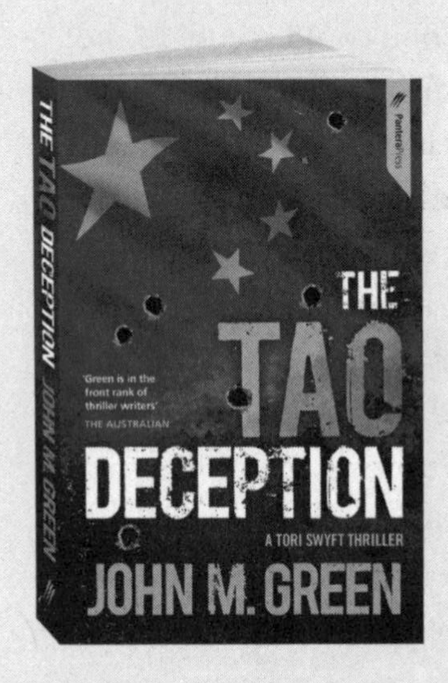

SPARKING IMAGINATION, CONVERSATION & CHANGE